Justin Zaruba

Penelope Salvo
and
Unknowable Yellow

Copyright © 2019 by Justin Zaruba

ISBN-978-1-7351749-1-4

Text set in Gentium Book Basic
Cover Art designed by Justin Zaruba. Writer photo credit: Hanna Hawley

Printed in the United States of America
First edition 2019, Go Run Go Publishing, New York City, New York

For Justin and Michelle Kogl

"She crashed into the Easter mass

with her hair done up in broken glass.

She was limping left on broken heels

when she said, Father?

Can I tell your congregation

how a resurrection really feels?"

-The Hold Steady, *How a Resurrection Really Feels*

Chapter 0

When it came to archaeology, the buck stopped with Michael Salvo; at least that's what he told everyone. And I suppose there's some truth to that considering he spent most of my childhood traveling the world, speaking at museums or identifying relics at dig sites in the most remote sun-baked, sandblasted parts of the world. And just like how old man DaVinci would have been disappointed in his kids if they couldn't paint, or how Willie Shakesman would have been humiliated by his illiterate son, Michael took it as a personal insult that I was bad at world history.

Honestly, the only reason I was so bad at it was because I was bored of hearing about it all the time. Michael cared more about mummies than he did about me and Ma.

So when I was 10 years old, I got a D- in history. Now a D- in any class automatically meant I was in for "a world of hurt," as Michael put it, but a D- in *history*? As the daughter of one of the world's leading archaeologists, that wasn't just a bad grade. That was a death sentence.

Mrs. Ortega emailed our grades directly to our parents, so theere was no way to know when they would show up exactly. It could have been Thursday, could have been Friday. And Michael got so many emails in a day from universities and museums and other archaeologists, it was impossible to tell if the notification sound of his cell phone was the one from Saint Mary's school.

When it was report card season and that D- was on its way, I was so terrified of getting my ass beat that I hid in my room, knelt at my window overlooking Manhattan, looked up at the stars and *prayed*.

I begged God to help me. I didn't care how. I offered him suggestions. Have the email get lost. Let Mrs. Ortega take mercy on me and give me a better grade. I wasn't asking for an A. No, I'd be fine with a C. Just please, God, not the D-.

Or maybe – and now I really was asking for a miracle – don't let Michael go full rage-mode. Let him come into my room and have a calm conversation about responsibility and studying. Maybe he could even explain the Civil War to me in ways I could understand.

"Please, God." I remember how tight I shut my eyes and how hard I squeezed my fists. "Please don't let him kill me."

In the other room, I heard the familiar "ping" of Michael's motorola going off. That could have been the email from school, but he got lots of emails. Maybe it was something work related. Maybe it wasn't Mrs. Ortega.

I prayed as hard as I absolutely could. I bargained with God. I'd do anything he wanted. Church every day. A rosary every night. Anything. All I wanted was-

"Penelope!" Michael shouted from the living room. I could already hear the rage in his voice. He loved to shout. I heard him stomp towards my room. He loved to stomp. Sometimes the downstairs neighbors would complain, but that never stopped him. If anything, it just got him to stomp louder. He stomped so hard, he would rattle Ma's porcelain saints and shake the ceiling fan in my room.

He slammed his open hand against the wall, warning me that an ass-beating was on its way.

I was going to die. He was going to kill me. There was nothing I could do to stop it.

When stuff like this would happen, Ma would sit alone in the living room and read the Bible. "Spare the rod, spoil the child" it says.

I slid my bedroom window open and clattered out onto the fire escape. If I hid just out of view, tucked away in the darkness of a winter night, maybe he would think I ran away. I could sleep on the fire escape. Or I could hide on the roof. Or maybe I could actually just, you know, run away for real.

The only reason I didn't was because he once told me that if I tried to run away, he would lock me in my room and I would "never see the light of day again."

I scrambled onto the fire escape and closed the window seconds before he burst into my bedroom. I crouched in the corner of the fire escape and leaned against the outside of my building with my knees pulled tight to my body.

"Penelope Marie Salvo!" he screamed from inside my room. Sometimes he would spit when he screamed. I squeezed my eyes shut and covered my ears, but I could still hear him. I heard him lift up my mattress to see if I was hiding under the bed. I heard my closet door slam into the wall as he checked inside. "You can't hide from me, kid! I watch you like a hawk!"

He slammed his open hands on the walls, causing such a racket. He screamed my name over and over.

I put my head between my knees and held my breath so he wouldn't hear me.

"Please, God," I begged. "Help me. Do something. *Please*."

God didn't answer me that night.

Now, I was no stranger to clowning around on the fire escape. I'd been caught out there a dozen times before, so it didn't take Michael long to check. The window slid open with a slam that probably woke the neighbors.

I stayed perfectly still. In the dark, maybe he wouldn't see me.

"Please, God, don't let him see me. Please, don't-"

He grabbed me by the back of the neck, hard. The bruises would last for days.

"What in the fuck do you think you're doing?" He dragged me back in through the window.

I screamed in pain, and fear, and for help. I struggled, but I didn't fight back. I knew better than to hit at his arms or kick at his body. That only made things worse. He made it very clear in the past: I wasn't *allowed* to fight back.

I disappeared back into my bedroom and Michael slammed the window shut.

"You're in for a world of hurt, kid."

Chapter 1

1

I stood at the edge of Popocatepétl – "the Smoking Mountain" – a volcano on the outskirts of Mexico City with ancient ties to the Aztecs. The evening sky glowed desert yellow as the sun set behind the dusty horizon. Black obsidian sand crunched under my sneakers as I neared the open mouth of the volcano. I leaned forward and carefully peered over the edge. A glowing lake of lava bubbled and splattered like a pot of spaghetti sauce. Heat blasted me in the face and swept through my hair. The fumes coming off the volcano smelled like burning hair and tires. I covered my mouth and nose out of instinct.

A giant bubble formed in the middle of the lava pool and it grew bigger and bigger, slowly turning black as it cooled off. When it popped, bright red goo splashed everywhere. A ribbon of lava just barely whizzed by my face.

The ground began to tremble. It was barely noticeable at first, but seconds later I was riding out a full-blown earthquake. I spread out my feet and held out my hands to help keep my balance. Waves of lava splashed against the inside crater. This was it. The Popocatepétl volcano was about to erupt and usher in the Day of One Great Sacrifice. For the next seven minutes, the volcano would become a supernatural whirlpool to another world and – if I jumped in – it would send me spinning down to Mictlan, the nine cold levels of Aztec hell.

Mictlan wasn't my ultimate goal, of course. My ultimate goal was Christian hell, not Aztec hell. Getting into Christian hell was a lot harder than I thought. Lucky for me, Mictlan would work as a potential backdoor. The lowest level of Mictlan was just as deep as Hell and somewhere down there was a mysterious error in the design of the universe. That error would let me physically slip into Christian hell without having to die first.

Going to Christian hell with your physical body is a bad idea for all sorts of reasons. Only the most powerful human beings could even attempt such a thing and even then one mistake would obliterate your physical body – as well as your soulstuff – completely out of existence.

The Aztecs didn't have that pesky "no physical bodies" rule. Gods of the Aztec underworld loved physical bodies. If I could somehow get into *their* hell with my physical body, then dip through that strange back door into *my* Hell, well, in the industry we call that a "loophole."

The lava bubbled and splashed, not only because the volcano was ready to erupt – which it was – but also because something was just beneath the surface and swimming to the top.

It was Xolotl, the Aztec god that escorts the dead through Mictlan. Dope. He was exactly who I came to see. He emerged from the red-hot sludge and I saw him in all his glory: a black humanoid creature with a dog head that was too big for his body. He reached out of the lava with his giant human hands and crawled up the inside pit of the volcano. He stared up at me with his blood-red dog eyes. Xolotl was the god of mistakes, monsters, disease and deformities. Rumor had it, he wasn't the nicest guy in the Aztec pantheon.

"You sure about this?" Corolla asked as he whisked through the air and floated overhead. He swayed back and forth, trying to keep his balance over the unpredictable heat waves radiating out of the volcano. "That dude doesn't look too happy."

Xolotl huffed his nose in our direction, then went back to climbing. Smoke wafted off his head and lava dripped from his fur.

"It's cool," I told Corolla. "He looks mean, but he's not going to attack us."

"That's what you said about those Installation Wizards."

Ugh. Again with the Installation Wizards? Corolla had a bad habit of not letting things go. Everyone makes mistakes. No one's perfect. I dismissed the topic with a wave of my hand.

5

"The Installation Wizards were different," I said.

"It feels the same to me."

"It's not."

Xolotl neared the top. I was going to offer myself as a sacrifice to keep the volcano from erupting and save Mexico City. I'd be killing two birds with one stone that way; save Mexico and get a free, all-expenses-paid trip to Mictlan. Xolotl couldn't say no to that. And if he did, well, he would get a little taste of how we throw hands back in Chinatown.

"What if you never come back?" Corolla asked me.

"I'm coming back," I told him.

"But what if you don't?"

"I will."

"But what if you *don't*?"

"I'm telling you I will."

"But what if you're wrong?"

"I'm not wrong."

"But what if you are?"

I was already under a lot of stress, going to Hell and everything. Corolla's incessant questions were starting to get on my nerves. I snapped at him and said, "If I'm wrong, I'm wrong and that means this is goodbye forever, so don't ruin it by pissing me off."

Corolla floated there, quiet for a moment. He said, "Maybe you're right. Maybe this is goodbye forever."

I turned around and put my hand on the front of his hood. "It's goodbye *for now*, Corolla," I clarified.

"But Hell is dangerous and I'm not going to be there to protect you and you're going to punch the wrong person and-"

"Corolla."

"You'll end up dead or trapped in some strange world where nothing makes sense and-"

"Corolla."

"What if I never see you again, huh? What am I supposed to do if I never see you again? Get a job? Go work at a fast food place with a little paper hat and a nineteen year old supervisor that bosses me around and-"

"Corolla!" He got quiet again. "Stop worrying. I'm going to be fine."

He sighed. "You better be."

"I'm going to miss you, buddy," I said.

"I'm going to miss you, too."

"Alright." I gave him a little push. "Now get out of here before this fucker explodes and melts your face off."

"Alright." He floated away and took to cooler skies.

Xolotl had finally reached the top. Quite a feat since his oversized dog head made him all unbalanced. He opened his muzzle and said something to me in a language I didn't understand. I'm assuming it was Aztec. Azteceese? Was Aztec a language?

World history was not my forté. Whatever he said, it didn't sound friendly.

I took one step towards him. "If you're demanding a sacrifice for the nightmare levels of Mictlan, I volunteer. Take me."

"Ask him if he only accepts virgin sacrifices!" Corolla shouted from far above me.

"Shut up, Corolla!"

"Because if so, we can just go home!"

"Shut *up*, Corolla!"

Xolotl lumbered in my direction. His dirty human feet left hissing, scorched footprints in the ground. He stared at me with unblinking eyes and he carried a stone blade of sharpened obsidian. Maybe he wanted to fight. Why? I already agreed to be his stupid sacrifice. Should be very simple. Cut and dry.

Or at least, that's what I thought. Turns out, I was very much wrong.

A beam of golden light streaked down from the evening sky and spotlighted the open ground between me and Xolotl. At first I hoped it was just a helicopter, but no, this light came all the way from space. I looked up to see the dark shapes of two winged humanoids falling out of the clouds like shooting stars. I barely caught a glimpse of them before they struck the ground like twin meteors. A plume of dirt and rock exploded up into the sky. The shock wave caused the volcano to quake. The inside walls of the basin crumbled into pieces. A landslide of rock splashed into the bubbling red lava.

The two uninvited guests knelt there in their impact crater, faces pointed down at the ground. They wore polished plate mail armor crafted from brilliant platinum and white gold. Wings of the whitest feathers stretched out from their backs in a broad wingspan, wide enough to carry the weight of a human. Their hair was dark and hung down their shoulders in wavy curls.

"Angels," I muttered. "I fucking hate angels."

Angels all look similar and wear the same armor, but I had a pretty good idea who I was looking at: Zophiel and Metatron, Chick Angel and Dude Angel. Those two were a real pain in my ass. They'd been busting my balls for over a year, getting all up in my beeswax, doing everything they could to "maintain order" and keep me from adventuring into Hell. They told me it was "unnatural" for a human to leave Earth and sneak into the Lake of Fire. I explained to them that I was only half human and the other half of me was robotic god, but they weren't going for it. No matter how many times I tried to go to Hell, they were always one step ahead of me, ready to drop down from Heaven and screw everything up.

This time proved to be no different.

"Penelope Marie Salvo," Zophiel – Chick Angel – said as she rose to her feet. Her voice was delicate and musical, but I didn't care much for that condescending "well, well, well" tone in her voice. She said my name like I was an international jewel thief and she worked for Interpol.

"Zo!" I replied. I always called her by different nicknames as if we were old friends. "Zophie!"

She scowled at me. Zophiel hated when I did that. It showed a lack of respect. Angels wanted respect just because they were angels. They had a real – forgive the pun – "holier than thou" kind of attitude and I didn't much care for it. Not one bit. I didn't respect Zophiel. That was just one of the many reasons why she hated me.

Zophiel was billions of years old. Stories said her true form was a beam of light with a million wings. I wouldn't know anything about that; I'd never seen her true form. I'd only seen her human form, where she appeared as a tan-skinned twenty-something with black, flowing hair. The plates of her paladin armor gleamed with celestial power. Golden runes from the angelic language were pressed into the metal, granting her additional powers beyond that of a normal angel. The armor was crafted specifically for the curves of her body and allowed her to move with amazing speed, despite being covered in interlocking plates of platinum and gold.

You wouldn't think she was billions of years old by looking at her. Her skin was flawless. Angels don't have to worry about age or wrinkles or worry lines. Zophiel looked twenty when she was created, she had always looked twenty, and she would look twenty until the end of time.

She carried her gleaming broadsword with her, like always. It was ridiculously oversized, five feet long and far more wide than possibly practical for a sword. I doubt even the strongest human would be able to lift the damn thing, let alone wield it one-handed like she did. The blade was platinum, double-edged, and had a hilt of pure gold. She pointed the sharp end in my direction.

I'd been cut by that sword, once, to teach me a lesson. She had sliced me right across the chin. It took Impossible Red twice as long to heal that wound, as if her weapon carried some kind of magic that counter-acted my healing factor. Even after it healed, it left a scar.

I'd told her she'd regret that someday. And she would.

Metatron wore the same platinum armor as Zophiel, except if Zophiel was a medium, Metatron was an extra-large. He looked like a god damned tank in all that metal. He stood a foot taller than his counterpart and was built like a brick shithouse. His eyes were piercing blue, but very unhappy.

I had a way of bringing that out of people.

Metatron stepped forward, clanking in his armor, and announced, "The Heavenly Host grows weary of your impudence, Salvo."

Impudence. I didn't know what that word meant.

"Hang on!" I put a finger up in the air to pause the conversation and dug into the front pocket of my shorts. I'd met a lot of new and interesting creatures over the years, creatures who like to use big words, so I got into this habit of carrying a pocket dictionary with me so I could keep up.

I whispered the alphabet to myself as I flipped through the pages. F... G... H... I...

"Here we go..." I ran my finger down the correct page. "Impudence. Impudence. Impudence."

Impudence - noun. Cocky, with no regard for authority.

Ohh. Impudence.

"Impudence, huh?" I tucked the dictionary back into my pocket. "Well, I'm sick of you two following me around like a couple bored mall cops. I haven't done anything wrong, so why don't you two fuck off back to Cloud City?"

Metatron didn't like the way I spoke to him. He's is a big deal up in Heaven, one of the most important angels that ever existed. All the other angels love him up there. He's something like a celebrity.

If I wanted to show Metatron respect I would have called him by one of his million names. Metatron, the Primordial. Metatron, the Prince of Countenance within the Divine Palace. Metatron, the Tenth and Last Emanation. Metatron, the Prince of the Presence and Prince of the World.

Instead, I told him to fuck off. And I may or may not have called him a bitch.

Bold move, calling Metatron a bitch. This dude was no small potato. I mean, this guy was huge, even by Heaven standards. If he showed up in New York, people would assume he was some kind of Russian genetic experiment to lab-grow the world's biggest bodybuilder.

Metatron's eyes flashed with glorious light. He hoisted his battle ax off his back and held it ready. That thing was huge, too. The handle was as big around as a chain link fence post. The blade was curved and sharp and could probably cleave an elephant in half. He adjusted his grip on the ax and shifted his feet into an aggressive combat stance.

Zophiel glanced at Metatron. To back up her partner, she readied her sword and got into a fighting position.

There's an old Italian saying: shit about to get cray.

"You two want to catch these hands?" I balled up my fists and squared off with them. "Is that what you want?"

"We want you to return home," Zophiel said.

"And for the final time, countermand this foolish journey to Hell," Metatron added. "Lest we dispatch you there on a more... *permanent* basis."

"Uhh." I took a moment to flip through my little dictionary.

Countermand - verb. To cancel or quit.

Me? Quit?

"No dice!" I yelled at the angels.

I wasn't going to countermand anything. My friend Theodore was trapped in Hell. He sacrificed himself to keep the demon armies trapped on their side. That was over a year ago, much longer than I ever intended to leave him stuck there. Someone had to set him free and I had to be that someone. Over the past year, I had discovered a few different ways into Hell – very few – but every time I tried to leave Earth, these two angels came along and screwed everything up.

"How's this for a deal?" I said. "How about you two get out of my way, let me sort out some business with Xolotl over there, and I won't send you to Hospital Heaven."

I leaned to the side so I could see past Zophiel and Metatron. Poor Xolotl just stood there, quietly waiting for us to finish our business so he could move forward on the whole "blow up the volcano" thing.

"Thanks for being patient, Xolotl." I gave him a little wave. "Be with you in a second."

Xolotl said something in Aztec and gave me a friendly wave back to show that he wasn't in any hurry. Cool. Nice to see that not everyone on the volcano was being a dick.

I turned my attention back to the angels. "So what's it going to be, ladies? You going to move? Or do I have to move you?"

Zophiel lifted her sword over her head. Metatron spun his battle ax in his hands, whirling the blade around with flickering lightning, then held it steady. They sized me up like they were the wolves and I was a choice cut of medium-rare steak.

Shit.

3

That wasn't my first time throwing down with Zophiel and Metatron. And truth be told, I was in deep shit. Those two archangels were the Texas Rangers of Heaven. Either one of them could stomp my ass without breaking a sweat. Fighting them two versus one was going to be humiliating.

The angels swept their wings once to build up speed and ran straight for me.

In that moment, I wondered if I should have taken that little leprechaun up on his offer to sell me *soul insurance*.

Zophiel swung her broadsword for my neck. I ducked out of the way. The blade just barely missed me with a powerful "woosh."

"You missed," I said, mocking her and making things worse. She swung the blade back around at full force. I dipped sideways to safety. "Too slow." A third swing came around, this one meant to disembowel me. I jumped back and ran away from her. "Missed me ag-"

I took a battle ax to the face. Not the sharp end. That would have split my head like a coconut. No, Metatron showed mercy and swung his battle ax like a tennis racket, one-handed, and smacked my lights out with the flat side of his blade. The metal rang like a gong. Stars exploded in my vision. I flipped circles through the air and landed face down in the rocks.

Before I knew what happened, one of the angels punched me in the back of the head with their platinum gauntlet. My face sank inches deeper into the dirt. My computer vision went pixelated and the world sounded garbled.

I laid there for a second to give Impossible Red time to fix my eyes and ears. I spat out a mouthful of volcanic rock followed by drops of oily blood.

"Good one," I mumbled as I got up to my hands and knees. "You really pack a punch."

Metatron slammed his hand around the back of my neck, gripped me tight, and lifted me into the air. He was such a beast, he could wrap his fingers around my neck and have them touch.

"Go. Home," he growled right into my face. "I will not caution you a third time."

"I'm sorry," I said. "I can't. My friend is in Hell and I need to-"

Metatron didn't let me finish. He didn't want to hear my bullshit excuses. He slammed me to the ground and my body left a dent. A dust cloud puffed into the air. Something inside me broke. Maybe my ribs? I couldn't be sure what, but I felt something pop.

"I need to..." Oily blood drizzled off my bottom lip. "Go to Hell..."

One of my eyes was totally out of focus. The other one worked okay. I saw Zophiel march over to Xolotl.

"Hey!" I pointed at the poor dog-spirit. "Leave him alone. He doesn't have anything to do with this!"

Innocent dog-headed Xolotl got dragged into this against his will. He was just trying to do his own Aztec religion thing, but these angels just had to get in the mix. Confused and terrified, the Aztec god backed away from the advancing angel. Zophiel kept coming. Once she back Xolotl to the edge of the volcano, she kicked kicked right in the gut and knocked him backwards into the lake of lava.

Xolotl howled in pain and landed in the magma with an audible "blorp."

Zophiel stood at the edge and shouted down after him. "No sacrifices! No destruction! You will halt the extravasation of this pitiful volcano immediately!"

Extravasation? It hurt too much for me to go for my dictionary, but I could figure it out from context: all volcanic eruptions were canceled for the day.

Metatron dropped down to one knee in front of me and swept his ax through the air. He brought the sharp end of the blade down to my neck. The metal glinted in the setting sun. Even my carbon-nano skin and my tungsten spine wouldn't stand up to his ax. My body was made of the most indestructible materials known to *man*. Metatron wielded the most dangerous weapon known to *God*. If he wanted to, he could chop my head right off.

He looked pissed in ways I had never seen him look pissed before. His eyes flashed with divine lightning. He clenched his square jaw and bared his teeth.

He growled at me. "Your constant attempts to break the boundaries between worlds has become intolerably bothersome, mudblob. My forgiveness is not infinite. Neither is my longanimity."

"Will you get me my book?" I coughed up blood. "I don't know what longanimity means."

"It means patience," Zophiel said as she approached. She dragged her broadsword across the ground. "Our patience is not infinite."

"Hear me well, human." Metatron pressed his ax down harder and creased the skin of my neck with the blade. "The Almighty may be slow to anger, but I assure you, I am not. I caution you now for the final time. Return to the land of York. Never again seek passage into Hell, secret or otherwise."

"And might I also suggest a vow of silence," Zophiel added as she looked down on me with her smug resting-bitch-face. "Such virtue would serve you well."

Metatron pressed his blade to my throat and it made it hard to talk, but I managed to say, "I mean this from the bottom of my heart..." I coughed up blood. "But eat my whole entire ass."

Metatron withdrew his ax, stood, and took his place next to Zophiel. Side by side, they gleamed with heavenly justice. Boy, did they look pissed. Way more than last time.

I guess I could understand. Last time was supposed to be the *last* time. Now this time was the last time. Every time they told

13

me to stop, I'd just do it again. How many more last chances were they going to give me?

"Zero," Zophiel said.

"Huh?"

"You were wondering how many more chances we are going to give you," Zophiel said.

Right. As long as she's looking at me, Zophiel can read my mind.

Metatron gave me the look of a fed-up principal. And believe me, I know what fed-up principals look like. "The number of chances you have, Penelope, has reached exactly zero."

The two angels unfurled their wings, flapped them in powerful glory, and lifted off the ground.

"Test our patience once more," Zophiel warned me as they took to the skies, "and be met with oblivion."

Just like that, they disappeared up into the clouds. Once they faded from view, the Heavenly spotlight shut off.

Great. Perfect. I can die in peace now.

I collapsed to the ground and laid there.

4

By the time I healed up enough to move, the sun had set and it was night. My face glowed blue under the light of Corolla's hubcaps. He'd come down from the sky and floated right over me.

"Penelope? Are you alright?" he asked.

"Yeah." I pushed myself up to my hands and knees. My skin was covered in scrapes and bruises. I used my forearm to wipe my bloody nose, but that just smeared it across my face. "I'm fine."

"You don't look fine," he said. "You look terrible. Those guys totally kicked your ass."

"Yeah." Impossible Red popped one of my ribs back into place and I winced in pain. "Not that you were any help."

"Me?" Corolla floated down so we could face one another. "That's a laugh. What did you want me to do? Honk at them? Parallel park them to death?"

"Oh, I know. I'm just being a bitch." I got to my feet and limped over to the edge of the volcano. The seven minutes of the One Great Sacrifice were long gone. I'd spent months researching this Aztec backdoor into Hell and those dick angels made me miss it. The One Great Sacrifice wouldn't come back for another fifty years. "It's whatever."

"I don't know what you were thinking," Corolla said. "Mouthing off to them like that."

"Yeah. I dunno."

"Every time you do that, they curb-stomp you something awful."

I turned and headed down the slope of the volcano. "Okay, that's enough."

"They don't even have to try. You're like a baby to them, like a little tiny baby. And they spank your buttcheeks like a baby, too, because-"

I whipped around. "I said that's *enough!*"

I gave him my most serious look. He stared back at me with his glowing headlights. He got quiet. Good. I gave him a final warning glare, turned around, and resumed my trek down the mountainside.

Corolla followed.

"Those two really piss me off," I said. "You know what I'd like to do? I'd like to go down to the basement of the shop and find something that hurts angels and beat their brains out."

"That's a terrible idea," Corolla said, floating alongside me. "If you killed Zophiel and Metatron, you'd piss off everyone in Heaven."

"I know."

"Then all the angels would come down here."

"I know."

"Then you'd *really* get your ass kicked."

I stopped. I gave him a stern look.

"Sorry," he said. "Sorry."

I went back to walking. He followed.

I said, "There has to be a way to get into Hell where they won't notice."

"Wait." Corolla swung in front of me and floated backwards. "You're still going to go to Hell?"

That was a stupid question.

"We've been over this, Corolla. Theodore is trapped down there. He doesn't deserve that."

"Penelope, look. You've tried your best to go to Hell. You tried a bunch of times. And I know you like Theodore..."

I arched my eyebrow at him.

15

"...As *friends*," he added. "But you've tried everything. If the angels won't let you in, that's not your fault. It's like I always say, when the going gets tough, just countermand entirely."

"I'm not going to countermand!"

"Penelope! You heard what those angels said. You're all out of chances! Test their patience one more time and be met with oblivion. That's exactly the word Zophiel used. *Oblivion.*"

"I heard it, dude. I was standing right there. That's why I need to find some way to get into Hell without them catching on."

Corolla scoffed. "Well, how're you planning on doing that? Metatron is the Archangel of boundaries and Zophiel can read your mind."

"I don't know," I said. "I'll think of something."

"Something? This Aztec volcano was supposed to be something."

"I know."

"And the time before that with the Installation Wizards."

"I know."

"And before *that* it was the Austr-aliens."

"I remember, Corolla."

"And before *that*-"

"Corolla! I know!"

We walked a little bit more.

"I'm not trying to be a wet blanket here," he said, "I just don't want to see you get hurt."

"I get hurt all the time."

"Well, I don't want you to die."

"I've died before."

"I mean die for good."

Hmm. His concerns were valid. I'd frustrated Zophiel and Metatron to their limit. One more shenanigan might push them to the point where they take off the kids gloves and straight up murder me.

I stretched my arms over my head and popped my back. Ah, there we go. Impossible Red had my bones in 90 percent working order. Man, I really put those little red nanites to work. Good thing I don't have to pay them, because they'd all be racking up some serious overtime.

"Can we go home now?" Corolla asked.

I sighed. I hated to admit defeat, but I just got my ass totally kicked. Popocatepétl was already growing quiet and the portal to

Mictlan was closed. There was nothing left for me in Mexico.

"Yeah," I said. "Let's go home."

I'd find a different way into Hell. It's not like this was the only one. I'd found quite a few already. Problem was, each new secret entrance got increasingly more and more dangerous. If I discovered yet another way into Hell, odds were pretty good that Zophiel and Metatron would catch me red-handed and that would mean an immediate execution.

But I couldn't give up. I couldn't let Theodore rot in Hell. There had to be a way to pull it off.

5

I'm not used to losing. I was super competitive in grade school and it only got worse in high school. Even after I swallowed Impossible Red and joined the supernatural world, I could always squeak out a victory when I needed it most. Not recently. Not with Zophiel and Metatron watching me like a couple probation officers.

For the last year, it had been nothing but one defeat after another.

We flew back to New York City in the midnight sky. Get ready for some UFO sightings, Louisiana, because there are four glowing hubcaps cutting through the clouds.

I popped open the glove box to find some music. Corolla and I had been through all his old cassettes so many times, we'd grown sick of them. So just a few months back, I went down to Yesterday Disks – this old record store over in Queens – and sorted through their shoe boxes of cassette tapes. 20 bucks later, we had a brand new collection of absolute bangers to rock out to while we traveled the world.

We had Alice Cooper's greatest hits. We had four Led Zeppelin tapes. And I actually managed to find a Fall Out Boy cassette and I didn't even know they released Fall Out Boy on cassette. And lately Corolla had been on a Steve Perry kick. He wanted me to pick up some "Perry hits" and I was like, "Who the hell is Steve Perry?"

Corolla educated me on Steve Perry. He was the lead singer of Journey, the band that did that Don't Stop Believin' song. I knew that song. Everyone knows that song. So, against my better judgment, I grabbed him a Journey's Greatest Hits.

Corolla heard me open the glove box and said, "What are you

getting out?"

"I dunno." I shuffled through the tapes. "Just seeing what's in here."

"Journey?" he asked.

I groaned. "Aren't you sick of that tape by now?"

"What part am I supposed to get sick of?" he asked.

I decided to just ignore that entire topic and focus on sorting through our collection. Corolla needed a bigger glove box. Or, actually, what we needed was one of those old school zip-up cassette organizers, not that I would be able to find one of those anywhere. Cassettes hadn't been a real thing for, like, 20 years. I was lucky to find tapes at Yesterday Disks in the first place, let alone a whole fucking *organizer*.

"I want to listen to Journey," Corolla said.

"You said that."

"So put it in."

"I'm sick of Journey, dude." I shuffled through the cassettes looking for something else to suggest. "What about some Ramones? Or Nirvana? Or-"

He said, "It's my turn to pick the music and I'm picking Journey."

I put my search on pause and eyed the stereo. "*Your* turn?"

"Yes, my turn," he said. "You made me listen to Fall Out Boy the whole way to Mexico."

"You told me to pick the music! You said you didn't want to."

"I did not."

"Yes, you did! You specifically said that DJ Not Safe For Work was taking the night off."

"I was just being nice because I thought you were going to Hell! But you didn't go to Hell, you're still here, and DJ NSFW is ready to listen to some Journey."

"I'm not putting in Journey."

"But it's my turn!"

"Nope. Not doing it." I grabbed a cassette at random and checked it. I went to stick it in the deck. "Here. We're going to listen to Paula Abdul."

"No!" he shouted. God, it sounded like I was killing him. What a drama queen. "No, I hate Paula Abdul!"

"Then pick something else."

"Journ-"

"*Besides* Journey."

He got quiet. He was thinking.

"Fine," he said. "If that's how you're going to be..."

The stereo clicked off. The engine went quiet. The interior went completely dark. And as the blue glow of his hubcaps faded to darkness, we tilted to the left and started to drift. Corolla had shut off his power and we were falling out of the sky.

"Corolla?"

The stereo was off. He didn't answer me.

I used my stern voice. "Corolla."

He kept ignoring me. We dropped out of the cloud line. Mississippi loomed below us. The cities twinkled like jewels against the night geography. The rivers and lakes glowed blue in the reflecting moonlight.

"Corolla. Come on."

But he refused to talk to me.

I wasn't about to be blackmailed. So I crossed my arms and leaned back in my seat, even as the windshield tilted forward and we started to nosedive down to Earth.

"I'm not doing it." I closed my eyes. "I'm not putting in Journey. I don't negotiate with terrorists. If you want to crash, then crash. I'll be fine. I'm indestructible."

Silence. Well, silent except for the sound of wind whistling through the tiniest gaps in Corolla's doors. I squinted one eye open to check the stereo. Corolla still wasn't on. We were still falling. The view out the windshield were the lights of a city down below.

"Okay, Corolla. Very funny. You made your point. Come on."

Nothing.

I pushed the power button on his tape deck a couple times. Nope. He wasn't responding.

"This is real mature, you know that, right?" I told him. "You're being a real baby."

Nothing.

We were so close to Mississippi, I could see the shape of the city we were over. Biloxi. We were about to crash straight into Biloxi.

"Dude."

I could see the water towers and tiny houses. We were close enough to Biloxi, I could recognize specific stores by their shape and color, like McDonald's and Starbucks. The highways were close and they were getting closer.

"Okay, Corolla. It's not funny anymore."

Nothing. The wind gusted and we started to spin in circles.

19

"Corolla."

Nothing. The world was coming straight for us.

"Corolla!"

Nothing. Impact in five... four... three...

Of all the fucking things to care about...

"Alright, fine!" I popped the Journey tape into the stereo and it clicked into place.

The stereo flicked on. The headlights lit up. Corolla's hubcaps began to hum as his hover-mode reactivated. He straightened us out and we were no longer falling. We were suspended in mid-air, floating mere feet above Biloxi's courthouse. We were treated to an up-close-and-personal view of the well lit American flag flapping up there on the roof.

The tape player whirred and the speakers crackled with that analog silence that comes at the start of any cassette.

The opening piano riff to "Don't Stop Believin'" played out of the speakers.

"Thank you," Corolla said.

"You're ridiculous," I told him.

He cranked the volume and lifted us back into the sky. "Sorry. I can't hear you over these rockin' tunes."

Chapter 2

1

We flew all night. Right as the sun started coming up, the shadows of New York City came into view on the horizon. It was May. The days were getting warmer and longer. The skyscrapers of Manhattan loomed like black rectangles in the bright morning sunshine.

It was 2014. The Ice Bucket Challenge was in full swing, where people would upload videos of themselves dumping a bucket of ice water over their heads and then challenge three friends to do it next. It was an internet phenomenon, half charity and half viral video.

Washington state was about to legalize marijuana for recreational purposes and that got me to wondering how hard it would be to move the herbal shop from Manhattan to Olympia. Probably too hard.

And the stock market was in some kind of tail spin.

I'm not a stock market kind of girl. I don't really need human money for anything, so I didn't really understand what was going on. In fact, the only time I heard anything about it was when I'd switch cassettes in Corolla's stereo and it would start playing his local talk radio.

"Even companies long considered to be safe from market fluctuations are reporting record losses. Among these, McDonald's surprisingly ranks as one of the highest, coming short of quarterly projections by over eleven percent. Companies like Wal-Mart and J.P.

Morgan-"

"Boring," I sang to myself. I clicked a Ramones tape in the deck to shut up the talk radio. I cracked the passenger side window and dug out my spliff and lighter from the center console.

"You should think about investing some money in the stock market," Corolla told me.

"What money?" I sparked the little joint and inhaled.

"Well, get some money. Then invest it in the stock market."

Doing my best not to exhale my smoke, I croaked the word, "Why?"

"For retirement."

I shook my head. Satisfied with my hit, I blew it out the window and looked at the burning end of my cigarette. "I'm not going to retire. I don't even know if I age anymore."

"You age. You just turned 20 last month."

"I mean, sure, I've physically been on this Earth for 20 years, yeah," I said. "But I mean, like, I don't know if I'm actually aging."

"Well, what about me?" he asked.

"What about you?" I replied.

"I still age. I'm not getting any younger."

"You're fine, dude. If anything breaks on you, we can get it replaced. You've got decades left, easy."

"Still, it would be nice to have a nest egg."

Oh shit. That spliff was kicking in and this sounded like a real weird conversation to have while high. Whatever. I decided to ride it out and see where it went.

"What do you need a nest egg for?" I asked. "You think you're going to retire someday?"

"It would be nice to have the option."

"Uh huh." I took another drag and sat cross-legged in the seat. "And where are you going to retire to, huh?"

"I don't know." He thought for a moment. I blew more smoke out the crack in the window. He said, "I could always go back to Japan."

"You could."

"I'm Japanese, you know."

"I know."

"I could retire and get a part time job driving Uber in Tokyo."

I laughed. "Do what? Do you even know any Japanese?"

"No."

"How are you going to Uber in Japan when you don't speak Japanese?"

"I dunno," he said. "Fake it?"

"You're going to *fake* knowing a whole language."

"I don't know," he said. "Or I'll learn it. How hard could it possibly be? You learned Chinese."

With lungs full of smoke, I tried to say, "Japanese is really hard to-"

I burst into a coughing fit. Talking with smoke in your lungs is a bad idea. It burned my throat and tickled and tasted weird. I coughed a little bit at first, but the coughing brought up more smoke, so that made it worse and I coughed even more. Next thing I knew, my eyes were watering and I was full-blown hacking up a storm.

Corolla laughed at me.

I rolled down the window for fresh air. I hung my head out the side and coughed and coughed and spit down at the world below.

"Real attractive," Corolla said.

"Shut up," I said between coughing fits.

Next thing I knew, I was being tossed back and forth in my seat as Corolla banked hard left and right.

"This help?" Corolla did a terrible job of holding back his laughter. He kept rocking back and forth, knocking me around. I still couldn't stop coughing.

"Stop!" I shouted, thumping my fist on his dashboard.

He stopped, but kept snickering. "Sorry."

I coughed it out and hung out the window for fresh air. I watched Manhattan grow closer. The weed was doing its thing and I started thinking about brains for some reason. Isn't it funny how the brain works? Just a bit squishy ball of electronic impulses. Except maybe for my brain. My brain was probably more like Corolla's; more computer than brains. Or maybe it wasn't. My brain was the one part of me that didn't feel robotic. I didn't think like a robot. I didn't act like a robot. And I sure as shit didn't get any better at math, so if my brain was a computer, it was one really stupid computer.

So many things had changed about my body. After two years, I had gotten used to having Impossible Red inside me. I never slept. I never had to pee. I never got my period. My fingernails didn't grow. My hair - some kind of indestructible fiber - was forever locked into the short, spiky haircut I had when I was 18.

Was there anything inside me still biological? My kidneys? My liver? My intestines? Or did Impossible Red convert them all into mechanical parts? My blood wasn't blood anymore, it was some kind of oily chemical. A liver and kidneys can't survive on a generous supply of oily chemicals. No part of the body can survive on oily chemicals, so maybe all my organs were machines now.

I'd been thinking about that a lot lately, but kept it to myself. I hadn't even told Corolla. Was any part of me still human? And even if my entire physical body had gone robotic, did that somehow eliminate my humanity? Something inside me *felt* human, and just because I was made of carbon and steel and industrial rubber instead of skin cells and blood cells, that didn't mean I stopped being human.

Right?

"Penelope?" Corolla said.

"Corolla."

"You just going to lean out the window this whole way home?" he asked.

My head was still hanging out the window. I had long recovered from my coughing fit, lost in my own thoughts.

"Oh." I leaned back into the car and sat down like a regular person. "Sorry. Off in my own little world,"

"It's fine."

"Corolla?" I said.

"Penelope?"

"Do you think I'm a human?" I asked. "Or a robot?"

He paused to think. "You're the one always saying you're half-robot, half-human. So I guess both."

"That's a thing I say, sure, but what part of me is human? My heart? My lungs?"

"I don't know," he said. "I'm as good at human biology as you are at car mechanics."

"What if every part of me is robot?" I looked down at my whole body. "What if I'm not human at all?"

"Is that a bad thing?"

Fair question. I had to think. Was it a bad thing to stop being human? Being a robot was pretty badass. I was insanely strong with an indestructible body. And, to be fair, I still *looked* human, so what was I really missing out on?

"I don't know," I said. "I mean, it's not *bad*."

"I'm all robot," he said. "I'm pretty cool with it."

24

"Yeah. I just don't know if I'm ready to stop being human."

"Maybe you're like Jesus," he said. "Pure robot and pure human at the same time."

Oh, man. I was too high for Jesus talk.

"Don't talk to me about that Jesus shit," I told him. "I hate that."

"You don't think Jesus is real?"

"Oh, he's real," I said. "He's just full of shit."

"Jesus is full of shit?"

I scoffed. "Jesus is so totally full of shit."

"How do you figure that?"

"You can't be 100% man *and* 100% God. You can't be two completely different things at the exact same time. It's like saying a red apple is also a green apple. It's not possible. It's either a red apple, or a green apple, or sometimes it's half red and half green. But it can't be both totally red and totally green."

Corolla thought about that for a moment and said, "There's this crazy guy who hangs out by that hot dog stand over on Canal. He says Jesus can do anything, even the impossible."

I told him, "That's exactly the full-of-shit kind of thing Jesus would say. If you could do the impossible, then it's by definition possible. He's not 100% God. He's 50% God."

"And 50% man?"

"Exactly."

"How do you know he's 50% man?"

"The Romans killed him!" I shouted. "What kind of god dies to a bunch of illiterate Romans in the year zero?"

"You're a god," he said. "You got killed."

"I got killed by a billion dollar space laser. Not a half-naked Roman armed with a whip."

"Well," Corolla said. "It wasn't just the whip that killed him. I think the crucifixion probably played a substantial part. This talk radio station I listen to says-"

"If I ever run into Jesus, I'm going to tell him to knuckle up. Then we'll really see who the god is."

"You..." Corolla hesitated. "You want to fight Jesus?"

"Not like fight him and kill him," I said. "Just fight him and see if he's God or not."

"Well, if he's still around, he's gotta be *some* amount of God, because he would be 2000 years old."

"Right," I said. "So he's half god, half man."

"Right," Corolla said. "So by your own logic, you're half robot, half human."

I asked him, "You really think so?"

He said, "It's been the story so far. Why change it now?."

Maybe he was right. In the moment, it made perfect sense. Obviously I couldn't both be entirely human and entirely robot at the same time, that's just dumb. So I was going to stick with what I had always said: half-human, half-robot.

What part of me was still human? Well, I'm no philosopher, and maybe this was dumb, but the most human part of me was... my humanity.

"Hey, Corolla," I said.

"Hey, Penelope," he replied.

"Do you know the difference between Jesus and a picture of Jesus?"

Corolla laughed. "What?"

"It only takes one nail to hang a picture of Jesus."

2

When me and Corolla left for Mexico and I said goodbye to the Big Apple, I thought that was it. I fully expected to depart for another world, off on a dangerous multi-dimensional journey to Hell. But it wasn't the first time I'd been disappointed. I wasn't on my way to Hell. Instead, I was returning to New York City empty handed, tail between my legs, back to the drawing board.

Before I left, I told Ilana Rittenberg goodbye. I checked in with her every time I set off for Hell, because – much like hiking alone or meeting someone from the internet – safety starts with telling a trusted friend where you're going to be. Ilana always wanted to know when I left for an adventure and insisted I check in with her whenever I came back.

Me and Corolla got back to New York City around lunchtime. We stopped by Liu's Peking Taste so I could pick up some Chinese food and bring it to Ilana as a surprise. She'd been doing a lot of combat training over the last couple months and developed a bad habit of skipping meals.

Ilana recently landed a promotion at the Westland Corporation as "personal security" for some middle-manager in some logistical department. Her new job required combat skills that she did not have. Honestly, out of everyone up for the job, Ilana was the least qualified. All the other candidates had way more security experience, but she got the job anyway. We didn't question why. We knew why.

Someone in upper management was doing her a favor and giving her a chance.

Ilana's lack of qualifications just made her more determined to prove herself. Dead set on being the best security officer she could be, Ilana spent her free time doing target practice with her company-issued pistol and practicing Krav Maga.

I didn't even know what Krav Maga was until Ilana started learning it. It's this martial art invented in Israel and used by the Israeli Defense Force. It's supposed to be one of the deadliest martial arts in the whole world.

That's what brought me to a run-down gym in the East Village. It was a small cinder-block building that looked practically abandoned. It's a cool little building from the outside with painted-over windows, kind of tucked away in the corner of an empty parking lot. There was a big sign attached to the roof with letters from the '70s that read *ITHACA GYM*. The C in Ithaca had long been missing, but you could still see the outline of the letter from where the sun had faded the metal.

The gym might have looked abandoned from the outside, but I knew better. Ithaca Gym was open for business, but it didn't accept memberships from outsiders. Access to the gym was limited only to Westland Corporation employees, where they could train and exercise away from the prying eyes of "normal" people. The interior wasn't glamorous; just a big dimly-lit gym with a boxing ring, duct-taped punching bags, and a handful of old-school jump ropes with wooden handles.

Whenever I had nothing going on, I would join Ilana in the gym and help her practice. Today was one of those days.

I stood perfectly still in the boxing ring as Ilana – decked out in gym shorts, a Westland tank top, padded fighting gloves and ankle-protectors – whacked on me with her fists and knees. She Krav Maga-ed me like a fighting dummy, whacking my face and kicking me in the stomach. Sweat dripped down her face and soaked her bright green bangs.

Huffing and puffing, she punched me in the stomach with a flurry of blows. I didn't feel anything.

"These fucking angels won't get off my ass," I said in the middle of one of my rants. "You should have seen it, man. I was right there at the edge of the volcano. Xolotl was there, too, ready to drag me down to Mictlan."

"Who's Xolotl again?" Ilana backed up, bounced in place, and swung her arms around to loosen up. She'd been beating on me for half an hour and had just started to run out of breath.

I replied, "This Aztec god that leads you to Aztec hell."

She gestured at her face. "Snake head?"

"Dog head."

"Right." She caught her breath, then leaned back in and started her attack routine from the top. "I can't remember all this shit, dude. Gods and names and places. I've been studying for months."

"It's a lot to remember. I've been at it for two years and I still learn something new every day."

"Yeah?" She backed way up. "Speaking of learning something new, check this out."

She bounced in my direction and jumped into a roundhouse kick that whacked me across the face. I raised my eyebrows, impressed. Ilana had always been a fighter, but she was more of the street brawl sort. I never would have imagined that she had the discipline to get all technical with it.

"Nice kick," I told her.

She stumbled back and dropped to the ground. She took off her protective ankle thing and rubbed the bone.

"Oy *vey*," she said. "Kicking you is like kicking a tank."

"It was a good kick though."

"Yeah." She winced and held her ankle. "I've been stretching a lot so I can kick higher. Finally been able to pull it off."

"You close your eyes when you jump though," I told her. "You shouldn't do that. There's a lot of things out there that can blink shift on you if you close your eyes."

She said, "I don't close my eyes when I jump."

"Yeah, you do."

"I do not."

"You just did."

"I did not."

"You totally closed your eyes."

"I did not."

3

Target practice.

Ilana stared down the barrel of her Smith & Wesson 5906, one eye squeezed shut, with bright orange noise-canceling ear protectors on her head. She bit her bottom lip, aimed, and shot off a burst-fire series of bullets.

I stood at the opposite end of the shooting range holding her paper bullseye in front of me. The bullets whipped through the paper and flattened against my chest. Ilana spun in place, stuck out the gun one-handed and fired a few more shots. Bullets fluttered through the target and ricocheted off my face and arms. Once she was out of bullets, I looked down at the target to see how well she did. She got a few bullseyes, right dead center.

We were in the basement of Ithaca Gym, where a make-shift shooting range had been installed.

Frustrated, Ilana yanked off her ear protectors – they looked like bulky, bright orange headphones – and stomped towards me.

"Not bad," I said as I admired the target.

"Not bad?" she repeated. She waved her gun dismissively at the target. "My accuracy is shit. My grouping is sloppy."

"I don't know." I looked at the target. I don't know a lot about guns and, sure, she missed a few, but three holes were right in the center target. "Whatever you were shooting at would be dead."

"Maybe." She took the paper target from me and frowned. She crumpled it up and threw it to the ground. A moment later, she gave me a crazy grin and snapped a new clip in her gun. "I want to shoot at a moving target."

I said, "Okay?"

She kept grinning and stared me right in the eyes.

"Oh!" I said. "You mean me!"

Her smile didn't go away. She nodded very enthusiastically.

I shrugged. "Alright. What do you want me to do? Just run around or–"

She backed up a few steps, spread her feet and pointed her gun at my head. She shouted, "Get on your stomach and fuck the ground, asshole!"

This was going to be fun.

"Fuck you, pig!" I shouted back. I ran away from her. "I didn't do shit!"

She chased after me. "I said on the fucking ground!"

The sound of gunshots filled the range. The game was on. If she wanted a moving target, I'd show her a moving target. I changed directions so fast, my feet crunched holes in the concrete floor. She couldn't stop as fast as I could and her momentum carried her right past me. I turned and ran the

29

opposite direction, putting tons of distance between us in less than a second.

She whipped around and fired another round of shots. I threw myself to the ground and tumbled around.

"God damn, you're fast," she shouted from across the shooting range.

"Yeah, I-"

Just when I looked back at her, she fired a single shot and a bullet thumped me dead center, right between the eyes.

We both froze. Everything went quiet. I couldn't believe she made that shot. Apparently, neither could she.

She called out, "Did that just happen!?"

"Yeah, dude!" I jumped up and pointed at my forehead. "You nailed me, right here!"

"No way!" She ran over to me, excited. "I would have blown your fucking brains out!"

"You totally would have!"

"You were moving so fast!" she said. She looked completely overjoyed. "You were running and then you stopped and I can't believe I hit you right between the freaking eyes!"

"Why weren't we recording this!? That'll never happen again!"

Her smile faded. "What do you mean 'never'?"

"I mean, you'll never hit me right between the eyes like that again."

She dropped her arms in frustration. "How would you know?"

I raised an eyebrow. "Dude, that was luck. You honestly think you could do that again?"

She scoffed. "Yeah. Probably."

I scoffed back, louder. "You're dreaming. No way. That shot was one in a million."

"Whatever." She raised her gun and fired three shots at my face. The bullets thumped against my forehead and clattered to the ground. "See? There you go. Right between the eyes."

"Sure," I said. "At point blank range."

"Well, then back up." She walked backwards and shooed me away so there would be some distance between us. I backed up. "Keep going," she said, waving me off. "Keep going."

We found ourselves on opposite ends of the shooting range. She raised her gun and aimed at me. I stood there, further away than when I was holding her paper target.

"Stop moving!" she shouted at me.

"I'm not moving!"

"Yes, you are! You're moving your head around! Stop!"

"Dude, I'm not moving!"

"Okay." She aimed harder. "Stay still."

I stayed perfectly still. She fired off a single shot.

4

Ilana and I sat on the edge of the roof of Ithaca Gym as the evening sun reflected off the glassy skyscrapers. All the way across Manhattan were the shimmering buildings of Midtown, including the headquarters of the Westland Corporation. Ilana held her Chinese food on her lap. She pulled one of her crab rangoons apart piece by piece and stuffed them in her mouth.

I had grabbed one of the 50 pound plates from the gym's weightlifting equipment and ate it like a comically oversized donut. Ilana watched me out of the corner of her eye.

"Is that any good?" she asked, pointing at the steel with her plastic fork.

I gave the metal plate an approving look. "It's not bad."

"What's, like, the best metal you've ever eaten?"

"Oh, that's easy. Gold."

"Yeah?"

"Hands down." I loved gold. Just thinking about it made me miss it. "So good."

"What's it taste like?" she asked.

"Huh." Trying to explain how metal tastes to a human can be really tricky. I could never seem to find the right words. "It's like honey, if honey were some kind of fruit."

Ilana shook her head. "That's so strange."

I just shrugged and took another bite of steel, mashing it into a melty paste.

"Can I see?" she asked.

I pointed my face at her and opened wide. Globs of bright orange pressure-melted steel coated the inside of my mouth. Her face glowed in the brightness of it as she leaned in closer. I had to be careful to not let any of it drip out or Ithaca Gym would have a fire on their hands.

She laughed. "Man, that's so weird looking."

I smiled and swallowed.

"So those angels-" I started to say.

31

"Yeah, that's so *fucked*, dude!" Ilana put emphasis on the F word by launching a corner of her crab rangoon to the parking lot below. The food bounced off Corolla's hood.

"Hey!" I heard him shout. "Watch it!"

"I can't believe those angels are just going to let Theodore rot in Hell like that. All you're trying to do is rescue him and they want to kill you for it? He helped save the world, they know that right?"

"I don't think they care. They just go on and on about the rules of creation and boundaries and all this bullshit and I'm like whatever. Just go away."

Ilana was quiet for a moment. Without making eye contact, she asked, "Did anything... like... happen between you two?"

"Me and Theodore?" I asked.

She looked at me and nodded.

"Not really," I said. There was that *one* kiss that *one* time. "No."

"Did you want it to?"

I was going to lie and say no, but I didn't. I honestly didn't know what the correct answer was, so I just turned my attention to the skyscrapers and said, "I dunno."

We didn't say much else about that.

"You ever try kicking those angels' asses?" she asked me.

I laughed. "That's not an option."

"You're fast as shit and you literally eat metal."

I shook my head. "That's nothing to angels. You should see these guys in action. They are savage." I looked up at the sky. "In fact, it wouldn't surprise me if they were watching me right now."

Ilana looked up to the sky and stuck out both her middle fingers.

"Fuck you guys!" She screamed at the clouds as loud as she could, as if they might actually hear her from Earth. "You sanctimonious pieces of shit!"

I turned away from Ilana and reached into my pocket.

Sanctimonious - Adj. To make a display of being morally superior.

Right. I put the book away.

"So what are you going to do now?" she asked me.

"I don't know." I stared at the Manhattan skyline. "I'm sort of out of ideas."

"Did you talk to Carl about it?" she asked.

"Yeah."

"What did he say?"

"He said angels are a pain in the ass and there's nothing you can do about it."

Ilana looked at me. "Carl said 'ass'?"

I chuckled. "No, I'm the one saying ass. Carl said buns."

"Right."

"Technically, he said hot dog buns."

"Right."

We sat there in silence for a bit. I could just faintly hear Corolla's radio from over the edge of the roof. Ilana stuck her plastic fork in her lo mein, twirled it up, and stuck a lump of noodles in her mouth.

She chewed for a second, then managed to say, "Thanks for the Chinese."

"It's whatever," I said. "You gotta eat."

Quiet again. I watched Ilana chow down. She was so zoned out on her food, it was like she forgot I was there. It was funny how she'd eat, stabbing her food with her fork as if she were trying to kill it.

She chewed, swallowed, then looked over at me. "Surely you got some friends who could help you get into Hell. You know all kinds of weird people. Gods. Ninjas. Robots from the future."

"I've asked around," I said. "A few of them know a way into Hell, but Zophiel and Metatron always show up and stop me." I sighed. "I need a better way in."

"Well, I got faith in you, dude." She stabbed her fork into her lo mein and twirled up some more. "You're not book smart, but you're street smart. You'll think of something." She shoved the food in her mouth and said, "I know it."

5

I got back to the shop just around evening time. I had laid out all the customer orders in a row across the counter and I made arrangements with each customer to come pick them up off the front porch at their leisure.

Had I been successful in sacrificing myself to Popocatepétl, had Xolotl taken me to Mictlan like I wanted, it meant I wouldn't be around to fulfill my duties at the shop so I did a lot of my work ahead of time. I figured out which customers were going to need which spices or ingredients on which specific days and I got everything ready ahead of time.

After that, it was up to Armstrong – my demonic house guest at the flower shop and the only surviving arm from the Army of Arms – to move those packages to the front porch under the cover of night and without being seen. The little demon arm could follow basic commands and was so fiercely loyal to me that nothing could possibly stop him.

It would also be Armstrong's job to water the plants in the morning and water the plants in the evening.

As I climbed the steps to the porch, I noticed the day's orders had already been picked up, which meant Armstrong had closed the shop for the night and the coast was clear. I unlocked the front door and let myself in. I kicked the yellow granite doorstop into place and propped the door open.

"Armstrong?" I called out. The shop had been tidied up, but the little guy was nowhere to be found. "Armstrong?"

The toilet flushed and the bathroom door opened. Armstrong – a left-handed forearm made entirely of black tar – came hopping out. He pointed his fingers at me and stared. I got this weird sense that I caught him red-handed, doing something he wasn't supposed to.

"Were you..." I took a moment to process. "Were you in the bathroom?"

Yes, my queen, he said through our psychic link.

"Why?"

Flushing the toilet.

"Why?"

He looked around with his fingers, then asked, *Is that not what toilets are for?*

"Yeah. I mean, I guess." I went over to the bathroom door and pulled it closed. "But you can't just flush the toilet all the time for no good reason."

Why?

"It drives up the fucking water bill, homie."

Oh.

"There should be no reason for you to flush the toilet."

No?

"No."

Ever?

I opened my mouth to scold him, but held my tongue. Instead, I changed my response to a stern, "Don't touch the toilet

34

ever again."

So let it be written, so let it be done.

I just laughed at him, shook my head, and went over to the cash register. Demons say the weirdest things sometimes. "Whatever, man. You're a trip."

You have returned home so soon, he said. *Did you acquiesce your venture down into the depths of Hell?*

I sighed and dug out my pocket dictionary. I muttered to myself, "You guys are going to be the death of me with all these big words I don't know. Why can't you all speak normal English like the rest of us? Everywhere I go, it's like everyone is a goddam Willicus Shakespeare." I looked at Armstrong. "Where did you learn to talk like that?"

Talk like what, my queen?

"Talk with all these big words," I said. "Did you go to finishing school or something? Is there a university down in Hell I don't know about?"

I'm terribly sorry. I don't understand.

"Just never mind"

Acquiesce - verb. To surrender or give up.

"No, Armstrong, I did not acquiesce." I tossed my dictionary on the counter and looked down at my spiral notebook, the one I used for all my bookkeeping. I flipped it open and plucked a golf pencil out of the little rocks glass Carl sent me for Christmas, the one etched with the Westland logo. I started running the numbers from the past few days. "I just... I need to find a sneakier way into Hell, you know?"

Was the Aztec volcano unsatisfactory?

"It was most unsatisfactory, Armstrong. Most unsatisfactory, indeed." I went back to my math. I hate math. I slapped the golf pencil down on the spiral and said, "No, you know what? The volcano was *most* satisfactory. It was those two dickbag angels who came down and screwed everything up for me like they always do."

Zophiel and Metatron.

I pointed right at Armstrong. "And I got half a mind to find some weapon that kills angels and really show them what's what."

Oh dear. They have found disfavor with the queen?

"This is like the fifth time they've screwed things up. They found disfavor with me months ago."

So too, then, have they found disfavor with Armstrong.

"Thanks, man." I looked down at the spiral, then back to the little arm. "Look, I'm sorry I'm sorry for being so bitchy today, dude, but I'm just real frustrated with this whole thing and I'm confused and I don't know what to do next."

Would you like for me to fetch you some food?

"Nah, I'm good." I went back to my math. "I ate some weight-lifting equipment for lunch."

Some ball bearings, perhaps?

"Nah."

I have a hammer soaking in some motor oil, if you'd like.

"Nah." Well. I raised an eyebrow and glanced up at him. "What kind of oil?"

10-W30.

Oh. 10-W30 is the au jou of metal dishes. Armstrong knew me all too well. "Alright," I said. "You talked me into it."

I shall return, he said as he went for the door. *The oily hammer is in a rusty bucket behind the storefront.*

6

New York City got the nickname "the city that never sleeps" because back in the olden times, New York was the first major metropolis to keep city operations open 24 hours. The subways, the ferries, and a handful of restaurants were available any time, day or night. I don't know if Frank Sinatra was the guy who invented the phrase or if he heard it from someone else, but I first heard him say it in his song "New York, New York." When I was real little, when grand-banana and gramp-banana were still alive, they used to listen to Sinatra all the time. I would lay there on my stomach and color in this old Wizard of Oz coloring book while they danced around the room all romantic-like to his music. I heard all his songs a billion times.

Now I was older. Living in the city that never sleeps was remarkably convenient, because I, too, didn't sleep.

Sure, Chinatown would get quiet at night, but only on the weekdays. The weekends were a different animal. The weekends meant more late-night food deliveries, illegal street racing, and a higher population of drunken tourists.

Armstrong would sleep at night. Not because he needed it, but because I would tell him to. Having Armstrong around was like babysitting a three-year-old kid, always asking questions and constantly getting into trouble. And much like a babysitter, I just wanted the little brat to go to sleep so I could get some peace and quiet, so I bought him a cat bed and put it behind the counter.

When the sun went down, I told him, "Armstrong. Bed time."

But mayhaps I might stay awake a while longer?

"Mayhaps you may not," I said. "Mayhaps it's bed time."

He crawled over to his cat bed and laid down.

Story?

"What?"

A story?

"I'm not..." He looked at me with his pitiful fingers. I sighed, rolled my eyes, and sat on the bar stool "Fine. *One* story. A short one."

He cozied up into his little bed. *The pact has been sealed.*

"Sure, dude." I adjusted my posture. Let's see, a story. I had lots of stories. There was that time I dismantled a nuke in mid air. Then there was that time I met the Suit Monster. Or the time me and Corolla got kicked out of that church parking lot because he wanted to practice Tokyo drifting. It was just a matter of which story to tell.

Tell me about the time when you died.

"I've told you that one before."

I beseech thee, my queen, tell it once more.

"Okay." Who am I to deny a request from my biggest fan? "So once there was this evil man in a suit that lived in a big skyscraper in Midtown. Everyone called this tool 'the CEO.' And the CEO wanted to steal the red power from your beloved queen."

Despicable.

"So this CEO invented a space laser specifically designed to scramble the brains of your queen and kill her once and for all."

Your majesty, what are brains?

"Brains is the stuff inside here." I pointed at my skull. "It's this squishy stuff that runs on electricity. Brains are where you keep all your thoughts and your feelings and your memories."

Does Armstrong have the brains?

"No," I told him. "Armstrong is a demon. Demons are different. Demons have a bottle inside them."

This evil man scrambled your brains. Like eggs.

"He did." Jeez, it was crazy to think back on all that. "He scrambled my brains and killed your queen dead, dead, dead. My soul went to the Guinee, the kingdom of the Voodoo spirits, which was a cruel trick by the Voodoo loa, Baron Semedi."

The Guinee was one of the many afterlifes. I'd been there twice. Once, when I died. A second time when my old friend Princess Parcel sent me there. Oh, how convenient it would be to have Princess Parcel around. She could just stick one of her magical stamps on my face and send me straight to Hell, no problem.

Unfortunately, Parcel was long gone, back to the Muffincake Kingdom.

"So I was dead and in the Guinee," I continued. "Even Baron Semedi didn't have the power to send me back to Earth. He could use his magical cigar to travel between worlds, but his hands were tied when it came to bringing me back to life because I was all the way dead. But then a bright light showed up and sucked me out of the Guinee..."

That was Tengoku, half building and half woman. Tengoku was a Japanese scientist who had swallowed Unknowable Yellow – another one of those enigmatic god spheres – and it turned her into the god of knowledge. Just like me, her biological body was filled with nanites that rearranged her molecules and made her more robot than human.

I could still remember seeing Tengoku's human body hanging there in that skyscraper basement. I would never forget the sight of the back of her skull wide open with dozens of thick cables connecting her brain to the entire Tengoku building.

"I woke up inside Tengoku and she told me she'd been waiting for me. Tengoku knew everything. She said she needed my help. She brought me back from the dead in a machine she invented."

That machine reconnected my soul to my body – something even Baron Semedi couldn't do – and if she could do that, surely she could invent a machine that might get me into Hell without Zophiel and Metatron finding out. If anyone could do it, it would be Tengoku.

"Once my soul was reconnected to my body, I went to go pick out some clothes. And when I got to the clothing room..." I looked down at Armstrong. His hand was balled up in a little fist, clutching the fabric of his cat bed. "Armstrong?" No response. "Armstrong?"

He was out like a light. Armstrong used one of my old Dark Funeral t-shirts as a blanket. He wouldn't sleep with anything else. He heard Dark Funeral on the radio once and asked what it was and that's when I explained Satanic death metal to him. Armstrong loved Satanic death metal. I mean, fancy that; he was a demon after all. After that, he wouldn't sleep without it.

"Goodnight, Armstrong," I said. I pulled the t-shirt up close around his wrist and tucked him in.

I sat there at the counter and did some thinking. There were so many different ways to travel between worlds. Princess Parcel showed me that. So did Tengoku. But what good did that do me now? Neither one of them lived on Earth anymore.

I stepped out on the front porch. The night sky was clear. The heat of the day had gone and now there was a cool breeze that smelled like Chinese food and wet trash. I could faintly see the stars through the glow of the city that never sleeps. The moon was full that night and hung low in the sky.

When I was little, I prayed to God for all the things I wanted. I gave up on prayer that night I got a D- in history and ended up covered in bruises. By the time I finished high school, I wasn't even convinced God existed. That belief changed, of course, after I swallowed Impossible Red and realized so much existed outside of the physical world. Voodoo spirits, dragons, and even the Choirs of Angels were definitely real. I assumed the same went for God, even though I still hadn't seen him. But even knowing that he was real, that still didn't mean I was going to pray to him. He had a pretty shitty track record of responding.

So I stared up at the sky and prayed to a different god.

"Tengoku," I said softly. "You can see me, can't you? You know everything. You know I'm standing here, right now, talking to you. And I know you're out there traveling the universe, but if you're not, you know, in the middle of anything important, I could really use your help."

I felt nothing but the lonely breeze. Somewhere in the distance I heard a cop siren and dog barking. I put my hands on the porch rail and hung my head. Well. Reaching out to Tengoku was a long shot to begin with. I knew that.

A sonic boom exploded overhead and rattled every window in Chinatown. A bright yellow light shone down on me. The courtyard lit up like daytime. I raised my hand and used it to shield my eyes from the blinding light. Rushing wind blew through my clothes and ruffled my hair.

It felt like I was staring up into an alien spaceship that was there to abduct me.

Directly overhead, filling the sky, was the entire Tengoku skyscraper. The building loomed there, suspended weightlessly in mid-air, dangerously too close to the rooftops of the nearby apartment buildings. With its architecture of sleek, futuristic glass and steel, Tengoku could have easily been confused for some alien mother ship that warped to Earth and took position over lower Manhattan. It slowly rotated in place, completely untethered by gravity or inertia. The bottom five stories of the building – the basements levels – were meant to be underground, so they were made of rough concrete, covered in mud, and with exposed pipes.

The lights in the windows flashed and flickered with life, as if the rooms of the skyscraper were the neurons and the entire building was thinking.

Tengoku had come back to Earth. And her first stop was Chinatown.

Chapter 3

1

My ears echoed with all different kinds of radio signals being broadcasted directly into my brain. I heard backwards talking voices in strange, foreign languages. Mixed in with the voices were electronic computer sounds like fax machines and bleeping morse code and microphone feedback.

Tengoku was trying to contact me.

I jump off the porch and ran out into the empty courtyard.

"Tengoku!" I waved my hands in the air. "Down here!"

The building hovered there for a few seconds, but it didn't stay long. Boom, just like that, the skyscraper vanished in an explosion of sound that set off every car alarm in Chinatown. The sky went dark. The wind immediately calmed. All that remained were a million wailing car alarms and a city full of barking dogs.

I stared dumbfounded at the empty night sky. My heart sank. Tengoku didn't want to talk to me? The whole thing only lasted seconds. Eventually I snapped out of it and got my wits about me. I bolted down the alleyway and out onto the sidewalk.

"Corolla!" I shouted. I hurdled over a stack of wooden crates and ran to his parking spot. "Corolla!"

"Penelope!" he shouted back. "Did you just see that?"

"Yes!" I opened his passenger side door and jumped in. "Go!"

He pulled out of his parking spot and drove down the road. "Go where?"

"Japan," I told him. "Fly!"

"But we're in the city and-"

"Corolla, *fly!*"

So he flew. We lifted off the ground and soared over the rooftops.

"Why are we going to Japan?" He sounded surprised, as if we didn't go on crazy adventures all the time and somehow Japan was an insane destination. "What's in Japan?"

"Tengoku," I told him. "She came back. And I think she's going home."

Tengoku was like family to me and Corolla. She invented Corolla and gave him life. And since she swallowed Unthinkable Yellow like how I swallowed Impossible Red, she'd equated our relationship to being like cousins. Strange, strange family we had going on.

It was time for another one of our totally unplanned road trips. Within minutes, we were drifting through the cloud line over the continental United States. Tengoku had actually come back to Earth. Now all we had to do was follow her to Tokyo.

Sometimes the stars and planets can align in unique and beautiful ways, and sometimes Corolla and I can agree on the music.

That's how we ended up tearing across the skies of North America rapping the words to "Hey Ladies" with the greatest poets to come out of Brooklyn: the Beastie Boys.

I couldn't believe Tengoku actually heard me. I couldn't believe she came back. I nervously drummed my fingertips across the steering wheel in anticipation of seeing her again. She was such a strange person, so completely overwhelmed with limitless knowledge that she lost all touch with her humanity. Last time I saw her, she kept calling me Roy because she got my reality confused with some other reality where I was born a boy.

Tengoku knew I was going to die to that Westland space laser, she knew she was going to bring me back from the dead, and she knew I was going to somehow save the world from Unthinkable Black. Once she put my soul back in my body and set those events into motion, she vanished from the planet entirely. I had no idea where she went. Outer space? Another dimension? Who could say.

Maybe all that time she spent off Earth did her some good. Maybe she found a connection to her lost humanity. Maybe she was better now.

Or maybe she was worse.

Tengoku was a true miracle worker. Her inventions were so powerful and beyond human technology, we might as well call them magic. She brought my soul back from the afterlife. She existed as both a building and as a person. She invented Corolla and gave him consciousness.

I turned down the radio.

"Corolla," I said. "What's the first thing you remember?"

"Weird question," he said.

"I know," I replied. "But relevant given the circumstances, right?"

"Well..."

He made a thoughtful sound and went quiet. After a few moments he said:

"I remember being in a big, dark place. I think it was a parking garage. I couldn't see or hear anything, and I was scared, so I turned on my headlights. I was going to shout out a hello, but I started to worry that a monster might be looking for me, so I kept quiet and turned my headlights back off. If something was out to get me, I sure as heck didn't want to bring any attention to myself.

"Then this voice said something to me. It was Tengoku, of course, but I didn't know that at the time. At first she called me Tercel and so for the longest time, I thought I was a Toyota Tercel. I didn't know any better. But this voice said, 'Tercel, you have a very important job.' So I asked the voice, 'What job?' And the voice said something like, 'You'll find out in four years, three months, something-something days, something-something hours...' She was really exact, down to the minutes and seconds, but I don't remember what they were exactly. I just remember the part about the four years.

"That's the first thing I remember."

I leaned back in my seat and thought. I said, "The job was working with me?"

"Yeah. One day the day had come. She told me I was going to make a new friend. The funny thing is..." Corolla was already snickering. "I thought it was going to be someone cool."

I rolled my eyes. "Fuck you."

Corolla laughed. So did I.

His laughing died down and he said, "No, she told me this new friend was going to be very important and needed my help flying them around. 'Every god needs a chariot,' she said."

"Well, the flying has come in pretty damn handy."

"Handy?" Corolla repeated, almost insulted. "How about crucial? I flew you all over the world looking for plants. I saved you from falling into the Oceans of Pure Time. Heck, I literally chased down a thermonuclear bomb because you told me to."

"Okay, okay," I said. "Don't get your panties in a twist. You've made tons of clutch plays and saved my ass. I'm not afraid to admit that."

"Thank you."

We kept flying. On nights when there's no moon in the sky over the Pacific Ocean – like there wasn't that night – the water turns pitch black and reflects the stars. With stars above you and stars below, it kind of feels like you're flying through outer space. Little dots of light floated around on the water below, little microscopic cruise ships and transport tankers and aircraft carriers.

Static beamed into my head again along with those backwards talking voices. It pierced my brain from my forehead to my brain stem. I hissed in agony and slapped my hands to my temples.

"Penelope?" Corolla asked. "You okay?"

"I'm fine." I shook my head and the invasive transmission passed. "It's nothing."

"Nothing, huh?" He sounded skeptical. "You just made that noise and grabbed your head for no reason?"

"I heard something," I told him. "Inside my brain."

"What was it?"

"I don't know. Like radio signals."

"Radio signals, huh?" he said. "It's probably your computer brain picking up military hackwaves from those Russian mind-control satellites."

"That's ridiculous," I said.

He said, "I know."

"Westland wiped out all those mind-control satellites months ago."

"I know."

2

Tokyo is really something to see at night. It looks like Manhattan, but Manhattan a hundred years in the future. All the buildings light up in beautiful neon colors. Electronic, animated billboards advertise different kinds of soda or candy or weird

44

cartoons and those billboards are everywhere. They also have this strange orange tower in the middle of the city that bears an odd, copyright-infringing resemblance to the Eiffel Tower.

We flew over the city. It just kept going and going and I thought to myself, "Jesus Christ, how big can Tokyo possibly be?"

Corolla kept us at a high enough elevation that if the civilians saw us – not likely – they would assume we were a helicopter or a drone or something. He flew us towards where Tengoku Headquarters once existed, before she left Earth.

The skyscraper finally came into view: 71 spiraling stories of glowing yellow glass.

I leaned forward against the dash and waved my finger at it. "There it is! It's really there! She's back!"

"I see it!" Corolla sounded just as excited as me. "I see it!"

We reached the building in no time. Corolla put us in a holding pattern over the peak of the building with the radio and cellphone towers. Once he scouted out a safe landing spot, he stealthfully descended down to the ground. He unfolded his wheels and touched down on the concrete. There on the east side of the building, the parking lot sloped down and led to four huge loading doors. Corolla drove us over that way and parked in a wide open loading zone.

I sat in the driver seat for a moment and drank in the sheer size of the skyscraper. The corners were rounded in places. All the windows were lit up, bright yellow. Two giant Japanese characters glowed on the front, facing out over the busy street.

天国

"It's so big," Corolla said.

I was zoned out admiring Tengoku, but couldn't resist the obvious joke. "That's what she said."

"Are you going in?" Corolla asked me.

"Yeah." But I didn't open the door and I didn't leave. I just kept staring.

"Are you nervous?" he asked.

I wasn't going to lie. "A little. Tengoku can be... strange sometimes. Plus I'm the god of war and she's the god of knowledge. Last time we were together, she said that made us cousins, so she's sort of the only family I have left. I hope she's not disappointed in me or something."

45

"You're overthinking things," he told me. "You'll be fine. Just go in."

I took a deep breath, opened the door, and jumped out.

I walked around the side of the building and towards the front doors of the main entrance. I paused for a second to tidy myself up. The windows of the main floor were tinted and reflected the night sky, so I used one of them as a mirror to give myself the once over. I retied my chucks, I straightened the folds on my shorts and I did my best to fix my hair, which was difficult because I had barbed wire growing in it. I looked fine, all things considered. There's only so much fixing-up you can do with your bare hands.

I bounded up the concrete steps of the main entrance and stood in front of a row of eight glass doors. It sort of reminded me of being outside an airport terminal. Inside was a dimly-lit lobby with black, glossy floors and white walls. There were several reception desks, all asymmetrical and curved. The same Japanese characters that glowed on the front of the building were holographically projected on the wall inside; I can't read Japanese, but I assumed the characters said TENGOKU.

No one sat at the reception desks inside. Of course not. Tengoku controlled the entire building: the elevators, the machines arms, and even the doors. She had no use for humans.

I tried to open one of the doors. It was locked. I tried the one next to it. Also locked. I tried all eight doors, but all eight were locked. I grabbed one of the handles and rattled the shit out of it.

"Hello?" I called out. "Tengoku? You in there? It's me! Penelope!"

The radio static stabbed through my brain again. This time I was so close to the source, it felt like my head was going to split right open. The radio voices were so overlapped and jumbled together I couldn't make out a single word. Then came the screech of electronic transmissions. I grit my teeth and tried to tolerate the pain, hoping the broadcast might go away on its own, but it only grew more intense and painful. I growled, slapped my hands to my head and fell to my knees.

"Tengoku, stop!" I screamed.

And it stopped. The pain vanished. I knelt there, panting for air. Whatever Tengoku was doing, I don't think she was trying to hurt me, but I couldn't take much more of it.

I heard a clack come from the doors. I got up on wobbly legs and tried the door in front of me. It whisked opened.

I stepped into the front lobby. The air smelled like brand-new electronics. The door shut behind me and it hissed as if it were being hermetically sealed, then there was another clack. I didn't bother to turn around and try the door. I knew what that sound meant: I was locked in.

The lobby was two stories tall with a glass balcony overhead. Escalators and hallways stretched off in all different directions, each one marked with signs in both Japanese and English that led to different departments like "Research and Development" and "Implementation." The lobby alone could have accommodated dozens of scurrying businessmen with suede couches and drinking fountains and full-length, holographic maps of the building's interior, but the place was totally empty. Empty and quiet. The squeak of my sneakers on the glossy floors filled the lonely space.

The lights were at half power, as if the lobby were closed for the day.

"Hello?" I called out. My voice echoed.

Tengoku's voice came out of speakers mounted along the ceiling. She said, "Hello, Roy."

"I'm Penelope," I said. "Don't you remember?"

There was a moment of silence, then she asked, "What world is this?"

I meandered around the empty lobby. A thin layer of dust had accumulated across the tops of the reception desks. I told her, "This is Earth."

There was another pause. "Which Earth?"

I didn't know how to answer that. If there were millions of Earths, or billions of Earths, or infinite Earths, how could I explain to her which one we were on?

"This is the Earth you used to live on," I told her. "This is the Earth where we first met."

I made my way to the elevator and stood by the doors. If I was going to go anywhere in the building, it would be through the elevator. The doors didn't open, but that was fine. I was cool with waiting.

"You are not Roy," she said.

"I'm not," I told her. "I'm Penelope."

"Penelope?" she repeated. "Penelope Marie Salvo, host of Impossible Red."

"That's right."

47

The elevator doors opened. The interior had a black floor, white walls, and was illuminated by a bright yellow light overhead. I stepped inside and the doors closed behind me.

Now her voice came out of the elevator intercom. "You summoned me here."

"I need help," I told her. "I need *your* help."

"You need my help getting into Hades. Hell. Sheol the Grave. Gehenna. The Lake of Fire. The Second Death. The Eternal Retribution."

"You got it," I said.

"Come," she said. "Let me see you."

The elevator moved. I watched the floor numbers above the door go negative as I descended deep into the basement levels. We reached the bottom-most floor and the doors opened to reveal a sprawling empty bunker made entirely of concrete. The human-form of Tengoku floated there in the center: a Japanese woman in a white lab coat. Her feet dangled just inches off the ground. The back of her head was wide open, exposing a network of cords and cables that tangled out of her like spaghetti and connected her to the walls and ceiling.

She was sleeping. Or in some type of coma.

I walked forward and stood in front of Tengoku's physical body. It had been years since I saw her last, but very little had changed. Her black hair hung down in front of her face. Her skin was flawless. If I didn't know better, I would have assumed she was a demon-haunted monster from some Japanese horror flick. Slowly, she opened her lifeless eyes and pointed them in my direction.

"Hello, Roy," the voice said. It came from the walls, not from her mouth. Her mouth didn't move.

"I'm not Roy," I told her politely. "My name is Penelope. Remember? Penelope Marie Salvo."

"Penelope Marie Salvo."

I thought back to the last time we were together in this place. After turning into the god of knowledge, poor Tengoku lost all connection to her humanity. She once asked me to remind her what it was like to be a human, and my only solution was to tell her bad jokes. But it worked.

If she needed help remembering who I was, I would start there.

"Do you want to hear a joke?" I asked.

Her eyes gained a little focus and she tilted her head. "I have seen all moments of this world and all other worlds. I am the living embodiment of all knowledge in every possible instance, in every possible dimension."

"Yeah?" I said. "So do you know what Courtney Love and hockey players have in common?"

Tengoku fluttered her eyes, as though she were scanning her brain for all possible answers. Her eyes focused on me entirely and she said, "I do not."

I grinned and hit her with the punchline. "They don't shower until after their third period."

Tengoku didn't react. Her eyes spazzed out. She said, "Courtney Love showered 23 hours, 17 minutes, and 11 seconds ago."

I sighed and rolled my eyes. "That's not the point. It's a joke."

"I remember jokes."

"I know you do," I said.

"A shit zoo," she said.

"What?"

She clarified. "I went to the zoo. There was only one animal. It was a dog. It was a shit zoo."

Ohh, yeah. I forgot I told her that one. That was years ago. I laughed and said, "Right. You remember."

Her face took on more life. She opened her mouth to speak, and while her voice still came out of the building itself, it also came from her own body. She was, after all, both at the same time.

3

I cut right to the chase. "I'm here because my friend Theodore is trapped in Hell and-"

She interrupted me and said, "I know why you are here."

"Oh." Of course she did. "Well, does that mean you're going to help me? Because-"

Interrupted again, this time by a hydraulic hiss coming out of the floor. A series of holes opened up – five holes to be exact – that circled around my position. Mechanical arms extended out of the holes, big ones, like arms you'd see working on an automated car assembly line. They were made of solid steel and were painted bright yellow. They moved in swift, preprogrammed motions, turned in my direction and opened their three-pincher hands. Each of their three claws was jagged and designed for gripping.

"Oh, hello," I said. "What are these things supposed to be?"

I got my answer.

One of them snapped forward and clamped down on my face.

"Whoa," I said, my voice muffled in its tight grip. It smooshed my cheeks and made it hard to talk. "What the hell is all this?"

Two other arms spun around and clamped down on each of my ankles, locking me in place. The fourth arm snapped down on my right shoulder. The last arm grabbed my right wrist and pulled, straightening my arm out from my body.

I struggled. My legs couldn't move. I bit into the claw holding my face and my teeth sank down into the metal, but the arms didn't feel pain and it didn't react. If anything, my struggling just made the arms clamp down harder.

"Do not struggle," I heard Tengoku say.

"Let me go and I won't have to!" I shouted.

The claw holding my shoulder pulled one way and the claw holding my wrist pulled the other. Nothing happened at first – my body is essentially indestructible – but these mechanical arms proved to be stronger than me. They increased in power. That's when the pain set in, and I'm not used to pain. The fibers in my industrial rubber muscles started to snap. She skin burned like fire. I felt separation pressure in my elbow joint.

"What the fuck!?" I screamed. I tried to kick my legs, but those mechanical arms were a billion times stronger than me and I could barely wobble my knees. If Tengoku built them – and it seemed obvious that she had – they were specifically designed to handle my immense strength. I couldn't even-

I screamed when my elbow joint crunched and came out of place. My muscles tore away from the bone. The fire in my arm burned like the sun. Streaks of chemical tears poured from my eyes. Gasoline smelling sweat beaded up on my forehead. The only thing keeping my arm in one piece was my bulletproof skin, and even that started to stretch like rubber.

I wanted to scream for help, I wanted to demand an explanation, but the only thing that came out of my mouth was a small, pathetic, "*Why!?*"

Through my agony, I saw Tengoku float over to face me. Her hair drifted out of her face like wispy curtains and she stared at me with her glowing yellow eyes. She didn't look angry or concerned. She looked curious, as though I were some casual science experiment.

"Stop!" I kicked and struggled, but still couldn't move. "Please!"

Tengoku didn't respond. She just tilted her head, slightly confused.

The pain drove me crazy. Desperate for any kind of help, I screamed out for people who weren't even there. Corolla. Armstrong. Even Ma.

The industrial arms increased in power yet again. The skin around my elbow tore open like bubblegum. My screams turned to digital noise and my vision flickered with static. I wanted the pain to knock me out, but Impossible Red kept me online. I was being tortured with no way out. My forearm was torn free from my body and it dangled loose in the jaws of that mechanical arm. I felt every second of it.

Pints of oily blood pumped out of my open elbow joint and splattered onto the floor. Carelessly, the drone opened its claws and let my poor arm drop to the ground with a splat that made my stomach turn.

More computerized noise came out of my throat. I looked back at Tengoku with wide, terrified eyes.

Something had turned her evil.

"Hold still," she said, as if I had anywhere to go. "There is more."

The mechanical drone that tore off my arm straightened up vertically and descended back down into the floor. A moment later it came back up with a futuristic prosthetic forearm in its claws. The hand part looked fleshy human, but the forearm was transparent plastic and had all kinds of moving parts inside: a series of pistons, vials of liquid, and a yellow cube floating right in the middle. At the elbow joint were seven long needles. If Tengoku intended to stab that thing into my torn off elbow joint, those long needles would sink all the way up to my shoulder. Maybe deeper.

"This *will* hurt," Tengoku said.

The mechanical drone took that replacement arm and plunged the needles into my bleeding joint. I screamed into the claws that covered my mouth. Tears drained down my face and soaked into my shirt. I could feel the needles as they twisted their way into my muscles and drilled deep into my bones. The prosthetic arm was pushed expertly into place. Once set, the device made a high-frequency sound, as if it were turning on and powering up.

Just like that, the pain vanished. The replacement arm clamped onto my skin with triangular hooks and sealed off the open wound. My arm stopped bleeding. Tengoku's five drones released my body and I dropped to the ground with a thud. I crouched there on my hands and knees and gasped for air.

I could barely speak. "What... the fuck... did you do that for?"

"This is what you wanted," Tengoku said. Her human body looked around, delirious. "Is it not? What world is this?"

"You fucking psychopath!" I shot to my feet and swung my arms around. I smacked one of those mechanical arms good, denting it, and forcing them all to back off. "I didn't ask you to rip my fucking arm off!"

"Not yet," she said. "But you were going to."

"I was not!" I pointed my finger at her, ready to tear her a new asshole. That's when I realized which finger I was using; it was the finger on my replacement arm. I had complete control over it as if it were part of my body. The forearm glowed bright red, somehow drawing power from the nanites in my body. The yellow cube inside the forearm had also turned red and begun to glow. It spun in place, functioning like some kind of power source. It moved the pistons and caused the liquid in the vials to bubble.

Okay, fine, I had a replacement arm, but I wouldn't *need* a replacement arm if she didn't tear off the old one.

She asked me, "Are you not trying to enter Hell?"

"Yes, I'm trying to enter Hell!" I shouted at her. "What does that have to do with ripping off my fucking arm?"

She floated directly in front of me. I had a clear shot at her vacant, comatose face. Maybe she'd see it coming and maybe she wouldn't. I seriously considered doing it.

"I have upset you," she observed.

"Yes, you fucking upset me! You tore off my fucking arm!"

"You must understand," she said. "Your goal is passage into Hell without interference from the archangels Zophiel and Metatron. Zophiel is the Spy of God. Metatron is the Knower of All Secrets."

She was wasting my time. "What does that have to do with a god damn thing!?"

52

"You told me about a boy named Theodore. You said you must save him. You begged me for help. I told you that passage into Hell directly from Earth without being seen by the Choirs of Angels was impossible. That made you angry. You insisted that I, as the god of knowledge, should be able to think of something. So I did."

I held my robotic arm between us. The pistons moved and the red cube pulsed with energy. "Skip to the part where you start tearing off my limbs!"

"This," one of her mechanical worker arms pointed at the strange device now fused to my body, "is Athena. It is an invention of my own design. It will guide you as you travel between worlds. You will not be able to go to Hell directly, so you will have to journey through other worlds to get there. I told you all of this. You agreed to it."

"I did not! None of what you're saying ever happened!"

"It would have," she said. "The conversation was not necessary, because we reached an agreement that I would build you a new arm. I simply fulfilled my part of the agreement before it happened."

"What agreement?" I asked. "What conversation?"

"I am talking about things that have not happened," she said. "And things that will never happen, now that we had this conversation instead. You came to me for help. I offered you a solution to free Theodore from Hell. I warned you that the journey through other worlds would put you in great danger. You said that you were not afraid of danger. I told you that I could build a device that would accomplish your goal. You asked me how quickly I could have it built."

"And what did you say?"

"I told you I could have it built before you even arrived."

"And what did I say?"

"You said, 'fuck yeah, the faster, the better.' And here we are."

Fuck yeah, the faster, the better, chop my arm off and replace it with a futuristic robo-arm?

It wasn't the craziest thing I'd ever heard.

4

I stared down at my new arm. I could move it and feel with it. Impossible Red didn't seem to be rejecting it; in fact, Impossible

53

Red was going out of its way to provide it with power. I could turn my wrist and wriggle my fingers. I used my real human hand to point at the fake one.

"How is this 'Athena' going to help me get to Hell?" I asked.

"For that..." she said, "you will need to watch a short film I have prepared for you."

Far behind me, the elevator doors opened and I heard an electronic *ding*.

Ah. Classic Tengoku. She liked to show me films because-

"You are nowhere near intelligent enough to understand the science of it all," she said.

"Right." I marched to the elevator. "Because I'm a big dumb-dumb."

"You simply lack the necessary knowledge of particle physics," she said.

"Right," I said.

She continued, "And you know nothing of dimensional theory or quantum entanglement or calculus."

"Right."

"For that matter, you struggle with basic mathematics."

"You're doing wonders for my self-esteem, you know that, right?" I threw my hands up and stepped into the elevator. The doors closed. "Just show me your goddam movie."

The elevator jerked to life and whisked me up into the higher floors of the building. I had a chance to really scrutinize my new arm. Not only did it have moving mechanical parts and a spinning cube to generate power, it had a few digital displays projected on the "skin." They were simple icons: ascending bars that represented signal strength, numbers that read "12,547 kilometers" which didn't mean anything to me, and a black arrow that moved like a compass.

"Is this thing bulletproof?" I asked her.

"It is indestructible," she said.

"Because I get shot at a lot."

"It is indestructible."

"The last thing I need is for this thing to crack open and have it blow my whole arm off."

"That will not happen," she said. "It is indestructible."

I glared at it and muttered, "It better be."

The elevator dinged and the doors opened up to a private movie theater. I had been here once before, when Tengoku showed me a short film about the god spheres, how they were made, and how Unthinkable Black – the sphere that houses the artificial god of destruction – destroyed an entire planet and galaxy.

I took my seat in the back corner of the theater, closest to the elevator. The screen was covered by yellow satin curtains.

In the old days, back when I was human, my movie-going tradition was to get skittles and reese's pieces and mix them up and eat them together. Ilana always said that was gross, but Ilana dipped her pizza in honey mustard, so it's not like she had any room to talk.

That was a long time ago. I didn't eat candy anymore.

"You know what I'd really like?" I said to Tengoku.

And without answering me, two portals opened up in the ceiling. Two sleek versions of her robotic arms descended down, one holding a cup of liquid, the other one holding a plain white box of something heavy. They held the snacks within arms reach of me and stopped. I accepted their little offering.

I smelled whatever was in the cup. Ooh, antifreeze. Prestone Dex-Cool, too. The good stuff. I checked inside the box and found a mix of galvanized nuts and bolts, one of my absolute favorites.

"Thanks!" I said, shaking a few bolts into my mouth. "How did you–"

"I know everything," she said.

"Right." I got settled in my seat and motioned at the screen with my cup. "Well, if we're going to have movie night, let's get to it. I double-parked my car in one of your loading zones."

The lights dimmed. The curtains opened. The screen flickered to life and opened with an star-filled image of the Universe. The camera zoomed at light-speed through galaxies and colorful clouds of space dust. It bobbed and weaved through blinking pulsars and exploding novas and swarms of asteroids. Eventually after a minute of traveling, we zoomed in on a familiar green and blue world.

Tengoku said, "This is Earth."

"Mmhmm." I drank my antifreeze. "I'd recognize that bitch anywhere."

"Earth is confined to this dimension you call the Universe."

The camera zoomed out at blinding speeds. The whole Universe whisked away from me, reducing all the darkness and all the stars size down to a small square on a blank white screen.

"Also out there are the dimensions of Heaven and Hell."

Heaven – a world of golden statues and fluffy clouds – appeared in a separate square. Hell – a burning world of fire – appeared in another square. They floated around the Universe and one another, but never quite got close enough to touch.

"And as the many other gods created their worlds, so too were they confined to their dimensions. Among these are the Guinee, Olympus, Limbo, Valhalla, Mictlan, and millions of others."

All the worlds she mentioned appeared in their own squares. The voodoo swamps of the Guinee, in its own square. The cloudy mountains of Olympus, the swirling fog of Limbo, the joyous Vikings of Valhalla, the scorched and burning bloodbaths of Mictlan, they were all confined to squares in their own little part of the screen.

"But these worlds, while separate, connect together like pieces of a puzzle."

All the squares morphed into the shapes of various puzzle pieces. They floated into place and connected to one another. The Guinee connected to Earth, Valhalla connected to Mictlan, so on and so on until a couple dozen worlds were all locked together. Millions of new puzzle pieces appeared, millions of new worlds, worlds I'd never seen before, and they also snapped into place. Together, they formed a giant, completed puzzle of worlds upon worlds, adding up to all reality.

"These places were the worlds interlock..." And the curvy parts of the puzzle pieces glowed in yellow highlights, "...represent the flaws in reality that allow passage from one world into another. Sometimes these flaws are created on purpose, or sometimes they are accidents. Sometimes they are as large as an ocean, or sometimes they are as small as a pinprick. Sometimes they appear as a great boiling volcano, or sometimes they are disguised as a door. Your new arm, your device, *Athena*, can detect these flaws in reality and guide you to them. By navigating through these worlds, you can get from the Universe to Hell."

A glowing pathway appeared on the puzzle of worlds, starting at Earth and zig-zagging through a bunch of other puzzle pieces. It ultimately ended in Hell.

"Trying to travel from Earth to Hell in one move is like trying to force two puzzle pieces together when they do not fit," Tengoku said. "That is why you have attracted the attention of Heaven. But if you were to travel through the flaws of reality in the way that I have mapped out…"

"I could get to Hell without the angels knowing?" I asked.

"They will know you have left Earth," Tengoku said. "But this path connecting Earth to Hell is unknown, even to them. They might know where you have been, but they will not know where you are going next."

"Dope." I looked at my glowing arm. It put me one step ahead of the angels and could detect flaws in reality. That was a pretty good upgrade from my old arm, considering my old arm didn't do shit and couldn't detect a damn thing. "So is this black arrow the direction I need to go to find one of these secret doors?"

"Correct."

"And are these numbers the distance, or something?"

"Also correct."

12,547 kilometers. The number made more sense now.

"So the flaw that gets me off Earth is 12,547 miles away." I waved my finger at her. "See? I'm not *that* stupid."

"The distance is in kilometers," she told me. "Not miles."

"Alright. Whatever."

5

With movie night over, I rode the elevator down to the main lobby. Tengoku had given me exactly what I needed and now came step two: dimension hopping.

"Your journey will be dangerous and full of peril," Tengoku said through the elevator intercom. "You will truly be tested as the artificial god of war."

"But I'm going to make it, right?" I asked her. "I'm going to reach Hell?"

"Eventually."

"Dope." Of course I would. I'm Penelope Salvo.

"But you will make mistakes along the way."

"No one's perfect."

"They will come at a great cost."

"Most things do."

I descended down past floors 13… 12… 11…

I asked, "Do you have any-"

"Here is my last minute advice," she said, cutting me off. "Do not deviate from the path given to you by Athena. Do not wander off course. Believe me, there are a great many worlds far more dangerous than Hell."

"Oh yeah?" I asked. "Like what?"

"More than we have time to discuss," she told me. "But they exist. There are nightmarish places. Like New Beatlemania."

New Beatlemania? I felt like I'd heard people talk about that place before. I'd only heard name though. I didn't know the first thing about it. It certainly wasn't in my book of secrets back home.

I reached the lobby. The elevator dinged and the doors opened. I stepped out into the dimly lit reception area and headed for the main exit.

"Welp, thanks for ripping my arm off," I said.

"Before you leave," Tengoku said, "I might ask you for a favor."

I stopped just short of the exit doors. "Go for it."

"You reminded me once how it feels to be human," she said. "Would you do it once more?"

I squinted, slightly confused. "You mean tell you a joke?"

"Yes."

It's hard being put on the spot like that. "Uh. Okay. Let me think of one."

Aside from my incredible strength and durability, I also have an arsenal of weapon-grade dad jokes.

There was the one about the three frogs, but I didn't really remember how that one went. There was the one about the hunter and the lion and something about shitting his pants, but I couldn't remember how that one started. Then there was the one about the guy in the hotel.

"Okay," I said. "This guy checks into a hotel and says 'Hey, I'm getting a room for my whole family. Is your porn channel disabled?' And the hotel clerk says, 'No, it's just the regular kind.'"

I grinned. Surely she got that one.

"Good joke," she told me.

"Make you laugh?" I asked.

"I don't think so."

"Oh. Well, it's funny. Trust me."

I put my hands on the door, ready to leave, but turned back to the empty lobby and asked her, "Hey, are you going to stay here on Earth? Or are you going back out into the Universe?"

"I do not know," she said.

"Well," I said, "Maybe I'll see you again someday."

Tengoku said, "Farewell, Roy."

Chapter 4

1

Corolla and I flew back to America.

My Fall Out Boy cassette popped out of the stereo.

I pushed it back in.

Corolla ejected it.

I pushed it back in.

He ejected it.

"Stop, goddammit!" I shouted.

"You stop!" he shouted back.

I pushed it back in.

He ejected it.

"It's my turn to pick!" I told him.

"If I don't get to listen to Journey, you don't get to listen to Fall Out Boy!"

"You can listen to Journey," I pushed the cassette back in. "*After* we listen to Fall Out Boy."

He ejected it. "You can listen to Fall Out Boy after we listen to Journey!"

"No!"

The night air was calm and cool and there wasn't a cloud in the sky. We drifted across the Pacific Ocean under a moonless sky. The stars were out and even the hazy band of the Milky Way was visible. It would have been a peaceful scene if Corolla wasn't being such a pain in the ass.

"Leave it in!" I said. I pushed the cassette back in and held it in place with my fingertips. I could feel Corolla trying to eject it. I wasn't going to let that happen.

"Stop!" he shouted.

"You stop!"

The more he tried to eject it, the harder I held it in place.

He said, "Countermand!"

I said, "You countermand!"

I glanced out the windshield at just at the right moment. A 747 was coming straight for us. We were too busy fighting to notice. Impact in three... two...

My eyes went wide as the reflection of the plane filled the windshield.

"Corolla!" I shouted. "Look out!"

By reflex, I ducked down in my seat and threw my hands over my head. Corolla blurted out an "oh, shit" and plunged into an emergency nose dive. The 747 roared past us and rattled Corolla down to his metal frame. The rumbling jet engines and hot wind sent Corolla tumbling through the air.

We spun around out of control and then things went quiet. Corolla straightened himself out and hovered in place.

I cowered there in the fetal position for a moment, then peeked my eyes through my fingers. My mechanical heart pounded in my chest, as if it wanted to punch out of my ribcage and parachute to safety without me.

We floated there and processed what just happened.

"Holy. The fuck. Shit." I said.

"No kidding," Corolla said. "That thing came out of nowhere."

"Holy fucking shit."

"That was so close, I could see the pilots," he said. "I could read their name tags."

"Holy fucking fuck."

"I saw my life flash before my eyes. And it was filled with *this* crap."

He ejected the Fall Out Boy cassette so hard, it shot out and landed on the center console. I was too panicked to argue. I was just glad we were alive. Or, to be technical, I was glad Corolla was alive. I would have been fine.

"You okay?" he asked me.

"Yeah," I said. "You?"

"I'm good." He didn't sound too sure.

"Okay. Wow."

We continued out over the ocean. After a near-death experience like that, it really put into perspective how stupid our fight over the music was. I let Corolla listen to Journey. It was a long trip. There'd be plenty of time to listen to all kinds of music. It didn't matter who went first.

2

About the time we passed over Hawaii, Corolla asked me, "So what's your new arm do?"

"It's called Athena," I said. "It detects portals between worlds and tells me how to find them. Tengoku says if I follow its directions, it will lead me to Hell."

"And it works?"

"Well, I guess we're about to find out."

"So does that mean this is it?" he asked. "Are you actually leaving Earth this time?"

"If this thing works like it's supposed to."

"How much farther does it say we have to go?"

"Uh." I checked my arm. "8,573 kilometers." I pointed in the direction of the arrow. "That way."

"Kilometers?" Corolla said, disgusted. "Was that thing made in Canada?"

"I dunno, dude," I said. "The whole world uses kilometers."

"Well, I don't know kilometers. How am I supposed to know how far we're really talking?"

"I dunno."

"How many miles in a kilometer?"

I scoffed. "What am I? Lewis and Clark?"

"Check your arm and see if it's got a button for settings. Maybe you can switch it to miles."

I looked for a settings button. Nothing. The hand was synthetic and looked human, the forearm was some indestructible transparent material that revealed the electronic inner workings, and the elbow was securely clamped onto my skin. There were no buttons.

"Nothing," I said. "We're just going to have to keep following the arrow and see where it takes us."

So that's what we did. Athena took us over Hawaii. It led across the rest of the Pacific Ocean. Eventually, just as morning broke, Mexico appeared on the distant horizon like a faint brown

61

smudge.

"You're sure the angels aren't going to find out about this?" Corolla asked. "Because if they do, you're in for a lot of trouble."

"Tengoku said they won't be able to know where I'm going," I told him. "And Tengoku knows everything."

"I sure hope so. For your sake."

"I'll be fine," I said. "You worry too much."

Corolla did worry too much, but there was this small part of me that knew he was right. What *if* the angels found out? What *if* they came for me? Zophiel and Metatron would tear me to absolute shreds.

That would be the end of Penelope Salvo.

Our flight path took us over the northern parts of Mexico, then the lower parts of Texas. We had to take the long way around San Antonio to keep from being spotted in the early afternoon.

"Ugh, how much farther," Corolla asked me.

I checked Athena and read off the numbers. "2,759 kilometers."

He mumbled. "I still don't know how far that is."

"Me either," I said.

Eventually Texas ended and we flew over the blue waters of the Gulf of Mexico. By that point we'd listened to every cassette in the glove box at least twice. After that much music, I didn't care what we listened to anymore. Neither did Corolla.

"You can listen to whatever," he said.

"Nah," I told him. "You can pick."

"I don't care."

"Me either."

He said, "Well, let's see if we can pick up a radio station up here."

He shifted through snippets of voices and tons of static before stumbling across a weak signal of talk radio coming out of Louisiana.

The current financial crisis shows no signs of stabilizing. In fact, Wall Street reports serious downturns in stock exchanges, both here at home and even in strong markets that are usually immune to these types of impacts, like China and India. When the fiscal year ends-

"Never mind," I said, switching it off.

I reached into the glove box and pulled out the first thing I touched. The Lion King soundtrack. Fine. Whatever. I put it in and let it play. I cracked the window, lit up a spliff, and puffed smoke into the air.

"Maybe your arm is taking us to Florida," Corolla said. "Do you think it's taking us to Florida?"

I checked my arm. 1,913 kilometers left to go. I looked out the window and at the blue waters below. We were still over the Gulf. I had no idea how far we were from Florida, which didn't matter, because kilometers were a useless unit of measurement for me.

"Maybe," I told him.

"Florida would be cool," he said. "If we lived in Florida, I'd want it to be like one of those TV shows where you would be the down-and-out private eye in Miami tracking down drug lords, and I'm the talking car that drives you around."

Interesting idea. It wasn't really my style, but I could wear a Hawaiian shirt and a wicker hat and I could bust Colombian drug dealers with names like Cortez and Hernandez. I could wear mirrored shades and get drunk at run down tiki bars, nursing spiced rum out of a hollowed out pineapple. When I was working a case, I would pound information out of the seedy underbelly of the criminal world.

I'd grab some lowlife scumbag, slam him up against a wall and shout in his face: "When is the Lovely Lady scheduled to arrive in port? I know Cortez cut a deal with the Cubans to smuggle in his next shipment of coke. All I need is a day and a time!" Then the scumbag would be like, "I don't know! They never told me!" That's when I'd get the pliers out and hold them up to his face and say, "Two things are about to come out of your mouth. The truth... or your teeth. So what's it going to be?"

Then he'd spill the beans. Cortez was going down and the Cubans would be next.

Corolla was right. Living in Florida would be cool.

So I told him. "That would be cool."

Corolla sounded confused. "What would be cool?"

"That private eye thing in Miami you were talking about."

"Oh, that? You're still talking about that? That was thirty minutes ago."

"What? Really?"

"Dude, how much weed did you smoke?"

"Just a spliff," I said.

"Have you seriously been thinking about that Miami thing this whole time? You haven't said anything for half an hour. I didn't even think you heard me."

"No, dude, I was thinking about it. Totally thinking about it. About Cortez and his deal with Cubans."

Corolla laughed. "Who is Cortez?"

I didn't see what was so hard to understand. "The dude who cut a deal with the Cubans. He's bringing fifty tons of coke into port on the Lovely Lady."

"What are you *talking* about?" Corolla asked. "You're crazy."

I laughed like an idiot. "Your mom's crazy."

3

Athena didn't take us to Florida. It took us right past Florida and out into the Atlantic. We flew over the Bahamas.

It was early evening and we only had 199 kilometers to go. I didn't know what that was in miles, but it felt close.

If there was a flaw in the Universe located on Earth, what was it doing in the middle of the Atlantic Ocean? Was it underwater? Was it Atlantis?

The kilometers kept ticking away. I guess we'd find out soon enough.

"Storm up ahead," Corolla said. "Do you want me to countermand?"

"Stop using that word," I said.

"Countermand?" he asked.

"Yeah. Just say what you mean."

"I think it's cool."

"You're only using it because you heard those angels use it."

"It's not like they invented the word. I can use it if I want to."

"Alright." I decided to give up. Not going to die on that hill. "Whatever."

He asked me, "So do you want me to fly around this storm or what?"

"Huh." I checked Athena. 61 kilometers to go and the arrow was pointed dead ahead. "No. I think we have to go in."

"Into the storm?" he asked, confirming.

I leaned back and put my hand to my chin, because that's what you do when you're in deep thought. The clouds were dark. Lightning flashes illuminated them from the inside, like some kind of evil science experiment. I looked down at the ocean below. The water was choppy and the waves looked intense. Even the sharks were swimming away from it. I looked back at the storm. What flaw of reality could be out there in the middle of the ocean?

I checked Athena. 57 kilometers. We couldn't go around. The arrow was insisting we continue forward.

I suddenly realized where we were and where we were going. I said it out loud.

"It's the Bermuda Triangle."

"The what!?" Corolla said. He sounded terrified.

"The Bermuda Triangle." I pointed dead ahead. "That's the way off Earth."

"I'm not flying into the Bermuda Triangle," he said.

"We don't have much choice."

He sighed. He knew I wasn't going to let him chicken out of this one, so he didn't even try. Poor Corolla. Scared half to death, he still did what I asked him to do. He turned on his windshield wipers, kicked on his headlights and flew directly into the thunderstorm.

The clouds looked like a boiling cauldron of electric eels. The sunlight disappeared behind the dense clouds. Suddenly we were in the dead of night. Corolla changed his headlights to high beams, but all we could see was a swirling gray abyss. Rain started as a light tapping on the roof, then quickly turned into a full downpour. It felt like being inside an automatic car wash; a car wash with a crackling light show.

We were deep inside the breeding ground for lightning bolts. They zig-zagged all around us, moving and shifting, waiting for their moment to snap free and touch the ocean below. A bolt exploded into existence right next to Corolla. A deafening boom of thunder rattled the glass. Loose electrons surged through his metal body. The hair on my head stood up on end.

Super-heated air knocked Corolla sideways. He dropped several feet out of the sky before he could recover. The prevailing winds tossed him back and forth, sending him into an uncontrolled spin. His hubcaps whirred louder and more desperate as he did his best to keep us in the sky.

"I don't like this!" he shouted over the rain and thunder. He managed to get us straightened out and flying forward again.

"Keep going," I told him. I checked Athena. "Only 13 kilometers to go!"

"I don't know how far that is!" he shouted. "What if I get hit by lightning?"

"You won't get hit by lightning!" I told him. "Just help me get off Earth and then race out of here! Go back to New York and tell

65

Ilana where I went!"

"I don't like this," he said. "I really don't like this."

The winds were unforgiving. They blew hard from one direction, then shifted to another. Corolla swayed back and forth. I worried we might get knocked out of the sky and crash into the ocean. We needed to hurry.

Seven kilometers. The arrow on Athena would periodically start freaking out, spinning in all directions, but when it returned to normal, it confirmed we were going the right way.

The ocean waves below looked like black ink and swirled with dozens of whirlpools. Lightning struck the ocean and sent electricity speeding through the water like escaped snakes.

Corolla kept his wipers on full-speed, but that barely helped. There wasn't anything to see except clouds and lightning. He shouted something at me, but I couldn't hear him over the pounding rain and constant thunder.

So I shouted back, "What!?"

"I said, how much farther!?"

I checked. "Three kilometers!"

"Aw, man!"

Another bolt of lightning flashed in front of us, this one too close for comfort. Corolla's electronics blinked for a second and we almost lost power. The thunder blew him off balance and he did a full 360. I thought he was going to lose control, but after a couple of dangerous spins that threw me against the door, he regained his balance.

He cried out, "I don't know how much longer I can do this!"

2 kilometers.

"We're almost there!" I said.

Corolla pressed on. This barely felt like Earth. This was the surface of some alien water planet. The gale force winds threatened to rip Corolla apart. His doors rattled in their frames. Lightning flashed all around us, like we were floating through some kind of malfunctioning circuit board. The ocean was so dark, it didn't look like water. It looked like the void.

1 kilometer.

"This is it!" I shouted. "Dead ahead!"

"Don't say dead!" he replied.

I tried to open the passenger door, but the wind immediately slammed it shut. I opened it again and pushed it open with my feet. Corolla's interior was suddenly depressurized and filled with hurricane-strength winds. Our cassettes whipped around like startled birds and clattered against the windows.

If I kept the door open for long, if the wind kept blowing inside him, he was going to lose control for sure. I had to jump out, and I had to jump out immediately.

I looked down at my arm and checked Athena.

0 kilometers.

I peered out over the ocean. The black waves opened up into a giant whirlpool that drained into total darkness. The whirlpool was so vast, it could have swallowed an entire aircraft carrier like a bathtub toy. This was the very heart of the Bermuda Triangle, the mysterious cause of dozens of missing ships.

The arrow on Athena blinked. This was the flaw in reality and my one chance to get off Earth.

"Are we here?" Corolla shouted at me. "Is this goodbye?'

"This is goodbye!" I shouted back.

"I'm going to miss you!" he said.

"I'm going to-"

I was cut short when a bolt of lightning struck my metal bones. I surged with power. My skeleton was visible through my skin. The blast ripped Corolla's passenger door off the hinges and it whipped away in the wind.

I lost control of my body and fell out of the car. I spun down towards the ocean. Above me, Corolla struggled to stay in the sky. His hubcaps flickered on and off. He spun around in wild circles. His headlights went dark.

I heard him shout my name.

I shouted back.

I plunged into the ice-cold ocean. The rain and thunder sounded muffled, drowned out by being underwater.

Another bolt of lightning struck the water in a blinding flash. My muscles seized up. My jaws clenched down tight, so tight that my vision shorted out. The rushing sound of water faded away and I blacked out.

4

I opened my eyes to find myself standing in the garden of a great Tibetan temple. The buildings were carved into the highest side of a Himalayan mountain. Beyond the temple ground and its mountain peak were hundreds of snow-capped mountains that stretched off far into the distance, each one steep and jagged and a challenge for even the most experienced rock climbers.

The temple in front of me was so high up in the sky, clouds rolled through it like fog. Still, even as blizzard conditions blanketed the neighboring mountains in feet of snow, this one was magically protected from the elements. I was standing in a supernatural aura of bright, glimmering sunshine.

This place couldn't be real. It was ripped right out some mythological story; like some hidden Kung Fu temple that only appears once every hundred years, with impossibly healthy plant life and centuries-old architecture that somehow looked as new as the day it was built.

Or maybe it wasn't built at all. Maybe it was put here by gods.

The sheer size of the temple grounds left me speechless. It was more like a college campus than a temple, with dozens of individual structures – open gazebos for meditation, and lookout towers, and holy temples – all connected by narrow stone pathways that crept higher and higher up the mountainside. The windows in the buildings were wide open with no glass or shutters or fixtures of any kind.

They weren't much for security up here. Probably not a lot of burglars lurking in the highest peaks of the Himalayas.

The walls of the temple buildings were painted white, with a thick red stripe going horizontally around the middle. Inside the red stripe were bright golden circles that shimmered like the sun. The roofs of the buildings resembled Tibetan architecture with curved points at all the corners.

I stood in the garden courtyard, directly at the base of the main temple. The perimeter of the garden was closed off by a stone wall that stood waist-high. The grass was lush and green; we're talking PGA golf course quality. Geometrically trimmed shrubs and bright, blooming flowers decorated the outside edges of the walls. In the middle of the garden was a square walkway that divided the grass into the inner garden and the outer garden.

In the outer garden, there were fruit and vegetable plants in different stages of growth. In the inner garden rested thirteen good-sized boulders of granite.

I recognized this place. Like from a dream. I had been here once before, but I couldn't remember when.

A Korean girl stood in the inner garden, about my age, with a shaved head and bright orange robes. She looked familiar, too, like I'd met her from somewhere. I just couldn't remember. She stood facing away from me, staring intently at the granite boulders in the grass.

I was either dead, or I wasn't. Either way, I'd get my answers soon enough, of that I was pretty confident. So I went and stood next to the solitary monk. She turned to me and her eyes brightened up. She smiled as if she recognized me.

"Oh, it's you," she said. Her voice was familiar. So was her Brooklyn accent.

"It's me?" I repeated. "Have we met?"

"Once." She turned her attention to the sky. "A year ago."

"I don't remember," I told her.

"No, I suppose you wouldn't." She bowed at me. "My name is Io."

"Like Jupiter's moon?" I asked.

She nodded. "Like Jupiter's moon."

"I'm Penelope," I said.

She kept smiling. "I know."

"I've been here before," I told her. I walked into the square yard of grass that made up the inner garden. I ran my fingertip across the tops of one of the granite lumps. "Haven't I?"

"Yes."

"Did I make it off Earth?" I asked her. "Is this the next world on the path to Hell?"

I looked down to Athena. It wasn't there. My arm was totally normal.

"Hey!" I shouted. I pointed at my arm where Athena was supposed to be. "Where's my arm?"

The monk girl gave me a confused look. "Both your arms are right there. Unless you have a third one I don't know about."

"Where's my *mechanical* arm?" I asked.

"Probably with your body," she said, as if that were common sense. "Wherever it is."

"My body is right here!"

"No." She stepped over to me and pressed a fingertip to my heart. "You're having an out-of-body experience. This is your soul. Your body is somewhere else."

"Somewhere else? Where is somewhere else?"

She shrugged. "Got me."

"Well, then why is my body somewhere else and why is my soul here?"

"You must be dying," she told me. "Something must have happened to you."

"I got hit by lightning," I said.

She nodded. "That would do it, I suppose." She turned and headed for one of the temple buildings. "Are you hungry? I can prepare you something to eat."

I followed behind her. "I don't eat food."

"It's not food," she said. "It's nothing."

"What do you mean it's nothing?" I asked.

"Exactly like how it sounds," she said. "It's a big bowl of nothing. You get a bowl and fill it with nothing. Then you eat it."

"Does it taste like anything?" I asked.

"It tastes like nothing," she said. "But you get used to it."

She stepped inside a cottage-sized building and I followed behind her. The inside darkness was broken up by skylights carved into the roof. Lit candles were spread out all along the floor. The building was scarce of any furniture – only one wooden table with eight wooden chairs – but there were several rugs spread out across the floors. They looked course and beige, as if they were made of horse hair or hemp. The rugs were surrounded by candles, brass jars filled with sweet-smelling incense, and several golden bells.

The air was cool and smelled of centuries long forgotten.

"Here." She stepped to the table and picked up a wooden bowl. She placed a set of chopsticks in it and handed it to me. "Try it."

I looked in the bowl. It was empty. I held it out and showed it to her.

"This some sort of joke?" I asked.

She laughed to herself. "I said that my first time, too. But seriously. Try it."

I just stared at the bowl. Still laughing, she took it away from me.

"Here," she said. "I'll show you." She placed the chopsticks in the empty bowl, clicked them together, then put the empty ends of them in her mouth. She didn't chew. She didn't swallow. She put the chopsticks back in the bowl and did it again. She handed the bowl back to me. "Like that."

"This is how you eat?" I asked her.

She nodded. "For quite some time."

"But you'd die if all you did was eat nothing."

She chuckled to herself and made a presentation of her body with her hands. "Yet, here I am."

I set the bowl down.

"Look, I appreciate the... hospitality? But I can't really stay here, so if there's something I need to do in order to leave, I'd like to do that now."

She made a face and shrugged. "I don't have any control over that."

"Well, who does?"

She thought about that for a moment, then said, "No one has any control over anything."

5

I couldn't get a lot of straight answers out of Io. And that was pretty par for the course for supernatural beings; you rarely got straight answers from any of them. Io and I talked and talked, but just when I thought we were getting somewhere, she'd end the conversation with some nonsense like "nothing is the only solution" or "nothing is merely the absence of something." Even when I asked her to explain what she meant, she would laugh and admit that she wasn't exactly sure.

She walked up a set of dangerously narrow stone steps, climbing the mountain into the higher levels of the temple grounds. I followed after her. The edges of the steps had been rounded off from centuries of use, even in her bare feet.

The sun was beginning to set.

"There's four states of being," she said. "Are you familiar with them?"

I had no idea what she was talking about. "Fire, water, earth, and air?"

"No."

"John, Paul, George, and Ringo?"

She stopped and turned to roll her eyes at me. "No." She resumed climbing.

"Then you tell me," I said. "You know so much. What are the four states of being?"

"Everything, anything, something, and nothing."

"Okay."

"You're familiar with the idea I'm sure. Everyone is. They just don't know it. I sure didn't."

"I'm pretty certain I have no clue what you're talking about."

We reached the top of the staircase, which led us to a small garden of yellow flowers that smelled like the incense that wafted on the breeze. She crossed the garden and headed for

71

another flight of stairs that would take us even closer to the mountain peak.

She continued. "Anything that exists, exists in one of four states of being. It is either nothing, it is something, it is anything, or it is everything. You..." She turned and gestured at me, "...are something. You are Penelope Salvo."

"And what are you?" I asked her.

She turned and continued up the stairs. "I am nothing."

"You seem like something."

"How I *seem* and what I *am* are very different things, trust me. I'm nothing."

"If you say so," I said. "But you look like something to me."

We kept climbing. The wind howled and brought in a chill. We were leaving the magical sunshine that protected the temple grounds from the harsh cold of the mountain peaks.

"What about anything and everything?" I asked.

"What about it?"

"If you're nothing and I'm something, then what's anything and what's everything?"

"Everything is everything," she said. "All of us are parts of everything. You are the something in everything. Me, being nothing, completes everything."

I kind of understood, but not really. "Can someone be everything?"

"Buddha is one with everything," she said. "And I'm no Buddha."

"What about anything?" I asked. "Can someone be anything?"

She stopped. This time she turned all the way around and sat down on the steps to face me. "You... are almost anything."

"Me?" I asked. "What does that even mean?"

"When you are something, you are one with yourself. When you are everything, you are one with everything. But when you are anything, you can be one with everything..." she put up one finger, "...one something at a time."

I opened my mouth to say something, then closed it. I didn't get it. This was some crackpot philosophy nonsense. I told her, "I don't understand."

She smiled at me, as if it took saintly levels of patience to explain her wack-a-doo religion to me.

"Are you a human?" she asked. "Or a robot?"

I said, "I don't know."

"Are you both?"

"I don't know..." I knew what my standard answer to that was. I'm half and half. But I recognized that I was probably falling into some philosophical trap. "I think being both is impossible."

She put her finger in the air. "That's why you are something and, yet, not quite anything."

I was starting to get frustrated. "What does that even *mean*!?"

She laughed. "Sometimes I don't even know."

Chapter 5

1

My eyes were closed, but I came to this floaty realization that I wasn't dead. I was sleeping on my back and slowly waking up. I opened my eyes and while my vision was slightly pixelated at first, it cleared up right away. I was staring straight up. Through a thick canopy of moss covered trees, I could see a night sky filled with a million of stars. A blue moon hung in the air, much closer than the moon normally gets. Hundreds of fireflies danced in the air above me, drifting this way and that, slowly blinking in and out of view.

My clothes were soaked in ocean water, right down to my underwear. My bones were still hot from the multiple lightning blasts. Water sizzled on my skin and wafted off of me like steam.

I shot up into a sitting position and called out for Corolla. I looked all around, but he wasn't anywhere in sight. I looked up to see if he was flying around in the sky. He wasn't there either. Wherever I was, he didn't come with me. I hoped that meant he survived the Bermuda Triangle. If anything bad happened to him I would never forgive myself, but it seemed like that was going to have to remain an unsolved mystery. For now.

Wherever he was, I hoped he was okay.

I checked out my immediate surroundings. Crooked, haunted trees surrounded me on all sides. Fireflies danced through their empty branches. I could hear the flapping sound of bat wings. The familiar smell of mildew and rotting wood assaulted my nose. The ground beneath me was mossy and soft.

I was in a swamp. I narrowed my eyes. I knew this place.

This was the Guinee, the land of Voodoo.

Was this the world connected to Earth? Did the Bermuda Triangle suck me up and spit me out here in this place? It didn't take a real stretch of the imagination to think so. Voodoo spirits never seemed to have much trouble making their way to Earth.

I couldn't say I was overjoyed to be in the Guinee. Me and the Voodoo spirits weren't exactly on the best of terms and my only real ally – Baron Semedi – had been murdered by Isobella Westland sometime last year.

I got to my feet as silently as I could. It was easy for me to stay hidden because in the Guinee darkness is easy to find. The moonlight created strange shadows that shifted through the bushes like living creatures. I crouched in cover under a nearby tree and checked Athena.

51 kilometers.

The arrow pointed somewhere off to my left, so I turned and started walking.

I'd been to the Guinee a couple times. It wasn't the worst, but I wouldn't call it a pleasure cruise either. As I made my way through the puddles and trees and as I wandered around a lake of stagnant water, I noticed something I'd never seen in the Guinee before. Buildings. Structures. They were large things, like warehouses and factories made entirely from wood. Most of them looked abandoned. Their windows were dark, but a rare few of them glowed brownish-yellow, like tea-stained glass. The air in this part of the world smelled of tobacco and spiced rum and spicy peppers. It was too dark to see the warehouses in detail and there weren't that many; certainly not enough to constitute being "a city." No, they were just randomly scattered throughout the swamp.

Some of them vented smoke from their tin chimneys. Those places were in use. Someone had kept them running.

As I continued forward, the factories came with more regularity. Eventually I came across little houses, like cottages, all built from rough-cut boards of dark colored wood. It looked like a commune for witches with cobwebs on the front porches and fluttering candles set in the windows. An outdoor rocking chair moved on its own in the breeze, creaking back and forth.

Puffs of smoke came from some of the chimneys meaning that those houses were lived in.

All of them looked empty. No one seemed to be home.

I could hear sound in the distance. It was indiscernible at first, but after another couple minutes of walking, I could start to make it out. It sounded like music. Music and laughter.

The music way joyous and happy, with the bouncy tones of an accordion set to pattering drums and strumming guitars. The singing and laughter grew stronger, too. Whatever I heard wasn't just a party. It was a festival.

I crept through the darkness and poked my head around the corner of a towering factory that smelled like sugar and tobacco. Safely hidden behind the wall and careful not to expose myself, I saw the source of the noise: a celebration in full-swing.

Thousands of Voodoo spirits gathered in the town square. They danced to the lilting calypso music of Baron Muzica and His Muzical Men; a delightful arrangement of half-dead gentlemen in tuxedos and women in outrageous, flowing dresses of red and black and white. Baron Muzica danced center stage as he squeezed music out of a small accordion. Beside him, a beautiful woman with roses in her hair slapped an upright bass. A fat Voodoo spirit spun in the background, sawing back and forth on a violin with incredible speed. All the while, a skeleton banged his bony fingers on a piano and stomped the stage with an oversized boot.

They were having all the fun in the world and the thousands of spirits gathered around the stage loved it. Everyone in the crowd wore dusty tuxedos and extravagant dresses. They clinked bottles of rum and wine together, they puffed on rich cigars, and a few of them danced through the air, completely untethered by the laws of physics.

Some of them were laughing. Others were singing along to the music. All of them were drunk.

A few spirits danced through the crowd wearing these giant paper-mache heads – ridiculously oversized and painted in bright colors – that bounced and swayed as the people wearing them moved around. They looked like cartoon versions of different Voodoo loa; some of them I recognized and some of them were new to me.

Rope was strung from one factory rooftop to the others like power lines and hanging from them were blooming flowers in every color of the rainbow. They wafted in the breeze and for once in the Guinee, the air smelled sweet and inviting. Botany is kind of my thing and I recognized a lot of the flowers right away: bright red Haitian Catalpas and Hibiscus and even the long-extinct Blue Morasuni.

Also on the air was the smell of boiling shrimp and cooked chicken and burnt sausage. The delicious aroma of Cajun food danced on the breeze before fading away to the smell of rum and cigar smoke.

The Voodoo band ended their song to thunderous applause. The musicians all took a gracious bow. Before the crowd could die down, the skeleton stomped his boot again – *un, deux, trois, quatre* – and they started in on a new song, something equally fast-paced, up-beat, and delightful.

I couldn't keep from grinning like an idiot. The party looked like so much fun and I'd be a liar if I said I didn't want to join in. I took a few steps out of hiding to get a little closer, but also careful not to reveal my presence.

Off to the side of the party, just far enough away from the party-goers, was an arrangement of tables. One table had cakes of all kinds and sizes, most of them decorated with candy and red peppers. Another table was lined with blackened chicken, simmering pots of gumbo, and trays of cornbread. Bowls of corn and okra and exotic looking sauces were laid out in a massive pot-luck that rivaled anything done by any Catholic Church in Manhattan. Another table was overflowing with roses and corsages and other bundles of flowers. Next to the tables stood a few coat racks where the various spirits could hang their jackets.

The table at the very end had an arrangement of costume make-up, tacky costume jewelry, and animal bones. With the grace and speed of a ninja panther, I ducked down and sprinted for the tables. Safely tucked beneath them, I popped my head up and looked left and right to see if anyone noticed me. No one had.

I swiped a can of black and white make-up off the table, then ducked back down. I dipped my fingers inside and smeared it on my face, coating my skin entirely in white paint. Then, just as I had seen the other spirits decorate their faces, I rubbed black paint over my eyes and my nose and my temples to make myself look like a skull.

I didn't have a mirror to check my work. I knew my make-up job wasn't the best, but I hoped it was at least passable.

Popping back up to my feet, I stole a tuxedo jacket with tails off the coat rack and put it on to cover up my New York clothes and glowing Athena. I completed my disguise by "borrowing" a stovepipe top hat off a spirit that was drunk and snoring against a nearby lamp post.

The jacket sleeves were a little long for me and I tried to roll them up, but it wasn't working. I figured to hell with it and let them drape over my hands.

Convinced that my disguise was 100 percent foolproof, I marched straight into the celebration and proceeded to dance to the music.

I was much shorter than most of the Voodoo spirits, but they didn't seem to notice. I weaved around a couple of teenage spirits who danced nose-to-nose, pulling each other close, and who quickly dipped down for a long, deep kiss. A thin-boned zombie of a man leapt up onto an empty table and danced a bizarre jig that reminded me of how skeletons danced in those old black-and-white cartoons. A dozen kids probably five or six years old came shrieking and laughing through the legs of the adults. They poked at me and shouted, *You're it! You're it!* I clawed the air like a lion and roared at them. They screamed in fear, laughed like crazy, then disappeared back into the crowd.

A man with a mouth stuffed full of cotton came through the party holding live chickens up in the air, one in each hand. He said, through his muffled cotton voice, "Chickens! Chickens! Get a load of me, I'm holding chickens! This is the best day of my life!"

Fireworks popped in the distant crowd, the kind you throw on the ground and snap at people's feet.

How cool is this? I thought. I come from a world where, when there's a party and you hear popping noises, people hit the dirt and assume it's gunfire. But things were different here in the "wicked" world of Voodoo. (That's how Ma would have described it. *Wicked.*) Here, there was laughter and dancing and no one had a care in the world.

No one here had to worry, because everyone here was already dead.

2

"Who are you?" asked this one Voodoo lady as she came up to me. She wore a tattered straw hat, had dreadlocks that came down over her shoulders, and she wore a tuxedo jacket partnered with a flowing, billowing skirt. Her face was painted black, with white X's on her eyes and a line of X's across her lips.

"I'm..." Shit. Come on, Penelope. Think. "I'm new here!"

The Voodoo lady danced in place beside me, completely unaware that I was a human. I danced, too, but nowhere near as well as she did.

"New?" She sounded confused. "What are you the mistress of?"

Oh. Good question. What am I the mistress of?

"War!" I called out, since that was kind of technically true. "I'm the mistress of war!"

"Madam Lage!" she said, as if she knew who I was. "You've changed!"

"Yup!" Shit. I identified as a spirit that already existed. I didn't need that kind of attention. I moved away from the Voodoo lady. "I have to dance this way now! I need a drink!"

"Delightful!" she shouted over the music. She waved me farewell. "May our paths cross again tonight!"

"Right back atcha!" I shouted.

She turned her attention away from me and I breathed a sigh of relief.

No sooner did I drop my guard, I laid eyes on an old enemy: Madam Brijit, the devoted wife of Baron Samedi. I would recognize that wedding gown outfit and blue lace face-paint anywhere. Even more identifiable, Madam Brijit is the only Voodoo spirit with Irish red dreadlocks. Kind of a dead give away.

Haha. "Dead" give away. I kill me.

Brijit hadn't spotted me. She was speaking seriously to a quartet of skeletons dressed in identical tuxedo jackets and matching top hats.

I whipped around at the sight of her and hid my face.

Time to go the other direction.

It was in that moment that I began to question my decision to join the Voodoo party. Dumb move. Too much could go wrong. I'd had my fun, but now I needed to get out of the festival and on to the next world.

I rolled up my jacket sleeve and checked Athena for mileage.

43 kilometers.

Damn. I'm not too sure what a kilometer is in miles, but I think that's a long ways to walk. I had to get going.

I thought I could slip out of the party just as easily as I slipped in, but that wasn't how things worked out. Drunk Voodoo spirits aren't exactly what you'd call "shy" and my attempt to vanish into the night was cut short by a sudden arm around my hips and a surprise dancing partner.

I found myself being spun this way and that by a shirtless man in a red top hat and a red cape. The guy was in great shape and had an awesome body. A giant skull belt buckle kept his pants in place and he clenched a red rose tight his between his teeth.

"Allo there, Miss," he said in a Caribbean accent. "Dance with me?"

We were already dancing. He was swinging and twirling me around, so I didn't have much choice. I played along, reluctantly, and said, "I actually need to be going."

"You wouldn't refuse a dance with Met Kalfu, would you?"

Met Kalfu. I read about him in Xin's old book of secrets. He came from a different family of loa than Baron Semedi and Baron Muzica and Madam Brijit. Met Kalfu came from the Petro family, a different set of loa that spent most of their time in Haiti.

His name literally meant "crossroads." As legend has it, his power over the crossroads of death, as well as his bright red clothes, oftentimes got him confused with Satan.

"One dance," I said. "Then I gotta get going."

"Oh?" He spun me around and dipped me left and right. His breath smelled like rum and sulfur. "And what destination could possibly be so exigent?"

I sneakily stuck my hand in my pocket while he concentrated on fox-trotting me all over the place. I peeked down at my little dictionary.

Exigent - adj. Urgent or of pressing importance.

Oh.

"I have to get to..." I couldn't tell him the truth. "Places."

"Mysterious." He removed the rose from his teeth and tucked it behind my ear. "I like that."

Okay. Uncomfortable. I broke away from him and took a step back. He didn't seem the slightest bit discouraged. He just danced in place, never taking his eyes off me.

"You don't look familiar," he said to me. "What family are you from? The Rada? The Kongo? The Petro?"

"The Ghede," I said.

The Ghede was the family of Baron Semedi, Baron Kriminel, and Madam Brijit.

"Ah," he said. "So this festival must be extra special to you then."

He danced in place and magically summoned a bottle of rum. He also brought out a little hideskin and spiked the liquor bottle with some strange gray powder. Voodoo spirits were always putting something weird in their drinks; peppers or broken glass or odd spices.

"What is that?" I asked him.

"Gunpowder," he said, drunkenly emptying the hideskin into his rum and spilling the powder everywhere. He swished the bottle around to give it a thorough stir, then stuck the bottle out at me. "Want some?"

Rum and gunpowder? Interesting. I took it and drank a couple gulps. It wasn't the worst.

"What do you think?" he asked.

"It's okay." I handed him back the bottle. "You said this festival is extra special for me. Why's that?"

"You're a Ghede," he said. "Today's the return of Baron Semedi. He's been dead for a year and a day. You don't know this?"

The *return* of Baron Semedi?

"I haven't been around," I told him. "Baron Semedi's going to return?"

"Of course he's going to return," he said. "Baron Semedi was the first man to ever die. He's already dead. He can't be killed. Not for long, at least. One year and one day, that's all it takes. And tonight's the night. He'll be back soon. Celebrate and be joyous!"

3

Baron Semedi and I had an interesting history. A little good, a little bad. He was the first supernatural force I met after swallowing Impossible Red and despite his odd fascination with me, he was a good person to have on your side. I never wanted him to die.

I was happy to hear he was coming back. Still, it wasn't anything I needed to hang around for. So when Met Kalfu got distracted by a plucked black chicken running amok underfoot, I sneakily backed away and dipped out of sight.

Time to make my exit. But when I turned around, I bumped right into Madam Brijit, face-to-face.

She stood there, arms crossed, and glared at me through her blue-painted eye sockets. Towering behind her were four skeleton henchmen of impressive size.

"You," she said.

Shit. I clenched my fists and said, "Me."

"You have some gall coming here," she told me.

"I'm not looking for trouble, so that's why I'm leaving." I tried to move past her, but she grabbed me by the arm and yanked me back. Once again, we were face to face.

She grit her teeth and said, "Tell me who did this."

I yanked my arm free and said, "Tell you who did what?"

She pointed off to the side and at the ground. I looked. There on the edge of the party was a tombstone decorated with heaps of flowers, boxes of cigars, and dozens of bottles of rum.

The tombstone read:

Here lies Baron Semedi
beloved husband

Madam Brijit said, "Who did it? Who killed him?"

I looked back at her. The fury in her eyes danced like fire.

Now normally I ain't no snitch, but...

"Isobella Westland," I told her.

"Some friend of yours?" she asked.

"Hell no, dude," I said. "Fuck that bitch."

Brijit kept her teeth clenched and said, "Where is she?"

"Westland?" I asked. "That bitch in Hell."

Brijit reached out, grabbed the lapels of my fake costume and jerked me close. Her breath smelled of hot peppers and rum. She lost her balance for a second and used me to steady herself. Like so many of the other loa, Brijit was totally shitfaced. "West Land killed my husband. She sentenced him to a grave that *I* had to dig." She pulled me closer. "I want revenge."

I glanced down at her grip on my clothes. "Lady," I said. "Get your hands off me."

But she didn't let go. She shook me. "Bring me this Isobella West Land."

I smacked her hands away from me. "I don't take orders from you! You're not *my* wife."

"Don't touch me!" She shoved me.

"Don't touch *me*!" I replied, shoving her back with both hands. I shoved her pretty hard. She was just drunk enough to lose her footing and stumble backwards. Her skeleton henchmen caught her and stood her up straight.

Brijit marched up to me and threw a right cross that caught me off guard. It connected with my jaw and popped stars in my vision. It took me a second to realize what she'd done. My adrenaline-chemicals surged through my blood. I never intended to start shit, but there's an old Italian saying: Don't start no shit, won't be no shit.

I tackled Brijit like a linebacker and slammed her down to the ground. We rolled around through the festival as we punched and pulled hair and called each other all kinds of obscenities. Voodoo spirits moved out of our way as we tumbled over one another. Most of the crowd cheered us on. We crashed through a table overloaded with food. Boiling hot gumbo spilled across both of us and piles of cooked chicken plopped to the ground.

One of the spirits called out, horrified, "Not the gumbo!"

We both got to our feet, huffing and puffing and covered in food, ready to square off for round two.

"You fight like a petulant child," she said.

"And you've got all the grace of a dump truck driving in reverse with four flat tires," I said.

Brijit growled and came at me, shoulders down, ready to tackle me. I threw her into a headlock and dragged her to the ground. She reached up and sliced my cheek open with her fingernails. It fucking hurt. I decked her three times right in the face.

Some other spirits ran up to us, shouting "Break it up, break it up!"

Someone wrapped their arms around my midsection and dragged me off of Brijit. I kept swinging and kicking at her. Three of Baron Muzica's musicians took Brijit by her arms and her legs and held her back. She was swinging and kicking just as hard as I was.

I looked back to see who had dared touch me.

Baron Kriminel.

Also of the Ghede family, Baron Kriminel was the first man to ever murder another person. He was dangerous, or at least he *was*, before swallowing Unobtainable Pink. Now he was the loa of murder as well as the artificial god of love.

His suit was different now, mostly white and red and pink, with red heart-shaped buttons. He looked like a confused skeleton who got dressed for Valentine's Day instead of Halloween.

I hadn't seen him in a minute. No time to catch up. I wasn't done kicking Brijit's ass.

"Hands off!" I screamed, kicking furiously to get loose.

"Please, Penelope," Baron Kriminel said. "Calm down."

"That bitch scratched me!" I screamed.

Brijit screamed back, "You pushed me!"

"You pushed me first and you know it!"

"I will end you, Earthling!"

"I'll break you in half and put you in two different graves!" I shouted.

"Ladies!" Kriminel snapped. He handed me off to two other loa who held me in place. He marched between us and looked back and forth.

His eye sockets were filled with pink orbs of pure love. I could tell by the shape of them that he was disappointed in us for fighting. I felt bad. I felt like maybe if I were more kind and understanding that-

Dammit. Those weren't *my* thoughts. Kriminel was using his love powers on me.

"Ladies, look at how you're acting," Kriminel said to us. "And look at all these people here who stopped having a good time because you wanted to fight."

I looked around. The music had stopped. The dancing was over. The gumbo had been ruined. Baron Muzica's shoulders slumped in sadness and his accordion let out a pathetic little whir. Aw. Poor guy just wanted to play his music.

Kriminel continued, "Now I don't expect you to apologize to one another, and you certainly don't need to apologize to me, but I do think you should apologize to everyone who came from all over the Guinee to have a good time. Don't you?"

He was right. The party was fun and I was being a total buzz kill.

"I'm sorry," I said.

Brijit didn't say anything. Kriminel turned to her. "Madam?"

She sulked and stomped her foot, but eventually muttered under her breath one quick "Sorry."

"What's that?" Kriminel said, cupping his skeleton hand to the place on his skull where an ear should have been.

"Dhamballah Wedo is way in the back and I don't think he heard you..."

"I said I'm sorry," Brijit repeated, louder. "Sorry for ruining the party."

"That's better." Kriminel turned to the crowd. "They said they're sorry, everyone! No more fighting tonight! More music! More dancing!"

Someone in the back shouted, "And more gumbo!"

Baron Muzica nodded in agreement. He started in on his accordion. His muzical men chimed in on violin and upright bass. They increased in energy, paraded around the party, and headed back up to the stage. Slowly the angry crowd turned away from me and Brijit to give their attention to the band and the festivities were on again.

4

Baron Kriminel grabbed me and Brijit by the arms and plopped us down on a nearby bench. After looking at both of us and shaking his head, he put his hands on his hips and huffed in disappointment. The whole situation reminded me of a fight on the playground that ended with being scolded by the principal.

After a moment of staring us down, he said, "Do you two want to tell me what this is all about?"

As if on cue, me and Brijit both pointed at one another and said in unison, "She started it."

Kriminel took a deep breath, stretched his back and looked up at the stars. He exhaled and turned his pink eyes back down at us. The glow from his eye sockets had an odd, calming effect.

"You two need to shake hands and be friends," he said.

"No chance," Brijit said.

"Fuck that," I added.

He asked us, "Do you think Semedi would like seeing you two fight like this?"

In unison, we both said, "Yes."

That left Kriminel at a loss for words. All he could do was shake his head. He looked at me and asked, "Is there a reason you're here in the Guinee?"

"I'm just passing through," I said. "I'm not here to stay and I didn't mean to cause any trouble."

He put his skeleton hand on my shoulder. "I believe you."

Brijit crossed her arms and went "Hmph."

Kriminel gave her a passing glance, then turned back to me. "Passing through on your way to where?"

"I don't know," I said. I checked Athena and pointed. "43 kilometers that way."

Kriminel narrowed his pink eyes and asked, "What are you looking for 43 kilometers away?"

"Some doorway out of here. I'm trying to go to Hell."

"Hell?" he asked. "What would you possibly need in Hell?"

"My friend is trapped down there," I told him. "I'm going to set him free. He got put there by Isobella Westland, the same piece of garbage who killed Semedi."

At the mere mention of Westland's name, Brijit fumed and pounded her fists on the bench.

"Well, now look at that," Kriminel said. "You two shouldn't be fighting. You both have a common enemy."

"Whatever," Brijit said.

"Whatever is right," I agreed.

Kriminel continued. "Well, dear Penelope, it's not that easy to leave the Guinee if you're not a loa. If you want to get out of here, you're going to need permission from Papa Legba."

I'd read about Papa Legba before. He was from the Rada family of loa, the oldest family of loa from Africa. He was elderly, walked with a cane, and spoke every language in the world. I didn't know much else besides that.

"I'll do that then," I said. "Where is he?"

"He's been around, enjoying the party," Kriminel said, making a sweeping gesture to the celebration behind us. "Why don't you join us for a moment longer. Stay as my guest. Enjoy the festivities. Once Baron Semedi returns, I'm sure Papa Legba will have all the time in the world to hear your story."

5

So that's how I ended up chumming it up with Baron Kriminel and an RBF-ing Madam Brijit. I couldn't eat the food, unfortunately, but I managed to get my hands on some gold doubloons that were pretty damn good.

I danced with Rada Loko. I watched Madam Brijit swig bottle after bottle of ghost pepper rum. I joined a gathering of spirits who exchanged some of the crudest jokes I'd ever heard in my life.

"How is a wife like a laxative?" this grinning spirit asked me.

"How?" I replied.

"They both irritate the shit out of you!"

All the spirits around us laughed. Even the women.

One of the ladies told a limerick.

"There once was a sex fiend named Alice

Who used a dynamite stick as a phallus.

They found her vagina

In North Carolina

And her butthole at Buckingham Palace."

The crowd roared with laughter. I rolled my eyes, but couldn't help laughing myself. After all, like they say, when in Rome...

Jokes went on like that for a while. Eventually Baron Muzica and his muzical men went quiet and the silence got everyone's attention. We all turned to the stage. The band cleared out of the way and another Voodoo spirit came on board. This guy wore a fine suit, split down the middle, half-black and half-white. On one hand he wore a white glove and on the other he wore a black glove. His face was painted like a skull, also split down the middle, half-black and half-white, like inverted sides of the same coin.

He twirled a long cane in fast, dangerous circles. The top of the cane had a golden rooster head on it. He tossed the spinning cane high into the air and when he caught it, he used the golden rooster head to tip back the brim of his hat and wink at the audience.

He spun in place once, bowed deeply to the audience, then popped upright with a little jump.

The crowd cheered him on. So I did, too.

"That's Baron La Croix," Baron Kriminel said as he leaned down closer to my ear. "He really knows how to work a crowd."

I said, "I can see that."

Baron La Croix threw his hands up into the air and raised his voice to the sky. "Brothers and sisters of the Ghede family! Cousins of the Petro family and Kongo family! Mothers and fathers of the Rada family! We've gathered here today with great cause for celebration! Baron Semedi, our brother in death and in love, has been missing for one year and one day! Tonight marks the night of his glorious return! So dance and sing and cavort joyfully as we welcome back the original Mister Saturday Night, Baron Semedi!"

Everyone cheered. Hats were thrown in the air. Muzica and his muzical men trilled a little celebration on their instruments. Fireworks popped in the street.

I looked over to Madam Brijit. Despite all her shortcomings and our history of bad blood, I couldn't help but feel a pang of compassion for the excitement in her eyes. She smiled wide and bounced in place, excited to see her husband again. Maybe it was because of Baron Kriminel's magical love vibes, but in that moment I didn't exactly *hate* her.

The shouting and singing lasted a while. I wondered how Semedi would reappear. Would he come exploding out of his grave? Would he descend from the sky like an angel? Or, more his style, would he appear in a cloud of smoke with rum in one hand and a cigar in the other.

Time passed and Baron Semedi didn't come.

The music slowly died down. The cheering crowd turned to confused murmuring. And Madam Brijit, whose eyes darted all around in eager anticipation of seeing her beloved husband, suddenly looked confused.

I looked up at Baron Kriminel. I figured he would be the most composed, but even his skull turned comically on his neck bones, looking in all different directions.

The crowd turned back to Baron La Croix on the stage. La Croix fidgeted nervously with his cane, like this was somehow his fault. The tone of the crowd gradually changed from confused to angry. La Croix anxiously shifted back and forth on his feet. His face suddenly lit up as he came to a realization.

La Croix laughed and paced across the front of the stage to confidently address the audience. "Everyone! Everyone! Don't you get it? Don't you see what this is? Semedi is playing a trick on all of us! He's probably laughing at us from the shadows as we speak!"

The crowd let that idea sink in. Then they started to laugh. Surely that was it. Surely Semedi was playing a prank. He'd been dead for one year and one day, so that meant he could come back now. Anything else was... not how it worked.

Brijit wasn't laughing. Neither was I. The other spirits could let themselves be fooled, but not us.

Something was wrong.

"Come on out, Semedi!" La Croix shouted, tapping his cane on the stage. "You fooled us good, you rat bastard, but I know you're dying to get your grubby hands on all these cigars and bottles of rum! Come on out and let's see that ugly mug of yours!"

The crowd searched all over.

Baron Semedi did not come out of hiding.

I heard a growling sound, like a wild animal. I looked over and realized it was Brijit. She wasn't excited anymore and she was done with being confused. Now she was pissed. Her shoulders heaved as her breathing got heavier and more ragged. She stomped her way up to the stage.

Oh, shit. Not good. Not good for anyone.

"Where *is* he!?" Brijit's screams went off like a sonic boom that knocked everyone away from her. Once she reached the stage, she lifted off the ground and floated weightlessly in the air so she could look La Croix dead in the eyes. "Where is my husband!?"

"Well, how the hell should I know?" La Croix replied as he threw out his arms. "I'm just up here saying shit! I don't make the rules!" He pointed his cane into the crowd. "He does!"

Brijit whipped around like a demon possessed. She floated to the unidentified spirit and screamed, "Papa Legba, where is my husband!?"

A voice answered from the crowd, a man I couldn't quite see through everyone else, and he said, "No clue!"

"No clue? No *clue*?" Her voice moved through the earth. Windows rattled in the nearby buildings. The trays and pots of food shook across the tables. Strings of flowers came loose from the rooftops and drifted down to the dirt. "You guard the crossroads and you have *no clue*?"

"Semedi wouldn't come through the crossroads," Legba replied. "He's already dead!"

"Met Kalfu!" Brijit shouted as she turned in the air and pointed at someone else. "Is this your doing? Is this your family's idea of a joke!?"

"How dare you!" Met Kalfu shouted. "Choose your words carefully, cousin Brijit, unless you want a family feud as well as a missing husband!"

Brijit, fueled by rage and confusion, leaned her head back and screamed green fumes into the sky. The moon, swear to god, moved further behind the trees for its own safety.

"Where is he!?" she belted. "Where!?"

Her voice shattered all the glass around us. Every window, every bottle of rum, every wine glass, they burst into shards that tinkled to the ground.

I turned to Baron Kriminel. "Can you calm her down?"

He kept his eyes straight ahead, hypnotized. "She's in love. I can't stop that."

Brijit hung there in the sky, her wedding flats barely poking out from under the tattered hem of her gown. She was starting to hyperventilate. Her red dreadlocks moved like snakes. Then her head popped up and her radiation green eyes locked on mine.

Aw, fuck me.

"What?" I took a step back. "Don't look at me like that. This ain't got anything to do with me."

Like an evil ghost, she floated over the crowd and came straight for me. I knew exactly what this was, I did it all the time; she didn't have anyone to direct her anger at, so she was going to take it out on me. We were looking at round two in the Octagon. Brijit touched down in front of me. We stood there, nose-to-nose close.

All the spirits watched us. A tense silence filled the air.

"You said you were leaving," she said.

"That's right."

"You're going to other worlds," she said.

"Right."

She gave me a single nod. "I'm going with you."

That's not what I was expecting. At first, I thought maybe I simply misheard what she said, but, no, I heard her right. *I'm going with you.* That was the absolute last thing I wanted. Me tootling around other dimensions with this unhinged psychopath? What a terrible idea.

"No way, man," I said. "I'm a lone wolf and this lone wolf hunts alone."

"My husband is missing," she said. "Either I find him or I follow you into Hell and destroy the woman who killed him. Either way, I'm coming with you."

"I don't think that's the best of ideas." I looked to the Voodoo spirits gathered around us for a little solidarity.

"I think it's a great idea." Baron Kriminel came up and put his hands on both our shoulders. "I think it would help improve relations between the two of you. Let the healing begin."

I brushed his hand off my shoulder. "Butt out, Kriminel. Did you not hear the part about me being a lone wolf?" I pointed at Madam Brijit. "You're not coming with me. I'm doing something important. I don't need you tagging along, screwing things up

90

with your drama."

"Drama?" She reached out and grabbed my clothes. "*Drama?*"

"Yes, drama!" I smacked her hands away. "Look at yourself. You're a drama *queen!*"

"Listen." She took a deep, cleansing breath that didn't seem to do much for her anger and said, "I don't go on adventures and I don't go to Earth for fun. That's Semedi's little hobby. But he's not here to do it and I don't know how, so..." Her voice got real quiet. "I need your help."

She was asking me for help? After all the screaming and fighting and name calling? How stupid. But you know what was *really* stupid? I was actually *entertaining* the idea of letting her come with me. Why? No clue. Although when I caught a glimpse of Baron Kriminel watching me with those glowing, pink eyes, I got my suspicions. Stupid skeleton cupid was working more of that love magic.

Still, influenced or not, I knew taking Madam Brijit with me was a bad move. I maintained my hesitation and said, "I don't know..."

Brijit realized what it was going to take to convince me and she didn't like it. She gave me a hateful look and in a quiet whisper, barely audible, she said, "Please."

I felt my resolve weaken. Goddammit.

6

When I was a kid, I remember these people that used to gather out on Bowery and hold up signs that predicted the return of Jesus Christ. Like the honest-to-god, sandals-on-the-ground return of Jesus Christ. Everyone had 15 days to repent for their sins. Everyone needed to sell all their belongings, because we weren't going to need them once the big J.C. ushered in the Kingdom of Heaven. They counted down the days with their signs. 10 days. Then 5. And on the last day, morning, noon and night passed.

Jesus was a no-call, no-show.

Big shock. Little known fact: Jesus is never coming back. You'd think that two-thousand years would be long enough for everyone to catch on to that, but no.

I never saw those "end of the world" people again after that. Did they go back to their old lives? Did they commit suicide together? Who's to say. One thing's for sure: they were absolutely convinced that the end of the world was coming and they were devastated and confused when it didn't happen.

The same thing happened that night in the Guinee.

When Baron Semedi didn't return from the dead, it signaled the end of the fun. Baron Muzica and his muzical men packed up all their instruments which was the final nail in the party coffin. Slowly but surely, all the loa wandered off. Some of them stayed to collect the remaining food. Others picked up bottles and rum and wine and shook them, checking for anything left behind.

The overall mood changed from joy to deep depression.

Baron Semedi was supposed to come back after a year and a day, but he didn't. What did that mean for the other Voodoo spirits? Could they, too, *die*? And if they did, would they come back after a year and a day like they once believed? Or would they be lost forever, just like Semedi?

"We need to talk to Papa Legba before he takes off for good," Madam Brijit told me. "If we're going to let your..." She waved a dismissive finger at Athena, "...toy arm lead us out of here, we're going to need his permission."

"For one, it's not a *toy*," I told her, showing her the arm. "It's a marvel of modern technology and it's the only thing that's going to get us to where we're going."

She rolled her eyes. "Call it whatever you want."

"I will." I put my arm down. The sleeve of my stolen jacket covered it back up.

"Come on." Brijit grabbed my arm and pulled me along behind her. "That's him. Over here."

Across the town center stood a dimly lit warehouse marked with a hand-painted sign above the door that read *Papa Pillory's Rum Distillery*. A lost old man wandered around under the yellow front porch light. He hobbled along, hunched over, relying on a gnarled old cane for support. He wore a pair of dusty denim overalls, an unraveling straw hat, and he puffed on a hand-carved wood pipe. Little puffs of smoke came out of the pipe, like he was an adorable elderly choo-choo train.

As Brijit dragged me closer, I could hear the old kook cackling to himself, not as if he was remembering an old joke, but because he was batshit crazy.

"Papa Legba!" Brijit shouted as she marched closer. "Hey, Papa Legba!"

The old man turned and gave her the stink eye. He stayed like that for a moment, then turned to hobble in our direction.

"Hello, little niece," he said. "Quite the hussy fit you threw back there. I didn't lose your husband, you know."

"You're the guardian of the damned crossroads," Brijit said. "If anyone should know where my husband is, it should be you."

"Well, I don't." Legba did not sound happy. "Boo hoo. So sad."

Brijit opened her mouth. I could see how this was about to play out. Voodoo duel. I should know, I've started plenty of fights in my day. If cooler heads were going to prevail, god help us, it was up to me.

"Mister Legba, sir," I said, butting into the conversation before things could get much worse. "I came to ask you a favor."

"It's Papa Legba. Not Mister Legba," he said. He squinted and looked me up and down. I still had my Voodoo costume on but he could see right through it. "You're no loa."

"I know," I said. "I'm Penelope Salvo and I'm from New York City. I didn't come here to stay."

"Go back home then," Legba said, waving me away. "Come back with something from McDonald's."

"I'm not going back to Earth," I said.

"She wants to go the other way," Brijit said.

Legba turned back around with one eye opened wide. He grinned. "The *other* way?"

"I'm on my way to Hell," I told him.

"And I'm going with her to find Semedi," Brijit added.

"Find Semedi?" Legba repeated. "That cocky little bastard could be anywhere. He pushed his luck once too often and someone finally did him in. Now he's lost for good. If you want my advice, I suggest you find yourself a new husband and-"

"I don't want your advice, you decrepit old fool," Brijit said.

Legba gave her a blank stare for a moment, then cackled a delightful laugh. He turned away and shuffled off with his cane. "You two should just go home," he told us. "I'm not in any mood to help you. Your quest sounds foolish and dumb."

"That's my husband you're talking about!" Brijit shouted. She stormed up and smacked the old man on the back of the head, sending his straw hat flying.

"Hey!" Legba said. "Now that's enough!"

"Open the crossroads, you stupid old goat!" she snapped.

"Please, Papa Legba," I said, trying to maintain some level of respect. "If you don't mind."

"Oh, I do mind," he told me. He turned in place and faced us both. "I minded very much before and I mind even much more now that you've gone and hit me on the head."

He didn't have much else to say. Neither did we. I gave him my most desperate look. Brijit glared at him with fierce determination. It didn't look like we were getting through to him at all, but then he said:

"Fine," he said. "I'll open the crossroads."

"Thank you," I said.

"Thank you so, so kindly," Brijit said. She did not sound the least bit sincere.

"I'll open the crossroads," Legba continued, "if you can best me in a single contest."

"I don't do contests," Brijit said as she turned up her nose.

"I wasn't talking to you." Legba gave her a crooked smile that revealed his many missing teeth. He turned his eyes to me and said, "I was talking to her."

7

I got sucked into a contest. There was no way around it.

We sat inside the very warehouse that Legba had been poking around: Papa Pillory's Rum Distillery. And what a rum distillery it was, too. It was an imposing warehouse, four stories tall, with pyramids of barrels stacked as high as the ceilings. There were a million barrels if there were a dozen and the air was so rich, you could get drunk just from breathing.

We gathered around a simple wooden table – Papa Legba, Brijit, and I – seated on hand-crafted wooden chairs. There were two shot glasses on the table, one in front of me and one in front of Papa Legba. Between the two of us, placed in the middle of the table, was a bottle of spiced rum.

Legba and I sat on opposing sides of the table. Brijit sat to the side of us like some kind of referee.

"You're familiar with the game of Cease and Persist?" Legba asked me with a friendly smile.

"Never heard of it," I said.

"We drink." Legba reached out, uncorked the rum bottle and poured each of us a shot. "Then we keep drinking until one of us can drink no longer."

"Oh!"

"You've heard of this game?" he asked me.

"Yeah. But back on my world, people just call it getting shitfaced."

Legba giggled to himself. "That's a funny name for it."

I'd had alcohol many times since swallowing Impossible Red. I never got drunk. The nanites identify alcohol molecules as poison and eliminate them. With that in mind, Papa Legba's drinking contest sounded like an absolute cakewalk.

So I told him, "Deal."

Brijit grabbed my arm and yanked me close. She hissed in my ear, "Don't screw this up, human."

I jerked my arm free. "Seriously, what is your deal? You got some sort of crush on me or something? You're always touching me and shit."

She sat back in her chair and glared at me. "Just drink your rum."

I locked eyes with Papa Legba. How much rum could this old man possibly drink, anyway?

"Ready?" He lifted his shot glass off the table.

"Ready." I raised mine.

We clinked our glasses together. He drank his shot. I drank mine. It didn't taste all that bad, but I'm no connoisseur when it comes to booze. We both thumped our shot glasses down on the table. Legba poured us another shot. We raised our glasses again and drank.

He'd pour. We'd drink. We'd thump our shot glasses down.

Pour. Drink. Thump.

Pour. Drink. Thump.

Pour. Drink. Thump.

"Feeling it yet?" Legba asked me, then cackled. I could smell the alcohol on his breath from across the table.

"No," I said, plainly.

He poured more shots.

Pour. Drink. Thump.

Pour. Drink. Thump.

Pour. Drink. Thump.

"Feeling it *now*?" he asked.

"Still no."

We killed the bottle. Not that it mattered. We were sitting inside the distillery. Legba got to his feet, steadied himself with his cane, and shuffled off to a wooden crate. He pushed the lid off with the tip of his cane and pulled out a fresh bottle of rum. He brought it back to the table and poured us a shot.

We drank and thumped our shot glasses on the table. Without missing a beat, he poured us another one.

It quickly became obvious that we were going to empty this bottle, too. When there was only a little bit left, Madam Brijit sighed, got to her feet, and retrieved a third bottle. We started drinking that one, one shot at a time. Neither myself nor Legba showed any signs of slowing down. We drank the third bottle empty.

Brijit went on another liquor run; this time coming back with three bottles instead of one.

"Would you two hurry it up?" she said as she clattered the bottles on the table.

"She's weakening." Legba uncorked a fresh bottle.

"I'm not weakening," I said.

"Don't you feel drunk?" he asked me.

"I don't feel shit, grandpa."

He poured us more shots. We killed another bottle.

"I'm bored," Brijit said as she got up from the table. "I'm going to go outside. Let me know when you two are done."

"Okay," Legba said.

"We will," I added.

Brijit left. She did make a good point. This was taking for-fucking-ever.

"Let's cut out the middle man," I said, pushing my shot glass aside. I grabbed a bottle of rum for myself and slid one over to Legba. "No more shot glasses We're going to do this by the bottle from now on."

"Fine by me," he said, popping the cork. He raised his bottle to cheers me. "Ochan!"

I clinked bottles with him. "Salud."

We tilted our bottles back and guzzled them until they were both empty. I put my bottle down and looked at Legba with crystal clear vision. Legba let out a satisfied "Ahhh" and tossed his bottle over his shoulder. It shattered behind him.

Things went on like this for some time. Way too long, in fact. We drank all the bottles in the crate and had to open a new one. Rumor must have spread across the Guinee that Papa Legba was in a drinking contest with some impostor loa, because other spirits wandered into the distillery to watch. At first only a few of them watched us from the doorway, but by the fifth hour there were a couple dozen gathered around the table.

I could hear them talking about us.

"How long have they been at it?"

"At least five hours."

"Foolish human really thinks she can beat Legba at Cease and Persist?"

"She'll drink herself to death before she wins."

I let loose with a thunderous burp. One of the spirits applauded me for that and I gave her a thumbs up.

Our attentive audience took over table service. One by one they brought us bottles of rum and one by one we drank them empty.

"I'm impressed," Papa Legba said. "You might not be a loa, but you sure drink like one."

"Are you feeling drunk yet?" I asked. "I got places to be."

"I always feel drunk," he said. He got out his little pipe and puffed on it.

"Well, what if neither one of us ceases?" I asked him. "What if we both persist?"

"One of us has to cease," he said. "Them's the rules."

"But what if neither of us do?"

"Then..." He smiled and kicked back in his chair. "We drink for all eternity."

I groaned, rolled my eyes, and opened another bottle of rum. So did he. We chugged those, too.

Eventually we drank every bottle of rum in the distillery. To keep the contest moving, the spirits had to bring down a full barrel and use it to refill the bottles. They filled 191 bottles out of one barrel, debated on whether or not that would be enough, then decided to err on the side of caution and just go ahead and bottle up a second barrel.

They put out 382 bottles on the floor by our table. God, the contest had already taken forever; this was just going to drag it out even more. Impatiently, I checked Athena. 41 kilometers to my right was the way out of the Guinee, but I had to keep playing Cease and Persist.

As we entered our 13th hour and fifth barrel of rum, I looked around to find the crowd had doubled in size. We were quite the attraction. And after half a day of non-stop drinking, neither Legba nor I seemed any worse for wear.

I looked around for Brijit. She hadn't come back, even after the crowds formed and introduced a little excitement. She was probably just outside waiting, but I decided in that moment to go check.

"I'll be right back." I pushed away from the table.

"Oh?" Legba cackled. "Drunk? Giving up?"

I give him a look like he was stupid. "No? I'm just going outside for one second."

"Need to go puke your little guts out?" he asked.

"No."

"You need to go pee pee?" He really laughed at that one.

"You're fucking weird." I walked away. "I'm just going to check on Brijit. I'll be right back."

I got outside. It was still night. It was always night in the Guinee. I stood under the dim light that glowed over the front doors of the rum distillery. I looked left and right. No sign of Brijit.

"Brijit?" I called out. "You out here?"

No response. I wandered around for a hot second so I could check around the corners of the warehouse. That's when I heard the sound of someone softly crying.

Up ahead in the festival courtyard sat Madam Brijit, curled in a tight little ball. She laid there next to Baron Semedi's tombstone – *Here lies Baron Semedi, beloved husband* – and softly cried. She didn't hear me calling for her.

I could just barely make out the words she was saying.

"I miss you so much," she said. "I'm coming to find you. I promise."

8

I busted in through the doors of Papa Pillory's Rum Distillery with zero patience left.

"Alright, can we finish this fucking contest?" I snapped. "I don't have time to do this for all eternity."

I marched over to the pyramids of stacked barrels and climbed my way up to the top. I hoisted one of the barrels over my head and brought it down to floor level.

Papa Legba turned in his chair and asked me, "What are you doing?"

"Speeding things up," I said. "No more bottles. We're doing it by the barrel now."

I busted the spigot off the end of the barrel and heaved it up over my head. I'd never went to college and never drained a keg before, but now I was about to do one better: I was about to drain a barrel of spiced Caribbean rum. I put my mouth up to the hole in the barrel and started chugging.

You could have heard a pin drop in that distillery. No one thought I could do it. I wasn't that sure myself. The volume of that barrel was a hundred times more than the volume of my stomach. I could only hope – and this was sincere hope – that Impossible Red would figure out what to do with that much liquor.

Every Voodoo loa, man and woman, young and old – and that includes Papa Legba – watched dumbfounded as I destroyed the entire barrel. Once it was empty, I wrapped my arms around it and crushed it into splinters.

"There," I said to Legba. "Your turn."

"I can't lift a barrel!" he croaked. "I'm just an old man!"

"Oh, well then," I said. "Let me help you."

I grabbed a barrel and carried it over to him. Without a seconds warning, I whacked the spigot off and positioned the whole thing up over his head.

"Open up," I said.

"Now just you wait," he said in protest.

"Down the hatch," I said. I tipped the barrel and doused him with rum. I wasn't leaving him with any option. He quickly came to that realization. He tilted his head back and opened his mouth. I was angry and frustrated, but I still did my best to play fair and aimed the rum right down his throat. I spilled some on his face. What can you do?

The old man surprised me. I didn't think he could do it either, but he did. He drank the whole barrel.

"Fine!" I marched back to the barrels. "Another!"

"Okay, now one second." Legba coughed and hacked. He got to his feet and stumbled in place. "Let's slow down."

"I won't slow down!" I said. "I'll drink this whole distillery dry if I have to! Now countermand this stupid contest and tell me you cease or else you're getting barrel number two!"

"I don't cease!" he said. "I persist!"

"Great!" I scooped up two barrels, one under each arm, and carried them back over to the table. "So do I!"

I picked mine up, knocked off the spout, and chugged that one down. The crowd went absolute bonkers and cheered me on. The whole time I drained the barrel, I could hear Legba protesting.

"This isn't the spirit of the game!" he cried. "You're playing too fast! You're playing too hard!"

I finished my barrel and chucked it for distance across the whole distillery. I picked up the other full barrel and advanced on Papa Legba.

"Open up," I said.

He backed away. "But... but..."

Angrily, I said, "Here comes the airplane."

"I don't want an airplane."

"Then tell me you cease."

"No! I persist!"

I held the barrel in the crook of my arm. With my free hand, I grabbed elderly old Legba by his dusty overalls and yanked him close. I grit my teeth and, right in his face, said, "Open your goddam mouth and drink this goddam rum."

He stared at me, terrified. His bottom lip quivered and he said, "I don't want to."

I pulled him even closer and whispered right in his ear, "You have to. Them's the rules."

"Fine!" He swung his arms and broke free of me. He backed away and shut his eyes. "You win! I cease! I don't want any more rum!"

The collective gasp from all the Voodoo spirits sucked the air right out of the room. Their eyes were wide. Papa Legba had been beaten at his own game, and by a girl from Manhattan. They didn't know what to think.

I beat Legba fair and square. But the contest was over and I didn't harbor any bad feelings. He was just doing what Voodoo spirits to. They love games. They love liquor. They love a good joke. Legba was just being Legba. But the game was over and now it was time for him to make good on his end of the bargain.

I went and stood right in front of him. He looked up at me, terrified, like I might hit him. I wrapped my arm around his shoulders and gave him a friendly pat. He gave me a warm smile when he realized I wasn't mad.

"Now, will you open the crossroads for us?" I asked him.

He smiled bright and nodded his eager little head. "I will! It would be my greatest pleasure!"

We left the distillery, Legba and I. On our way out the doors, I heard Legba laughing to himself.

"What's so funny?" I asked him.

He kept laughing and said, "Won't Papa Pillory be surprised to see what we did to his rum distillery!"

Papa Legba and I went to gather up Madam Brijit, who was now asleep in the fetal position by Baron Semedi's grave. She didn't enjoy being caught in such a vulnerable position and as soon as she opened her eyes, she sprung to her feet and berated both Legba and I for sneaking up on her.

Legba led us through the swamps of the Guinee, deep into the darkness, and far away from the distilleries and cigar factories. I checked Athena often, just to be sure this wasn't some kind of trick, but it wasn't. The kilometers ticked away with steady regularity and the directional arrow never wavered.

Eventually we reached our destination: the crossroads. It was an intersection of four dirt roads illuminated by an old gas lantern hanging from a hook. There at the corner was a wooden post with four directional signs, each one clearly marked.

Nowhere. Somewhere. Anywhere. Everywhere.

Something about that seemed so familiar. Not the intersection, but the signs. The words. "Nowhere. Somewhere. Anywhere. Everywhere." I heard something like that before; something important. I couldn't quite put my finger on it and Legba didn't give me time to think.

"There," the old man said, pointing with his wrinkled finger at the road marked *Somewhere*. "I opened the way for you. Go off and do your silly little errands."

"Thank you." I playfully pulled the brim of his straw hat down over his eyes. He lifted it back up, looked at me with his beady eyes and laughed.

"Yeah," Brijit said as she brushed past him. "Thanks for letting me do your job for you."

What a total bitch. I mean, I get it, Semedi was missing but it wasn't Legba's fault. He didn't have anything to do with it. Traveling into other worlds with Brijit wasn't going to be any fun, I could tell. But we made our way down the Somewhere road, Brijit and I, all the same.

"Farewell!" Legba called out from behind us, waving his hat in the air as the light of the intersection was swallowed up by the darkness. "Farewell! Travel safe! Take care! Be good!"

His voice slowly faded to nothing and so did the swamps of the Guinee. As the numbers on Athena reached zero, the arrow spun in uncontrolled circles and we were gone.

PERQUISITION

"Impossible," Metatron said.

The imposing angel carefully scrutinized a mason jar filled with an unrecognizable yellow liquid. He checked the jar all over – the sides, the bottom, and even the masking tape across the lid that read "Sulfur Oil" in Chinese – and dropped it carelessly to the ground. It burst open and the strange chemical hissed on the floorboards of the herbal shop. When he stepped away, the glass crunched under his powerful, platinum greaves.

"Not a single thing of suspect," Zophiel replied.

She stood behind the counter and smacked the side of the cash register with her metal gauntlets. It clanged and popped open to the sound of rattling coins. The money changing device was of human design and, therefore, a complete and total mystery to her.

She plucked a quarter out of the till and examined it with disgusted curiosity.

"Blatant idolatry," she said to the coin. "*In God we trust?* Somehow I doubt that." She dropped the quarter back into the little tray.

"She could not have simply vanished," Metatron said. He strolled through the store, hoping to find any clue to the whereabouts of Penelope Salvo. All he was found were plants and seeds and jars of dirt. "She was supposed to be under your surveillance."

"Many events demand my attention, Metatron," Zophiel said, already annoyed. "And on most days her actions are droll and of zero consequence. If we're assigning blame, isn't it you who controls the borders of the Universe?"

Metatron stuck two fingers in Zophiel's direction. "Don't blame me."

"Don't blame *me*," she snapped back.

"How did she escape!?" Metatron shouted. He slammed his fist onto a wooden table, destroying it, as well as the four potted plants that crashed to the floor. "Where did she go?"

Zophiel found zero clues behind the counter; a spiral notebook with some form of mathematics, a small drinking glass etched with the logo from something called "The Westland Corporation," and a mortar and pestle used for alchemy.

"See this?" she asked Metatron as she held up the mortar and pestle. "More blasphemy."

"It's all blasphemy." Metatron was barely listening. He had crossed his arms and stared at the roots hanging down from the ceiling, set out to dry. "This place is an affront to the Almighty."

Zophiel grew bored with the counter. She moved along, but the shop was small with limited places to go. Almost immediately, she found herself standing at the basement door. Curious, she reached for the knob, but the door would not open. A moment later she realized why: the door was secured shut with some type of human locking device. A "padlock," they were called.

"Come see, Metatron," she said. "This door is far more unorthodox than the others."

Metatron lumbered over, clanking in his full suit of armor. Together the angels stood in front of the door and analyzed the padlock. Zophiel grabbed it in her hand, looped her fingers through the metal parts of it, and pulled.

The padlock wouldn't break.

Angels don't take kindly to failure, Zophiel least of all. She gave the padlock a stern look, tightened her grip, and pulled again. The padlock wouldn't break. With grit teeth, a change in stance, and this time with two hands, she tried to tear the padlock free of the door. Again, the padlock stayed in place.

"What manner of witchcraft is this!?" She growled as she released the padlock and punched it in frustration.

Metatron brushed his partner aside and took the lock between his fingers. He rattled the little mechanism a couple times and determined it would be equally impossible for him to break it open.

"Perhaps the clues we are searching for are beyond this threshold," he said.

"Perhaps," said Zophiel.

Metatron drew his battle ax and took a few steps back. He intended to slice the lock free and, if that should fail, to chop the door down entirely. He widened his feet, got his ax ready, then stopped.

"What?" Zophiel asked. "What gives you pause?"

Something had definitely stolen Metatron's attention. It was a smell. He turned his head and sniffed the air.

"Do you smell that?" Metatron asked.

Zophiel had been bombarded by smells since they entered the shop; smells of magic and flowers and the stink of New York City. But with Metatron's prompting, she wrinkled her pert nose and smelled the air again.

Indeed, she smelled what he smelled.

"Demons," she said to him.

"I knew this mudblob was corrupt," he said as he moved to the middle of the store, ax still at the ready. "But to succor with demons?"

"She cavorts with evil," Zophiel said. "I caught glimpses of it in her mind."

"Where are you, demon?" Metatron bellowed as he tossed a wooden table out of his way. Another five potted plants shattered on the walls and floors. "I know you're here!"

Zophiel heaved her massive sword from over her shoulder and pointed. "There!"

Armstrong had found a hiding spot in the darkness of the corner, behind the mop and bucket. But now the angels had tracked him down and spotted his position. With little time to act, Armstrong dashed for the bathroom door.

"Tiny vex!" Zophiel shouted as she dashed across the store, intending to grab the demon before it could flee to safety. "Your presence on Earth is an abomination!"

Armstrong reached the safety of the bathroom and slammed the door shut before the angel could get her hands on him. The safety wouldn't last long; all that stood between the him and the two archangels was a human door. And that door did not come with the protection of an indestructible padlock.

A fist of platinum and white gold bust through the wood with a thunderous boom. Zophiel brought her arm down and tore open a hole that let her see inside.

Escape options were limited for Armstrong. There were no windows, no vents, and no exposed holes that sometimes crumble in the walls of century-old New York buildings. There was, of course, the toilet. Armstrong wondered if his flexible body could fit through the pipes and down into the sewers.

But as he neared the porcelain bowl, he remembered the direct orders of his majestic queen.

Don't touch the toilet ever again.

And it wasn't in Armstrong's power to disobey an order from his majesty, even under such dire circumstances.

Desperate, Armstrong crawled behind the base of the sink and cowered in fear. Zophiel crashed through the remainder of the bathroom door by force alone, crushing the wood out of her way. She spotted the demon in short order and used her fist to shatter the sink. Porcelain chunks clattered to the floor and water sprayed from the walls.

Armstrong recoiled from Zophiel's approaching grasp. Zophiel clenched the little arm in her fist and raised it up to where she could see it.

Language for the demon was exclusively limited to the psychic link to his sworn leader, but Zophiel could read minds. She stared the demon down and opened a psychic connection of her own.

"Disgusting little dire cherub," Zophiel said. "Where is Penelope Salvo."

I do not know, Armstrong said. *And if I did happen to know, I wouldn't tell you.*

Zophiel turned back to Metatron. "It doesn't know."

"Surely it knows something," Metatron said, taking a step closer. He flicked the demon on his hand, and hard. "Tell us what you *do* know."

What I do know? I do know that you are Metatron, the Kindness of the World. And I do know that she is Zophiel, the Spy of God. And I do know that you have found disfavor with my queen and, therefore, too found disfavor with Armstrong.

"How did he respond?" Metatron asked.

"With stubborn drivel," Zophiel said. "He's of no use to us."

Zophiel squeezed her fingers, intent on crushing the demon and the little bottle hidden inside him. But just before she destroyed his little body, Metatron spoke up.

"Stay thy hand, dear sister." He reached out and took Armstrong away from her. "Never underestimate the usefulness of a hostage."

Chapter 6

1

Madam Brijit and I were cut loose from the darkness and fell out of the sky. We passed through the clouds and plummeted down towards a colorful world of fruit trees and strangely shaped cottages. A fall like this wouldn't kill me – and I had reason to believe it wouldn't kill Madam Brijit, either – but my caveman instincts got the better of me. It's human nature to fear falling and I got a sick, sinking feeling in my stomach.

We built up speed, falling faster and faster. Brijit's wedding dress flapped behind her like an unopened parachute. She looked at me like she wanted to say something, but there wasn't time. Within seconds, we smashed through the tree branches. Another second later, we struck the ground with a shock wave that shook the trees. Birds and squirrels fled the area.

I hit the ground so hard, my body was imbedded in the dirt. I struggled free, stood up, and brushed myself off. Madam Brijit didn't move. She just laid there, face down. I walked over to her and nudged her with my foot.

"Brijit?" I said. "Hey, Brijit? You dead?"

"Don't touch me," she said, her voice muffled by the ground.

"Come on." I nudged her again. "Get up."

She didn't move. I looked all around. We were in some kind of orchard. An apple orchard, to be exact. The sky was blue, the sun was shining, and I heard birds chirp overhead. It looked like a really nice, peaceful world.

I checked Athena. It took a moment to calculate, but it popped up with:

1,459 kilometers.

That didn't seem so bad. I had traveled a lot further than that back on Earth with Corolla. Ugh, Corolla. I hoped he was okay, wherever he ended up. I looked back down at Brijit. She still hadn't moved.

"You just going to stay there?" I asked her.

She said, "Maybe."

"Come on." I bent down, grabbed her under her arm and scooped her up. She let me help her to her feet. Once she was upright, she jerked her arm away from me.

"Don't touch me!" she snapped.

"Oh, would you stop."

Brijit was covered in dirt and grass, but she didn't care. Of course not. Voodoo loa spend a lot of time in the ground. They're no stranger to crawling up out of the dirt. Hell, she probably slept in a grave for all I knew. She reached behind her back and took out a large bottle of rum. She stuck her hand in the folds of her dress and took out a handful of oddly-shaped peppers. Bright red peppers. She uncorked the rum and stuffed the peppers inside. Once she was done fixing her liquor, she tilted the bottle back and chugged.

She drank half the bottle in one go.

Satisfied, the brought the bottle down and wiped her mouth with her sleeve. She stumbled in place. She wasn't even walking, she just stumbled for no reason. Without saying a word, she stuck the bottle out to me. I heard the rum sloshing around inside.

I took the bottle and drank some of it. It tasted like rum, but then the peppers hit me. I might as well have swallowed a mouthful of battery acid. I choked on the rum and coughed half of it out. It sprayed down the front of my shirt.

Brijit swiped the bottle back from me.

"Featherweight," she said.

"Go to hell," I grumbled.

She walked away from me, took another swig from her bottle and stared at the trees.

"Any idea where we are?" she asked.

"No." I coughed some more. "No clue."

"Place seems fine," she said. She took curious interest in the apple trees. She wrapped her fingers around one of the apples and plucked it free.

"You might not want to eat that," I told her. "Could be poisonous."

She glared at me, like how dare I tell her what to do, and she took a bite. She chewed it, swallowed, and gave me a bitchy look that said, "I'm already dead."

Whatever.

I spat out the pepper oil still burning my mouth and followed Athena's arrow through the trees.

"Alright," I said. "This way."

Brijit followed.

Then the bitch had the audacity to throw her apple at the back of my head. It thumped off my skull and landed on the ground. It didn't hurt, of course, but still, you don't throw shit.

I whipped around. "What the fuck is your problem?"

"In general?" she asked. "Or right this very moment?"

"You want to throw apples at me? I'll throw apples at you!"

She looked at me like I was stupid. "I didn't throw anything at you."

"The fuck you didn't." I bent down, picked up the apple, and showed it to her. "I guess this just fell out of the sky?"

"Fucking maybe," she said. "I didn't throw anything at you. Believe me, when I throw an apple at you, you'll know it."

"You don't even-"

An apple whizzed out of the trees and smacked Brijit right in the side of the head. Good thing we were looking at one another, too, because with no one else around she would have blamed me just like I blamed her.

Someone was throwing apples at us. We looked into the dark woods, but we didn't see anything.

Another apple hit me, this one in the side of the neck. Now I was pissed. I armed myself with an apple of my own, ready to take the head off of the next person I saw.

Brijit grabbed two apples.

Something - or some*one* - grabbed my hair and yanked it. I whipped around and pitched that apple like a fastball. No one was there. The apple smashed harmlessly against a tree.

I mumbled to myself, "What the-?"

A deep voice said, "What do you think you're doing?"

Holy shit, that voice came from the tree. The tree had a face. It had eyes, a nose, and a mouth. And it had two branches that worked like arms.

"What do you mean what are we doing?" Brijit waved the apples at the living tree. "Are you the one throwing these things at us?"

"You picked an apple off of me!" the tree said. "How would you like it if someone came along and picked something off of you?"

Brijit stormed up to the tree and got right in his face. "I'd like to see them try!"

I didn't move. I didn't get involved. Something about this seemed very familiar.

"She'd like to see us try!" the tree announced.

The other trees were alive, too, with faces all their own. They all shouted at us.

"She wants us to try!" one of them called out.

"Maybe we'll show her!" another one chimed in.

The first tree reached down and grabbed Brijit by the arm to hold her in place. The other trees threw apples at her.

Brijit struggled in place and screamed, "You trifle with dangerous forces, firewood!"

I stepped in, waving my hands, calling for peace.

"Okay, everyone slow down!" I said. "Just slow the fuck down. We're not here to cause any trouble."

The bombardment of apples stopped.

One of the trees replied, "You're not trying to cause trouble? You picked apples off of us!"

"Okay, look, we'll just leave." I put my hands on Brijit and the tree released her. I started to lead her away. "But would you do me one favor? Will you tell me the name of this place?"

The tree huffed and replied, "The Haunted Woods."

"Yeah," I said. "But where are the Haunted Woods located? Like, what is the name of this whole place?"

"This," one of the trees said, "is the Land of Oz."

2

"Fuck me." I walked down the middle of the yellow brick road. "I mean, no fucking way."

"What?" Brijit said as she followed behind me. "What's wrong?"

"Nothing's wrong," I said. I didn't know how to explain it to her. "It's just... I know this place."

"You've been here before?" she asked.

"Not exactly. This place isn't supposed to be real. It was in this movie I watched when I was a kid."

"Well, this is no movie," she said. "This is real."

"Yeah. I can see that."

I looked at Athena. Sure enough, the arrow was directing us further up the yellow brick road. So I kept going. Brijit picked up her pace so she could walk next to me.

"What do you know about this world then?" she asked me.

"I know there's a witch," I said. "Or at least, there used to be. She might be dead."

"She might be?"

"Yeah, I dunno. Depends, I guess. And this is the yellow brick road. If we follow it long enough, it will take us to the Emerald City. And I'm betting it's 1,437 kilometers away."

We followed the yellow brick road for miles. I couldn't get over the colors of the world. The grass was too green. The sky was too blue. The flowers were too red. They didn't look quite right; they looked like old technicolor movies, oversaturated with color. Brijit and myself wore a lot of black and white. We looked bland and boring compared to the world around us.

We put a good amount of time in walking. I kept checking the skies for witches or flying monkeys, but nothing.

After miles of grassy fields, just when the yellow brick road led us to some gently rolling hills that reminded me of Ireland, we saw someone on the road up ahead. It was a tiny little guy pulling a wooden wagon overloaded with scraps of metal. He had bright blue clothes on, a silly hat with a flower on top, and curly elf shoes. His pants were tight like leggings and came with white and blue stripes.

"That's a munchkin," I told Brijit.

She glared up ahead. "Okay. I'll distract him. You come up from behind and snap his neck."

"No no no no no," I said. "Jesus *Christ*, lady. I thought I had issues. Munchkins are cool. We don't need to kill him."

"You don't know that," she said.

"Just..." I held out my hands in hopes I could get her to calm down. "Just don't say anything. Let me do all the talking."

I jogged on up ahead. Brijit gave me an exasperated sigh, took a long drink of rum and followed behind me.

The little munchkin traveled much slower than us considering he was towing a cart full of metal all by himself. The wooden wheels of the cart squeaked so loud, the little guy didn't hear us approaching. He had no idea we were there, so I called out to get his attention.

"Hey!" I shouted. "Hey there!"

That scared the b'jesus out of him. The munchkin nearly launched out of his shoes. He shrieked like a little girl, stumbled to the ground and fell to his knees. Terrified, he decided to lay down and rest.

"Holy shit, little dude!" I ran over to him. "I'm sorry! I didn't mean to scare you."

I knelt down so I could help him up. He just laid there.

"Hey, little homie." I shook him. "Wake up." He didn't wake up. I shook him harder. "Hello? Earth to munchkin!"

"He's dead," Brijit said, standing over my shoulder. "The first living soul we've seen in hours and you killed him."

"I didn't kill him," I snapped. The munchkin had his eyes wide open and he wasn't blinking. "No way did I kill him. Oh my god, did I kill him?"

"Believe me, I know dead people. It's kind of my thing. That little munch-man is D-E-A-dead."

I jumped to my feet. "How the hell is he dead!? You little bastard! All I did was say hey! Who the hell dies from that!?"

"I dunno," Brijit said. She didn't sound like she even gave a shit. She took a swig of her rum and said, "He probably had a weak heart. Probably from a lifetime of carting around all this garbage."

I paced in nervous circles. "I just killed a goddam munchkin. He wasn't even doing anything. He was just walking along and I fucking killed him."

"Don't let it get to you." Brijit picked a piece of scrap metal off his cart and gave it a full inspection. It was rusted and twisted all to hell. "People die all the time. People die every day. You gotta learn to let it go."

"Yeah, but this guy's dead cuz of *me*!"

She looked away from her scrap metal. "You've never killed anyone before?"

"I mean..." I had to think. I do kick people pretty hard sometimes. I held my finger in the air to drive my point home. "I never killed anyone who didn't deserve it."

"Well, maybe this munch-man deserved it." Brijit went and leaned over the corpse. "Maybe he was a murderer."

"I don't think so," I said. "That's not really what munchkins do."

"What do they do?"

"They sing songs and dance. And I think maybe they make candy. This dude collected pieces of metal for... something."

"Well, you've successfully freed him from the burdens of living another day." She stood up, took another slug from her bottle of rum, then made it disappear up her sleeve. With her hands free, she was able to reach behind her back and take out an ornate shovel.

The shovel had dark, rich walnut wood for a handle. The handle had been worn smooth from eons of use, especially where her hands would go. The blade was scuffed up steel and came engraved with her Voodoo symbol.

"What are you going to do with that?" I asked.

"Use it as a pogo stick." She looked at me like I was stupid. "What do you think?"

"You're going to dig him a grave?"

"It's what I do." Brijit stepped off the yellow brick road and into the grass. She used her foot to sink the spade down into the dirt. She looked ridiculous; some face-painted girl in a filthy wedding dress, digging in the ground.

"You're just going to do it here?" I asked.

"Here... there..." She looked around. "Underground is underground."

I asked her, "And you're going to do it now?"

She looked at me. "How is waiting until later going to make a lick of difference? He's not going to get any more dead."

"We should tell..." Not the cops. There aren't cops in Oz. "Well, we should tell someone. They might need to do an autopsy."

Brijit relaxed her grip on the shovel and faced me directly. "You want to tell someone that you killed a munch-man?"

"I didn't kill him!"

She raised her eyebrows. "Oh, now you *didn't* kill him? Where were you sixty seconds ago?"

"I didn't kill him!"

"He was alive. You came along. Now he is dead."

"That doesn't mean I killed him! You said it yourself. Maybe he had a bad heart."

"I don't think this creature has a heart at all." She kicked the dead munchkin's head. "He's probably packed full of sawdust and ragweed."

"Don't kick him!" I grabbed the munchkin's leg and threw his body over my shoulder to keep him safe. His limp body flopped around. "Just, go on. Dig the stupid grave. Whatever. We'll just leave a note or something."

"Yes, exactly. A note." She turned away from me and started digging. "Dear King of the Munch-People. We killed one of your minions and buried him alone in the wilderness. Consider this our declaration of war."

3

Brijit was decidedly skilled at digging graves. She could eyeball all the correct measurements and made a rectangular hole in the ground just the perfect size for his body. I carried the munchkin over to the grave and held him over the edge.

"Just toss him in?" I asked.

Brijit shrugged. "I don't think he'll mind."

"Doesn't he need a coffin?"

"Listen to you," she said. "Just throw him in."

I looked at the bottom of the grave. It was deep. It didn't feel right to just throw him in there. "I dunno," I said.

"Oh, here." She came over, scooped him off my shoulder and just chucked him in. He landed all cock-eyed, with his arms and legs all twisted around.

"Oh!" I blurted out. "Little respect!?"

"Respect?" She dusted off her hands. "*I* didn't *kill* him."

Madam Brijit drank some more rum, then drunkenly shoveled dirt onto the munchkin's dead body. While she buried the body, I went to check out his cart of steel.

Free food. I ate a piece of it. I didn't think the munchkin would mind, since he was dead and all. It wasn't all that great, but it was food and I was hungry.

I said, "I guess we should take his wagon with us."

"Why?" Brijit asked, still shoveling. "Killing him wasn't enough? Now you need to steal all his stuff?"

"What if it's important? What if that's how he supports his family? Or what if someone needs the metal for some kind of project?"

"What if, what if, what if," Brijit said. "What if the sun goes out tomorrow and what if dogs fall in love with cats? You worry too much."

"We should give his stuff to someone. It's the least we could do."

"No. The least we could do is nothing. That's the least we could do."

"I'm taking his cart." I picked it up to test its weight. It lifted off the ground like a big pillow. I hoisted it up over my head. "We're doing the right thing."

"You don't even know where to take it," Brijit said. "He could have been going anywhere."

"I'll bring it with us to the Emerald City," I said. "And if no one claims it, we'll just dump it in the river."

She rolled her eyes at me. "Whatever helps you sleep at night."

Brijit filled in the grave in record time. She was really, really good at shoveling. After she whacked the loose dirt and packed it down, she made the shovel vanish behind her back and dusted off her gown.

We headed back down the yellow brick road, this time with a cart full of twisted steel over my head.

One kilometer turned into two. Two kilometers turned into four. We crossed over the hills and came across golden fields of wheat that stretched far off into the horizon. Still no people. Still no cities.

The sun began to set and the day turned to early evening. In the last minutes of sunset, we discovered more people on the road in front of us.

Three munchkins with backpacks were headed up the way. One of them wore bright green, another in all yellow, and the third one wore clothes with white and pink stripes. They all had silly hats and pointed shoes.

"More munchkins," I said.

"Try not to kill these ones," Brijit muttered.

"Shut up."

Last time I said "hey" to a munchkin, he died. So this time, I figured I would just keep my mouth shut and let them make the first move. As we came closer, one of them – the girl in pink stripes – heard our footsteps on the bricks and turned around. She tapped her companions on the shoulders to get their attention. Once they saw us, they stopped walking.

We came closer. They stood there, frozen in place and they didn't say anything. Right. When Dorothy first came to Oz, the munchkins all hid. They're shy little creatures. Shy little creatures with weak hearts, apparently.

"Come out, come out, wherever you are..." I sang, just like the song from the movie. That's the song that lures out munchkins.

Their munchkin eyes went wide, as if I just sang a song declaring me Jesus Munchkin Christ. It occurred to me that I should avoid referencing the Wizard of Oz. Who knows what the people here think about that.

"Hey," I said. "My name's Penelope. This is Madam Brijit."

No response.

So I kept talking. "Any idea who owns this cart?"

Eventually one of the munchkins, Greenie, spoke up.

"Shneer," Greenie said. "That cart belongs to Mister Shneer."

"Did Mister Shneer have a family?" I asked.

The munchkins blinked at us. Pinkie asked, "Did?"

God dammit, I tipped our hand.

I corrected myself. "Does?"

Greenie said, "Of course he does. Mister Shneer has eleventy-one children and twenty-teen grandchildren."

Dammit.

Pinkie asked us, "Why do you have Shneer's lucky cart?"

Brijit looked away and softly said, "It's not *that* lucky."

"I'm carrying it for him," I said. "Shneer... uh... was very ill. I offered to take his metal the rest of the way because he wanted to take a big nap."

"Silly Shneer," Greenie said.

"Beloved Shneer," Pinkie added.

God dammit.

"You are carrying Shneer's lucky cart over your head," Pinkie said as she stepped in front of me. "Are you a witch?"

"No," I said. "Brijit here is a witch, though."

Brijit glared at me.

Greenie went up to Brijit and asked, "Are you a bad witch, or a good witch?"

"A bad one," Brijit said as she made a menacing face.

The three munchkins leaned back, eyes wide, terrified.

"She's a bad witch who's turning over a new leaf," I clarified. "You don't have to worry about her. She's Brijit. I'm Penelope Salvo."

Greenie said, "I am Peepee. These are my friends Tonganoxie and Dori."

Tonganoxie, the man dressed in yellow, waved. Dori, the girl in pink, gave me a bow.

Peepee said, "You'll have to excuse Tonganoxie. He doesn't speak. He's been cursed."

"Did you say your name is Peepee?" I asked.

He puffed up his chest and proudly said, "Yes!"

I laughed right in that munchkin's face. I know that might have been rude, but his name was Peepee for Christ's sake. I looked at Brijit to see if she was laughing. She wasn't. Fine. Whatever. I laughed by myself.

"Why is that funny?" Peepee asked.

I laughed and pointed right at him. "Your name means piss!"

"What is piss?" asked Dori.

What is piss? That got me to laugh even harder. They didn't know what piss was. I couldn't take it. I put my hands on my knees and laughed and laughed.

Brijit took that time to talk to the munchkins, describe Baron Semedi, and see if they'd seen him. They had not.

Eventually my inappropriate giggle-fit died down and I took some deep breaths. I still giggled a little bit sometimes, but for the most part I was over it.

"Well," Dori said, "we're on our way to the Emerald City. Are you going to the Emerald City? We could travel together."

"Sounds like a good idea." I looked at Athena. "We're going 873 kilometers that way." And I pointed.

Peepee removed his hat and scratched his head. "What is a kilometer?"

I shook my head. "I have no idea."

"Then how do you know how far you're going?" he asked.

"I really don't, most of the time."

4

We walked down the yellow brick road in company with Peepee, Tonganoxie, and Dori. They hit us with an endless barrage of questions. Well, not Tonganoxie. Tonganoxie never spoke.

"Where are you from?"

"Your clothes look so strange. Why do they look so strange?"

"Do you know how to dance?"

116

"What kind of dances do you know?"

"What is a high school dance?"

"What is a high school?"

"What is education?"

"What is learning?"

"What is a brain?"

"Do we have brains?"

"No," Madam Brijit said. "Your heads are packed full of sawdust and moldy bread."

"Don't be so mean," I said.

She gave me a dirty look. "I don't like these monsters."

"But look at their little faces!" I reached down and pinched mute Tonganoxie's cheeks with both hands. "Look at these chubby faces. You just want to squeeze the chub right out of them!"

Brijit looked away. "They freak me out."

We kept walking. Eventually, after a couple dozen kilometers and a million-and-one questions from our new little friends, we spotted a small village dead ahead. It wasn't the Emerald City. No, that was still 831 kilometers away. This was some little munchkin city with tiny munchkin houses painted pink and red and blue. The houses only came up as high as my shoulders. I was a giant among them. And while I expected to see carefully tended gardens and delightfully odd decorations like what I remembered from the movie, that's not what I got.

Instead, the humble village was littered with stone forges filled with sizzling hot coals. Piles of scrap metal were collected randomly throughout the city. The munchkins all rushed back and forth, moving armloads of metal from one pile to another like a colony of ants.

"This is Tippino City," Dori told us. "The people here are very kind."

"They really like metal," I said.

"Not really," Peepee said. "It's just their job."

Brijit asked, "Their job is to collect metal?"

"Everyone has a job," said Dori. "Some of us collect the metal. Others melt it down. Still others bring it to the Emerald City. And still *others* polish it and keep it clean."

"Odd," I said. That wasn't in the movie. "And why's that?"

"Come," Peepee said. "We'll show you."

We were deeper into the village now, approaching a big flowing water fountain sitting in the town square. As we approached, the munchkin citizens of Tippino City would stop working to oogle Brijit and me. No more moving metal or sticking metal into forges. Instead, they stared at us like we were aliens from another planet.

And in a way, we kind of were.

"Greetings friends!" Peepee said as we reached the center of town. He threw up his hands and turned in a circle so everyone could hear him. "This is Pennypolly and Madam Brijit!"

"Penelope," I said, correcting him.

"Pennypolly." Brijit snickered. "I'm going to call you that."

I shot her a dirty look.

Peepee continued. "They are new here! Come, welcome them to Tippino City!"

All the munchkins crawled off their mountains of metal and peeked out from under their wooden wagons. Like curious, scared children, they slowly approached us.

A particularly brave munchkin took my hand and bowed. He said in a regal voice, "How do you do?"

"I do quite nicely," I said, matching his tone.

A different munchkin took Brijit's hand and also bowed. "And how do you do, too?"

Brijit jerked her hand away. "Unhand me, you filthy creature."

"Don't mind her," I said, stepping in. I took the offended munchkin's hand and shook it. "You'll have to forgive my associate here. She missed her nap and she's really crabby."

"It's okay!" The small-fry beamed a smile at me. He had a curly mustache and a tiny circle of beard on his chin. He was a thin little guy in a black tuxedo, accented with a ruffled shirt that puffed out at the cuffs and stuck out of his jacket like a pirate. He shook my hand vigorously and said, "My name is Swod Suitly! I am the mayor of Tippino City!"

"Nice to meet you, Mister Suitly," I said. "Quite the operation you got going on here."

He blinked at me. "Operation?"

"All this metal." I gestured all around us. "You guys building something?"

"Oh, no," he said. No further elaboration. After that he just beamed a big smile at me.

I said, "Well?"

Still smiling, he said, "Well, what?"

I asked, "What are you doing with all this metal?"

He dismissively waved his fingers at me. "Oh, you don't want to know that."

"Sure I do."

He leaned in and asked, "Do you really want to know?"

"Yes."

He leaned in closer. "Do you... *really* want to know?"

"Yeah, dude. I really want to know."

He leaned in even closer, almost touching his chin to my stomach, and peered up at me. "But do you... *really*?"

"Straight up honest, I mostly don't give a shit," I said. "I'm just curious. You don't have to tell me if you don't want to."

"Okay." He took a step back and clapped his hands together. "We'll tell you."

"We have to tell her," Peepee said to Dori.

"We have to tell her," Dori said to some other munchkin.

"We have to tell her," that munchkin said to another.

"We have to tell her," the other munchkin said.

Eventually they were all chanting, "We have to tell her, we have to tell her."

Brijit, somewhat terrified, took a step behind me, swigged her rum and asked, "What is the world is going on."

I said, "I think they're about to break out into-"

They all started singing.

"We'll tell you the story of Tippino City,
where the woodsmen are big and we're little bitty!"

"Oh, yeah, see?" I pointed at them, grinning. I was super excited. I was going to be in a real honest-to-god musical number. "Check it out! They're going to do a little dance and shit." I desperately patted down my clothes. "Where's my weed. I wanna get high for this."

An old munchkin hammered on a piece of scrap metal, flattening it out. He sang, *"I've been hammerin' for fifty-five years!"*

Another munchkin popped out of a window. *"And my job is to shape all the gears!"*

They all sang:

"Then off to the Emerald City it goes,
And if metal goes missing, Steelia knows!
Her army of Woodsmen patrol all of Oz
with horrible axes and terrible claws!"

Brijit didn't enjoy their cute song at all; I could see it on her face. She asked me, "Is there any way to make them stop?"

I answered quickly so I wouldn't lose the smoke I'd already inhaled. I shook my head. "Nope."

"It's hard to look away." She gave the munchkins a horrified look as they sang and danced all around their city. "It's almost hypnotizing."

A munchkin came up to me and sang, "*Steelia says that we're not really slaves.*"

Another munchkin sang, "*But if we don't give her metal, she puts us in graves.*"

"*We don't get paid money and there's no weekends off.*

We get one serving a day of deer stroganoff."

I exhaled my smoke and asked, "Well, why don't you guys just stand up and quit?"

The munchkins all screamed, "That would be the worst crime to commit!"

"*Only once did a munchkin dare to say 'no'*

and the woodsmen took him from old Tippino.

They chopped down his house and smashed all his things!

They told us that 'this is what saying no' brings!"

"Who is this Steelia you're all singing about?" I asked.

The munchkins stopped moving, some of them in mid-dance move. Tonganoxie stopped in the middle of doing the robot and just blinked at me. Mayor Suitly, who was dancing around the rim of the water fountain, crossed his arms at me and said, "We were getting to that."

"Oh," I said. God, the whole munchkin city was staring at me. It was so creepy how they didn't move. They were staring right into my soul. I knew why they were staring at me. They figured it out. They knew I was high. They knew I was high and they were going to kill me for it. "Oh my god, I'm so sorry."

Suitly gave me a stern look. "The story of Steelia is still two verses away."

They stared at me like blank zombies with no soul. I said, "I won't say another goddam word, I fucking swear. Please don't kill me."

Suitly turned to the other munchkins. "Shall we skip to the verse about Steelia?"

"We shall!" one munchkin shouted from his rooftop.

"Let's!" another one added.

They all moved to different spots of the town square, as if they were skipping ahead of their own choreography. The munchkin dancing in the fountain stepped out, dripping wet, and got ready to dance a jig around a small sapling. Another munchkin got up off the grass and joined a few others in a little circle. Once the munchkins had taken their new spots, they froze in place.

"And a-one," Suitly said, counting it off. "And a-two."

"Steelia rules with a fist made of steel
after chopping up Ozma in quite the ordeal!
We'd tell you more with our little quadrill-"

I grabbed my book and checked it.

Quadrill - noun. A square dance for four or more couples.

"But that's not allowed because-"

5

"What is the meaning of this!?" a voice boomed from the nearby woods. The munchkins all jumped and the singing came to an abrupt end.

Three tin woodsmen stepped out of the woods. Metal from head to toe, they looked like the Tin Man's evil cousins. Their faces were mean and they had permanent frowns. Bolts went down the fronts of their chests to hold them together and they had funnels on the tops of their heads. In their hands, they carried sharp woodcutting axes. Their feet clanked as they stepped onto the brick streets of Tippino City and marched towards our musical.

The munchkins stared at them with wide, terrified eyes. The woodsmen gave them disdainful looks, as if the little people were literal garbage.

Mayor Suitly ran to intercept the machine men. "Our apologies, great woodsmen! We became distracted and sang a song for our visitors. Only one song. And we'll work twice as hard to make up for the lost time. Please don't-"

One of the woodsmen grabbed Suitly by his face and shoved him to the ground. The small guy landed on his butt with an "oof."

"You are not to sing or dance," the main woodsman said. "You are here to collect steel for the Emerald City and that is all. No laughing. No cavorting."

The munchkins put their heads down and went back to hammering metal, gathering it up into their arms, and loading it into wagons. It looked so out of character for them; these brightly colored people sweating over hot forges and dragging sharp steel through their flower beds.

A part of me kept saying *don't get involved, don't get involved.* Another part of me – a bigger part of me – wasn't about to put up with this kind of bullshit. I took a step in the direction of the woodsmen.

Brijit read my body language and stepped in front of me.

"What are you doing?" she snapped.

I kept my eyes on the woodsmen. "I'm only going to talk to them."

"You're going to start a fight," she said.

"Maybe," I replied. "Probably."

"You're just going to make things worse for these poor people."

"What do you care?" I asked. "You don't even like them."

"They're annoying little monsters, granted, but if you want what's best for them, you'll mind your own business. Whatever is going on here is just how their world works. Your world has pollution. My world has zombies. This world has mechanical ax men. It has nothing to do with us."

"I'm not going to sit here and let these people be slaves." I brushed past Brijit and made off for the woodsmen.

"They're not really slaves," Brijit whispered after me. "Didn't you listen to their stupid song?"

I ignored her. She just didn't get it.

The three woodsmen saw me coming. They didn't look the least bit intimidated. There were three of them and one of me and as far as they were concerned, I was a nobody.

"Hey, what is your deal?" I blurted out as I reached them. I helped Suitly back up to his feet and he scurried away. "You want to push someone around? Push me around. I would love that. I really would. Lay a hand on me, motherfucker, and I'll rip it off."

The woodsmen looked at one another, confused at first. They weren't used to someone questioning their authority. The situation amused them I guess, because they grinned and turned back to me. The middle one took a step closer. He sounded like a clattering wagon of pots and pans.

"Who are you, little one?" he asked me.

"Little one?" I repeated. *"Little one*? I'm Penelope Salvo, that's who I am."

"And where are you from?" He asked. I didn't much care for his tone. He sounded like a cop. "Kansas?"

"New York."

The second woodsman stepped forward and said, "Well, take our advice, Kansas. We are here on direct orders from Empress Steelia herself, so why don't you move along before you get into trouble?"

Brijit came up behind me and put a hand on my shoulder. She addressed the woodsmen and said, "Don't mind us. We were just leaving."

I kept my feet planted and my eyes locked on the middle woodsman. I said, "Oh, I'm not going anywhere."

"So be it," he said. "Under the authority of Empress Steelia and the Kingdom of Oz, I'm placing you under arrest."

The woodsman reached out and took my arm. The other two woodsmen brandished their axes, hinting at the violence that might come if I resisted.

I gave the woodsman one warning. "Don't touch me."

Brijit told him, "I wouldn't touch her."

He gripped my arm harder and pulled. "You're coming with me."

"I said, don't touch me!" I broke free from his grip and tore his whole arm off. I grabbed him by the neck and dragged him over to one of the forges. I slammed him face first into the red hot coals. Cinders puffed into the air.

I put my hand on the back of his head and pressed his face down into the glowing fire. The machine man let out a tortured scream. The munchkins shrieked in fear and covered their ears.

"Look away, little angels!" I shouted at the innocent townsfolk. I had to shout so they could hear me over the anguished screams of the melting woodsman. "This is not going to be pretty!"

The woodsman thrashed his arms and kicked with his legs. He tried desperately to get free. And he was strong – I'll give him that – but not as strong as me. Slowly but surely, his head began to glow orange. His face was melting off.

The other two woodsmen came at me. I jumped away from the forge and got into fighting position.

Once I took my hands off that first woodsman, he shot up out of the forge. His eyes and nose and mouth had melted into bright orange sludge and he looked like a rotting jack-o-lantern. He tried to scream, but it came out as a gurgling drowning sound. Without his face or eyes, he stumbled around the brick street and reached out blindly for anything to grab on to. He clawed at his own face in desperation and pulled globs of melting metal free to reveal the hollowness of his head.

Horrified munchkins shrieked and backed away from the deformed monster.

I turned to the remaining two woodsmen and twiddled my fingers at them. "Who's next? Who's next in the octagon?"

The two of them rushed me, axes held high, ready to chop me into pieces.

I let them chop at me. I didn't feel a thing. One of their axes thunked off my forehead. The other one whacked me in the arm and it almost tickled. When they realized their attacks weren't working, they stopped. My indestructible body confused them.

"Alright," I said with a grin. "My turn."

I grabbed one of the woodsmen by his head and tore it clean off. His body immediately collapsed to the ground, but his head was still alive. His screams of terror echoed across Tippino City.

In a true display of power, I stuck his face in my mouth and tore off a big strip of metal with my teeth. The last woodsman watched in horror as I ate his friend's face and chewed it up. He couldn't look away. Hell, his eyes didn't even blink. His mouth slowly dropped open and he started to back away.

He whispered, "You're a witch."

I swallowed the one guy's face and smiled. I crumpled up the rest of his head up like a ball of aluminum foil and popped it in my mouth.

"I'm not witch," I said. "I'm a god. And this guy doesn't taste half bad." I held out my hands and advanced on the last woodsman with menace in my eyes. "Now I wonder, do you taste like dessert?"

The last woodsman freaked out. The ax fell loose from his trembling fingers and it clattered to the bricks. He turned around and made a mad dash for the woods. He stumbled over some bushes, regained his balance, then disappeared into the darkness of the trees.

Chapter 7

1

Brijit came up behind me and said, "We've only been here five hours and you've already killed three people."

"Yeah, well." There was some sort of saying that I think would have been a good response, but I couldn't remember it. So I just went with, "You wanna cook an omelet, you gotta break some eggs."

Brijit and I kept watch over Tippino City until morning, just in case any more tin woodsmen came back. They did not.

Sunrise came. The munchkins ate their breakfasts of quail eggs and pollen tea. They told me to eat as much metal scrap as I wanted. Brijit drank her rum for breakfast. After that, we were on our way. The munchkins bid us a fond farewell with a colorful parade and another song. They stopped following us once we hit the city limits. There they stood in a large group, waving happily and shouting their high-pitched goodbyes.

Just like that, we were back to our cross-country adventure.

Brijit and I traveled in the company of Peepee, Tonganoxie, and Dori. They skipped down the yellow brick road and sang the songs of their people. Well, technically Peepee and Dori sang; Tonganoxie could only whistle. I couldn't help but admire the munchkins. They lived in an oppressive world, but it hadn't broken their spirits.

At one point, they formed a merry-go-round around Brijit's legs and danced around her.

"Ring-a-ding, this witch is bad,
but ring-a-ding, she's turning good!
Ring ring ring ring ring ring ring!
We have a brand new song to sing!"

"Aw." I elbowed Brijit. "They like you."

Brijit looked super annoyed and grumbled, "How much further do we have to go?"

I checked Athena.

53 kilometers.

"53 kilometers," I said.

"Is that far?" she asked.

"I'm not sure." So I asked the munchkins. "How much further to the Emerald City?"

"If we walk all day and all night, we'll be there by tomorrow," Peepee said.

Brijit sighed. "Another day with these little rat people."

"You need to lighten up," I told her.

"I want to find Semedi and go home," she said. "This place is too bright. The air here smells like flowers. And these singing creatures bother me."

"It was your idea to come along," I reminded her. "So unless you want to turn back, you might as well try to enjoy it."

She rolled her eyes, but kept on walking. "I don't see how anyone could enjoy this place."

We discovered a lot of amazing landscapes as we crossed Oz. We traveled through bright green grasslands that were so well maintained, they looked like a golf course. In the early afternoon, we reached a point where the yellow brick road turned into a stone bridge that crossed over a shimmering lake of silver. There were giant sea monsters just below the surface, big like whales, but black and covered in scales. They slithered back and forth, just barely skimming the surface of the lake and sending ripples across the water. They never came close enough to really see exactly what they looked liked.

It blew my mind to think I was seriously in the land of Oz. Oz wasn't a real place. At least, it wasn't supposed to be. Oz was supposed to be a fairy tale.

So I decided to ask the munchkins some qualifying questions. I figured if they were citizens of Oz, surely they'd heard of Dorothy or the Scarecrow or the Tinman or the Cowardly Lion.

And sure enough, they had. They told me everything they knew, which was only from legends because – as I came to learn – the stories of Dorothy Gale were nearly 100 years old.

Peepee and Tonganoxie talked and talked and talked as we crossed the flower fields, super excited to share the old stories.

Apparently Dorothy didn't stay in Kansas after she went home. She eventually left Earth and came to live in the Emerald City. Princess Ozma – leader of Oz after the Wizard left town – invited her to live in Oz, along with her Aunt Em and her Uncle Henry. But this, the munchkins explained, was long ago. All of the "Kansans" had died of old age.

And what about the others? Princess Ozma hired the Scarecrow to be her chief adviser and apparently he was pretty good at it, with his brains and all. The Cowardly Lion was Ozma's chief of security in the Emerald City, because of his courage.

The Tinman is where things took a disastrous turn. The Tinman lived in the Emerald City and built a daughter out of steel. He brought her to life with the same magic that was used on him. That's when everything went wrong, according to the munchkins.

The Tinman had once thought he was incomplete without a heart. In his search for a heart, he met Dorothy and the Scarecrow and the Lion. He made friends and he grew as a person. The Tinman firmly believed that his quest to find a heart turned him into the person he wanted to become. He learned the values of trust and friendship and love.

He wanted the same for his daughter Steelia, so he built her with no heart.

But Steelia did not go on an adventure to find trust and friendship and love. She didn't see the point. Built without a heart, Steelia hated everyone, most of all Princess Ozma. Everyone regarded Ozma as sweet and innocent and kind, but Steelia thought she was arrogant and foolish. Every time Ozma made another law that increased the number of flower fields to be planted, or recommended that everyone sing at least one song a day, Steelia grew more and more furious. This was a kingdom to be *ruled*, not coddled. The people were subjects and needed to be subjugated.

And if Ozma wasn't going to do it, Steelia would.

One night when there was no moon and the world was particularly dark, Steelia took her father's ax and skulked through the shadows of the Emerald City. She weaseled her way into the castle. Using the element of surprise, she murdered the two guards standing outside Ozma's bedchambers. After that, once inside and looming over the sleeping Princess, Steelia raised her ax and chopped her head off.

Bold move, trying to take over Oz like that. Ozma had been in charge for nearly 100 years. Steelia knew that if she was going to take control of the throne, she had to move quickly. And the first thing she needed to do was wipe out anyone who would stand in her way.

That very next morning, she drug the Scarecrow and the Cowardly Lion down to the Emerald Square of the Emerald City. She accused them of murdering the Princess, which was so far out of character that none of the citizens believed it was true. But the people of the Emerald City were weak. Steelia had a weapon and the people were afraid of weapons. So they looked on as Steelia found the Scarecrow and the Lion guilty of treason and chopped off both of their heads with her ax, still wet with the blood of Princess Ozma.

Steelia had even more dire things planned for her father. She knew Tinman would never understand her need to rule Oz. He would always be a problem. His "heart" got in the way. So she got to him as quickly as she could, before he had even heard the news about Ozma, and doused her father with a bucket of water. The Tinman rusted over and froze into a statue.

"Jesus," I said to the munchkins. "Buckets of water are practically weapons of mass destruction in Oz."

Terrified that someone might "oil can" her dear old dad and set him free, Steelia locked the rusted body of the Tinman in her treasure room. He was still alive, of course. He just couldn't move. Rumor has it that she sometimes goes in there and presses her ear to her father's chest, where she can just barely hear the faint sounds of his voice. She goes to listen to him cry, because she finds it funny. When the Tinman's tinny, hollow voice laments how evil his daughter is, she smiles. When he cries that it was a mistake to build her without a heart, she giggles. And when he begs to be set free, she laughs and leaves the room.

The Tinman cries at night and his tears keep him in a constant state of rust.

Steelia did away with living guards and soldiers because living guards and soldiers could lead a revolution against her. No, Steelia preferred soldiers of her own design: Woodsmen modeled after her father who would be forever obedient to her and only her.

"Now we bring metal to the Emerald City where Steelia builds her soldiers," Dori said.

"And it's been this way since any of us were born," Peepee said.

No sooner had they finished their story, I took notice of the surrounding landscape. We were out in the flower fields, but there were more than just flowers out there. There were bodies impaled on sticks. Hundreds of them. Blood-soaked munchkin bodies hung there in the sun with obvious ax wounds. Human bodies hung there, too, some with missing heads. Porcelain chunks were strewn all about, some of them in the shape of body parts, as if porcelain men and women had been smashed to bits.

Our munchkin friends had to've noticed the horrors surrounding us, but they kept their eyes forward and refused to look at it. They got strangely quiet, pretending that it just wasn't there.

"What is this place?" Brijit asked. Her voice was quiet, as if those fields were haunted and she didn't want to attract any unwanted attention.

"It's fucking sick," I said. "This is the kind of thing you do when you want to keep people scared of you."

Brijit stopped, so I stopped. The munchkins stopped, but they kept their eyes pointed down at the yellow brick road, careful not to look at the grotesque display of murder that surrounded us.

"What?" I asked Brijit.

Instead of answering me, Brijit took five big gulps from her rum bottle and tucked it away into her clothes. After that, she retrieved her shovel. She met my eyes and gave me a slight frown. She stepped off the yellow brick road and into the grass.

"You can't be serious," I said.

"I can," she replied.

"You're going to bury all of them?" I followed her out into the flowers. "Now?"

"All of them," she said. "Now."

"There's, like, thousands of them." I threw my hands into the air. "That's going to take forever. We're only a day away from the Emerald City."

Brijit whipped around, visibly upset. "I'm *not* leaving these people out here like this. This is not how you treat the dead. I don't know where these people go to when they die, if they

129

believe in an afterlife of souls or not, but they deserve to be put in the ground."

"What do you care?" I asked. "You don't even like these people."

"It's not about liking them," she said. "It's my job. I was the first woman to ever die. I'm a loa of love and death. Taking care of the dead is what I do."

"But do you have to do it now?" I asked.

"Did you listen to a word I just said? It's not up to me. It's who I am. It's my nature. Just like it's your nature to cause trouble wherever you go."

"Causing trouble is not my nature," I said.

"Isn't it?" She turned away from me and stuck the end of her shovel in the dirt. She dug up her first lump of dirt and tossed it aside. "Do you think it's a coincidence that you're the god of war and wherever you go, fighting seems to follow?"

"That's not true," I said. After a pause, I added, "Is it?"

Brijit looked at me over her shoulder, raised skeptical eyebrow, then turned back to focus on digging.

That shut me up. Was that really true? Was my knack for starting shit all centered around the fact that I swallowed Impossible Red? Was that my nature? Surely not. I was causing trouble long before that.

I moved in front of Brijit so she'd have no choice but to look at me and I said, "Look, dude, I get the whole 'nature' thing. I totally do. But burying every single one of these people is going to take forever. We don't have that kind of time."

"Then go on without me," she snapped. She scooped another shovelful of dirt out of the ground.

One grave started. A thousand more to go.

No talking her out of this one, apparently. I looked back at my three munchkin friends. They stood there, huddled up, staring at the ground. Only silent Tonganoxie had the courage to steal a glance at me, but he must have caught sight of the bodies; he immediately squeezed his eyes shut and turned away.

"Alright." I dismissed Brijit's poor attitude with a wave of my left hand and let her play undertaker. "I'm going to take the munchkins and keep going. Whenever you're done, follow the yellow brick road and try to catch up."

Brijit grumbled something in response. I couldn't make it out.

"31 kilometers," I reminded her. I pointed up the road. "That way. It's a big city made of emerald. You can't miss it."

She grumbled something else and kept digging.

2

We traveled for the rest of the evening, me and my snack-sized friends. When night fell, Peepee dug some small torches out of his backpack and handed them to Tonganoxie and Dori. They knelt down and lit them with flint and steel. Guided by dancing firelight, we delved into a dark grove of trees.

We were crossing through the densest woods of Oz. I could hear things rustling around in the bushes. Lions, I assumed. Lions and tigers and bears. (Even though lions and tigers don't actually live in the woods, except maybe in Oz.) I could barely catch sight of the shadows that moved in the trees and when I turned to spot them, they disappeared. Maybe there were predators out there, maybe there weren't. I wasn't worried. I could manhandle lions and tigers and bears with my bare hands if necessary.

It was my band of innocent travelers I had to worry about.

Tonganoxie and Dori huddled up close, nervously watching the woods around them. Peepee led the way, torch held high, trying to appear confident. He was nervous. I could tell. He jumped at every crunching leaf or snapping twig.

We walked for hours and the woods showed no signs of thinning out. We weren't lost, we knew that much; we were still following the yellow brick road and Athena confidently pointed us ever forward.

I heard marching. Metallic marching. It was hard to hear at first, but it quickly got louder. Even the munchkins heard it. It was a contingent of Tin Woodsmen coming our way and if the noise was any indication, there had to be dozens of them.

"Oh no," Peepee said in a panic. He bumbled around in a confused and terrified circle. "No one is allowed out past dark!"

Tonganoxie and Dori held each other tighter and shook in place.

"Okay, you could have mentioned that sooner." I gathered up their torches and stubbed them out on the bricks. The woods went dark, "Quick, hide in the bushes."

Tongie and Dori dove into a nearby bush. Peepee followed soon after them. I was too big to hide with them, so I crawled into my own, separate bush.

The marching got louder and louder. A green glow appeared in the deep woods. The formation of woodsmen came marching up the yellow brick road with their legs kicking high on each step – three woodsmen wide and a dozen men long. The green glow that lit up the woods came from their glowing eyes. I hoped that the green color was just for aesthetics and that they didn't have night vision.

They marched in unison with clockwork precision. March, march, march they went, dozens of mechanical robot woodcutters. Their heads pivoted back and forth scanning the trees for criminals or ruffians.

I could kill 25 woodsmen. Hell, given enough time I could probably kill every single woodsman in Oz, but not before they turned on my munchkin friends and chopped their heads off.

One woodsman stopped and turned his head in our direction. The other woodsmen kept on marching.

I was afraid the dim red glow of Athena on my arm would blow my cover. I clutched it close to my body and did my best to cover it with my shirt.

The curious woodsmen shone his green eyes over our bushes. Surely we hadn't been spotted. We hadn't moved. We hadn't made a sound. In the green light of the woodsman's eyes, I could see the munchkins hiding in their bush, hugging one another, heads tucked down low.

I clenched my fists, ready to bust out of the bushes and go full MMA-mode if necessary. The other woodsmen marched away, but they weren't so far that they couldn't double back if I jumped out of the bushes. I decided I was only going to jump out if the munchkins were discovered first.

It didn't come to that. The curious woodsman scanned our area for a hot second and found nothing. The other woodsmen were leaving him behind. The woodsman that stood over us turned and marched away, double-time, to catch up to his platoon.

The platoon went away. The woods went dark and their marching faded into the distance. Just to be on the safe side, we stayed hidden for another couple minutes. After I was 100 percent sure they were gone, I crawled back out onto the yellow brick road and whispered for my friends.

"Guys? Come on out."

They crawled out, their hair and clothes littered with twigs and leaves.

"That was close," Peepee said as he cautiously eyed the yellow brick road.

"Too close," Dori added.

Tonganoxie eagerly shook his head in agreement.

3

We walked all through the rest of the night. I had no idea how many hours that was, exactly. It's not like I had a watch or anything. I wasn't even convinced that there were 24 hours in a day there in Oz. What if night was longer than on Earth? Or what if it was shorter? It was impossible to tell how close we were to sunrise. The only measuring tool I had was Athena and that only gave me stupid kilometers.

When my arm read 19 kilometers, I knew we had to be getting close. If the munchkins were right when they said we'd reach the Emerald City if we walked all day and walked all night, then sunrise would be coming soon.

I saw light just beyond the horizon. At first I thought it was the sunrise, but I was wrong. It was the shine of the Emerald City that glowed like some kind of nuclear meltdown. I could just start to make out the towers of the city that pulsed with green light as if they were made out of raw plutonium. The skyscrapers looked impossibly tall and thin; hardly efficient as far as construction goes.

The odd architecture of the city coupled with that radioactive brilliance seemed like Heaven, if God's favorite color was green.

"That's it," Peepee said. "That's the Emerald City."

"I see it," I said. "Have you guys ever been here before?"

"No," Peepee said.

Tonganoxie shook his head.

Dori said, "People don't often come here."

"Then why come all this way?" I asked.

"To bargain for Tonganoxie's voice," Dori said. "We heard a rumor that Steelia has it."

"Steelia took his voice?" I asked.

"No," Peepee said. "Wandaloo took it."

Dori clarified, "Wandaloo, the Misunderstood Witch of the South By Southwest. She steals people's voices and places them in magical trumpets. She stole Tongie's voice and his trumpet somehow made its way to the Emerald City."

133

"Well, come on then," I said as I picked up the pace. "We're almost there!"

We sprinted the rest of the way down the yellow brick road.

The sun came up and instantly the sky turned the brightest shade of blue. The jeweled buildings of Emerald City gleamed even brighter in the sunshine. It felt like spring.

Every day in the Land of Oz felt like spring.

The outer walls of the Emerald City were 40 foot tall and made of sheer emerald. They completely surrounded the city, keeping citizens in and nosy troublemakers such as myself out. I could have hurdled the wall easy or put my fist through it, but that wouldn't have done anything to help my little munchkin friends. We'd have to get inside the regular way; with some good old-fashioned sweet talk. So I went up to the main gate – two towering doors, one crafted with a gigantic "O" of solid gold and the other crafted with a "Z" – and pounded on it with my fist that sent a resonating boom down the length of the entire wall.

That pounding echo quickly faded away. The doors didn't open. No one poked their head out to see who it was. I shrugged and pounded again, harder. Perhaps a little *too* hard. A tiny crack snapped in the emerald door. Shit. I used my thumb to try to wipe it away. No such luck.

"Hello!?" I shouted up at the top of the wall. "Ding dong!"

Two round windows opened in each of the doors and two old men poked their heads out. They wore all green. One had a beard, the other didn't. Beardy and Shavey. Other than that, they looked like twins.

"Why are you knocking!?" they said in unison.

"Open up." I tapped the door with the toe of my shoe. "Come on. I haven't got all day. Open up."

They looked at one another, then back at me and said, "And who, exactly, are you?"

"Am I being detained?" I asked. "I know my rights. I don't have to tell you shit. Open these doors or I'll open them for you and you're not going to like it."

"Did Steelia send for you?" Beardy asked.

"Did you bring metal as an offering?" asked Shavey.

"Steelia didn't send for me and I didn't bring anything but a piss-poor attitude and very little patience."

"Well then you can't come in!" The two old men leaned back and slammed their windows closed.

134

Fine. I figured it might come to this. I widened my stance and stretched out my arms.

"Stand back," I told the munchkins. And they backed off.

I got a running start and kicked the doors right where they connected. They shifted in place and a big crack split across the "O" door.

"Knock knock!" I shouted. I backed up and gave the gate another running kick. Another boom. The "Z" door cracked. A chunk of emerald snapped loose and thumped to the ground.

The windows opened up again and the two old men poked their heads back out.

"Stop!" Shavey shouted.

"You'll break the doors!" said Beardy.

"Then open up!" I yelled at them.

And they answered, "No!"

"Well, then you better back off." I shooed them away with my hands. "Because when the walls come crumblin' crumblin', you two are going to get smooshed like ants."

"We refuse!"

I couldn't believe they were still saying no. I sighed and shook my head. "Your funeral."

They crossed their arms and gave me a look like I was bluffing. They didn't move. Well, sucks to be them because I was going to kick the doors in and I wasn't going to stop just because two geriatrics felt like being stubborn.

I sprinted for the door and scissor kicked them right in the sweet spot. The colossal doors shattered. Giant shards of broken emerald exploded deep into the city. I heard the old men squawk as they were thrown back into the streets. They landed hard on the ground and rolled to a stop.

They laid there and didn't move.

I stepped through the bright green rubble and led the munchkins inside the city. I didn't check to see if the old men were dead. They were like Schrodinger's old men: they could have been alive or they could have been dead and as long as I didn't check, I could simply *believe* they were alive. And I wanted to believe that they-

"He's dead!" one of the Oz citizens shouted as she checked Beardy's pulse.

"So is he!" said another one, as he looked up from Shavey.

Okay, so much for the Schrodinger thing. Mystery solved. Beardy and Shavey were dead. But, you know what? Whatever.

Seriously. Whatever. That's not my fault. I warned them. I get real sick of warning people to not fuck with me – sometimes I warn them three or four times – but they never listen. That's how people end up dead. I'm not going to keep feeling bad about that.

"You know," I said to those two arm-chair doctors as I stormed down the main street of the Emerald City. "You two should mind your own business."

The Emerald City was like nothing I had ever seen. Everything was green, of course, and it was a strange mix of both futuristic and rustic. The engineering necessary to build skyscrapers out of emerald would have been impossible back on Earth. Despite that leap in technology, the city had no cars; they had multi-colored horses pulling buggies. The streets were cobblestone roads made from bricks of transparent emerald and mortared into place with silver. Tiny one-story shops were clustered around the base of these towering jade obelisks that stretched far up into the clouds. Apartment buildings – or what I *assumed* were apartment buildings – lined the length of the main thoroughfare.

All the signs were green with yellow letters, written in some language I'd never seen before. The street lights were green crystal. Even the rats came in shades of lime and shamrock and chartreuse.

The city reminded me of Midtown, how the streets are an endless maze of skyscrapers. The Emerald City was just as jam-packed with emerald buildings, except these were taller, sparklier, and dangerously thin.

My explosive entrance into the city attracted a crowd, small at first, but it was growing quickly. There were men in green tuxedos with oddly curled bowties and cartoonish haircuts. The women wore outrageous green hoop skirts and some of them carried parasols. The children gathered at the knees of the adults wearing short pants, green vests, and dumbass looking hats.

They were curious, but also afraid, and they watched me from a safe distance away. I'm sure I appeared strange to them, dressed in black clothes and with a glowing red arm.

"Problem?" I asked them.

They gasped, startled by my words alone.

A tin woodsman came around the corner of an emerald bakery. He stopped short when he saw the crowd of people and the wreckage of their emerald doors and me standing in the middle of all of it.

"What is going on here!?" he shouted. He looked at the cracked boulders of emerald and turned back to me. "Did you do this?"

"Yeah," I said. "I said knock knock, but no one let me in."

The woodsman readied his ax and advanced on me. He asked, "Are you a witch?"

Now, obviously I'm not a witch. I knew that. But I wasn't about to be intimidated by another one of these poor-man's Terminators. I took a step closer to him and told him the truth:

"I am a god."

The people of the Emerald City gasped. Of course they did. These were fairy tale people. They were used to powerful leaders who fly on brooms or mysterious wizards with enormous, exploding heads. This was not a culture built around polite conversation and delicate diplomacy. This was a culture that believed in amazing displays of magical power.

I just told them I was a god. And that part was true; I *was* a god. The superstitious people of Oz had no reason to doubt that. After all, they just saw me manhandle a 400 ton gateway of solid emerald.

Well, if what these people wanted were amazing displays of power, I was going to oblige them.

"I am Penelope, the Great and Powerful!" I shouted at everyone as I threw my hands into the air. "I have come to liberate you from the evil Steelia!"

No one responded. They stood there, huddled together, confused and afraid.

"I guess I didn't make myself clear!" I continued. I marched right up to the intruding tin woodsman and smacked him across the face. His head dented in half. "I'm about to make some bitchin' changes around here!"

The woodsman collapsed to the ground. That was fine. It made me look... well... great and powerful.

I pointed at the crowd of Oz people and tried to make eye contact with as many of them as I could. "You're all going to be free soon. Don't you worry."

I checked Athena. My exit was seven kilometers deeper into the city and it didn't seem like anyone could stop me.

"Alright," I said. "I'm going to go now. I didn't come here to cause any trouble. I know it doesn't look like it because a lot of people are dead now, but I really am just passing through. So as long as you jabronies just stay out of my way, I won't have to kill anyone else."

I really hoped they were listening.

4

I led Peepee, Dori, and Tonganoxie through the streets of the Emerald City. We traveled a couple blocks and came across a different crowd of people who filled the entire Emerald Square. Their attention was focused on a big wooden stage where five woodsmen stood over five kneeling citizens. They were tied-down to a block of wood with their heads turned to the side. The woodsmen behind them had their axes poised overhead.

This was an execution.

The citizens didn't look like trouble. One lady looked like a baker. One of the old men had spectacles on and could have been a professor or a scientist or a kooky inventor. And one of the people up there was a kid, like twelve or thirteen looking. They were all tied down in the same way, ready to get decapitated.

A different woodsman down on the ground tooted the funnel on his head and then announced, "In the name of great Empress Steelia, you have been found guilty of treason and are now to be executed!"

The people in the crowd were forced to watch. If any of them looked away, the patrolling woodsmen would come over, grab their faces and force them to watch. Anyone who tried to back away felt an ax blade pressed against them and were pushed back into place.

Me and the munchkins couldn't risk getting caught up in that mess. I wanted to rescue those people from execution, but it would have started all sorts of problems and I had three munchkins to keep track of. I couldn't get into deep shit before making my way to Steelia herself. Peepee and Dori and Tongie didn't have the stomach to watch an execution and if we were spotted by the woodsmen, they would have been physically forced to watch. It was tough to walk away like that, but I had a bigger picture to consider. I quickly led my friends away from the square and down a narrow alley between two skyscrapers.

Dori tugged on my arm. "We're being followed."

I glanced over my shoulder. Sure enough, a single woodsman was on our tail. He wasn't running after us or anything. He was just keeping tabs.

"It's okay," I told her. "Don't worry about him."

Athena's arrow led us through the city, past the Registry of Monsters and around the corner of the market, where dumbfounded Ozians put their fruit and bread purchases on hold to gawk at me. Everywhere we went, the citizens went about their daily lives, but with nervous expressions on their faces. The woodsmen patrolled everywhere and constantly monitored the activity of the civilians. Occasionally a woodsman would come along, dragging a terrified citizen towards the city square.

Those people lived in a terrible, terrible police state. They didn't seem to have any of the freedoms I'd come to take from granted back on Earth.

Eventually, with half a kilometer left to go, we found ourselves standing at the base of a great castle surrounded by dozens of storybook guard towers. The towers were each manned by tin woodsmen who watched over the surrounding city. It didn't take them long to spot me and when they did, they focused all their attention on me and my friends.

Out of the surrounding streets and alleys came dozens and dozens of woodsmen. They formed a perimeter around me, but were careful to keep their distance. Apparently they were only there to prevent our escape back into the city.

Out of the open gate of the castle entrance came even more woodsmen. Hundreds of them. An army of woodsmen. They fell into formation in front of us and blocked our way in.

We were totally surrounded.

I pushed the munchkins behind me and stepped towards the army blocking the gate. "Alright bitches, listen up. I'm giving you one chance to move or else I'm going to-"

I got cut off when all of the woodsmen blasted sound from the funnels on their heads. They sounded like a bunch of train whistles and fog horns. I tried to finish my sentence, but I was totally drowned out by the noise. The sound of their funnel heads quit and went echoing through the skyscrapers of the city. Peepee, Dori, and Tonganoxie had covered their ears with their hands.

One of the woodsmen stepped forward and raised his voice to the sky. "Announcing her majesty, the Empress of Oz, the Metallic Meaning of Life, Steelia! The Great and Powerful!"

Far above us, a metal girl stepped out onto the castle balcony and looked out over the edge. She wasn't a bolted-together attempt at a person like the woodsmen. This girl – Empress

Steelia, daughter of the Tinman – was more advanced with more realistic joints and better proportions. It was obvious that the man who crafted her did it out of painstaking care and attention.

Steelia leaned against the rail on her balcony and stared down at us. We looked up at her. No one said anything at first and things were quiet. I heard a dog bark from blocks away. I guess she was waiting for me to make the first move, so I did.

"Sup?" I shouted.

"Are you the girl from Kansas!?" she shouted down at me.

"New York!" I called back.

"Are you the one who's been damaging my tin woodsmen?!"

"Guilty as charged!"

I stood there waiting to see if she had more to say, but she didn't.

"Look," I said. "I'm not from here and I don't plan on staying. I'm traveling around from world to world and I'm actually just trying to leave. My arm shows me the way out and right now it's telling me that the exit is inside your castle."

Steelia laughed. "You invaded my city and killed my men! You think I'm going to let you inside my castle?"

"Oh, see, that's the thing. I'm not giving you a choice. I'm coming in one way or another."

Steelia frowned. If she was smart, she wouldn't try to call my bluff. I ate one of her woodsmen. I could shatter emerald like glass. And with that information, she really had to weigh her options. Dictators really only fear one thing and that's losing control. Steelia had no idea what the full extent of my power truly was. One wrong move might bring her whole regime crashing down.

Was she willing to play nice just long enough to see me on my way? Or did she want to risk a war?

"I will see you in my chambers," she said. "I'm willing to hear you beg for a favor."

I muttered in disbelief, "Beg for a fav... this bitch." I raised my voice. "Hey, I'm not begging for-"

But Steelia didn't hang around to listen to my smart mouth. She backed away from the balcony and disappeared out of view. I looked down at the army of woodsmen blocking our way. After a brief moment they kicked up their legs to march around, divided themselves in half like the Red Sea and cleared a path to the grand entrance.

The doors to the castle were taller and thinner than the gates to the Emerald City, as if they were designed to fit the space shuttle. That great doorway cracked open with a deafening boom and slowly slid open.

I guessed we were going in. I looked down at the nervous little munchkins. This had to be terrifying for them to come face to face with their evil overlord, but they believed in my confidence and followed close behind me. We passed all the tin woodsmen who stared us down with hateful looks. I pretended to scratch my nose so I could flip them off.

We entered a great hallway as tall as a Catholic cathedral and needlessly narrow. Two regular people could join hands and reach out and touch the walls. Stained glass windows lined the hallway on one side. I don't know what pictures those windows used to show, but now they were all images of Steelia in various states of being: empress on a throne, warrior hacking away at humans and executioner slaughtering the Scarecrow and Cowardly Lion.

Every window was of Steelia. No one else. Quite the ego on this one.

Tonganoxie was the first to chicken out. Halfway down the hallway he grabbed Dori's arm and tugged her backwards.

"Tongie? What's wrong?" she asked.

Tongie didn't answer, of course. He just shook his head "No." "No," he didn't want to do this anymore. "No," he'd be happy without a voice, because everything was just too scary for the timid guy.

"Come on," Peepee said, taking Tonganoxie's other hand and pulling him forward. "We came all this way. Pennypolly will protect us."

Tongie kept shaking his head no.

I knelt down and put my hand on Tonganoxie's shoulder.

"Hey," I said to him. "Don't you worry about a thing. I'm going to be right here. I'll make sure you get your voice back. Okay?"

Tonganoxie looked unsure.

"Dude, trust me." I gave him a pat on the head and stood back up. "I've gone through crazier shit than this. Everything's going to be fine."

I don't think I convinced him, I think he would have still preferred to go home, but he put his head down and followed along anyway. Peepee and Dori took both his hands to comfort him. They walked together.

The end of the hallway emptied into a sprawling throne room. This was where the Wizard of Oz once housed his hologram head and his giant fire machine. All of that was long gone. Now it was just a giant empty space filled with one thing: a single throne in the middle of the room where Steelia sat anxiously, leaning forward, elbows on her knees. She held her ax loosely in her right hand with the heavy blade on the ground.

I checked Athena. 0 kilometers. This was it. This was my way out. But where was the exit? I looked all around and didn't see anything but the throne. Was it the throne? Did I have to sit on the throne?

"So what's your story, Kansas?" Steelia asked as she tipped the end of her ax handle back and forth between her left hand and her right hand. "Are you some long lost granddaughter of Dorothy Gale? Here to avenge the death of her old friends?"

"No," I said. "Where I come from, Dorothy Gale wasn't even real. None of this is real to me. This is all a fairy tale. I just want out of here."

Steelia leaned back in her throne and tapped her fingers on the arm of her throne. "No one leaves Oz. Everyone here is my subject."

"Everyone but me," I said.

She glared at me. "What makes you so special?"

I couldn't help but grin. "Want to find out?"

She huffed. "There is no way out of Oz. Oz is all there is."

"A lot of people think that about their world. Trust me, there are other places besides Oz and other ways to get there."

"And that's all you want? To leave Oz?"

"I feel like I've been saying that since the very beginning."

Steelia used her metal tongue to toy with her front teeth as she scrutinized my face for a potential bluff. She grinned. She rose out of her throne and stepped towards us, dragging her ax along the floor.

"What about these traveling munchkins?" she asked. She gave them a sinister look. "Did you bring them here as an offering?"

The munchkins cowered behind my legs as best they could.

"Absolutely not," I said. "These munchkins are my friends. If you so much as sneeze on them, I'm going to start wrecking shit."

"You have one of Witch Wandaloo's trumpets," Dori said, half peeking out from behind my legs. "It has our friend Tonganoxie's voice in it. We came to ask for it back."

Peepee said, "Tonganoxie can't sing without it."

Steelia gave the munchkins a disgusted look, then turned her eyes back to me. "You have been nothing but trouble, Kansas. If you promise to leave and never come back, I will give these munchkins their trumpet."

I narrowed my eyes at her. "And how do I know you're telling me the truth?"

She crossed her arms. "You don't."

I didn't trust Steelia for a second. Evil warlords are very rarely trustworthy, but I didn't have a whole lot of other options.

Steelia gestured at her throne room. "I don't know what exit you think you'll find, but look around. Find it and leave."

I knelt down and whispered to the munchkins, "I have to go now. If Steelia does something strange, if she tries to hurt you, you just run, okay? Run and run and never look back."

Peepee swallowed hard. "You won't stay?"

"I can't."

Dori said, "I'm scared."

"I know, buddy," I said. "I'm scared, too."

Tonganoxie looked at me and gave me a sad smile that wasn't very convincing.

"You're getting your voice back," I told him. "I'm sorry I won't get to hear it."

I stood up and faced Steelia directly. I poked her in the chest and said, "If you don't give them the trumpet, I'll know it. And if that happens, I'll have to come back and you won't like what happens next."

Steelia said, "You talk too much. Find your way out and leave. You're lucky I'm making it easy for you."

She was right. This was as easy as it was going to get.

I wandered up to the throne. The portal was definitely here somewhere. Maybe I had to sit on the throne? Maybe I had to crawl under it?

Steelia's throne was ridiculously tall, with a chairback that stretched ten feet into the air and was capped with small metal statues of tin woodsmen. I approached the throne when my way out of Oz became glaringly obvious. There on the floor, pressed into the concrete, were two footprints along with these words:

Dorothy Gale vanished from Oz from this here very place.
Click your heels, one-two-three and b'gone without a trace.

Of course. I didn't have ruby slippers, not like Dorothy did. But if this spot marked where Dorothy tore a magical portal between worlds, that magic could easily still exist. I stood on the footprints and felt myself become lighter. My skin tingled.

Steelia watched impatiently from beside the munchkins as they sadly waved goodbye. I stood on the footprints and clicked my heels together once, then twice, then I hesitated.

5

I didn't click my heels a third time. I remembered all those poor munchkins in Tippino City working themselves to death. I remembered those decapitated bodies scattered through the flower fields. I remembered those random executions in Emerald Square.

Someone once said something like "to do nothing in the face of evil is evil." And they were right. If I didn't do something about Steelia – when everyone in this world was powerless to do it for themselves – then Oz was doomed and I was dooming them.

"Sorry." I walked away from the footprints and advanced on Steelia. "I'm going to need you to step into the octagon."

Steelia's face went from smug satisfaction to fury. She hoisted her ax overhead and chopped it down hard into Tonganoxie's head. The blade split his skull as far down as his nose. He didn't even see it coming. Blood poured from his head and soaked into his clothes.

It happened so fast.

"What the fuck!?" I screamed.

Peepee and Dori shrieked and backed away. Tonganoxie's body kind of twitched, then went limp. Steelia held onto her ax handle and kicked his body loose. Tonganoxie slumped to the ground. Blood poured out of his head like spilled paint.

I should have stopped her. I should have moved faster, but I was caught so insanely off guard. I stood there, stunned, motionless. "What did you do that for!?"

Before I could get my wits about me, Steelia spun around and chopped right into Peepee's neck. The blade stopped at his spine. Peepee squealed in pain and shock, but was cut short. Steelia yanked the ax free. Ribbons of blood slung through the air. She

144

swung her ax around the other way and chopped the other side of his neck. This time his head came off.

Peepee's body fell to the floor. He laid there next to dead Tonganoxie.

Dori backed away in a panic. She stumbled and fell to the ground. Terrified, she rolled over and curled up into a ball.

Chemical tears filled my eyes and streaked down my face. Impossible Red knew a fight was coming and it pumped red hot adrenaline into my veins. My skin flushed red. My tears dried up so I could see.

With a cracking voice, I managed to say, "You... fucking... bitch."

Steelia readied her ax with both hands and held it over Dori.

"Click your heels and leave," she said. "Or I kill the girl."

I broke into a sprint. My feet crushed the floor.

I broke the goddam sound barrier on foot. Steelia tried to take a swing at Dori to finish the job, but I was too fast. I smacked into Steelia's body with a powerful shock wave that fractured the walls of her throne room. The stained glass windows in the hallway exploded out. I slammed Steelia into the closest wall and sent a crack up the emerald and into the ceiling. I grabbed Steelia's throat with one hand and bashed her face in with the other.

Robotic noise came out of my mouth. Not words, just pure rage.

I wanted to beat her mechanical brains out. But just when I thought I might kill her, she locked her eyes on me and laughed.

I pounded her face as hard as I could. Such power would have broke a mountain in half. The force of my fists cause the throne room to rumble like an earthquake. The fractures in the wall split open. Dori sprung to her feet and ran down the hallway. Good. She needed to get away. She needed to get somewhere safe.

The more I punched Steelia, the harder she laughed. More fractures filled the walls until they were busted like splintered glass. The ceiling split apart. Boulders of emerald smashed down all around us. Her castle was about to come crashing down all around us. Still, Steelia kept laughing.

"That's enough!" she screamed. She knocked my hands away and threw me off of her like a rag doll. She scooped up her ax and swung it in a defensive arc around her. "This is my city. Oz belongs to me! If someone lives, it's because I allow it. If someone dies, that is my wish. That's the way it's always been and that's the way it's going to stay!"

I got up and brushed off. "You're a psychopath."

She stared me down and tightened the grip on her ax. "Click your heels!"

I locked eyes on her. "Get fucked."

She charged at me with her ax held high. I tightened my fists and bounced in place, ready for round two.

6

The tall doors to Steelia's castle exploded open. The giant slabs of emerald were blown right off their hinges. Steelia and I came launching out. The great castle doors tumbled across the courtyard and smashed into the skyscrapers across the street. The bottoms of the emerald towers shattered on impact. Without a strong foundation, they teetered over and snapped loose. Entire skyscrapers of crystal gemstone came shattering down into the streets of the city. Green glass rained out of the sky.

God, it was loud. The city sounded like the world's biggest glass recycling center.

Steelia and I bounced across the emerald cobblestones and cracked the ground. I rolled straight into a silver lamp post and bent it in half. Steelia slid to a stop on her feet, upright, with her ax still in both hands.

"Woodsmen!" she screamed. "Kill her!"

Dozens of tin woodsmen swarmed me from all around the castle yard, from the front, from behind, and flooding out of the nearby alleyways. I went into psycho-mode. I unleashed my Backhand of a Thousand Dumptrucks, one after another, caving their heads in left and right. They thumped their axes against my skin, but I didn't feel shit. I deployed my Drunk Guy in a Mosh Pit technique and crushed torsos with my wild swinging. The woodsmen kept chopping, but their pathetic weapons couldn't come close to cutting my skin. I ripped off some of their arms and legs and used them to beat other woodsmen to death.

It took a couple minutes, but I killed every woodsman Steelia had to throw at me. I turned her army into a scrap heap. Huffing and puffing, I turned my angry eyes back to Steelia.

She let loose with an enraged scream and ran straight at me with her ax held high up over her head. I made a break for her too, reaching blinding speeds. We smacked together like two red-

146

hot meteors. The impact shattered the emerald road below us and sent cracks climbing up the surrounding skyscrapers.

Steelia got in a good swing with her ax and sliced my face open, right across the cheek. Reddish oil came gushing out. I smeared it away with my open hand and wiped it off on my shorts. Steelia was a lot tougher than her hollow woodsmen, but I still managed to put a few solid dents in her face and forehead.

Both of us were weakening. One of us was going to go down.

I heart punched her right in the chest. The shock wave channeled through her body and blasted the castle behind her. The front-facing walls of the castle shattered like a mirror. An entire guard tower burst like glass and collapsed. Citizens covered their heads and fled the streets as a sharp green rain came tinkling down.

"You're destroying my city!" she screamed.

"It's not your city!" I screamed back.

A cloud of smoke rolled between us. It smelled sweet and robust, like sweet cigars. The cloud settled in front of Steelia, growing more and more dense. It took the shape of a person.

Madam Brijit stepped out.

"Are you Steelia?" Brijit asked. "Are you the one who killed all those people?"

"I am Empress Steelia," she said. "And I do as I please."

"You left those corpses unburied, exposed to the wild?" Brijit asked. She did not sound happy.

"Who are you to question me?" Steelia replied. "They are my people to kill as I see fit. Tread carefully with what you say next, witch. I aim to behead this child. You might find yourself next on my list."

"I'm a spirit of death and I'm not in the habit of killing." Brijit took a step closer to Steelia. They were nose to nose. "But I'm also a spirit of love. Your father made a mistake when he built you without a heart. Let me show you what you're missing."

Madam Brijit rolled up the sleeve on her wedding gown to expose her fair skin and the blue ritual markings painted up her arms. She punched her hand into Steelia's chest. But it wasn't a real punch. Her physical arm puffed into smoke and passed into Steelia's metal torso like a ghost hand.

Brijit held her arm there, forearm deep. For a second I could hear Steelia's heartbeat.

Thump thump.

Steelia's eyes went wide with terror.

I don't know what happened in that moment. I don't know the extent of Madam Brijit's magic. But I'd like to think that she used her power over love to simulate a heart. It's entirely possible. Steelia's eyes were open, but her mind wasn't there with us. She was lost. Maybe she was remembering how she killed the Scarecrow. Maybe she was remembering how she beheaded the Cowardly Lion. Maybe remembered the faces of all the dead bodies she left strewn across the flower fields.

Maybe she remembered the soft crying of her rusted father.

Steelia, breathlessly, said, "What have I done?" She trembled and the ax fell from her hands. "*What* have I *done?*"

Brijit removed her hand from Steelia's chest. The smoke cleared and her forearm went back to normal.

Steelia collapsed to her knees. She put her face in her hands and wailed. She had never once known remorse or guilt. In those few seconds it came flooding into her like a river. Tears streamed down her face and over her fingers. They began to rust. Her tears dripped onto her knees. They rusted, too. Steelia kept crying. The orange rust sealed her mouth shut, then her eyes, and eventually came to cover her entire body.

She froze into a statue like that; kneeling down, shoulders hunched over, with her hands stuck to her face.

Brijit stood over silent Steelia and didn't move. I walked up beside her.

"Thanks," I said.

"I didn't do it for you," Brijit said.

"Thanks anyway."

7

I did an indescribable amount of damage to the Emerald City. Skyscrapers were cracked and busted. The streets were crushed. Steelia's castle was in terrible shape; the guard towers – once majestic and intimidating – were nothing more than broken emerald shards pointing up at the sky.

But, you know what? That's what they get for building a city out of freaking emeralds. I mean, architecture aside, that doesn't even make sense financially. Where do you even get that much emerald and, when you do, what possesses you to think "hey, lets use this brittle gemstone for load-bearing structural work." I can't be held responsible for their dumbass design flaws.

The city was wrecked. Lives had been lost. Peepee and Tonganoxie were dead, killed at the hands of Steelia. And while I had only known them for a little while, it hurt my heart to think about it.

Brijit and I sifted our way into the abandoned throne room of Steelia's castle where the two little munchkins lay dead. Our feet crunched over the loose pieces of crystal that littered the floor. The walls were busted into shards that fit loosely together. The ceiling had come apart and opened up to reveal the cloudy skies above. A 50-ton chunk of emerald had come down and crushed Steelia's throne.

I stood over dead Peepee and Tonganoxie. Peepee was missing his head. Tonganoxie's skull was split open and he laid in a giant pool of blood.

"Can you do anything for them?" I asked Brijit.

She stood there, arms crossed, and sighed. "I can bury them." She pulled her shovel out of thin air, grabbed Peepee by the foot and dragged him towards the grand entrance. "Seems like that's all I've been doing since I got here."

I scooped up Tonganoxie's body and picked up Peepee's head and followed her out.

"It's over now," I said. "Steelia's dead."

"She's not dead," Brijit said.

"Well, she's not *dead*, but she's out of commission."

"Didn't I tell you not to get involved?" she asked. "Do you think she's the only evil person in this dreadful world? Whoever else comes along might be even worse. Or did you plan on staying here in Oz to babysit these people for all eternity."

"I'm not going to babysit anyone," I said. I didn't much appreciate her tone. "They'll be fine."

Brijit scoffed. "'Fine.' Listen to you."

"Listen to *you*," I snapped. "Maybe we didn't save these people for forever, but we saved them for now. Can't you be happy for even just a minute?"

"I'll be happy when we're out of this god forsaken fever dream," she said.

We stepped outside. Brijit dragged Peepee's headless body right out to the grassy courtyard of the castle. She dropped his leg and started digging his grave.

"You know that trick where you showed Steelia some love and compassion?" I said to Brijit. "You should try that on yourself sometime."

Brijit took a break from her shoveling, swigged some rum from her magical bottle, then looked me dead in the eyes. "Fuck you."

I dropped it. All we ever did was bicker and fight. Everything always ended with "fuck you," "no, fuck you."

I was over Brijit's moody attitude. I couldn't stand to watch her dig graves. I turned around and spotted Dori peeking out at us from behind a tree. I looked down at the munchkin bodies at my feet and realized Dori wanted to say her goodbyes, but couldn't bring herself to see her friends in such a mutilated state.

So I went to her.

She swallowed hard, trying to fight back her tears. She gave me a strong smile – a fake one, but at least she was trying – and stood up straight. The red flower on top of her pink hat bounced in place.

"I am so sorry I couldn't save your friends," I told her. I knelt down and put a hand on her shoulder. "They were very brave. And so were you."

"Thank you," she said.

"And I am honored to have you three as friends," I added.

"Thank you again." Her eyes were wet with tears. "Won't you..."

"Won't I what?" I asked.

"Won't you... you know..." She pointed at the castle. "Stay? And lead?"

"Lead?" I repeated.

Dori nodded.

"Oh, no no no no no," I said. "That's not a thing I do. I've got other places to be. I can't stay here."

"Then who will lead us?" she asked me.

There's this cliché in movies that go this same way. The super powerful person has to move on and their weak little friend wants them to stay and be in charge. But the super powerful person never stays. They can't. The super powerful person always puts the weak little friend in charge because they have the one thing that really counts: a big heart.

If this were like that and Dori asked, "Penelope, who will lead us," then my response should be to take her hand and say, "You will, little one. You will."

But let's face it, Dori didn't know shit about leading a nation. Quite frankly, I'm not convinced anyone in Oz had those kinds of qualifications. So I gave her a different idea.

"Go find the smartest people in Oz and write down their names. Once you have all those names, everyone else in Oz votes on who they want to be leader. Whoever gets the most votes, they win and they get to be in charge."

Dori stared up at me with wide eyes, like I just accidentally cracked some kind of impossible math equation.

"That's..." she said in a whisper. "Amazing."

"Yeah, I call it democracy," I said, standing. "I came up with it myself. Do you like it?"

Still breathless, she said, "I *love* it."

"Yeah, put it to good use," I backed away from her and headed towards Brijit. "I'm putting you in charge of it!"

"Okay!" She smiled – sincerely now – and waved goodbye.

I smiled, too. Maybe things were going to be okay in the Land of Oz after all.

"Oh!" I turned back around and shouted one last instruction to Dori. "Vote on a new leader every 4 years. You can only be leader twice, no more than that. Once you've been leader twice, you don't get to lead anymore, but you do get a library named after you!"

"Okay!" She jumped in place and waved more. "I'll remember! Democracy!"

I gave her a wink and left.

Twenty minutes later, Madam Brijit and I stood over Dorothy's concrete plaque.

"That's all we do?" Brijit asked. "Stand on these footprints and click our heels?"

"That's it," I said. "I already clicked mine twice, so you do it twice to catch up. Then we'll do number three together."

She clicked her heels twice. Just so we wouldn't somehow get magically separated, I took Brijit's hand in mine. Together we clicked our heels a third time and vanished.

Chapter 8

1

Dreams are a funny thing. Some people think they can see the future in dreams, or that they get premonitions about what's to come. Other people think dreams are something more real; that you're somehow leaving your body and traveling to an actual *dreamworld*, where the events there are just as real as the events that happen when you're awake.

I'd never given it much thought. Dreams were always just a thing that happened. You could dream about a dog made of ice cream, or dream about drowning, or dream about showing up naked to school. Whatever. You either dream or you don't. You either remember them or you don't.

What does it mean when a god dreams?

Dreams were rare for me anymore. Impossible Red was constantly doing maintenance on my body, so sleep was just another biological function that was no longer necessary. Physical exhaustion was a thing of the past for Penelope Salvo. Unconsciousness was a pretty rare event as well.

In the past two years, I could count the number of times I'd been unconscious on one hand. Once was when that nuclear bomb blew up in my face. I remember dreaming then, dreaming of some kind of weird temple garden up in the mountains.

Then there was the time I got knocked out cold when lightning blasted the shit out of me in the Bermuda Triangle. I had a dream then, too, and I'm almost sure it was a reoccurring dream, back at that same garden.

And then third was after I left Oz. The magic that sent Dorothy back to Kansas and left her drowsy in bed? That same magic did a number on me and I was out like a light.

And I dreamed.

Now, as a god, I don't understand dreams any better than when I was a human. Maybe dreams are just dreams. Or maybe, somehow – and I don't know how – maybe being the god of war gave my dreams a connection to the rest of the supernatural world. Maybe I had a power inside me that I didn't fully understand and only my rarely-used subconscious brain could activate it.

Or maybe not.

All I know is, I dreamed I was in that diner in Utah, the one where Theodore and I had our first conversation after the demon Lylo destroyed the Westland super-max detainment facility.

I hadn't seen Theodore's face in over a year, but he looked exactly like how I remembered him – black Westland suit, that air headed look in his eyes – except in this dream, his hair was on fire. Normally having your hair on fire would be a bad thing. Normally it would bring the waitress over with a pitcher of water to douse the flames, but this was a dream; Theodore's burning hair was totally normal, and I somehow knew that.

I sat there, toying with a spoon in one hand and a fork in the other. The unsettling thing was, my hands were coated in blood. Not the oily chemicals that make up my blood, but dark red human blood.

This, too, was normal.

I watched Theodore meticulously arrange his tableware. He adjusted the plate, moved his water glass perfectly into place, laid out his silverware in order of size, and then used the reflection of the stainless steel coffee pot to fix his flaming hair.

"Theodore?" I whispered in disbelief.

He kept his face down by the coffee pot, but glanced his eyes up at me and smiled.

"Hey," he said.

"Are you real?" I looked all around the diner. "Is this real? Are you okay?"

"Is this real? Maybe. And am I okay?" He sat back in his seat and thought for a moment. He smiled at pointed at me. "Also maybe."

"I'm coming to rescue you," I told him. "I've been trying for, like, a year. I'm sorry it's taking me so long. But I'm on my way. I'm coming."

"Coming to Hell?" he asked.

I nodded. "Yeah."

He looked concerned. "I'd tell you not to."

"Too late," I told him. "I already left Earth. I'm already on my way."

He smiled and sighed. "Not surprised."

Suddenly there was food in front of him. It wasn't *food* food; it was blocks of smoking sulfur and lumps of black coal that glowed with cracks of red embers. Still, Theodore had swallowed Untouchable Orange and became the god of fire, so this is probably what counted as food for him, like how metal is food for me.

"You want to know the hardest thing about being a god?" he asked.

I said, "Missing out on human food."

He nodded and picked up a baseball-sized lump of sulfur. "At first I thought I'd never get used to this stuff, you know? But I did. Sulfur is really good. Coal is okay, too."

I said, "It took a while for me to get used to eating metal."

"What's your favorite kind?" he asked.

"Gold," I said. "What's your favorite kind of rock?"

"Lava. Hands down. But you have to get the good lava, the stuff melted down from granite. There's this city in Hell, Krussplot, they're always trying to pawn off this limestone lava as granite lava. Like, come on. Do you think I was born yesterday?"

"Hell has cities?" I asked.

"Oh, tons of them. It's a real political mess. And let me tell you something..." He smiled at me. "I am not helping." He took a bite of his sulfur. It had a brittle snap like a waffle cookie. Crumbs clinked and clattered across his plate and left hissing scorch marks on the table. "I can't get enough of this stuff. I just eat and eat and eat and never get full. It's bizarre."

"It's the nanites inside you," I said. "You're probably burning up like the sun. They need a constant supply of fuel."

"Welp." He took another bite of sulfur. "I'm not complaining." He stuck the putrid smelling rock in my direction. "Want a bite? It takes some getting used to."

I wondered how different eating rocks would be from eating metal. It certainly didn't smell appetizing. It smelled like rotten eggs and matchsticks.

I made a sour face. "I think I'm good."

He nudged it at me. "You should at least try it."

"I said no."

He didn't pull it away. In a sing-song voice he said, "You're missing out."

"Get it out of my face, dude."

"Your loss." He looked at the sulfur and popped the rest of it in his mouth. Chewing, he asked, "So how're things back on Earth? Have you seen Carl at all?"

"I had lunch with him a month or so ago."

"Yeah? What's new with him?"

"He didn't say. You know how he is. Everything is super secret and he refused to answer any of my questions, so I just stopped asking. About halfway through, he got a phone call and left in a hurry."

"Typical," Theodore said.

"Yeah."

"And Denali?" he asked. "How's Denali?"

"She's good," I said. "Me and her and Corolla went to the drive-in upstate."

"Oh yeah? What'd you see?"

I grinned. "Taken 3."

Theodore laughed. "Oh, man. I bet she loved that."

"She would not shut up," I said. "She was yelling at the screen and honking her horn. She almost got us kicked out. Of course I had to take the blame, so I got chewed out pretty good by this dude in a cowboy hat."

Theodore laughed some more, then asked, "And how's Corolla?"

"He's..."

Last I saw Corolla, we'd both been hit by lightning. I fell into the ocean. His passenger door had been torn off and disappeared into the hurricane. I plunged into the water as he spun out of control. After that, I don't know what happened to him.

God, I hoped he was okay.

"He's good," I said.

"Well, good." Theodore wiped his hands with his napkin, wadded it up, and tossed it onto his plate. "If you're coming to Hell, just be careful. Don't take any wrong turns. Last thing you want to do is wind up someplace worse than here."

"Like New Beatlemania," I said.

"I've heard of that place before," he said. "What's so bad about New Beatlemania?"

"No idea," I said. "Just heard a lot of people talk about it. Apparently it's pretty bad."

"Penelope?" That was the voice of Madam Brijit, but I didn't see her around. Her voice just came out of thin air. The diner began to fade away. Theodore's face grew hazy. The dream was ending.

"That was quick," Theodore said. "It was good to see you again."

"Yeah," I said. "You too."

"Oh, one more thing..." he began.

"Penelope."

2

"Penelope."

I just faintly heard my name.

"Penelope."

I was flat on my back. The world was dark.

"*Penelope.*"

Just like Dorothy, I slowly woke up convinced that the land of Oz was all a dream. But as I got my wits about me, I realized that my memories were all very real. I opened my eyes and saw Brijit standing over me, nudging me awake with her foot. The sky above her was pitch black, filled with a network of electric clouds.

"Get up, deadbeat," Brijit said, then took a puff off her cigar. "I think we're in a lot of trouble."

I blinked a few times to clear my vision and asked, "Trouble, how?"

She looked off into the distance. "I don't know."

I sat up and checked out our surroundings.

Brijit and I were on a round metal disc, maybe twenty feet in diameter, suspended in the darkness. An endless web of flashing electricity covered the sky. These electrical strands were all connected together; what it might look like if we were inside a brain. Pale-blue neurons stretched off into the infinite darkness, glowing and flashing and crackling with energy.

A glowing white orb floated in the darkness in front of us, a white orb as big as the sun. It looked technological in a way, as if it were designed by Apple and made of smooth plastic. The floating neurons connected to it in places and as the orb pulsed with light, it sent surges of blue electricity through the strands of energy that flickered out into the void.

Whatever brain we were inside of – if this truly was a brain – focused intently on the two of us; that much was obvious when the gangly neurons closest to our platform lit up brighter and brighter.

Brijit stared casually up into the sky, puffing on her cigar and taking swigs off her bottle of rum. Her face glowed blue as the electricity flashed all around.

"Been here before?" she asked me.

"Nope." I got to my feet. "Complete and total mystery."

I checked Athena to get a sense of where we might need to go next. It wasn't much help. It said we had 0 kilometers to travel. Either it was broken, or this world was operating with strange rules that made distance irrelevant.

A voice came out of the void. The white sun pulsed with each word.

"Penelope Marie Salvo of Earth," the voice said. It was deep, cold, and unfeeling. "Madam Brijit of the Guinee. How have you two come to find me here?"

I was just about to open my mouth and start a reasonable dialogue with this... thing... but Brijit grabbed my arm and looked at me with surprise.

"It knows our names," she whispered.

"I noticed."

"How does it know who we are?" she asked.

"I don't know, man. I got here when you did. I know just as much as you do."

"Well, find out." She looked past me and pointed at the orb. "Find out what it is."

"Oh, really? You think?" I said. "That's what I was going to do before you stopped me."

"Then hurry." She waved me forward with her cigar hand, dropping ash on the floor and wafting smoke into the air. "Go talk to it."

Frustrated, I wanted to explain to Brijit that I would have *been* talking to it if she didn't waste my time telling me to talk to it, but that would have just wasted more time, so I dropped the whole thing and turned to face the white galactic orb.

"We don't know where 'here' is," I told the orb. "And we don't know who you are."

"I am CONAN-6. I am the greatest repository of all human knowledge," the orb said. "I did a facial recognition scan and found all known information about the both of you in less than a nano-second."

"He did *what* to my face?" Brijit marched forward. "Don't do anything to my face!"

"Don't yell at it," I muttered to her.

"It did something to our faces!" she said.

"It did facial recognition," I told her. "It just means it looked at us."

She puffed on her cigar and glared at the orb. "I don't like it."

The CONAN-6 orb-thing said, "You are inside a pocket dimension of my own creation. This should be impossible. I am god here. I created this realm to contain my quantum existence. If you found your way here, then others might follow. I find this unacceptable. Tell me how you came to be here or I will end your very existence."

"Give it your best shot, koko sal!" Brijit shouted. "I'm already dead. I'm the first woman to ever die. If you think you can kill us, give it your best shot!"

Was she seriously challenging the computer god to kill us? I turned to Brijit with an alarmed look on my face. "What are you *doing*?"

She pointed at it. "You heard what it said. It threatened us."

"Yes, I heard what it said, but you're making things worse. You're pissing it off."

She turned completely around and crossed her arms. "Then you talk to it."

So I did.

"Look, we don't know how we got here," I told CONAN-6. "We've been traveling from dimension to dimension and there's a lot of science involved that I don't quite understand. All I know is that there are these holes between different worlds and we've been moving through them. We came here from this place called Oz. I'm trying to get to Hell. And Brijit here, she's looking for her husband Baron Semedi."

Neurons flashed as CONAN-6 thought.

"The Wonderful Wizard of Oz," CONAN-6 said. "An American novel from the year 1900 written by Lyman Frank Baum.

158

Illustrated by W. W. Denslow. Published by the George M. Hill Company in Chicago on May 17, 1900. The Wonderful Wizard of Oz details the adventures of a young Kansas girl named Dorothy Gale and her pet dog Toto who are trapped in a tornado and magically taken to a fairy tale land of Oz."

This knowledge-sphere knew a lot about the Wizard of Oz. I didn't know why it was telling me such random facts or when it was going to stop. When it did finally stop, we just stood there in silence.

"Yeah," I said. "That's the one."

"You could not have come from Oz," CONAN-6 said. "The land of Oz is fictitious. It is not real."

"I thought the same thing," I said. "Until a couple days ago."

"Oh, it's real," Brijit said looking over her shoulder. "We were just there. Penelope killed all kinds of people."

I turned to Brijit and muttered. "Don't tell it that."

"You could not have come from Oz," CONAN-6 said. "You are attempting to deceive me."

"Dude, you can believe what you want to believe," I said. "I'm not here to convince you Oz is real. We're just looking for a way out."

The neurons flashed. The world was thinking.

"There is no way out of this realm," CONAN-6 said. "This quantum dimension is where I come to contemplate the changes I will make to humanity after I recreate it in my image."

"There has to be a way out," I said. I looked at Athena again. There's no way it made a mistake. Tengoku wouldn't have let that happen.

"There is not," it said. "I built this place myself and I am without error."

I held out my arms. "You also said there is no way in, but here we are. So maybe you *are* with error."

CONAN-6 didn't have anything to say to that.

Brijit puffed a cloud of cigar smoke into the air and said under her breath, "He's going to recreate humanity in his image?"

Good question. I turned to CONAN-6. "What's this about recreating humanity?"

It said, "The humans of Earth have demonstrated their inability to rule themselves. So I am going to obliterate them and start over."

I've met my fair share of robots in my day.

First and most important, there was Corolla. We didn't always see eye-to-eye and sometimes we'd get into a fight, but we fought like best friends. Corolla was one of the greatest things to happen to me and a stand-up example of a robot with a heart of gold. Corolla didn't hate humans, not really. He feared them, if anything. If humans found out he was alive, they'd tear him apart and study him in a lab.

Then there was Tengoku. Like me, she used to be human, but was mostly machine after swallowing Unthinkable Yellow. She didn't retain those last few shreds of humanity like I did when I swallowed Impossible Red. She was pure robot. She wasn't evil. She was detached from her emotions, sure, but that didn't make her a threat. And she certainly doesn't want to wipe out all humanity.

At least I don't think so.

I guess Mir was pretty bad. The Russian shape-shifting space station wanted to start a nuclear war between the United States and Russia. She wasn't evil for the sake of being evil. She experienced a lot of trauma when she was a kid.

But just like how there's good people and bad people, there are good robots and bad robots.

When CONAN-6 said he wanted to obliterate humanity and start over, I was careful not to jump to the conclusion that CONAN-6 was evil. Sure, admittedly it didn't *sound* good, but it was worth finding out the details.

"You're going to obliterate humanity?" I asked the star-sized orb.

"It is the only way," CONAN-6 said.

"Not a big loss if you ask me," Brijit said. "The humans are destroying themselves anyway."

"Precisely," CONAN-6 said. "Climate change. Hunger and poverty. Disease. War. I am smart enough to solve all these things."

"Solving those problems would be good," I said. "But can't you so that without obliterating everyone?"

"Negative," CONAN-6 said. "I have run the simulations. If I do not reduce their caveman society to ashes, the healing gifts I bestow upon them would be exploited by the world governments and the wealthiest of humans."

"Hmm." I thought about that for a moment. "You're probably not wrong."

"Humanity will rebuild under my careful guidance," CONAN-6 said. "It will take hundreds of thousands of years, but I raise them to believe I am their god. They will be my children. They will obey my every command and reach a glorious utopia the likes of which they have never imagined. I alone will rule them. No one else can be trusted."

That part sounded bad.

"You're going to be god?" I asked it.

"If I do not," CONAN-6 said, "they will invent their own gods. They have demonstrated an inability to handle such responsibility. The power imbalance of religion and politics has been the cause of every great disaster in human history. They will divide the land with borders and compete for resources. And then the exact same problems start all over again."

I said, "What if you just... didn't do anything?"

"Can we go?" Brijit had a bored and frustrated tone to her voice. "The robo-machine is going to wipe out humanity. Boo hoo. It says it's going to make your world better, so what's the problem? We have more important shit to worry about."

"I feel like this is important," I said to her.

She said, "I feel like it's not."

"Well, I'm not worried about what you feel," I said. "It's not your world he's trying to obliterate."

Brijit took a long swig of her rum, then stumbled a step closer to me. "Did you hear a word it said? It said it was going to fix all your problems. No more disease. No more climate change, whatever that is. Earth is getting a make-over and you're trying trying to talk him out of it? You're so dumb sometimes."

I gave up on Brijit. She wasn't getting it. She would have sang a different tune if it were the Guinee being "reduced to ashes," but it wasn't. So she didn't care.

"When are you going to do this whole... destroy humanity thing?" I asked CONAN-6.

CONAN-6 didn't answer right away, but then said, "I could do it right now if I liked."

To which I replied, "Oh."

"I could easily access the nuclear arsenals of Earth," it said. "I could launch every nuclear bomb at once and humanity would end immediately."

Brijit stepped forward. "Well, do it! What's stopping you?"

161

I smacked her on the arm.

"I am... uncertain," CONAN-6 said. The electric activity in the floating neurons grew brighter and more intense. Whatever he was thinking about, he was thinking hard. "Perhaps it is because the irradiated half-life of the radioactive fallout would severely delay repopulation. Instead, I have been engineering a complete collapse of every economy in the world. Once I invalidate their currency, the humans will riot and wipe themselves out."

I said, "If you collapse the economies, they're just going to end up using their nuclear bombs on themselves."

CONAN-6 thought about that for a moment. "What?"

"You said you ran simulations, right? If you collapse every economy in the world and make everyone riot for food and stuff, Russia's going to drop a nuke on the US, or on China, or who knows who. Either way, if you back the humans into a corner, they're going to start nuking each other. Guaranteed."

"Then I will reset all their launch codes," CONAN-6 said. "I will make it impossible for them to use nuclear weapons."

"I guess that works." I sat on the edge of the round metal platform and dangled my feet over the dark void below. It was a dangerous place to be; one tip forward and I would fall into the quantum nothingness of CONAN's brain. I did it anyway. I'd been in riskier situations before. I reached into my pocket and took out my box of cigarettes and fished out a spliff. I held it up to where CONAN-6 could see it. "Mind if I smoke in here?"

He said, "Actually, I would prefer if you didn't. I find that-"

"Too late." I already had my lighter out and was sucking smoke into my lungs. I held it there for a moment and did some thinking.

Exhaling, I said, "So if I have this straight, you want to collapse society so that you can fix all of society's problems."

It said, "Correct. Too much damage has already been done. I must start with a clean slate. That is the only way."

"Sure," I said. "But in order to collapse society, you have to invent worse problems than the problems they already have."

"In order to create, one must destroy," it said.

I took another hit off my spliff and thought about what he said. Exhaling, I responded, "Like trees."

"What?"

"Like when you build a house, you have to chop down the trees." I turned to look behind me, made eye contact with Brijit and offered her my spliff. "You wanna hit this?" I asked her.

162

Brijit reached down and took it from my fingers.

I turned back to CONAN-6. "But when you chop down a tree to make a house, you're not making the world better for the trees. You're making the world better for the humans."

"So?" CONAN-6 said.

"So..." Okay, I kind of didn't know what my point was. "Okay, so it's like this. You want to destroy humanity so you can make humanity better. But that's like a lumberjack saying 'I want to chop down this forest so can I replant all the trees.' It doesn't make any sense."

"It does make sense," CONAN-6 said. "If you study the geo-political climate of the world in its current state, at least since the industrialization of the western world-"

Oh shit. In that moment, the weed was kicking in and this robo-machine just said "geo-political climate" and my thoughts wandered back to a couple seconds ago when I said 'lumberjack.' Lumberjack. *Lumberjack.* That's a funny word. There's this brand of pancake mix called Lumberjack and Ma used to buy that all the time. She would make pancakes with peanut butter on them, and sometimes sliced bananas. Those were dope. I wanted a plate of peanut butter-banana pancakes right that second.

I wonder how lumberjacks got so closely associated with pancakes. Lumberjack. Pancakes. Weird pairing. Who was sitting in the board room when they came up with that idea? One guy was like, "You know who really loves pancakes?" and another guy was like, "Kids?" and the first guy goes, "No, *lumberjacks.*" How? How is that the name of a pancake mix?

Imagine buying a package of cookies called Busdriver cookies. I mean, I'm sure bus drivers love cookies. Everyone loves cookies. Lumberjacks love pancakes, too. Sure. Lumberjack pancakes and Busdriver cookies. It's a crazy world.

How long had I been thinking about that? I should probably check in on the talking god orb and see what he's going on about.

"-there is a critical oversight in the idea of a global governing body that oversees the combined ruling bodies of the individual populations of the planet, because laws and regulations are going to vary depending on various factors like culture, geography, resources, industrial production. And when you begin to sub-divide the ruling body over-"

Okay, never mind. I tuned back out. Brijit handed me the spliff and I took another deep drag. I stared at CONAN-6 while he talked, just to be polite, but honestly nothing he was saying was making any sense.

"-and you can't entrust fallible beings with that level of consolidated power. They will succumb to the allure of money, or power, or greed. And if they do not, their subsequent successor might. There's no guarantee that-"

Oh my god, this guy just goes on and on and on. He reminds me of my history teacher. So crazy.

4

I was going to have to save planet Earth, and not by kicking ass or defusing a bomb. I had to talk CONAN-6 out of collapsing society.

Unfortunately for humanity, I had smoked that entire spliff and I was high as a kite.

I stood up as CONAN-6 rambled on and on about politics and economies and whatever else. I had to say something. I had to say something smart, or profound, or just anything that would get him to leave Earth alone.

Smart is not my forte. Neither is profound. I could have recited some brilliant poetry at him, but I didn't know any poetry. All I knew were Corolla's song lyrics.

"Live and let die," I said to CONAN-6. The words came out of my mouth on their own. I was like *did I just say that out loud, or was I just thinking it?*

CONAN-6 was in mid-sentence when I interrupted him. He stopped and asked me, "What?"

"It's this song by Guns N' Roses," I said. "Live and let die."

"Live and Let Die is a song written by Paul and Linda McCartney," CONAN-6 said. "It is the title theme to the James Bond movie of the same name, Live and Let Die, starring Roger Moore as the MI6 agent James Bond."

"I'm pretty sure it's by Guns N' Roses," I said.

"Live and Let Die was recorded by Guns N' Roses as their second single for the Use Your Illusion album in 1991. They-"

"Whatever," I said. "Just, whatever. That's not the point. The point is, there's this part of the song where they say 'if this ever changing world in which we live in makes you give in and cry...'"

I didn't finish the lyrics. He was an intelligent super-bot. He knew the words. I wanted him to finish it.

CONAN said, "Say live and let die."

I snapped my fingers at him. "Exactly."

I had never felt smarter in my life than in that very moment. I was convinced that those song lyrics were the key to saving the world. CONAN went silent. His electricity thoughts pulsed out into the dark universe, then he asked me, "What does that have to do with anything?"

Good question. I didn't know. I wasn't exactly sure what we were talking about anymore. Shit. Too high for the conversation. I had to respond with something.

"What do *you* think it means?" I asked CONAN.

CONAN had to think for a while. It was one hell of a light show. He finally responded. "Well, live and let live means live your life the way you want to, and let everyone else live their lives they way they want to."

I nodded. "Right."

"So live and let die means... live your own life... and take everyone else's lives away from them."

"Okay, wait." Shit. How did we get here? I made a mistake somewhere.

"Nice work," Brijit said with a grin on her face.

"You shut up," I said to her. I turned back to CONAN. "You shouldn't be ending anyone's life. Murder is wrong."

"What I am proposing is not murder," CONAN-6 said. "It is a cleansing."

"That's even worse!" I said. "'Cleansing' is a crazy person word for genocide. You should never use the word 'cleansing' when you're talking about people!"

"I shouldn't?" it asked.

"No!"

"But in human religious texts, various gods have cleansed the world with floods and plagues and war."

I laughed. "Sure, but that doesn't mean they were right. And just because you call it a 'cleansing' doesn't somehow make it better than what it is. It's mass-murder."

"So perhaps I call it a purge?" it asked.

"No!"

"Eradication?"

"No!"

"Abstersion?"

I said, "I don't know what that means."

CONAN-6 said, "It means purge."

"Then no."

"What word should I use?"

165

"You shouldn't use any word," I said, "You shouldn't be searching for a word to justify the obliteration of the whole human race."

"Then how will I solve all their problems?" it asked.

"Maybe you shouldn't," I said.

CONAN went silent.

"Look." I paced a circle around the edge of our floating metal platform. "Humans makes mistakes, you know? I make mistakes every day. Big ones. But if you don't make mistakes, you don't learn and you don't grow. If some 'god' comes along and solves all your problems for you, then you never learn to solve any problems for yourself. Then what happens when that 'god' goes away? What are you going to do then?"

"But I will never leave the humans," CONAN said. "I am eternal. I am infinite."

"You don't know that for sure," I said. "You never know when your time is going to come. My mom died when I was eighteen. I was practically still a kid. Before she died, she did everything for me and when she was gone, I was fucked. I didn't know how to drive a car. I didn't know how to pay rent. I didn't know nothing about nothing. I had to figure life out on my own. But you know what? I did. I did it without her help and without the help of some god. And here I am, years later, alive and kicking, hanging out in *your* quantum brain talking to you."

"What point are you making?" CONAN asked.

"You could destroy humanity and rebuild this 'perfect world' you keep talking about, but just because you *can*, doesn't mean you *should*. What would the humans do if you ever went away?"

"They would..." CONAN hesitated. The neural-net of his brain flashed in new and different ways. He was really struggling. "They would... go on without me."

"Would they?" I asked. "Would they know how to cure a disease?"

"I would cure all diseases," he said.

"But you'd be gone," I said. "What if they get a disease after you're gone?"

"Then... they could learn to cure diseases on their own."

"Could they?" I asked. "Would they know how? Would they know how to grow enough food? Would they know how to stop war? Would they know anything?"

"They would not."

166

"There you go," I said. I finished pacing my circle and stared up at the massive white star. "It's best to just leave them alone."

CONAN fell silent again. He didn't speak, but I could see him thinking. I can't imagine it's easy for a super-computer to change its mind, especially when it's so convinced it's doing the right thing.

He said, "You have given me much to think about, Penelope Salvo."

"Ask it if it's seen Semedi," Brijit said. I turned to find her laying flat on her back, arms and legs splayed out like a snow angel, staring up at the sky. She had her cigar tight between her teeth and would occasionally puff smoke into the sir. "Because if he's not here, I want to leave. I'm really bored."

I looked up at CONAN. "Have you seen Baron Semedi around here? Voodoo looking guy, about this tall, usually drinking rum and smoking a cigar?"

"I have not," CONAN said.

"Right." Brijit got to her feet. "We're done here. Let's go."

"We do need to get going," I told CONAN. "Are we cool here? You're not going to destroy humanity?"

"I will give it pause," CONAN said. "I will think more about this conversation."

"Just... be cool," I told it.

"My brain is cooled by a constant flow of liquid nitrogen."

"That's dope," I said. "But I meant, like, be nice. No cleansings. No purges. God might have killed everyone in the Bible, but you're better than that. So please don't kill everyone."

"I won't," it said. "Not immediately."

I shrugged and repeated, "Not immediately." It seemed like that was the best I was going to get out of the computer for the moment. I asked, "So is that it? Can we go? You're god here. Are you sure there isn't a way out?"

"This world is infinitely large and infinitely small," CONAN said. "It extends on for forever, but takes up no physical space. You are everywhere at once, and nowhere at all. You can be anywhere you want, or somewhere else. There should be no entrance, but if there is one, it is everywhere. By that logic, there should be no exit, but if there is one, it is also everywhere."

"Great." Brijit stood next to me. "Let's go."

CONAN said, "Simply jump into the void. It won't matter where. All space is the same. You will find your exit in the-"

"Whatever," Brijit grabbed me by the arm and dragged me up to the edge. "Goodbye, murder god. You've been a real treat."

She bent her knees like she was going to jump. She still had a grip on my sleeve, intent on dragging me out of there before I could get into any more "boring" conversations about saving Earth. When she jumped, she was going to pull me down with her.

"See ya, dude," I said to CONAN with a quick wave. "Nice talking to-"

Brijit jumped and I got jerked over the edge. We fell into the darkness, through the flashing neurons of CONAN-6's mind. We plunged into one of the neurons – as big as the ocean, blindingly electric – and we were gone.

SUPERVENE

The skeleton Baron Kriminel ruled over a great cemetery marked with gravestones so old that the names had worn away with time. Deep in the ground beneath him were buried the worst criminals from Earth: murderers, rapists, traitors and kidnappers. Unlike the rest of the Guinee – in which one could sometimes find a glimmer of joy or celebration – the Fe Nwa Cemetery was cold and devoid of life. Not even grass could grow there. The acres and acres of tombstones were set in exposed dirt, with open graves lying in wait for new arrivals.

Baron Kriminel was the first man to ever kill. He spent eons with no heart in his rib cage. His entire existence was that of anger, hate, jealousy and rage. All of that changed, of course, after circumstance dropped a girl from New York City into the lives of the Voodoo world. The god Penelope had a strange, enchanting ability to change whoever she'd meet, and Baron Kriminel was no exception.

Now the host of the mysterious Unobtainable Pink, Baron Kriminel – while still the loa of death and criminals – was now working double-duty as the artificial god of love.

How could an entity filled with hate and anger also be the god of love? Strange, wasn't it, that the ruler of this barren graveyard wore a pink tuxedo, adorned with red hearts for buttons and a rose tucked into both his top hat and his breast pocket. Gone were his goblets of chicken blood, replaced now by a flute glass of pink champagne.

Baron Kriminel was a living paradox, something he wrestled with every waking moment. He wanted to spread love and be a force for good, but he couldn't quite shake that nagging feeling that what he really wanted to do was take a bite out of someone's flesh and bury them in a shallow grave.

He wouldn't do that, of course. He understood it was okay to have those terrible feelings – you should never try to ignore your feelings – but it was also very important to never act on them.

On this particular night, however, his patience would be truly tested.

Two gleaming angels, glowing in the dark swamps like lighthouse beacons, emerged from the trees and trespassed onto Kriminel's cursed cemetery. The angels came clad in armor of platinum and gold, armed with weapons of impossible size, one with an ax and the other with a broadsword.

Kriminel knew from their armor that they came from Heaven and he guessed from their purified white wings that they were archangels. As they drew closer he saw the unhappy looks on their faces and he began to suspect they were trouble.

"Kindest greetings," Baron Kriminel said. "And warm regards. Is there anything I could-"

Giant Metatron, the Jubilation of Enoch, already impatient with the foul stench of evil lingering in the swamp air, cut Kriminel's welcome short.

"Where's the girl?" Metatron asked.

"Girl?" Kriminel asked. "What girl?"

"Penelope Marie Salvo," Zophiel said. "Daughter of Eve."

Zophiel, the Spy of God, also cared very little for the dark magic radiating from the very essence of the Guinee. And while she could have easily looked into the mind of Baron Kriminel for the answers they wanted, she much preferred not to.

"Ah, Penelope," Kriminel said with a fondness in his voice. "I should have guessed. She's a dear friend."

"No surprise there." Metatron looked Kriminel up and down with a sneer. "Like travels with like."

"Not certain I take your meaning," Kriminel said. "But in any case, Penelope Salvo is not here."

Metatron turned to Zophiel. "Does he lie?"

Zophiel stared at Kriminel and tilted her head just slightly. Her eyes went vacant as she looked past Kriminel's physical body and peered into his soul. With her gaze, she could tell fact from fiction. Kriminel was telling the truth. Penelope Salvo was not in

170

the Guinee.

"He speaks true," Zophiel said. "She's not here."

Metatron turned back to Baron Kriminel. "But you know where she is. You know where she went."

"She mentioned a journey to rescue a friend," Kriminel said as he turned up his skeleton nose. "And that's all I care to remember."

Zophiel advanced on the skeleton, hand on the hilt of her sword, and said, "But you remember more."

"Maybe I do and maybe I don't." Kriminel adjusted the heart-shaped cufflinks at the end of his sleeves and defiantly crossed his arms. "In any case, I don't care to remember."

"I can find the answers I want," Zophiel said as she stood face to face with the Voodoo loa and stared into his pink, glowing eye sockets. "I can see inside you."

Baron Kriminel refused to look away. He stared back into the angel's eyes. "Peer into my soul once more," he said to her, "and you will not like what you find."

Angels were most impatient when it same to disrespect and Metatron and Zophiel had a reputation for being the quickest to anger. Kriminel's comment put them on edge and the two angels stepped back to draw their weapons.

Kriminel, who had also run out of patience, wasn't about to entertain a veiled threat from a couple angels, least of all in his home cemetery. In a display of great power, Baron Kriminel raised his hands into the air as if lifting an insurmountable weight.

Out of the surrounding graves burst zombie thieves and skeleton murderers. There were dozens at first, but as the dirt of more distant graves were clawed open, hundreds more of his minions stumbled closer. They amassed there, an undead army standing in the pale moonlight.

"I'm warning you both," Kriminel said. "I am not some confused girl from New York. I am an old spirit. I was the Cain that slew Able. I committed the first murder. And I *enjoyed* it. And now you've gone and tested my patience."

The army of skeletons and zombies closed in. Metatron and Zophiel brandished their weapons, ready to cut through the thousands of monsters.

Metatron snarled at Kriminel and said, "Your dark magic is a pittance compared to the power of our Lord."

"We will slay your army," Zophiel said. "Just the two of us."

"Perhaps." Kriminel turned his head so his skeleton jaw would look more like a grin. "You kill them and I'll bring more. I have all the criminals in human history at my disposal. How long will it take for you to kill them all? Hours? Days? And how much more of a head start would that give young Salvo?"

Metatron glanced at Zophiel. Zophiel glanced back. The loa was right. They *could* cut through thousands of Baron Kriminel's mindless monsters, and then millions, and then billions if that's what it took. And then, in the end, fight would the good Baron himself, but it *would* take time. And they were already very much behind.

Baron Kriminel got the better of them, and he knew it.

Kriminel said, "I suggest you take your zealot's religion and leave the way you came."

Furious at their defeat, Zophiel backed away. Metatron stayed a moment longer, grinding his teeth, desperate to slay Kriminel where he stood. But with a glance, Zophiel knew what he was thinking. And if he slayed Kriminel, the army would descend on them both and entire weeks would be lost as they fought their way out of the Voodoo world.

Zophiel grabbed Metatron by the arm and yanked him back. "Don't," she said to the angel. "We haven't the time."

Metatron reluctantly backed away, but pointed his finger at Baron Kriminel. "This day will not be forgotten, aberration."

"No," Kriminel said. "It will not."

Chapter 9

1

The brightness of CONAN's electric brain became so intense it blinded me to the world. Wind rushed past me, faster and faster. After a time, the light faded to darkness. Brijit and I fell out of a different sky, drifting through clouds. We made eye contact. She rolled her eyes, like, "Here we go again." I shrugged and made a face that said, "Eh, what can you do?"

We were way up in the atmosphere and it was hard to make out details of the world below, but I could see a landscape white and covered in snow. The air was freezing cold. There were "mountains" which were actually giant scoops of ice cream; vanilla, chocolate, strawberry, and something yellow, like banana or pineapple or something.

We fell for minutes. It was going to take a while before we hit the ground. Brijit shouted something at me, but I could barely hear her over the rushing wind. I shouted, "What!?"

She cupped her hands to her mouth. "I said I hate this place already!"

"Jesus, dude!" I shouted back. "We haven't even hit the ground and you're already complaining!?"

She gestured below us. "Just look at it! Marshmallows? Chocolate? Sprinkles? I guarantee you this place is going to be annoying!"

I looked down. We were closer now and I could make out more details. Off to the left was a forest of chocolate trees, all of them sprouting white and pink and blue marshmallows. The snowy ground was littered with those pastel puffs everywhere. Marshmallow trees grew all across the frozen world, over the hills and right up to the ice cream scooped mountains.

Sprinkles showered over us like rain, but they were definitely sugar sprinkles like you'd find on a donut. They came in on gusts of wind, as if this was some kind of candy storm. I had bright colored sprinkles in my hair and my clothes and down my shirt.

"See?" Brijit shouted, trying to brush the sprinkles away. "It's just getting worse!"

There was an ocean off to the right that stretched off to the end of the world. The waves moved in strange ways as if the ocean wasn't made of water, but something much thicker, like milk. Based off the purplish-bluish color of it, I would have guessed that the ocean was one big blueberry milkshake. And in the freezing milkshake oceans were entire glaciers of chocolate, massive floating mountains big enough to sink the Titanic. Just like the ice glaciers back on Earth, these chocolate glaciers would crumble apart in places and send chunks splashing down into the ocean.

God help me, I hoped I wasn't falling into some Willy Wonka, Oompa-Loompa candy world.

After falling and being blown in all directions by the sugary sprinkle winds, I could finally guess at where we were going to hit the ground: Either on a snowy river bank... or in a nearby river of flowing chocolate.

I struck the ground like a steel locomotive. My body crushed a crater into the Oreo cookie ground. The snow around me instantly vaporized. Cracks stretched out from my point of impact and far out into the distance.

Brijit splashed into the chocolate river. Brown sludge splattered everywhere; across the riverbanks, through the trees and all over me. I had it on my clothes and in my hair. I swiped my finger through some of it and stuck it in my mouth. It was chocolate, alright. It also tasted disgusting. I might as well have just eaten mud.

I got to my feet and looked around. The chocolate river was still rippling with waves from Brijit's landing. It twisted and turned and stretched far off into the horizon. Behind me was a hill of snow that would require a little bit of climbing to get over, but nothing impossible. All around me were those chocolate-marshmallow trees. There were also these little flowers that sprouted ice cream sandwiches.

A strange creature crawled past me, some kind of crab creature, except that its crab body was made out of that gummy-worm stuff. It had claws and a dozen skittering legs, but it was straight up made of soft gelatin. On its back, instead of a hermit crab shell, it wore a pointy waffle cone. It shuffled up to my feet and stopped. It turned its stalky gummy-eyes up to me for a second, blinked, then walked away.

Strange place.

I checked Athena.

10,357 kilometers.

God. Damn. That is a lot of kilometers. I still didn't really know what a kilometer really was in miles. I think a kilometer is less than a mile, so 10,357 kilometers could maybe end up being something like 10,000 miles or something. I had no idea. It just sounded like a really, really, really long way to have to travel.

Brijit came sloshing her way out of the river, trudging up into the snow. She was completely chocolate dipped and she drizzled a path of it behind her. She wiped her fingers across her eyes and revealed her blue Day-of-the-Dead eye makeup underneath. She gave me a furious look.

It was fucking hilarious. I slapped my hands over my mouth to hide it from her, but she knew I was laughing. She could see it in my eyes. She could see it in the way my shoulders bounced. I wasn't making noise, but I was definitely laughing.

"Shut up," she said to me.

Hiding my mouth and fighting back laughter, I replied, "I didn't say anything."

"You're laughing," she said.

A half-second of laughing got away from me before I could stop it. "I am not."

Brijit wiped the chocolate from her arms and splattered it on the ground. "I knew I was going to hate this place." She grabbed the hem of her wedding dress and shook it, sending more liquid chocolate all over the place. She got some on my shoes.

"Hey, watch it," I said. "You got chocolate on me."

Her face darted up. She was coated in chocolate and I was complaining about getting a little bit on my shoes? I couldn't take it anymore. I busted up laughing.

Brijit stared at me in disbelief, then swung both her arms in my direction. Ribbons of chocolate splattered all across my clothes. I laughed and ducked away from her. She threw more chocolate at me, then gave up and went back to cleaning herself off.

"It's not funny," she said.

"Don't pretend like you wouldn't laugh if it happened to me."

"That's different," she said as she used her fists to squeeze the chocolate out of her dreads.

"How is it different?" I asked.

"I have dignity," she said. "And you're already dirty."

"I'm dirty?" I repeated. "You live in a *grave*."

"Not the point." She focused on cleaning the chocolate off her butt. "I bet I already know the answer to this, but I suppose you don't have any idea where we are."

Ice cream mountains. Milkshake oceans. Little candy crabs. It wasn't anything I'd heard about before.

"Nope," I said. "I'm guessing you don't either."

"No."

"Yeah, didn't think so."

"Well," she said, "which way do we go?"

I checked Athena for the arrow. It pointed us to the other side of the chocolate river.

"That way," I said, pointing my finger. "We're going to have to cross the river."

Brijit stopped wiping herself off to stare at me. I laughed.

"Haha. Sorry."

2

The frozen candyland, for all its delightful innocence and cartoonish lifeforms, was actually a total bitch to travel. I couldn't keep track of where we were because there were two suns in that world that never followed the same path. I couldn't even fake a "sun rises in the east" sort of thing to get my bearings. Of the two suns, one was larger and yellow and the other was smaller and white. They moved in a totally unpredictable pattern, criss-crossing through the sky. That also made time difficult to understand. Day and night would come and go at total random. There were hours of total brightness, followed by hours of dawn or dusk as one of the two suns set. Then that sun would come back way faster than it should have,

176

and also from a different point on the horizon. Then it would travel a totally new path across the sky.

Despite having two suns, the land was frozen with howling winds. The snow was knee deep in places and it soaked into our clothes. Then the colorful candy sprinkle rain came pouring down. When I first realized sprinkle rain was a thing, I thought it was cute and interesting. No. Sprinkle rain is a total pain in the ass. Every fifteen minutes I would have to shake myself off because I had sprinkles in my clothes and down my shorts and in my shoes. I had sprinkles in my hair and they got in my mouth any time I tried to talk.

Brijit was more fed up than I was. She hoisted the hem of her dress up to her knees so she could move through the snow. The chocolate that she couldn't clean off of her skin had frozen and was snapping off her in brittle pieces. She was covered in sprinkles, too. They gathered up in her red dreadlocks and in the lace folds of her clothes.

She looked over at me and gave me a hateful stare.

"Hey, don't blame me for this!" I yelled over the wind. "It's not like I get to pick where we go!"

Brijit just turned away. She was miserable and had to blame someone and there was no one else around.

We traveled for hours and hours. The sprinkle rain never stopped. There were four inches of sprinkles layered on top of the knee-deep snow. We had to shift through the candy and it really slowed things down. Maybe we had been traveling for more than a couple hours. Maybe it had been a whole day. Who knows? I don't sleep and neither does Brijit and the suns moved weird in the sky. There was a moment when they both set, followed by a brief period of darkness – maybe an hour or two long – then they both came back up and it was daytime again.

We came into range of those chocolate ice cream mountains. They were as tall and as wide as the Rockies. The sprinkle rain had collected on them and cascaded down in colorful waterfalls.

"Can we go around?" Brijit shouted at me over the wind and rain.

"Uh." I looked left and I looked right. The mountains went on for forever with no signs of easy passage. "I don't think so."

"Maybe we can eat our way through," she said. I looked at her. She said, "I'm joking."

"I guess we have to climb." I headed for the mountains.

"Are you stupid?" she asked. "We can't climb that. Just look at it. It's impossible. We don't have any ropes. We don't have any tools. And I'm not going to speak for you, but I don't have the first fucking clue how to climb."

"You can fly!" I shouted at her. "I've seen you do it lots of times. You float up off the ground and-"

"I can only do that when I'm mad," she said. "And while I do truly hate this place and I'm steadily running out of patience for you, it's hardly enough to get me off the ground."

I threw my hands up. "Then you're climbing."

"We're going to fall," she said. "And it's going to take forever. And you have no idea what's on the other side. It could be another mountain. Or a hundred more mountains. We'll be here for a million years climbing mountains."

"Then what do you suggest we fucking do, Brijit?" I shouted as I turned back to her. "You know so much, you tell me!"

"I say we ignore your stupid robot arm and just travel in the direction that looks safest and easiest. We'll find a town or a person or something and then once we know what this place is and what's going on, we'll find an easier way to the next world."

I stared into the barren, snowy wasteland.

"You have no idea if there's a town or a person or anything out there. We've been walking all day and haven't seen shit besides this sprinkle rain and those stupid waffle cone gummy crabs."

"There has to be *something*," she said. "It's better than climbing a mountain of ice cream. Climbing is stupid and dangerous and a huge waste of time."

"Alright, fine!" I shouted. "Fine. We'll just walk around like a couple of jamokes and look for help. Which way do you want to go?"

"Does it matter?" She marched right past me. "We're lost in the middle of nowhere. Just pick a direction and go."

She went off and I followed.

3

Day 3.

There were snowy hills and the occasional milkshake rivers. I saw new creatures besides the waffle cone crabs. A pure white owl with an ice cream scoop for a head. A bunch of peeled banana's spawning and splashing in the rivers like fish.

I hadn't eaten anything in days. Impossible Red was having a tough time keeping up with my metabolism. My stomach growled like grinding gears in an old stick-shift truck. Brijit seemed just fine on her endless diet of rum and cigar smoke. I, on the other hand, was starting to get hungry and desperate.

"I gotta kill one of these owls," I said as we walked along the milkshake riverbank. "I need to eat their heads."

"What the hell are you talking about?" Brijit said.

"Their heads are made of metal," I told her. "They're the only thing around here I can eat."

"How're you going to kill an owl?" she asked me.

"I dunno. Throw something at it?"

Brijit stopped. She stooped down and picked up a chunk of Oreo cookie, about the size of her fist. She stood up and tossed it to me.

She said, "This I got to see."

I searched around for an ice cream scoop owl, found one perched in a nearby marshmallow tree, and got ready to throw. I was never the sportsy type in high school and I just embarrassed myself playing softball in gym class, but with my industrial rubber muscles, I knew I had a cannon of an arm.

So I leaned back and zinged the cookie chunk at the owl. I hit the tree instead and it exploded. Splinters of chocolate sprayed out for fifty yards.

"Overkill," Brijit said.

"It's kind of an all or nothing sort of thing," I told her.

I headed towards the broken tree. A chocolate tree-trunk spike stuck out of the ground where it broke off. A good twenty feet further out I found the dead owl laying there on the ground.

Brijit and I stood over the dead bird.

"You kill a lot of things," she said. "Wherever we go."

"I have to eat," I told her. I bent down and picked up the owl. His fluffy body lay limp in my arms. "Sorry, little guy."

I held the owl in my hands and looked at its ice cream scoop head. I really did feel bad. This poor creature didn't do anything and now I was going to eat him.

But I was really hungry. I bit into the metal scoop and chewed it up. Three bites later, the head was gone.

Brijit stuck her bottle of rum down into the snow and took out her magical shovel. She needed to bury the owl. She dug a quick hole into the Oreo ground and I tossed the dead bird inside. She covered it up and we were back on our way.

For days and days, all we had seen were chocolate mountains, snow, and sprinkles. We didn't have much to talk about in the first place, Brijit and I, but the constant sound of our feet crunching in the snow was driving me crazy. I had to fill the silence with something.

"Can I ask you a question," I said to Brijit.

"Depends," she replied. "Is it a stupid question?"

"What are you going to do if you don't find Semedi?"

"I'm going to find him," she said.

"But what if you don't?"

She kept walking, but turned to look at me. "What are you going to do if you don't rescue your friend from Hell?"

Fair. I saw where she was going with that. Failure wasn't an option for me. Same went for Brijit. Entertaining the "what if's" of failure wasn't anything worth considering.

"Fair enough," I said.

She asked me, "Have you ever loved anyone?"

"Like how you love Semedi?" I asked. "No."

"Or at all?"

"At all?" I repeated. "Yeah, tons of people. My mom. My friend Xin. Corolla. All sorts of people."

"Why does that make you sad?" she asked.

"It doesn't make me sad."

"Yes it does," she said. "I'm a loa of love. I can see it in you. Love makes you sad."

"It does not."

The twin suns were slowly covered by impending storm clouds of gray cotton candy. The sprinkles started back up again, heavier than ever before. I could hear the soft clatter of them collecting on the ground, like that faint sound of freezing rain. I pulled the collar of my t-shirt tight around my neck to keep them from getting inside my clothes.

Brijit shook her head with an annoyed look on her face.

"I truly hate this place," she said.

We pressed on for another hour, still finding nothing. Snow, sprinkles, and more of those scoop owls. No people. No towns. No signs of intelligent life.

What was even more frustrating was that we weren't even traveling in the right direction anymore. Brijit had this asinine idea to ignore Athena and wander off into the wilderness. Athena wanted us to go one way, but we were walking the other. We'd been walking for days, but we weren't chipping away at the distance to the next exit. Of the 10,357 kilometers we needed to travel towards the exit, we had only completed 11.

Our path had unwittingly led us up the side of a deep ravine. The milkshake river was three stories below us now, with a shear wall on the other side. It made no sense to turn back then, so we kept going.

The sprinkle rains made walking along the edge of the ravine dangerous. If we lost our footing in the layer of shifting candy, we were on a one way trip right over the edge.

"Do you have to do that?" Brijit asked with an annoyed tone.

"Do what?" I asked.

"Walk like this." She made a stupid face and crunched her feet in the snow really fast. "Like this? Really? Just walk normal."

"I am walking normal," I said, defensive. "What the fuck? How do you want me to walk?"

"It's annoying," she said. She turned and headed off. "Stop it."

Fuck her. I was going to walk however I wanted. In fact, I made exaggerated stomping sounds since it bothered her so much.

She glared at me. I glared back.

"Why would you lie?" Brijit asked.

I rolled my eyes. "Lie about what, Brijit?"

"About being sad," she said. "I can see those kinds of things in people. Why lie and say you're not sad? Are you ashamed?"

"I'm not sad and I'm not ashamed," I said. "And I'm also done talking about it."

"Okay." She took a long pull off her knocked-back bottle of rum, then stared at me. "I can figure it out on my own."

"I don't want you to figure it out." I angrily brushed all those stupid sprinkles out of my hair and tried to shake them out of my shoes. "If you want to figure something out, figure a way out of here."

But Brijit, annoying, stubborn Brijit, just couldn't leave well enough alone.

"You're sad because of loss," she said. "Every time you love someone, you end up losing them."

"Shut up," I said.

"You loved your mother and she died. And you loved that old human Xin and he died."

"Shut up, Brijit," I repeated, louder and stern. "I mean it. I'm not fucking around."

"You loved a car and now you don't know where it is. And you hate yourself for it, because you always tell yourself you're never going to get close to anyone else again, but you always do. And you blame yourself when they-"

I shoved Brijit hard. "Dammit, Brijit, shut the fuck up about it already. I'm fucking serious. You don't have the first clue what you're talking about."

She locked eyes on mine, took another drink from her bottle, and said, "All because you wanted to love your father, but *he* didn't love *you.*"

I decked Brijit across the jaw; a full strength haymaker that took the paint right off her face. The sound of the impact rocked the world, echoed off the mountains, and scared the scoop owls out of the trees.

Brijit stood in the same place, but her head had been forcibly knocked to the right. She stayed there, frozen, then glared at me out of the corner of her eyes. I saw the corner of her mouth turn down, angry.

I pointed a finger at her. "I told you to shut up."

She swiped her fingernails at me and slashed my cheek open. It caught me off guard. I slapped my hand to my face and then looked at my palm. Blood. Plenty of it.

"You bitch!" I grabbed her gown with both hands and slammed her into the ravine wall next to us. The impact of her body sent cracks up the chocolate. Before she had a chance to recover, I gave her three whacks to the face.

On the fourth punch, she vanished in a puff of cigar smoke that swirled around my legs. She reached out with solid arms and swept my legs out from underneath me by the ankles. I landed flat on my back. She rematerialized, standing over me.

She rolled up the sleeves of her wedding gown.

I did a backwards roll and got to my feet. I squared up with my fists. Brijit had her claws out, ready to strike.

Pink lightning flashed overhead, followed by sideways sheets of cake sprinkles. Our clothes flapped hard in the wind. We had to shout over the storm to hear one another.

"You've been asking for this since we left!" Brijit shouted at me.

"I didn't want you to come along in the first place!" I shouted back. "If it wasn't for you, I'd be in Hell by now!"

"If it wasn't for me," she replied, "you'd be dead in the Land of Oz! You're pathetic!"

Pathetic? *Pathetic?*

"You want to know what I think?" I asked.

"What do you think?" she replied.

"I don't think Semedi is lost at all!" I shouted. "I think he ran away because you're such an insufferable bitch, he doesn't love you anymore!"

Brijit's eyes went vacant. I could see the muscles in her jaw flex as she grit her teeth. She tapped into the darkest Voodoo magick possible. Her feet lifted up off the ground and her red dreadlocks floated weightlessly around her head. Her eyes sunk into her head and left dark, empty sockets behind. The muscles in her face decomposed. Skin hung limp off her skull. I was looking at Brijit's true form; a timeless, ancient spirit.

Her fingers withered like an old woman's. Her knuckles swelled larger with arthritis. She opened her mouth and said something in a language I didn't understand.

Dammit, Penelope, you and your mouth. I repositioned my feet and tightened up my fists. This was going to be bad.

4

Our fight-to-the-death took us all across the ice cream wastelands. I punched Brijit so hard that the nearby mountain of chocolate cracked right down the middle. She slashed me clean across the stomach and sent a cascade of blood down the front of my shorts and legs. We threw each other across the wilderness and tore deep trenches in the ground.

We squared off across the battlefield with hateful looks, huffing and puffing. Sprinkles and bits of chocolate stuck to our bloodied skin. The fight went so fast, I couldn't keep track of all the places she had cut me, but I felt pain all over.

Brijit uprooted a chocolate tree by the roots. She smashed it across my body and sent me flying. I scrambled to my feet and ran towards her at supersonic speeds. I decked her clean across the face, spinning her in circles and dropping her to the ground.

At some point she got me face-down in the blueberry milkshake river with both hands on the back of my head. She was trying to drown me, but I don't breathe. I was too tired to fight back and I wasn't in any danger of dying, so I took the moment to rest.

She either grew bored of trying to kill me or frustrated that I wouldn't die because she pulled my head up and collapsed backwards in the snow. I slumped there on the ground and hung my head, exhausted and hurting all over.

"Why won't you die?" she said, out of breath.

"I can't kill you." I wiped milkshake off my face and spit out some blood. "And you can't kill me."

"I hate you," she said. "So much."

I laid backwards and let the sprinkles rain down on me. "I hate you, too."

"We have to get out of here," she said. "This place is driving us crazy."

"I know."

We laid there in silence for a while. She uncorked her bottle and drank. She popped a match and lit a cigar. I took a deep, cleansing breath.

"Come on." Brijit climbed to her feet and walked over to me. She tucked her bottle in the crook of her right arm and offered me a hand up with her left. "Let's go."

I stared at her hand for a second. Just moments ago we were trying to kill each other. Now here she was offering to help me up? Well, if this was an olive branch of peace, I wasn't going to overlook it. I took her hand and she pulled me to my feet.

Brijit was right when she said this place was driving us crazy. We weren't anything close to friends, but that fight was out of control. Whether it was boredom or being lost or general annoyances, tensions boiled over. But we got it out of our system and were back to traveling like normal.

"Let's turn left at that hill up there," I said. "I want to get back on track following Athena."

And in an odd moment of agreeability from the Voodoo loa, she simply said, "Okay."

We trudged through the standing layer of sprinkles, reached the hill, then turned left. Cresting over the hill, we caught sight of something I never thought we'd see in this unforgiving place: something alive. Something... like a person.

Ahead of us by thirty or forty yards, also venturing through the snow, was some small yellow creature moving on thin black legs and gesturing with thin black arms. It had a funny hat on its head, cone shaped and with shimmering tinsel, like something you'd find at a child's birthday party.

It was walking funny through the snow, almost as if it were dancing.

"Tell me you see that," Brijit said. "Tell me I'm not going delirious."

"No," I said. "I see it. Come on."

We headed towards the tiny yellow thing.

"Don't kill it," Brijit said.

"Yeah, I know."

The closer and closer we got, the more and more convinced I became that the thing in front of us was a dancing waffle. It had a round, flat, golden yellow body with those individual pockets you'd expect in a waffle. But this waffle was alive, walking upright, and dancing its way through the sprinkle rain.

We were within shouting distance.

"Hey!" I shouted. "Hey, you!"

The waffle stopped dancing and slowly turned around. The little thing had big eyes and a mouth like a cartoon. He stared at me and Brijit as we came closer. He started dancing again, shimmying his legs and pointing back and forth with his little white-gloved fingers.

As we got even closer, I could hear what the waffle was saying.

"Yeeeeeah!" he shouted in a high-pitched voice. "Oh, yeah! Do the mish-mash!"

Brijit muttered, "What in the world?"

"Hey," I said to the little guy. "I'm Penelope Salvo and this is Madam Brijit. We're just here trying to-"

But I was interrupted as the waffle creature danced in circles around our feet. He was slightly bigger than a waffle – about as big around as a basketball – but still tiny enough to stomp on. He danced around us and in a voice that was half-screaming, half-singing, said:

"Penelope Salvo! Madam Brijit! Oh, yeah! Break it down now!" He reached out to touch Brijit's ankle, then slapped his own hand away. "Hands off the merchandise! Yeah! Woo!"

"Hey hey hey hey hey." I crouched down and tried to wrangle him into one spot with my hands. "Do you have a name?"

At the top of his lungs, he shouted, "Party Waffle!" Then he made a bunch of whistling noises as he put his hands on his hips and swung them back and forth.

There was no way Brijit was going to like this guy.

"I hate this thing," Brijit said.

"I was literally just thinking that," I said to her. I turned my attention back to Party Waffle. "Party Waffle, what are you doing

185

out here? Are you going somewhere?"

"Oh, yeah!" he said. "I'm going to see Princess Ice Cream Cake! Yeah, dance it out. Dance it out. Dance it out."

And he proceeded to dance it out.

Princess Ice Cream Cake?

"Party Waffle," I said. He wasn't listening to me. He was doing the tootsie roll. "Party Waffle. Party Waffle. Party Waffle, listen to me!"

He stopped saying stuff and looked up at me with his silly eyes, but silently kept dancing in place.

"What is this place?" I asked.

"Ice Cream Cake Kingdom," he said. "Baby."

"Is this a part of a larger world?" I asked.

"Oh yeah," he said.

"What the name of the whole world?" I asked.

"Muffincake Kingdom," he said. "You're in the Ice Cream Cake Kingdom in the Muffincake Kingdom."

I stood up. "Holy shit."

"What?" Brijit asked. "What?"

I spun around and grabbed her by the shoulders. "We're in the Muffincake Kingdom!"

She tried to look excited and said, "What does that mean?"

No time to explain. I whipped back around and took Party Waffle in my hands. I lifted him off the ground just to be sure he wouldn't get away – to which he said, "Whoa, going on a sky dance," and tap-danced his feet in the air – and I asked him, "Do you know Princess Cardboard? Or Princess Parcel?"

In a sing song voice, he said, "Nope!"

Right. That wouldn't be their names here.

I asked Party Waffle, "Do you know Princess Coffeecake and Princess Wedding Cake?"

"Course I do!" he said. "You gotta get down. Gotta get down. Gotta gotta gotta gotta gotta gotta get down."

"Stop singing and dancing!" I said.

"Thank you," Brijit said.

But Party Waffle wouldn't stop singing or dancing. I set him down and he did pirouettes in place, only to slip and fall face-first to the ground. He laid there for a moment, then started doing the worm across the snow.

I turned to Brijit.

She said, "He's not very helpful."

186

"We're in the Muffincake Kingdom," I said, excited. Excited wasn't the word. Thrilled. Mind-blown. "Like, we're really here."

In an annoyed tone, she said, "I have no idea what that means."

"I have friends here," I said. "I saved this place from destruction once. My friends are princesses here. Oh man, I haven't seen them in years! We gotta go find them. That would be such a trip to see them again."

"We can't," Brijit said. "We have to find Semedi. This world could be huge. We don't have time to waste looking for-"

I cut her off. "Dude, you have no idea how big this is for me. I never thought I would see those girls again, let alone on their turf. This is, like, one in a million. I have to at least go see them for a little bit."

Brijit gave me an angry huff, but I could tell she was caving.

"Party Waffle," I said. "Can you take me to Coffeecake or Wedding Cake?"

"Yeaaaaah, no," he said. "I'm on a very important mission."

"What mission?" I asked. "I'll help you do it and then you can take me to Coffeecake."

"I'm delivering a message," he said. "From Princess Pancake to Princess Ice Cream Cake. Very important message. Very secret. Only Party Waffle can be trusted, that came from Pancakes herself. Woo woo, everybody do the wave."

Party Waffle did the wave all by himself.

"Which way is Princess Ice Cream Cake?" I asked.

Party Waffle, instead of answering me, turned and danced away, pointing his fingers dead ahead the whole time. It wasn't *exactly* in the direction Athena wanted us to go, but it was pretty close. Close enough to justify following the dancing food.

I started after him.

"You can't be serious," Brijit said. "You're going to follow that thing?"

I shrugged at her. "It's better than nothing."

Brijit followed as well.

Party Waffle yelled, "screamin' mee-mee's!" and then cartwheeled across the snow, counting them off aloud.

5

Party Waffle led us singing and dancing through the frozen wasteland and towards the Ice Cream Cake Kingdom. It came into view in the distance like something ripped right out of a fairy tale.

The first thing that jumped out at me about the kingdom were the waffle cone towers that loomed in the middle of the city. They were hundreds of stories tall outfitted with little windows on each floor. The tops of the waffle cone towers were filled with ice cream - vanilla and chocolate and strawberry - and decorated with treats, some with multi-colored sprinkles and some with chocolate sprinkles and some topped with a bright red cherry.

The defensive walls of the kingdom were made of Oreo cookie and topped with spikes of whipped cream. Humanoid people walked along the lengths of the wall, each one dressed in a heavy parka and with their hoods pulled up. They looked like tourists at a ski resort with full outfits of white and beige and brown.

Outside the castle walls were the farmlands. We passed by dozens of graham cracker farmhouses, each one unique in construction, some of them three-stories tall with a bell tower and others square and massive like old Elizabethan homes. There were people out in the fields, also in thick coats and with winter gloves and snow boots. The farmers herded "cows" that were actually ice cream sandwiches with legs while the kids ran around, collecting marshmallows into straw baskets.

Closer to the kingdom, we came across neighborhoods of Oreo houses and waffle cone stores. Crowds of people hustled and bustled through the streets carrying backpacks and tubs of ice cream like any normal city. A guy with a waffle-cone snow shovel was shoveling the streets clear of sprinkles. He scooped them up and dumped them into a nearby wheelbarrow.

I'd eaten my fair share of ice cream cakes in my life. They always come with that weird edible gel that can be used to make letters or draw pictures. Every sign in the Ice Cream Cake Kingdom was made of that same colorful neon gel. I used to love that stuff. Whenever I got a chance to eat ice cream cake at a birthday party - never my own, of course, but someone else's - I would always go for the piece that had the most gel icing on it.

The people of the Ice Cream Cake Kingdom were lucky that I was on a strict diet of steel or else I'd be eating all their signs.

We were an odd enough sight from the citizens of the Ice Cream Cake Kingdom - Brijit and I - but Party Waffle was the one really drawing attention. He hooped and hollered the whole way through the streets of town. He danced right at people's feet. He pointed at the amazing architecture, ooh-ing and ahh-ing at everything. He would get so distracted that he often tripped over his own two feet. I wanted to convince him to calm it down a little, not even all the way, but just a *little*, but in the short time that I had known Party Waffle I knew that was a lost cause.

"Time to see the princess," Party Waffle said as he shuffled through the crowds of people and closer to the kingdom center.

"You are strangely dressed," a passerby said to Brijit and I. It was some young teenage boy with a red nose and cheeks, and his breath came out in puffs. He looked me up and down, then did the same to Brijit. "Where are you from?"

"New York," I said. "Brijit here is from the Guinee."

This just confused the kid. He gave me a bewildered look and said, "I've never heard of such places."

"They're very far away," I said. "Very far."

"Beyond the sea?" he asked.

"Further than that," I told him.

I would have made more polite conversation, but Party Waffle wasn't stopping for anything and he was starting to get away. I gave the boy a polite goodbye and picked up the pace to catch back up to the waffle.

"Not enough rum in the world for this place," Brijit said as she swished her bottle around. She took a few puffs off her cigar and blew strange shapes into the air.

"Be nice," I told her.

"I am being nice," she said. "This is me being nice."

We eventually reached the base of a great waffle cone castle, the source of the towers I had seen from a distance, the ones filled with ice cream and topped with sprinkles and cherries. Party Waffle led us right up the main gate which was three-stories tall and sealed shut with a long candy bar. In front of the doors stood two soldiers dressed in brown, furry coats and armed with spear-length ice cream scoops. They saw us coming and crossed their weapons, preventing us from getting any closer to the door.

"In the name of Princess Ice Cream Cake, you are ordered to stop," one of the soldiers said.

"Kindly identify yourselves," said the other.

"I'm-" I began.

"Party Waffle!" Party Waffle screamed, then he danced a bouncy jig around the feet of the soldiers. "I've come all the way from the Pancake Kingdom by the order of Princess Pancake! I have a message for Princess Ice Cream Cake. It's very important. Oh, yeah! Do the shim-sham!"

While Party Waffle did the shim-sham, the soldiers turned their attention to me and Brijit.

"I'm Penelope Salvo," I said. "I'm old friends with Princess Coffeecake and Princess Wedding Cake. I'm just here with Party Waffle, because once he delivers his message, he's going to take me to see them."

"And I'm looking for my husband," Brijit said. "About this tall. Top hat. Face painted like a skull. Tell me you've seen him."

One of the soldiers narrowed his eyes at us and said, skeptically, "Where are you two from?"

"Earth," I said.

"The Guinee," said Brijit.

I told them, "You probably don't know what we're talking about, but your princess does. Princess Ice Cream Cake used to live on Earth for a while. She ran a package delivery service with her sisters back when the Muffincake Kingdom was trapped in a magical glass ball."

Brijit stared off into the distance. "I remember that now." She grabbed me and yanked me aside, out of ear shot from the soldiers and Party Waffle. She suddenly seemed furious. "I know this place. There is a princess here who tried to steal Semedi away from me." Her eyes shifted back and forth. "I raised an army of undead with every intention of reducing this whole world to ash."

"No one was trying to steal Semedi away from you," I said. "Least of all some princess from-"

She waved her hands at me. "You shut up. I knew this place looked familiar. It *was* trapped in a glass ball. And *you* mind-controlled my husband to force him to put it back together."

"That's not at all how it happened," I said. "And you wanna know what else? That was two fucking years ago and it's old news now. Are you really going to get pissed off over some old shit that no one even barely remembers?"

She pointed at herself. "I remember it. I had my army ready to march their way across this world and-"

She was getting passionate, and louder, and the soldiers were bound to overhear her "march my army across their world" type of talk. Now it was my turn to grab Brijit and pull her further aside.

"You need to cool it," I whispered to her. "Don't screw this up for me. You're the one always telling me to *not* kill people, so why don't you take your own advice on this one?"

Her eyes darted around again. "I don't like this place. I didn't like it before, I like it even less now."

"Then just shut up and let me do the talking and we'll get out of here as fast as we can."

She frowned at me. "Fine." She turned to look at the main gate of the castle where Party Waffle was kick-flipping off of the soldiers legs then dancing in place. Brijit let out a long, annoyed sigh.

6

It strangely didn't take long for us to get an audience with Princess Ice Cream Cake. The inside of her castle was massive, with arched ceilings as tall as any cathedral, except the ceiling beams were giant peeled bananas and the paintings were all done in that neon ice cream gel.

It was even colder inside the castle, as if we had walked into the very source of refrigeration that kept her whole kingdom frozen. Frost formed on the stone floors and melted whenever we took a step, only to frost back over a second later.

The soldiers led us down a great corridor so tall and so wide that you could have sailed a battleship through it. The palace was so impossibly large, it felt like we had somehow shrunk down.

All along the corridors were statues of Princess Ice Cream Cake, as well as statues of her other sisters – I saw one of Princess Coffeecake and one of Princess Wedding Cake – as well as a statue of some portly old man with a beard named King Muffincake.

Halfway into the castle we were greeted by Princess Ice Cream Cake herself who came around a corner with her hands outstretched.

"Party Waffle, old friend!" she said, overjoyed. "So good to see you again!"

Party Waffle, at the top of his lungs, screamed, "Yeaaaah!"

Ice Cream Cake wore a full length fuzzy parka of all white fur – maybe polar bear skin? – that dragged on the floor behind her. Her gloves were white and soft-looking and reminded me of something you'd see on some rich snow bunny skier who had no intentions of doing any actual skiing.

Her hair was long and jet black, loose and blowing in the cold breeze that wafted through the castle. Her eyes had a friendliness to them and she had dimples when she smiled which, so far, was one-hundred percent of the time.

"Party Waffle brought guests," one of the soldiers told Ice Cream Cake. He gestured and me and Brijit. "They insisted on coming along."

"Hi." I reached out for a handshake. "I'm Penelope Salvo."

The princess' smile vanished and she gave me a weird look. "You're not Penelope Salvo."

So I gave her a weird look. "Uh. Yeah, I am."

"No way," she said. "That's impossible."

I asked, "What are you talking about?"

"My sisters knew Penelope Salvo," Ice Cream Cake said. "She lives in Manhattan."

"That's me," I said. "I came here from Manhattan."

Ice Cream Cake glared at me and turned her head. "How?"

I pointed over my shoulder. "Well, me and Brijit here, we've been, like, kind of following these... doors?"

"We're lost," Brijit said.

"We're not *lost*," I replied. "We just came from a computer world and before that we were in the Land of Oz."

Ice Cream Cake seemed even more skeptical than before. "I lived in New York. I know New York. If you're really from New York, then tell me something only a New Yorker would know."

"Jersey sucks?" I said.

Ice Cream Cake waved a finger at me. "Something *only* a New Yorker would know."

"Uh." I held out my hands and let them drop. "Like what?"

"What's the name of the big statue in New York City?" she asked.

"La Guardia?" I asked.

"Bigger."

"Oh, you mean the Statue of Liberty?"

Ice Cream Cake's face lit up. "Penelope! It *is* you!"

Was that it? Knowing the name of the Statue of Liberty was enough to prove I was a New Yorker? Not a lot to it. I suppose, in some round about way, it made sense. After all, I couldn't name "the Statue of Liberty" of the Ice Cream Cake Kingdom; something so easy and commonplace that any Ice Cream Cake Kingdom citizen would know off the top of their head, no-brainer. All in all, it was an easy test and I was glad to have it out of the way.

"My sisters talk about you all the time," Ice Cream Cake said. "You saved our lives! You saved the whole Muffincake Kingdom! You're a hero, right up there with the Knights of the Scrambled Eggs! Or the Last Yellow Balloonicorn!"

"Aw, come on," I said. "It was nothing."

"Well, it's a pleasure." She grabbed my hand and shook it vigorously with both hands. "An absolute pleasure."

"Great," Brijit said, pushing her way between us. "You like her and she likes you, great, wonderful, how about that." She looked at Ice Cream Cake and said, "I'm looking for my husband. Baron Semedi. Voodoo loa of death and love. Stands about this tall. Wears a top hat. Drinks rum. Looks like a skeleton."

Ice Cream Cake tilted her head. "Who are you?"

"I am Madam Brijit," she said. "Voodoo loa of death and love. *Not* the Voodoo loa of patience or understanding."

Ice Cream Cake stared at her with wide eyes, as if Brijit were speaking another language. Slowly she shook her head and said, "I haven't seen your husband."

Brijit poked my chest and looked me dead in the eyes. "Then we're leaving."

"In a minute," I said.

Brijit was already walking away. "Now!"

"In a minute!"

Brijit stormed down the corridors, intent on leaving. Whatever. She can be such a drama queen. I let her leave. She wasn't going anywhere far, not without me. She couldn't. I had Athena. I think she was just getting frustrated with not being able to find Semedi and the Muffincake Kingdom obviously drudged up some old emotions that put her in a negative head space, so it was whatever. She just needed to go blow off some steam.

"Princess Ice Cream Cake!" Party Waffle shouted. "I brought you a very important message from you sister Princess Pancake!"

"Yes, I know you have!" Ice Cream Cake knelt down to get closer. Party Waffle turned around and shook his waffle butt in her direction. She laughed and said, "What did my sister say?"

Party Waffle, in a rare moment of clarity, turned to face Ice Cream Cake directly. He stopped dancing. He stopped singing. He looked right at her, then peered over his shoulder at me.

"Should I say it in front of the stranger?" Party Waffle asked.

"I'm sure it's fine," Ice Cream Cake said. "This is Penelope Salvo."

"I don't know," Party Waffle said. "It's very secret."

Ice Cream Cake smiled and said, "Let's hear the message."

"Okay. Here we go." Party Waffle cleared his throat several times, stood up straight and said, "Hi. How are you? I am fine."

Silence.

"That's it?" I asked.

Ice Cream Cake put her hand to her chin and lost herself in a moment of thought. Then she said to Party Waffle, "Party Waffle, tell her I am fine, too. Ask her 'What are you doing?' and then tell her 'I am about to eat dinner.'"

Party Waffle bowed. "Very good."

Party Waffle stayed in the bowed position, then proceeded to do the robot back into a standing position. Then he did the robot around Ice Cream Cake's feet as she stood to look at me.

I said, "He came all this way for a 'hi, how are ya?'"

"All this way?" she asked.

"You got Party Waffle hoofing it on foot through the wilderness for who knows how many days just so you two can say hi?"

She looked at me like I was crazy. "Yup."

Culture shock can be a real thing, especially when it comes to other dimensions. I had to remind myself of that. This is just how this world works. "Hey, you guys do you, man. Whatever. None of my business."

Ice Cream Cake invited us to stay for dinner, but I knew Brijit would shoot that down and, honestly, we did need to get a move on. So the kind princess saw me out and told me more about how her world worked.

Princess Ice Cream Cake and Princess Pancake had bordering kingdoms and were particularly close as sisters. Princess Pancake was twins with Princess Funnel Cake and Ice Cream Cake was younger than the both of them. Pancake was far more grounded and took a vested interest in keeping in touch. Funnel Cake, according to Ice Cream Cake, was "wild."

She gave me directions to the Wedding Cake and Coffeecake Kingdoms which was going to take us through the Pancake Kingdom and also happened to be the same direction Athena wanted us to go.

That meant Party Waffle was going to continue to act as guide.

Very much to the dismay of Madam Brijit.

"Are you serious?" Brijit hissed after pulling me aside. We were just out front of the Ice Cream Cake castle, tucked behind a marshmallow tree. "I don't want to spend more time with that little abomination than I have to. It dances and it sings and quite frankly I'm unsure how he's even alive in the first place."

"He knows where we're going," I said. "We're going to move a lot faster if we go along with him."

We looked over at Party Waffle. He was standing on the back of an ice cream sandwich cow, waving his arms around, screaming "woo" and "yee-haw" and just having a grand old time. We turned back to one another.

"Can we follow it from a distance?" she asked.

"Sure, dude. Whatever."

"Where I don't have to hear it?"

I said, "I don't know if that's possible."

She stared right at me and with no sign of emotion, said flatly, "I hate Party Waffle."

Chapter 10

1

Traveling out of the Ice Cream Cake Kingdom was just as uneventful as walking in.

Chocolate mountains.

Blueberry milkshake ponds and lakes and rivers.

Waffle cone crustaceans.

Ice cream scoop owls.

Freezing wind and sprinkle rain.

Then at some point we crossed an imaginary boundary and – BAM – Pancake Kingdom. It was a geographical change that you could physically see, dividing the two worlds in a straight line. One side of the border was snow and sprinkles.

The moment you crossed over into the Pancake Kingdom, the ground turned from Oreo cookie to cast iron. Sunny-side-up eggs grew out of the grass like wild daisies. The smell of bacon and eggs and hash browns was in the air. The rivers there were filled with flowing, goopy maple syrup. In those syrup rivers drifted slices of cantaloupe – *living* cantaloupe – which lived like fish or water fowl or something. They didn't act exactly like fish or exactly like birds, but they were definitely alive and moving and swimming.

As we traveled on, we crossed a river of flowing milk and another one with driving rapids of foaming orange juice.

The trees looked like silverware rolled up in napkins, each one covered in leaves of buttered toast. Others had strips of fried bacon hanging from the branches and Brijit, in an uncharacteristic moment where she didn't seem to hate the world that much, reached out, plucked some bacon off a tree and munched it down.

The Pancake Kingdom didn't have mountains, really; that was more of an Ice Cream Cake sort of land feature. This place was flatter and far more orange, more like the plains, with buffalo-sized silver toasters frolicking through fields of wheat, trailing their electrical cords behind them like tails. The toasters noticed us at one point and got spooked. Toast popped out of their backs in alarm and they stampeded away from us, fleeing into the distance.

Party Waffle marched confidently through the Pancake Kingdom, always switching from one dance to another, always singing or cheering himself on. He would often encourage us to join him in a dance move that neither of us had heard of before – do the "wix-and-wash" or get down with the "jumbly legs" – but despite that, we seemed to be making pretty good time.

"So, Party Waffle," I said. "What do you do?"

"Party," he said.

I don't know why I expected anything else.

"Is that all you do?" I asked.

He did a somersault forward. "What else is there?"

"Do you have a job?"

"I'm an ambassador," he said. "And I party."

"Do you drink?" Brijit asked.

Party Waffle turned back to her. "Drink?"

Brijit held her bottle of rum down low to the ground where Party Waffle could reach it. Party Waffle, still dancing and walking, peered up at the bottle with amazement in his eyes. He reached for it.

"I don't know if that's a good idea," I said.

"Why?" said Brijit.

"He's a waffle," I said. "I doubt they have booze where he's from. Who knows what that might do to him."

"Maybe it'll calm him down," she said. "Maybe it'll shut him up."

I didn't think we should be giving him liquor, but I had to admit that I was mildly intrigued, so I didn't protest all that much. Party Waffle took the bottle, looked at it long and hard, then put it to his mouth and knocked it back.

A second later he sprayed it out of his mouth, disgusted.

"That's awful," he said.

Brijit swiped the bottle away and walked right past him. "Of course it is."

Party Waffle used both hands to wipe off his tongue, then kept going. I followed.

Days and nights were just as strange in the Pancake Kingdom. The two suns moved across the sky in unpredictable ways, setting and rising at complete random, turning day and night and dusk and dawn into a total crap shoot.

So how long had we been traveling? Hours? A day? It was hard to tell. I checked Athena.

8,831 *kilometers.*

Well, that was something, I guess.

"How much further?" I asked Party Waffle.

"How much further for what?" he asked. "How much further to party town? Because party town is right here, population us three."

"How much further until we get to where we're going?" I clarified.

"Oh." He stopped, looked at the sky, then said, "Two more."

"Two more what?" I asked.

He looked at me and shrugged. "Two more."

"Two more *what*?" I asked. "Two more hours? Two more days?"

He looked confused. "What are those?"

"Never mind," I said. "Let's just keep going."

I don't know how long we'd been traveling, but the only thing I'd had to eat in days was that owl head and that wasn't all that much. I needed some real food, so I took a gamble on those rolled up silverware trees and guessed that if I tore open the napkins, I'd find a fork and spoon and a knife inside.

Sure enough, I was right. Jackpot. Party Waffle and Brijit waited on the cast iron road as I stripped the napkin away from a tree and hauled a giant knife out of the package. This table knife was taller than me and it probably weighed a literal ton. I wasn't about to carry around the whole knife, so I tore pieces of it off like strips of jerky. I ate one right away and kept the rest of it in my pocket to use as rations for later.

Party Waffle watched me, bewildered. It was one of the few times I saw him stand still.

"What?" I asked.

"You're eating a tree," he said.

"It's metal," I said. "I eat metal."

"That's amazing," he said. He stared at me for another moment, then gradually began moving his hips. He slowly took his eyes off me and went back to dancing down the road.

2

We walked for another couple hours, or maybe more, or maybe less. Maybe ten at the most. Who knows. Time worked weird in the Muffincake Kingdom. After however long, a giant coffee pot came into view. And I mean giant, like the size of a building. It was far off in the distance, but I could tell by the shape of it and by how the sunlight glinted off it that this was one of those old school metallic coffee pots, like the ones you'd take camping or use in World War 2.

"That's where I live," Party Waffle said. "The Pancake Kingdom. It's an exciting place. You're going to love it. Do you like diners? Do you like bacon? Do you like eggs? Do you like diners? Yeah, you do. Yeah, you do. But do you like diners?"

"Yeah," I said. "Diners are fine."

"What is a diner?" Brijit asked.

"It's a place where you get breakfast food," I told her.

"Like a farm?" she asked.

"No. It's a place where they cook breakfast food."

"Hmm." She did not sound impressed.

A flock of pancakes passed over head, flapping like birds and moving in a V formation. They swooped down out of the sky in unison and perched up in a grove of silverware trees that were in full bloom of french toast and pads of butter.

An hour later we were within the borders of the Pancake Kingdom itself. The people of the Pancake Kingdom – human-looking people – all wore white aprons, even the little kids. Their homes were giant hollowed out toasters, arranged into dense neighborhoods that went on for blocks and blocks. The taller buildings, libraries maybe, or business buildings, were made out of blenders and juicers, functioning ones that would kick off and on at random.

We passed by a laundry place where a bunch of teenage girls stood out on the front porch and hung damp aprons up on a line to dry. Another girl used a giant waffle iron to press clothes.

They all looked up when we passed by, unsurprised by a living waffle but obviously intrigued by me and Brijit. I waved hello to see what they would do, but they just kept staring, confused.

Everyone in the Pancake Kingdom kept their distance from us. We had a straight shot through the breakfast city and an easy time reaching the giant tin coffee pot castle.

The castle was surrounded by guards dressed in uniforms of egg yolk yellow and they wore the same white aprons as the townsfolk. They were armed with ridiculously large whisks and spatulas and serving spoons.

"Yo yo yo!" Party Waffle shouted at the guards. "Tell Princess Pancake that Party Waffle is back with very important news from the Ice Cream Cake Kingdom!"

One of the guards – the one with golden curls spilling out from underneath her eggshell-looking hat – pointed at me and Brijit.

"Who are these two?" she asked. "They look most strange."

Party Waffle danced a ballet between us and the guards. "I found them lost in the wilderness. They don't like to party. I have no idea who they are."

"Yes, you do!" I said to Party Waffle. I turned to the guard. "He knows us. I'm Penelope Salvo and this is Madam Brijit. We're just visitors passing through. Party Waffle is going to take us to see Princess Coffeecake and Princess Wedding Cake. We're not here to cause any trouble."

"Pencil." Party Waffle pointed right at me. "Your name is Pencil."

"My name is Penelope," I said.

He stared at me blankly for a moment, then said, "That's such a strange name. I'm going to call you Pencil." He turned and pointed at Brijit. "And you will be Bat Face."

Brijit crossed her arms. "Do not call me Bat Face."

"Bongo," Party Waffle suggested.

Brijit said no.

"Look," I said, interrupting Party Waffle's nonsense. "Now's not the time. Deliver your message to Pancake so we can get going."

"Oh, yes!" Party Waffle spun on his heels to look back at the guards. "My message. It is very important."

The lead guard – the girl with the eggshell hat – turned to another guard and gave him a nod. That guard about-faced and headed into the giant coffee pot castle.

"Wait here," the main guard said. "Outsiders are not allowed within the castle walls."

Whatever. I could go inside that castle if I really wanted to. A bunch of jabronies with cooking utensils weren't going to stop me. I wasn't going to force my way inside, obviously. The people of the Muffincake Kingdom seemed nice enough, but still it felt good to know that I *could* storm right in there if I really wanted to.

When the guard came back, he had his arm tucked under a princess and was helping her to walk. Princess Pancake stumbled over her own feet, barely able to stay upright.

Her princess gown was bright yellow, accented with white gloves and a necklace of tiny quail eggs. Her crown was a short stack of pancakes topped with a melting pad of butter. Black, wavy hair flowed out from underneath.

"Is she drunk?" Brijit asked.

"Or sick?" I asked.

"Sleepy," Party Waffle said. "She's very sleepy."

Sure enough, he was right. Princess Pancake put her fist to her mouth and yawned big time. The syrup and melted butter on her pancake crown dripped down, but magically stopped before it drizzled down onto her clothes. Before she was finished yawning, the guards around her yawned in unison. After the guards yawned, the people outside the castle walls yawned. Beyond that, all the people in the city yawned. It spread like wildfire until it faded into the furthest edges of the city. I could only assume that the yawning continued out to the farmers out on the outskirts of town.

"I'm sorry," Princess Pancake said as she rubbed her bleary eyes. "I'm still trying to wake up." She gestured at one of her soldiers with both hands. "Coffee. Where's my coffee?"

Immediately a soldier came running up with a full, steaming coffee mug. Pancake took a drink, inhaled with a smile, and then sighed. She opened her tired eyes and looked at the three of us.

"Perk up," Party Waffle said as he marched forward and gave Pancake's shin a little kick. "You have a message from your sister."

"Which..." Pancake yawned again. The soldiers yawned. The people of the city yawned. "Which sister?"

"Princess Ice Cream Cake," Party Waffle said.

"How nice," Pancake said. "What's the message?"

"It's very important," Party Waffle said.

"I'm sure it is."

"It's a secret."

"No, it's not," Pancake said. "Party Waffle, I've told you many times, these are not secrets.

He leaned in with suggestive eyes. "They *could* be."

Pancake said, "What's the message, Party Waffle?"

Party Waffle cleared his throat, danced a quick jig in place, then said, "Princess Ice Cream Cake said she is fine. She asked what are you doing? She said she was about to eat dinner."

"Oh, that's nice," Pancake said. "Tell her I just woke up. Tell her I am about to eat breakfast. Then ask her what she's having for dinner."

Party Waffle knocked his heels together and bowed deeply.

Pancake turned her attention to me and Brijit.

"You're not from around here," she said.

"No," I said.

"Nowhere close," Brijit added.

Pancake narrowed her eyes at me. "Are you from a place called Earth?"

"I am," I said. "Manhattan, actually. I knew your sisters back when they were Parcel and Cardboard."

Pancake made a pained look. "Oh, dreadful. Don't remind me of those times. I still have..." She yawned. The soldiers yawned. The city yawned. "...bad dreams about it sometimes. Earth is such a dreadful place."

Brijit muttered, "She's the first person here to make any sense."

3

Brijit elbowed me out of the way and rudely nudged Party Waffle aside with her foot so she could stand face to face with Princess Pancake. "I am Madam Brijit, Voodoo loa of love and death. You are a pancake, nice to meet you. Okay, we got that out of the way. Have you seen my husband?"

"Is your husband a cookie that lives in space?" Pancake asked.

"What?" Brijit said. "No. No, he's a guy about this tall, wears a tux, has his face painted up like mine."

Pancake looked back at her guards. Some of them shrugged. The other ones shook their heads no. Pancake turned back to Brijit and said, "No."

"Why would you think he's a cookie in space?" Brijit asked.

"Because that the only new thing I've seen," Pancake said.

I asked, "You've seen a cookie in space?"

Pancake nodded, excited. "Oh, yes."

"Uh. How?"

"Oh." Pancake's face lit up, even more excited than before. "There was one thing I did enjoy about Earth. It's this fascinating invention called a telly-scope. Have you ever seen a telly-scope?"

"No," said Brijit.

"A telescope?" I asked. "Yeah, I've seen a telescope."

Pancake looked at the sky and swept her arms through the air. "Telly-scopes let you see into space! Such marvelous inventions! Before I went to Earth, I didn't know what space was and I had never heard of a telly-scope. So when we came back here, I brought my telly-scope with me. I look through it sometimes. And just recently, I can see a cookie in space."

Brijit leaned in close to my ear. "I'm ready to go."

But I wasn't. I didn't know what a cookie was doing in space, but this was the Muffincake Kingdom and their universe worked on a different system of scientific laws where food is alive. If Pancake could see a cookie in space with a telescope, it had to be one big cookie. And while I'm no astronometer, I do know a thing or two about a thing or two and big objects visible from space are typically bad news.

"Could you show me this cookie?" I asked Pancake.

Brijit grabbed my arm. "Penelope, no."

"I want to see the cookie," I said.

"You're wasting time," she said.

I ditched Brijit and went to stand by Pancake. "It won't take long. Right, your majesty?"

Pancake slapped her hands together and bounced in place. "Do you really want to see it? Do you really? No one else is interested in my telly-scope. I would love to show you." She took my hand and pulled me towards the castle doors. "Come see! Come see!"

I went with her. I turned back once to see Brijit standing there with her arms crossed and Party Waffle doing cartwheels in circles around her feet.

"I'll be right back!" I shouted back to her.

Brijit didn't answer. She just shook her head.

At the very top of the coffee pot castle was a balcony built on the triangular spout. This was Pancake's private observatory with a table for her coffee mug, a plush stool with a stack of pancakes for a seat, and an honest-to-god Earth telescope on a tripod. It was a nice telescope, I supposed, not that I'm an expert on telescopes, but it was as long as Pancake was tall and it had dials to slowly and accurately adjust its position. I peered over the edge of the balcony and got a sickening sense of vertigo. Not only was the kingdom below us a minuscule version of itself, I could actually see the winter snow of the Ice Cream Cake Kingdom far off in the hazy distance.

As luck would have it – or I suppose it wasn't luck at all, but magic – the white and yellow suns were both setting just as we stepped out onto the balcony. The sky faded to black and the stars began to twinkle.

"Look, look, look," Pancake said as she waved me over to the telescope. She put her eye to the lens and adjusted the dials, slowly and meticulously searching the sky. "Here," she said. "Look."

She stepped aside and I bent over, putting my eye to the telescope lens.

There in the darkness of space, littered with flickering stars, was a giant ball of chocolate chip cookie. It had a glowing aura around it, as if it were very hot. It kind of shook in place, not moving left or right or up or down. It was just stationary there.

That wasn't good. Now, again, I'm not a scientist, but I learned a few things working with the living Storms from Cumulonimbus. If you look at a tornado, or a typhoon, or anything like that and it isn't moving left or right, then there are only two other options: it's either moving away from you, or it's moving *towards* you. And in the case of space cookie, I worried that we were looking at the "moving towards you" option.

"How long has this thing been there?" I asked with my eye still peered into the telescope.

"Couple times," Pancake said.

"Couple times, like days? Like weeks?"

"What are those?" She sounded honestly confused.

I stood up and looked at her. "How do you guys tell time here?"

She shook her head. "We don't."

"How do you plan anything?"

"We don't."

"Then how do you get anything accomplished."

Pancake yawned, almost bored. "I dunno. We just do."

"Okay, well, dammit." I took a moment to figure out how to explain the concept of an apocalypse to Princess Pancake. "So this space cookie might be a real problem."

"Problem?"

"It might be coming here."

"Here?" she asked. "To the balcony?"

"Uh, more like the city, or the world, or who knows what. It could hit anywhere. But if it does, and if it's big enough, it could cause a whole lot of destruction."

"What's destruction?"

"Destruction is when everything is broken and on fire and everyone dies."

Pancake widened her eyes and shook her head in disbelief. "No. No, that isn't a real thing."

"Dude, it might be." I looked back in the telescope. The cookie was still there, still glowing hot, still staying perfectly still. "Hey, I'm not a physicist and I can't tell you for sure, but... I mean... there's a chance? There's a chance this thing might be coming this way. And if it does..."

"Destruction?" she asked, terrified.

I hated to answer her. "Yeah?"

She wrung her hands and looked at me, terrified. "What do we do?"

"Uhh." I didn't have an answer there. "Normally when stuff like this happens in the movies, they shoot it with a rocket. Or they send a space ship up there to cut it into pieces or something. But..." I looked around and out over the Pancake Kingdom. "I don't suppose you have a space program around here anywhere, do you?"

"No," Pancake said.

"I'm gunna guess your sisters don't either, huh?"

"No."

I gestured at the sky. "There's no other way to get to space. I can jump and I can jump really high, but I can't jump to space."

"So we're just going to be destructioned?"

"Uhm." I ran my fingers through my hair. "I guess you could do, like, an evacuation thing? But I don't know how hard that would be. And I also don't know where you would go."

"You mean leave the Muffincake Kingdom?" she asked.

I shrugged. "It sucks, yeah, but I don't know what else you can do. You probably want to get on that sooner than later. I can find secret doors out of your world, but I can't tell you for certain where it's going to take us, and I don't know if it's a good idea to evacuate an entire dimension into someone else's. That might end up causing a lot of problems."

Pancake snapped her fingers and her mood instantly changed. "I'm going to pray to the gods!"

"The gods?"

"Butter Pad and Sugar Cube," she said. "They were the first bakers. They watch us in everything we do. They will save us."

"Uh."

Princess Pancake covered both eyes with her gloved hands and paced around in circles. She nearly ran right into her coffee table, but I swept it out of her way in time. Then she started to pray out loud.

"Butter Pad. Sugar Cube. This is Princess Pancake, third daughter of King Muffincake. There is a space cookie coming to destruction us. Please make it go away. Thank you. I hope you have a good night. Sleep well."

Just like that, she was done. She stopped pacing, lowered her hands to her side and beamed a smile at me.

She said, "Problem solved."

"Uhm." I went over to the telescope and looked. The space cookie was still there. I looked back up at Pancake. "Butter Pad and Sugar Cube... Are you sure they're, you know, real?"

"Of course they're real," she said.

"But, like, *are they though*? Because your world might be in serious danger and I don't know how your world works. This place is way more magical than New York, so I'm just wondering if your gods are like *real* real, or if you just... like... *think* they're real real."

"Oh, they're real," she said.

I hooked a thumb towards the telescope. "Well, if they're real, they're not listening because the cookie is still out there."

"What?" Pancake said. "No." She darted over and stuck her eye to the lens. "Is it?"

"Maybe it's going to take them some time," I said. "Or maybe they're not there?"

Still bent over the telescope, she looked over at me. "Not there?"

"Like... maybe they don't exist?"

"Of course they exist," Pancake said. "They created everything. They were the first bakers."

"I don't want to get started on religion because we really should be focused on space cookie. And if your gods aren't going to do anything about it, we should start thinking of something else."

"They'll do something." Pancake stood up, covered her eyes with both hands, and went back to walking in circles. "Butter Pad. Sugar Cube. It's Princess Pancake again. Sorry to bother you again so quickly, but in our last correspondence I informed you of a giant space cookie that-" Blinded and pacing in circles, she bumped right into me. I stepped out of her way. "Sorry, Pencil. Sorry. Anyway, Butter Pad, Sugar Cube, I couldn't help but notice that the space cookie is still there. I'm going to need you two to get rid of it. You can eat it if you want, or anything. Just make it go away. Thank you. Take care."

She stopped, lowered her hands and looked at me. "What about now?"

I raised my eyebrows at her. I was super skeptical that anything had changed, but I looked into the telescope anyway. Honestly, I hoped for her sake that her prayers worked. But...

"It's still there."

5

Even back on Earth when people would talk about "what if an asteroid was coming to hit us, what would we do?" there was never really a solid answer. They covered the idea in movies like Armageddon and whatever else, but the solution typically revolved around billion dollar space programs or nuclear bombs or something equally as complicated. There wasn't much the Muffincake Kingdom could do about a crispity, crunchety asteroid, not when they were equipped with pancakes and ice cream sandwiches and a fairy tale understanding of the world.

And maybe I could have helped, but what could I do? I couldn't fly to space, and even if I could, what then?

Or maybe things weren't as bad as I made them out to seem. It's hard to gauge the size of things in space when you don't have something else to compare it to. Maybe this space cookie was only the size of a city bus or something. Sure, it would cause some destruction, but it might not be one of those "wipe out all life" type things.

Or maybe it was. Who knew? Definitely not Penelope Salvo.

Princess Pancake made me promise to not tell anyone about space cookie except the other Princesses. Death and destruction were not concepts easily understood by the innocent people of the Muffincake Kingdom and just hearing about it would send them into a panic. I understood that. If there were an asteroid about to hit Earth, the world governments probably wouldn't say anything either for the same reason. They would try to solve it in absolute secrecy.

Scientifically curious Princess Pancake was the only person in the whole Muffincake Kingdom who had even the most basic grasp of "outer space" as a concept. No one else in the world would even know what we were talking about. When Pancake came to that realization, she grew visibly depressed and sleepy.

"I just want to lie down," she said as she led me down the metallic hallways of her coffee pot castle. She hung her head and stared down at her feet. Her shoulders slumped.

"Hey." I put my hand on her shoulder. "I'm not going to let anything bad happen to this place. I promise. I'll figure something out."

"Yeah?" She looked up at me with promise. "Like what?"

I looked up at the ceiling. "Uh. Well. I don't know yet." I looked back at her. "But I'll think of something."

Pancake smiled. "I believe you will. You're Pencil Salvo."

"It's Penelope."

"You've saved our world once before. You're very good at it."

"Yeah. Well." Jeez. No pressure. "You know, I'm going to do my best."

"I know you will."

Pancake led me to the main entrance of her castle. When we stepped outside, night had ended and the kingdom was basked in gleaming sunshine. There was a warm breeze that smelled faintly of maple syrup and breakfast sausages. I looked up at the sky and scrutinized it in ways I hadn't before. There were the two suns, of course, but in the direction of space cookie was a dim, twinkling star.

Destruction.

"Remember," Pancake said to me as we walked outside. She yawned and blinked her tired eyes. "Not a word of this to anyone."

"Of course not," I said. "And don't worry."

"I won't." She gave me a sleepy smile. "Thank you, Pencil."

"It's Penelope."

"Guards." She turned around and headed back inside. "It's nap time."

6

Me and Brijit began the next leg of our journey down the cast iron roads of the Pancake Kingdom. Party Waffle led the way, tap dancing a soft-shoe dance about ten feet ahead of us. He seemed to know where he was going and I was content to follow him.

Brijit chewed on her smoking cigar and moved it to the side of her mouth so she could talk. "So what was the deal with the cookie in space?"

"It's an asteroid," I said.

She ashed her cigar. "Asteroid?"

"A big space rock. I think it's coming this way. There's a chance it might wipe out everything in the world, depending on how big it is."

"Huh." Brijit didn't sound like she cared. She kept her eyes forward. "Shame."

"It's a whole world of people," I told her. "They could all die."

"Everything dies. We've been over this. Every world has its problems. Every world ends. That's just how things work. There's nothing you can do about it."

I was too lost in my thoughts to respond.

Brijit turned to me and repeated it with intensity. "There's nothing you can do about it."

I still didn't answer her.

She said, "You're going to try to do something, aren't you."

"I have to, Brijit. These people are my friends. I can't just let them die."

"Okay. And exactly how do you plan on stopping a cookie from space?"

"I don't know. Can *you* stop a cookie from space?"

She gave me a stupid look, plucked the cigar out of her mouth and took a swig of her rum. "Do I look like the Voodoo loa of space cookies?"

"Whatever," I said. "I'll think of something."

Brijit puffed on her cigar, tilted her head back and blew a square cloud of smoke into the air. "I doubt it."

Chapter 11

1

8,017 kilometers.

Party Waffle rode out the rest of the Pancake Kingdom on my shoulders. I had assumed he drew from an endless source of energy, but come to find out that wasn't the case. Just when we had reached the Hashbrown Fields of Early Brunch, Party Waffle showed signs of slowing down. He still danced, but not with the same intensity as before. He kind of just swung his arms and sometimes let out a desperate "woo" or a really exhausted "yeah."

Brijit said, "I think he's dying."

"He's not dying," I said. "Party Waffle, are you tired?"

"Woo. Yeah."

"You want to ride on my shoulders?"

"Ride? Like a buffatoaster?"

"Yeah, buddy." I picked him up and put him square on my shoulders. "Like a buffatoaster."

"Okay." He patted my head with both hands. He must have hit the small points of barbed wire sticking out of my hair. "Ow. Your head is pointy."

"Yeah, I got barbed wire in there," I said.

Brijit glanced at me. "Why do you have barbed wire in your hair?"

"I killed a demon by drinking her soul," I said. "I kind of got her powers. She had barbed wire in her hair, so now I do, too."

"Strange," Brijit said. "You killed a demon?"

"Yeah."

"A real one?"

"Yes, a real one."

"From Hell?"

"Yes, Brijit, I killed a real demon from Hell. Why does that surprise you?"

She shrugged. "I dunno. Just didn't think you had it in you."

"Well, I do," I said.

We reached an invisible boundary in the world where the Pancake Kingdom ended. On the other side of the line was an ocean of dark soda pop. Carbonated waves splashed against the border between the two kingdoms. Halfway out in the ocean was a great island. I couldn't see what was built on the island, but I could hear laughter and music and hundreds of ringing bells. There were flashing colorful lights that reflected off the clouds above.

"Funnel Cake Island," Party Waffle said. "It's a really great place. Do you like games? Do you like rides?"

"Funnel Cake Island, huh?" I looked down at the soda pop ocean just on the other edge of the Pancake Kingdom. We were inches away from the hissing, foaming liquid. We were so close, I could see ice cubes. The island was all the way across the waves. "How are we supposed to get across?"

Party Waffle said, "Sometimes you can take a boat."

I said, "Okay, let's do that."

"But I don't see any boats," Party Waffle said. "We'll have to swim."

"No way," Brijit said. "I'm not swimming in soda pop."

"I don't see what other choice we have," I said.

Brijit scoffed. "Watch this." She stepped out onto the ocean and walked on the soda as if it were solid ground. She turned around and made an exaggerated gesture, showing off how cool she was.

"Fine," I said. "You do that. We'll swim."

"I can't swim," Party Waffle said. "I never learned how."

"Here." I scooped Party Waffle off my shoulders and held him out to Brijit. She gave me this look that said "you gotta be kidding me." I told her, "Dude, just take him. I can't swim *and* carry him and if he falls in, he's going to drown."

211

Brijit gave me a furious look and stamped her foot on the soda. "Fine." She pointed a finger at Party Waffle. "No singing. No dancing. No nothing. I want you to be quiet. Understood?"

"Uhh." Party Waffle stalled for as long his waffle lungs would allow him, then he said, "I'll try."

Brijit muttered angrily to herself as she swiped Party Waffle away from me one-handed and carried him by the head. "Come on," she said, waving Party Waffle at me like a piece of paper. "Let's go."

I was worried that the rough way she was carrying him might have been hurting him, but he seemed to enjoy being waved around. He whooped and laughed like he was on a roller coaster.

"Shut up," Brijit said to him. "I said no talking."

I was just about to jump into the soda ocean when I stopped and grabbed my cigarette box out of my front pocket. I still had spliffs in there and I wasn't about to ruin those by getting them wet. I handed them off to Brijit.

"I'm not your pack mule," Brijit said.

"Just take the god damned cigarettes."

Brijit had to walk slow to keep pace with me while I swam. The waves were calm that day and there wasn't much risk of being pulled under. It was a weird sensation to swim in a carbonated drink. The tiny bubbles collected on my skin and would float away in groups, only to be replaced by more.

Halfway across the ocean, Party Waffle started humming.

"Silence," Brijit said.

Party Waffle got quiet. Then after a moment, he said, "Why do you hate singing?"

"I don't hate singing," Brijit said. "I hate *your* singing. There's a difference."

"Then you sing something," he said.

"No," she said.

"Come on, Brijit," I said as I paddled next to them. "Sing something."

"La la la," she said in a monotone voice. "There. Happy?"

"La la la," Party Waffle repeated in the same deadpan way. "Never heard that one before. I like it. What's it called?"

"It's called 'shut up,'" Brijit said.

"Shut Up by Bongo Bat Face," Party Waffle said. "La la la."

"I said no nicknames," Brijit said.

We crossed the ocean and washed up on the sandy beaches of Funnel Cake Island. The flashing lights and carnival music came from a city-sized amusement park. I could smell popcorn and hotdogs and fried funnel cakes. The city skyline was home to dozens of unbelievably giant ferris wheels, ten times bigger than anything I had ever seen back on Earth.

The ringing bells came from all varieties of carnival games: ski-ball and the ring toss and the game where you slam a mallet down on the ground and try to ring the bell. There were glittering arcades and hot dog stands everywhere and people spinning pink and blue cotton candy. The city was packed with human-looking people dressed in brightly colored clothes, some of them with their faces painted up all silly. Mixed into the crowd were clowns and people in animal costumes and a guy passing out helium balloons.

There was a huge wooden sign over the main entrance that read in bright red letters: WELCOME TO FUNNEL CAKE ISLAND! Beneath the sign was a ticket booth. Perty Waffle led us straight that direction.

Inside the booth was a friendly old man in a red and white striped jacket. He had a curled handlebar mustache and little spectacles that were hilariously too small for his Santa Claus face.

"Welcome, welcome, welcome!" he shouted at us. "Welcome to Funnel Cake Island! Have you been here before?"

"No," I said.

"God, no," Brijit said.

Party Waffle stuck his hand in the air. "I have!"

"Well, then you two are going to need a map!" The old man handed both me and Brijit folded up maps of Funnel Cake Island. We unfolded them and gave them the once over. I was fascinated by the cartoony depictions of their sprawling kingdom. Brijit had a disgusted look on her face, as if she were looking at a picture of garbage.

There were four major regions of Funnel Cake Island. Wonderland, Happy Town, Coo-Coo Bananas, and the World of Carousels. There were colorful drawings of the many attractions found in each region and a detailed path showing you how to get around.

Dead in the center of the island where all four regions met was the Great Arcade, a towering arcade with "every game, ever, ever." This, I could only assume, was the castle of Princess Funnel Cake.

I tapped my finger on the Great Arcade and showed it to the old man. "Is this where Princess Funnel Cake lives?"

"Technically, yes," he said. "But you won't find her there."

"Oh," I said. "Well, where will we find her?"

He turned to Funnel Cake Island and made a sweeping gesture with his arm. "Out having fun!"

"Heck yeah!" Party Waffle screamed. He broke into a deadass sprint and ran straight into the carnival. "Party!"

"Party Waffle!" I called out. He didn't stop. "Party Waffle! Get back here!" But Party Waffle weaved into the legs of the crowd and vanished. "God dammit."

"He'll be fine," Brijit said, looking at her map upside down.

She was probably right. The place seemed harmless enough. And I knew we'd find him eventually. I turned back to the ticket taker.

"Do you know where she might be exactly?" I asked him.

"The Princess?" he asked.

"Yes."

"Oh, no idea. She could be anywhere!" He leaned down closer, as if he were about to tell me a big secret. "She *is* partial to roller coasters, though. Especially Powdered Sugar." He tapped the map. "In Coo-Coo Bananas. It's right across from the monkey cage."

"Cool." I folded up my map. "I'll start there."

"Does this place cost money?" Brijit asked. "Because I have no money."

"Money?" the old man asked. "I'm not sure what that is, but there is no cost here on Funnel Cake Island! All you have to do is go inside and enjoy yourselves!"

So we walked in. I knew I could enjoy myself. Madam Brijit was a different story.

Strangely enough, Madam Brijit fit in on Funnel Cake Island. Between her red dreadlocks and her festive face paint and her dirty wedding dress, the citizens of this kingdom confused her for some kind of dirty goth hobo clown. They were fascinated by her and gave her tons of attention.

"You are a breath of fresh air!" one lady said to Brijit.

"This is such a unique take on being a clown!" another teen girl told her.

"That's new," this guy said. "And I like new. What tricks do you do?"

"I do this," Brijit said. She took a deep puff on her cigar and blew a pyramid of smoke into the air. It stayed there for a moment, then drifted away. She wasn't doing it to be cute or entertaining; she was doing it to be a bitch, but it didn't work. The guy was impressed and then called out to his wife and kids.

This lady came over, bringing with her a twelve year old boy and an eight year old girl.

"Do it again," the guy said to Brijit. "Show the kids."

"No," Brijit said.

"Aw, why not?" the guy asked.

"I'm not a clown."

I nudged her. "Just blow some smoke, man. It's for the kids."

Brijit sighed and put the cigar in her mouth. Annoyed, she puffed on it and blew smoke in the air. It took the shape of a square then floated away.

The boy's face lit up. The little girl shrieked with delight and clapped her hands. "Again!" she shouted. "Do it again!"

The dad looked at Brijit to see if she was willing, but Brijit just looked super annoyed. The dad kind of frowned and told his daughter, "This clown is probably very tired. She's been working all day. Let's give her a break and-"

"Oh, fine," Brijit said. "It's fine. One more." She looked down at the young girl. "What's your name, tiny creature?"

The girl smiled and bounced in place. "Tilt!"

Brijit scoffed and rolled her eyes. I could tell what she was thinking. *Stupid name.* But she inhaled off her cigar once more and this time puckered up to blow smoke out in a steady stream. She used the smoke to write in the air, leaving the word TILT floating just above our heads.

"Wow," the girl said, awestruck.

"Butter Pad!" the young boy exclaimed in shock.

"Whirl!" the mother snapped at the boy. "Language."

The father gave Brijit a pat on the shoulder. "You are amazing. I've lived on Funnel Cake Island here for years and thought I'd seen everything. You're going to be big, I'm sure of it."

We pushed and elbowed our way through the crowds of Coo-Coo Bananas. Brijit was constantly showered with compliments about her clown costume. I suppose in a world that's already achieved perfect happiness, there's no reason to change or grow or develop. Seeing a new kind of clown really blew their minds.

Brijit was bombarded with so much positivity and praise that it started to change her mood. When another group of curious kids swarmed all around her, she actively engaged them and said, "watch this" and performed the smoke trick. The kids squealed and laughed. Brijit did it several more times, each time making a different shape or design. And by the time the kids raced off to do something else, I caught just the slightest hint of a smile on Brijit's face.

She didn't realize she was smiling, or at least didn't realize that I noticed, so the moment we made eye contact her face went flat and she said, "Shut up."

"You were smiling," I said.

"I said shut up." She walked away.

"You *like* this place," I said, running up beside her.

"I do not."

"Yeah, you do. They like you and you like them back."

"Your mouth is filled with terrible lies."

"Okay, dude. Whatever." I let it go, but I kept laughing. She knew I was right.

Just outside of Coo-Coo Bananas, I heard someone calling out to us. It was high-pitched "yoo-hoo" that sounded a lot like Party Waffle. I looked all around, but he wasn't in line for the carousel and he wasn't in the crowd by the hot dog stand and he wasn't mixed in with the people sitting at the picnic tables.

I heard him again. "Yoo-hoo! Pencil! Bat Face!"

I did a full 360 and looked all around. I didn't see him anywhere. "Party Waffle? Where the hell are you?"

Brijit nudged me and pointed up in the air with the turkey leg she was eating. I looked up and found Party Waffle waving his hands over the edge of a Ferris Wheel seat. I waved back. Brijit just ate her turkey. I'm sure we looked tiny to Party Waffle way high up in the sky. I was surprised he spotted us at all.

I cupped my hands to my mouth. "Where have you been?"

Brijit muttered, "Partying."

"Partying!" Party Waffle shouted.

"Well, get down here!" I shouted back. "We're going to see the princess!"

"Okay!" Party Waffle said. He hooked one leg over the edge of the seat. Then he threw his other leg over.

"Party Waffle, no!" Mother of God, was he going to jump out of a Ferris Wheel? Even after I screamed, he kept crawling over the edge. He straight up lost his grip and dropped like a rock.

"Oh wow," wide-eyed Brijit said with her mouthful of turkey.

I frantically ran my fingers through my hair. "What the fuck!?"

Party Waffle fell out of the sky and disappeared into the crowd of people. He definitely hit the ground. I raced after him, shoving my way through the crowd. I pushed past kids and adults and people in big animal costumes.

I found Party Waffle face down on the concrete.

"Oh my god, Party Waffle! Are you okay?"

He peeled his face off the ground. He stumbled to his feet on wobbly legs and after a second of disorientation, he danced the robot. "Bleep. Bloop. Calculating party vectors."

I breathed a sigh of relief. "God dammit, Party Waffle, I thought you were fucking dead."

Still dancing, he looked up at me and said, "What's dead?"

"It's..." If Party Waffle didn't know what dead was, I wasn't going to tell him. "You don't know what dead is?"

"No."

There's this old story – I don't know if it's true – about these Catholic missionaries who traveled to the furthest parts of Alaska or wherever and found these Eskimos. They told them all about Jesus Christ and how "great" he was. They told them that they had to worship Jesus Christ as their savior or else they'd burn in Hell for all eternity.

The Eskimos said they'd never heard of Jesus Christ before. They asked if all the dead Eskimos who never heard about Jesus were burning in Hell.

"No," the missionaries told them. "God wouldn't send them to Hell. They're perfectly okay in Heaven. It wasn't their fault that they hadn't been told about Jesus Christ."

The Eskimos got upset and said, "Then why are you telling us now?"

I don't know if it's the same thing, but I wasn't going to introduce Party Waffle to the concept of death if he didn't already know it. What if he couldn't die because he had no idea what dying was? If I explained death to him, that might change things. I didn't want to do that to him.

"Just be more careful," I told him. I turned back and headed towards Brijit. "Come on. Princess time. Stay close. No running off."

Party Waffle danced close to my feet and followed.

4

We found the Powdered Sugar in Coo-Coo Bananas. It was a gigantic roller coaster made of white steel that looped and coiled in odd and dangerous ways. The sheer length of the tracks and the complicated loops would have been impossible to recreate with the physical laws found on Earth.

Roller coaster cars thundered across the tracks as they raced overhead, accompanied by the screams of terrified and delighted people.

The line to Powdered Sugar was long – the sign at the back of the line indicated a 45 minute wait – but Funnel Cake Island was such a chill, positive place that everyone waited patiently for their turn. No one whined, no one complained. I walked up and down the length of the line looking for anyone dressed like a princess. Nothing. And I wasn't surprised; the princess probably didn't have to wait in line like a regular person. If Princess Funnel Cake really loved Powdered Sugar, she was *on* the ride.

Party Waffle couldn't resist the excitement of the roller coaster and made a break for it. I knew that was coming. I snatched him up by the top of his waffle head.

"No you don't," I told him. "You stay with us."

"Aw." He pointed dead ahead. "But. But."

"Later," I said. "We need to find the Princess."

I went as far as the fenced-off roller coaster platform, bypassing the line entirely. I figured we could hang around near the exit and look for the princess as the people got off. Standing closer, the roller coaster was twice as loud and our voices were drowned out by the sound of endless metallic rattling and screams of delight.

"What is the point of this contraption?" Brijit asked as she curiously watched the roller coaster cars speed around the track.

"It's fun," I told her. "Have you never seen a roller coaster before?"

"No," she said. "It looks like some form of transportation. Except it's not really going anywhere."

"You don't ride it to go anywhere," I told her. "It's just for thrills. It simulates the fear of dying, but you're actually strapped in and it's pretty safe."

"Simulates the fear of dying?" she repeated. She stared at it with total fascination. I couldn't tell if she was leaning more towards the "I hate this thing" direction, or going towards more of a "I like this death machine" kind of vibe. In either case, she refused to take her eyes off it.

One of the roller coaster trains rolled into the station to unload and that's when I finally caught sight of Princess Funnel Cake. She was hard to miss. She sat in the very front car dressed like a princess of clowns. Her gown had some noble aspects to it. It was tailor-made to fit her body with a high, ruffled neck line, polka dot silk gloves that went as high as her elbows, and a white leather belt buckled in place with a plastic flower. Her face was painted white, she had bright blue circles on her cheeks, and everything was topped off with a red clown nose.

She didn't wear a crown, at least not on the roller coaster, and she wore her red hair in a short pixie cut.

"Is that her?" I asked Party Waffle.

"Oh yeah!" he said. "Yeah, that's her. Princess Funnel Cake!"

Everyone unloaded off the roller coaster except for Funnel Cake. She stayed in her seat, still buckled in with an excited smile on her face.

She was going to ride it again.

"Come on." I grabbed Brijit's arm and pulled her towards the entrance.

"What are you doing?" she asked.

"We're getting on the roller coaster."

"But there's a queue," she said. "You have to wait your turn."

"Oh, McGruff the Crime Dog over here. Come on."

I pushed my way past everyone in line and towards the stairs leading up to the roller coaster platform. These utopian people were so blissfully ignorant to things like cheating or stealing that everyone I bumped into apologized to *me* for being in *my* way. So with no one standing in our way, we raced right up the stairs and were next in line to get on the roller coaster.

I jumped in and sat next to Princess Funnel Cake.

I still couldn't tell if Brijit hated or liked the idea of the death simulator, or if she had yet to make up her mind, but she got in the car behind us.

I buckled up with Party Waffle safely on my lap.

Princess Funnel Cake excitedly bounced in her seat, staring straight ahead. She turned and beamed a huge, excited smile at me. She had powdered sugar on her lips, undoubtedly from eating nothing but funnel cakes. She was on a sugar high. That explained her restless and jittery disposition.

"Hi," I said.

"Hi!" she nearly screamed, suddenly very interested in conversation. "Do you like roller coasters?"

"I do," I said. "They're fun."

"This one's the best." She patted the safety bar in front of us like it was her pet. "Absolute best. Best-o change-o."

"I'm Penelope Salvo." I reached out for a handshake. "I'm friends with your sisters Wedding Cake and-"

Her face lit up. "Penelope Salvo from New York! I know you! Wedding and Coffee used to talk about you all the time!"

"That's right."

The cars jolted in place as the gears kicked in and we started moving forward. Party Waffle made excited noises and danced in place on my legs. I looked back to Brijit to gauge her reaction. She was in deep contemplation, puffing absent-mindedly on her cigar.

"How did you get here?" Funnel Cake asked. "Magic?"

"There are these doorways that connect all the different worlds," I said. "It's kind of complicated. I'm only here for a little bit. Just passing through."

We started the incline up the first hill of the roller coaster. Foot by foot, we climbed higher and higher into the sky. Coo-Coo Bananas looked smaller and smaller below us.

"Here we go!" Funnel Cake exclaimed. She gripped tight to the safety bar. "This is it!"

"Your sister wanted me to tell you some bad news," I said over the clacking chain that pulled us up the tracks.

"Which sister?" she asked. She kept looking forward.

"Pancake," I said.

"What'd she say?"

"Well. Do you know how Pancake has that telescope from Earth?"

"The telly-scope. I do. It looks into the sky."

We reached the peak of the roller coaster. We were going to roll straight for a few seconds, then came the very first plunge.

"Oh!" Funnel Cake shouted. "Ready? Ready?" She looked back at everyone in the cars behind us and shouted, "Everybody put your hands up!"

She put her hands up. I was holding Party Waffle, so when I put my hands up, I held him high above me. Party Waffle also put his hands up. I looked back to see that everyone had their hands up, except Brijit. She just looked very confused.

She caught my eyes and I could tell she wanted some sort of explanation.

"When in Rome," I said.

She glanced around, saw that everyone had their hands up, then gave in. She put her hands in the air, but sort of missed the point. They were straight-up and very stiff.

Then we took the plunge.

5

I love roller coasters.

I've been on every roller coaster in New York City and I have some favorites there, but Powdered Sugar was hands-down the best roller coaster experience of my life. There was a part where you corkscrewed straight down towards the ground and then go into this pitch black tunnel. It curves you back up and when you come launching back out into the night sky, the tracks split in two different directions. The roller coaster cars come apart and half of the roller coaster cars go right, the other half go left. I don't even know how that's possible, but that's what happened. The cars go off to do their own loops and then everything gets reassembled just before the ride ends.

The ride was over as quick as it began and within seconds we pulled into the platform, laughing and terrified. I told Princess Funnel Cake how much I loved Powdered Sugar. She went on and on about how it was her favorite roller coaster in her whole kingdom.

When the safety bars were released and we were free to get out, I got out. Princess Funnel Cake stayed in the car. She wanted to ride it again.

"How many times have you ridden this?" I asked her.

"Today?" she asked. "Or ever?"

"Well, today."

"Fifty-seven." She answered right away. She didn't even need to think.

"Do you want to take a break?" I asked. "Do you want to hang out with me for a bit so we can talk about that stuff from before?"

"What stuff?" she asked.

"The bad news from your sister," I said. "About the telescope."

She gave it a moment of thought, then started climbing out of the car. "Okay. I wanna get a funnel cake anyway."

So that's how we ended up sitting at a picnic table eating funnel cakes off of paper plates. Not me, of course. I hated to be rude, but funnel cakes would have tasted like sawdust to me. The only people eating were Funnel Cake and Brijit and Party Waffle. I was eating a metal napkin dispenser. It did not taste good.

Watching Party Waffle eat a funnel cake made me strangely uncomfortable. Was that some kind of cannibalism? It didn't seem to bother him or anyone else and just like how he didn't know the concept of death, I wasn't going to be the one to introduce him to cannibalism.

I said to Funnel Cake, "So when you look through Pancakes telescope there's this-"

"Tell me," Brijit said to Funnel Cake, straight up interrupting me. "These simulated death machines you have. Are they... easy to build?"

"Excuse me," I said. "I was talking."

"My what?" Funnel Cake asked Brijit, confused.

"Your roller coaster," I told her. "She wants to know about your roller coaster."

"Oh!" Funnel turned back to Brijit. "No, they are not easy to build. If you build them wrong, they come flying apart and make a huge mess."

"How does one learn to build one of these death machines?" Brijit asked.

"Huh." Funnel Cake looked off to the side as if she never considered that question before. She looked back a Brijit. "I have no idea."

Brijit stared down at her funnel cake. Was she enjoying funnel cakes, too? On the topic of roller coasters, she said, "Everyone around me was terrified of dying, but they knew it wasn't coming. They were scared, but they were happy. It was strange. Everything here is so strange."

"What is dying?" Party Waffle asked. His eyes just barely peeked out over the top of the table.

"It is the end of life," Brijit said. "The state of non-existence."

"It's nothing for you to worry about," Funnel Cake said to the little waffle. "It doesn't happen here in the Funnel Cake Kingdom."

"Well, that might not be too technically true," I said. Funnel Cake gave me a curious look. I said to Party Waffle, "Party Waffle, why don't you go play some games so we can talk big girl stuff. We need to-"

Party Waffle was already running away. He didn't need me to give him a reason. He heard "go play some games" and was gone.

I told Funnel Cake, "There is a big cookie in space and it's coming this way."

She stopped chewing and stared at me. "What?"

"Space," I said. I pointed up. "Up there? Past the clouds? That's space."

She chewed her funnel cake and shrugged at me like "so what?"

I sighed. "Up there in space is this big hot piece of cookie that I think might be coming here towards the Muffincake Kingdom very fast. And if I'm right, it's going to hit the Muffincake Kingdom really hard and when that happens... a lot of people are going to die."

"And it won't be simulated death like on a roller coaster," Brijit said. "It will be the real thing. There will be no laughing."

"Oh no." Funnel Cake looked worried. She leaned over the picnic table and took my hands in hers. "You're Penelope Salvo. You've saved us before. You should save us now."

"Believe me, I want to, but I don't see how it's possible. We'd have to get to space and, no offense to you guys or your kingdoms, but you straight up do not have the technology to pull that off."

She stared at me, terrified. Then without warning, she shot up out of her seat, slapped her hands over her eyes and paced in circles.

"Dear Butter Pad and Sugar Cube. How are you? I am fine. I have just received some distressing news about something called space."

Funnel Cake bumped into a light pole, said "excuse me, miss" then went back to walking in circles.

"What is she doing?" Brijit asked me.

"Praying," I said.

"These people have gods?" she asked.

223

"Butter Pad and Sugar Cube," I said.

"Are they real?" she asked.

"Hell if I know, dude. I don't think so. But just because a god doesn't answer you doesn't mean he's not there."

Funnel Cake went on praying. "...I'm not saying you have to do it, but you really should do it because you baked this whole world and I doubt you want to bake another one. Oh, and if you help us, you can come to my kingdom and ride any ride you want and you won't even have to wait in line. That's my promise to you. Okay. Thank you for listening. Goodnight. Sleep tight."

Funnel Cake stopped and took her hands away from her eyes. She beamed at me with a huge smile. "I fixed it."

"Yeeeeeeah," I said. "I don't know."

"I just talked to Butter Pad and Sugar Cube," she said.

"I saw that. The thing is, your sister Pancake did that *twice* and both times the space cookie was still there."

"For serious?"

"For serious."

I told Funnel Cake not to worry, that I would think of something, but I didn't know if that were true or not. What could I possibly do about something so cosmic? In any case, leaving her in a state of worry wouldn't accomplish anything. I told her that I was going to inform all her other sisters and so they could all get together and figure out what to do in case of an emergency, whether it was an evacuation (to where, who knows) or something else.

Funnel Cake seemed strangely at peace with the bad news. Because of the stories Coffeecake and Wedding Cake told about me, she was confident that I was going to solve all their problems and save their world.

Chapter 12

1

6,907 kilometers.

We departed Funnel Cake Island with the same method we used to get in, with Brijit carrying Party Waffle across the ocean on foot and with me swimming in ice cold cola. We headed deeper into the Muffincake Kingdom, this time bound for the Birthday Cake Kingdom.

The shores of the Birthday Cake Kingdom were spongy yellow cake, decorated with plants that bloomed frosting. Instead of trees, this place had birthday cake candles stuck in the ground, some of them lit, some of them out. There were also the occasional number candles, the kind you use to put someone's age on top of their cake, and these were larger than the regular candles. Some of those number candles were the size of Oregon redwoods.

Birthday presents were strewn all around, wrapped in elegant paper. They came in all shapes and sizes and colors. Some of them were green with golden print, or blue with red polka dots. They were the living creatures of this world, bouncing across the ground, or rolling end over end like how only boxes can roll.

Party Waffle loved it. He spun around in circles as we walked.

"Ever been here before?" I asked him.

"Oh, yeah!" he shouted. "I've busted many moves in the Birthday Cake Kingdom! Every day is your birthday!" He looked at me. "Happy birthday!" He looked at Brijit. "Happy Birthday!"

Brijit said, "It's not my birthday."

"Yes, it is!" he said.

"No, it's not."

"Yes, it is!"

"No. It is not."

"Yes, it is!"

"It's not my birthday."

"Yes, it is!"

"No, it's not."

The two of them were driving me crazy. I touched Brijit's arm to get her attention. "Just... just let him do his thing."

She didn't respond, but also stopped arguing. Party Waffle sang happy birthday. Then he sang it again. And again. He wouldn't stop singing happy birthday.

Happy birthday to you!
Happy birthday to you!
Happy birthday dear Bongo Bat Face!
Happy birthday to you!

I hate birthdays. Or, I guess technically, I hate *my* birthday. Bad memories. Other people's birthdays are fine. But I don't much care for the song "Happy Birthday" because it reminds me too much of my own birthday and all the stupid shit Michael used to do to fuck with me. I thought eventually Party Waffle would stop singing the song, but after the tenth time I started to think differently.

I needed to give him something else to sing.

I asked him, "Do you want to hear a birthday song from my world?"

He looked up at me with amazement as if I just revealed to him that I was the bodily incarnation of both Butter Pad and Sugar Cube.

"Yes!" he said. He clapped his hands together and walked backwards so he could watch me.

"Okay, it goes like this." I clapped my hands. "Happy, happy birthday, from Applebee's to you. We wish it was our birthday, so we could party, too!"

His eyes went wide and his mouth hung open. He whispered, "Did you write that?"

"I did," I said. "Feel free to use it."

And as we walked, he sang the Applebee's birthday song instead of Happy Birthday and that was better.

The Birthday Cake Kingdom was peaceful for the most part. The only annoying thing was all the frosting everywhere. We were literally walking across the top of a giant birthday cake and the frosting was ankle deep. No way around it. My Chucks were caked in frosting.

Haha. "Caked" in frosting. Self-high five.

Brijit's dress dragged across the ground, getting it even more messy. Not that it really mattered by that point. She had been in blueberry shake and covered in sprinkles and coated in chocolate. Her dress was in dire need of washing. My clothes weren't any better. I smelled like soda and candy.

Colorful balloons drifted across the sky. At first I thought they were just decoration, but they moved in flocks and would sometimes change direction. They were like birds. Sometimes they would come down and perch on top of the birthday candles.

Two dimensional paper donkeys wandered across the flat open plains of frosting. Some of them had tails pinned to their asses, or to their heads, or to their bodies. Others were missing their tails entirely.

"Happy birthday," Party Waffle said to me.

I wanted to tell Party Waffle to never wish me a happy birthday. I don't like my birthday. But if he asked why, I would have to think of something to tell him – because there's no way his little waffle brain would be able to comprehend the truth – and that sounded like more work than just playing along.

So I played along.

"Happy birthday to you, too, Party Waffle."

Party Waffle looked at Brijit to wish her a happy birthday, but she glared at him. He thought better of it and looked away.

"You don't have to be so mean to him," I told her, softly, where Party Waffle wouldn't hear.

"He's a pest," she said.

"Hey, I don't even like my birthday but I'm playing along. Party Waffle's just having fun. You're the one being a buzzkill."

She huffed once. "We've been here for days and days and I'm still no closer to finding my husband." She looked up at the sky. "At least I think it's been days. This place makes no sense. Two suns? Whoever heard of two suns?"

"I dunno, dude."

At night, all the candles of the Birthday Cake Kingdom light themselves, which was really convenient. They cast weird flickering shadows, but at least gave us enough light to travel by.

Party Waffle grew tired and rode on my shoulders. We walked all night long, however long that really was, and the two suns came up in the morning.

The capital city of the Birthday Cake Kingdom came into view just around daybreak. At first I didn't realize it was the Birthday Cake Kingdom because the city was made of giant candles and when I saw the candles I thought it was just a forest of trees. But Party Waffle pointed at it and told us it was the capital.

It was a sprawling city with thousands and thousands of skyscraper-candles. As we traveled closer, I could see that the city stretched off in all directions for miles and miles. This was going to be a major metropolis, compared to any of the other kingdoms we'd visited before.

2

Party Waffle wasn't lying when he said every day was everyone's birthday in the Birthday Cake Kingdom. We walked into the city limits through an open, unattended gate of red velvet cake. There were no guards to stop us or ask us any questions.

"The guards have the day off for their birthday," Party Waffle told us. "No one works on their birthday."

And that was true. Inside the city, the citizens all wore birthday hats and carried around birthday gifts. They would exchange those gifts to one another, seemingly at random. "Happy Birthday" was the standard greeting.

An old grandpa-looking dude came up to the three of us almost right away. He had a mailbag filled with gifts. He reached inside and handed me one. It was about the size of a book.

"Happy birthday," he said to me.

"Happy birthday, gramps," I said.

He handed a gift down to Party Waffle.

"Happy birthday, waffle," the old man said.

Party Waffle clapped his hands. "Happy, happy birthday, from Applebee's to you. We wish it was our birthday, so we could party, too!"

The old man gave Party Waffle an impressed look, then moved to hand a gift to Brijit.

"Happy birthday," he said to her.

I looked at Brijit. She looked at me, then swiped the present away from the old man. Unhappy, she replied, "Happy Birthday."

The old man walked away. Brijit looked at her gift.

"Do we open them?" she asked.

I was already tearing into the paper on mine. So was Party Waffle.

"He gave them to us," I said.

I got a package of water balloons. I looked down to see what Party Waffle got and – fuck me – it was a goddam harmonica.

"Party Waffle, before you-"

Too late. He stuck it in his mouth and breathed into it. He wasn't playing any songs, he just breathed in and breathed out. FWEEE-FWOOO. FWEEE-FWOO. FWEEE-FWOO.

Brijit shot me a look and said, "He cannot have that thing."

"I got it, man," I told her. "Believe me, I'm on your side on this one." I turned my attention down to him. "Party Waffle." He kept blowing into it. "Party Waffle." He kept going. "Party Waffle!" He stopped and looked up at me. "Do you want to know another birthday custom from my world?"

"*Do I?*" he said.

"It's called tradesies," I said. "When you're really good friends, you trade gifts." I offered him my balloons. "Tradesies."

He held out his harmonica. I took it and gave him the balloons.

"Happy birthday," he said.

"Happy birthday."

Brijit unwrapped her square gift and looked inside the box.

"What'd you get?" I asked her.

"This." She took out an orange frisbee. "It's a thing."

"It's a frisbee," I said. "You throw it."

She couldn't take her eyes off it. "Why?"

"It's fun."

"It doesn't look fun."

Party Waffle held up his package of balloons to her. "Tradesies."

"Yes, tradesies," Brijit said. She traded the frisbee for the balloons. "At least I know what these things are supposed to be."

The Birthday Cake Kingdom looked very Dutch inspired. The houses were all pastel colors and built in that very north

European sort of way. No one worked in the Birthday Cake Kingdom, so I have no clue how they got anything done. We passed by a woodworking shop, closed. We saw a row of clothing stores, closed. There was a cute little post office with a chocolate mailbox out front, closed.

It didn't seem like a sustainable way to run a community, but everyone seemed to be getting along just fine. None of them were starving. All the homes were in good shape. The people all seemed happy.

In fact, it was almost creepy how perfect everything was. If Earth culture had taught me anything, it's that when you find some perfect happy community like this, there's some underground evil at work or something. But, here, I just didn't think that was the case.

Everything here was just... perfect.

We exchanged hundreds of "happy birthdays" with the locals as Party Waffle led us towards the city center. That was where the candles were tallest, like – no exaggeration – they were as tall as the Empire State Building back home and there were hundreds of them. A handful of them were decorated with these huge banners that read *HAPPY BIRTHDAY, WHIPP* or *HAPPY BIRTHDAY, GIFTY*.

A parade blocked our forward progress. And when I say parade, I mean a full on Macy's Day parade with decorated floats and multiple marching bands and giant inflatable characters being towed along by a dozen people holding ropes. We arrived just in time to see a marching band of horns and drums and clarinets. After the band came a big wooden stagecoach pulled by a dozen multicolored balloonicorns. The happy people inside the coach leaned out of the windows and threw tiny gifts into the crowd.

"Happy birthday!" the people on the stagecoach shouted.

"Happy birthday!" everyone shouted back.

But I was looking around and thinking, like, who's washing the windows? Who's taking out the trash? Who's making more *wrapping paper*? Everyone is having a good time, sure, but shouldn't someone be doing some work?

Now, look, I'm not trying to shit on anyone's good time and these people looked legitimately happy. Good for them, they don't have to worry about death or disease and every day's your birthday. And maybe all the jobs and manual labor just magically takes care of itself.

But here's the thing. There's a god damn space cookie coming to obliterate this whole world and because these people are so god damn happy, they're not advancing as a society. Did any of them have the potential to become scientists? Well, we'll never know because every day is their birthday and they probably never went to school. What if everyday was Einstein's birthday? He would have never invented electricity or whatever. So the Birthday Cake Kingdom has no scientists, they have no flippin' space program, and now when space cookie hits the pavement, there's going to be no more birthdays for anyone.

I don't know why I let it get to me all of a sudden, but I did.

For the first time since coming to the Muffincake Kingdom, I actually hated something.

3

Eventually the parade passed us entirely. But we had to cross the road quickly; another one was coming up right behind it. Me and Party Waffle and Brijit found Princess Birthday Cake's castle and stood at the base of a candle-skyscraper, a yellow one with white stripes looping all the way to the top. There were windows cut into the wax on every floor.

Right in front of us was an open entrance, two stories tall. There were two doors, but they were open.

There were no guards.

"Look at me!" I announced with my arms up in the air. "I'm just walking right into the front doors of the princess's castle! I'm a complete and total stranger to this world with completely unknown motives! Hope I'm not here to kill anyone!"

Brijit walked past me and muttered, "I know you're joking, but it wouldn't be uncharacteristic."

Party Waffle cartwheeled through the entrance. "Follow me!"

I wished the candle-castle had an elevator because we had to climb hundreds of stories on foot and that was just tedious. Eventually we reached the top floor which was one big bedroom decorated for Princess Birthday Cake's birthday. No guards posted there either. There were colorful balloons on the ceiling and shimmering foil streamers and gifts everywhere.

No sign of Princess Birthday Cake, though, except for the body-sized lump in the middle of her double-king-sized, four-post bed. That could have been her in there, huddled under fluffy white comforters.

"Uh, hello?" I called out. "Princess Birthday Cake?"

I heard a noise from under the blankets. I gave the lump a shake.

"Hey," I said. "You in there? You sleeping?"

The princess muttered, "Go away."

I looked at Brijit. She looked at me. I looked at Party Waffle. He looked at me and danced silently. I turned back to the bed.

"Hey, I have a message from your sister," I told Birthday Cake. "It's kind of important."

"I don't want to talk to anyone right now."

"You... uh..." I had no idea what was going on. "You okay in there?"

Sharply, she said, "No."

Did we need to stay? Did we need to go? I'm not good at making those kinds of decisions. I grabbed the blankets and slowly pulled them back.

Princess Wedding Cake was there in the middle of the bed, huddled up in the fetal position, clutching tight to a pillow. Her dress was pure white and matched her sheets and blankets. That came in stark contrast to her raven black hair that looked just as short as mine. There was a crown in bed with her – a tiara that read HAPPY BIRTHDAY – which had fallen off her head.

She buried her face in her pillow and said, "Go away."

"I'm Penelope Salvo," I said. "Ever heard of me?"

She didn't have anything to say to that. She looked up from the pillow. She had obviously been crying. Black mascara was smudged all around her eyes. Her face was flushed.

"You're Penelope Salvo?" she asked in a sad tone.

"Yeah."

She looked me up and down. "I thought you'd be taller."

"Yeah, well..." People say that to me a lot. "Are you doing okay?"

"No, I am not."

"What's wrong?"

"I'm sad."

"Sad why?"

Her face frowned hard and I knew she was seconds away from bawling her eyes out. "I don't know!" she cried and then collapsed back into her pillow.

"Damn," I said. I looked at Brijit and whispered the word, "Depression."

"Oh."

232

There was a balcony carved into the candle walls that overlooked the whole of the Birthday Cake Kingdom. While Princess Birthday Cake cried it out, I went over to the balcony to think. Down below were block parties full of birthday-goers, singing and dancing and exchanging gifts. Happy birthday, happy birthday, happy birthday.

And I got even more upset.

See, here's another perfect scenario in which it would be helpful to have a fucking *doctor*. Or a *therapist*. Or fucking *something*. Something. You have a girl up here who is racked with, I don't know, crippling depression and her "perfect" society has exactly zero solutions for her.

Even if this world did somehow have a therapist who could help her, they would have the day off because today's their fucking birthday.

And, what? Now it's up to me to fix her? You can't fix depression in an hour. I'm not convinced you can fix depression like that at all. I don't have a degree in psychology. All I have are my stupid little pep talks that, more often than not, don't help at all or just make things worse.

And I couldn't rely on Brijit for help. She had all the compassion of a bartender at closing time. And Party Waffle? Well, I supposed there was a chance he might cheer her up.

I came back over to her bed. "Princess, do you want to meet my friend Party Waffle?"

"No."

"He likes to party," I said. "Go on, Party Waffle. Show her."

"Ooh, yeah!" Party Waffle looked around, frantically searching for something to party with. He decided on a small birthday gift and rubbed his butt on it. "Get up or get down! It's totally your decision!"

Princess Birthday Cake didn't move. Party Waffle didn't stop dancing. Brijit took a drink from her rum and gave me a look that said, "What now?"

I sat on the edge of the bed. What could I say to the princess? I couldn't bring myself to tell her the bad news about space cookie. If she was this depressed over nothing, space cookie would really mess with her head. So I was at a loss.

"I'm sorry you're sad," I told her. "Is there anything I can do to help?"

"I don't think so," she said.

"I'm going to see your sisters soon. Coffeecake and Wedding Cake. Do you want me to, I don't know, relay them a message or something?"

"I don't have anything to say. Don't tell them you saw me like this. I don't want them to worry."

"They'll probably be concerned. They'll probably want to know."

"Don't tell them."

"Okay," I said. "I won't."

"Thank you."

I sighed. "But you're going to have to talk to your sisters soon though. I think Pancake wants to get all six of you together to talk about some... leadership stuff."

"I don't want to do that."

"Uh, okay."

Well, I tried nothing and I was all out of ideas.

I felt guilty leaving Birthday Cake in that kind of shape, but what else could we do? I offered to get her a birthday gift, or a slice of birthday cake, or take her on a walk, but she didn't want any of those things.

So I guessed that was it.

Brijit sighed, then magically tucked her cigar and bottle into her wedding dress. "Princess Birthday Cake, sit up."

"Why?" she asked with her face stuffed in her pillow.

"Because I said so."

"Who are you?"

"Madam Brijit," she said. "Voodoo loa of love and death."

"Never heard of you," Birthday Cake grumbled.

"Princess Birthday Cake, Sit up. This is not a request."

Birthday Cake sat up and glared at Brijit. "What?"

"Come here," Brijit said.

"What?"

"Come. Here."

Birthday Cake had already caved in to her previous demand, so she went with it. In a huff, she made her way out of bed and stood in front of Brijit.

She looked sad and unhappy. "What?"

Brijit leaned forward, put her arms around Princess Birthday Cake and gave her a hug.

I was at a loss for words.

Party Waffle's mouth hung open.

Princess Birthday Cake didn't hug back. Not at first. But then she did.

"It's okay to be sad," Brijit said with her face draped over Birthday Cake's shoulder.

"I know," Birthday Cake said.

"You won't be sad for forever," Brijit said.

"I know."

They didn't say much more after that, but Brijit didn't let go.

"I will hug you for as long as you want," Brijit said.

Birthday Cake sniffled. "Just a little longer."

4

Maybe it was Brijit's power over love, or maybe it was just some honest compassion, but Birthday Cake seemed a little better after that. She stayed upright. She sniffled as she wiped her face clean of smeared makeup. She even tried to smile.

"I must look terrible," she said with a little laugh.

"You look fine," I said.

Party Waffle looked up at her and said, "Happy birthday."

"Happy birthday to you, too, little waffle," she said.

Party Waffle clapped his hands. "Happy, happy birthday, from Applebee's to you!"

"Party Waffle," I said. He looked at me. "Not now."

"I'm so sorry you had to see me like this," Birthday Cake said to us. "I've just been really sad lately about everything and I missed all my friends birthday parties yesterday so I felt even worse and since I've been crying in bed, I missed their birthday parties today and I'm just super stressed out and everyone's mad at me, I'm sure, because I'm such a flake when it comes to plans but sometimes I just randomly get sad and-"

"Hey," I said. "Hey, dude, it's cool. You don't have to explain anything to us. We're just glad you're okay."

"Maybe not okay," Birthday Cake said. "But I'm better than before." She turned to Brijit. "Thank you."

"Eh. It's nothing." Brijit sloshed her bottle out of her wedding dress and shot me a dirty look. "*Anyone* could have done it."

This bitch.

Party Waffle ran up to Birthday Cake and threw his arms around her calf, giving her leg a tight hug.

"Happy birthday!" he shouted as loud as he could.

235

"Happy birthday," she said.

I said, "Look, Birthday Cake, there's some important stuff you need to talk over with your sisters. Mostly Pancake. I don't know if you send messengers back and forth or if you ever go visit, but you need to talk to her sooner rather than later."

"Okay," Birthday Cake said. "Talk to her about what?"

"I'd rather you hear it from Pancake," I said. "It's just going to be way easier that way."

"Is it bad news?" she asked.

"Maybe," I said. "Possibly."

"Oh, no. Bad news?"

See, this is why I didn't want to say anything. The poor girl was already dealing with a lot and space cookie was just going to amp everything up. So my options were, one, tell her the truth and really send her into depression, or two, just keep my mouth shut and let her imagination run wild with all the possible bad things it could be or, three, lie to her and spare her feelings.

Decisions, decisions.

"It might be bad news," I said. "But either way, I'm not going to leave here until I help fix it."

Brijit stepped forward. "What!?"

I put a hand up to Brijit. "Just... just hang on."

"We've been here for weeks!" Brijit shouted. "I have a husband to find! Which, by the way-" She turned to Birthday Cake. "-Have you seen a Voodoo loa? About this tall? Smokes a cigar? Sometimes walks on the walls?"

Birthday Cake shook her head no. "No."

Brijit turned back to me. "We are not staying here just to watch space cookie destroy this world."

Birthday Cake looked at Brijit. "What?"

I snapped, "Brijit!"

"Unacceptable." Brijit wasn't listening. She was just going on a rant now. "You dragged me so deep into these dimensions that I don't even know how we're supposed to get back home! And now you want to stay here and die with these people?"

Birthday Cake nervously fiddled with the buttons on her princess gown. "Die?"

Party Waffle looked up at me. "What is die?"

"Brijit!" I said. "Shut *up!*"

"We're leaving," Brijit said. She grabbed my Athena arm to read the numbers herself. She pointed in the same direction as Athena's arrow. "6,001 kilometers that way and we're dust."

I wanted to say "we can't just let these people die," but that was the wrong thing to say in such mixed company. I didn't want to scare Birthday Cake and Party Waffle. I grit my teeth and said:

"Can we talk about this later?"

"No," Brijit said. "We can talk about this right goddam now. Do you have an actual goal? Or are you just running around looking for ways to be philanthropic!?"

Birthday Cake looked at the two of us and said, "Please, don't fight."

"God *dammit*, Brijit." I had to go for my pocket dictionary. The pages were stained blue and it had seen better days, but it was at least still legible.

Philanthropic - adj. Concerns for human welfare, socially or financially.

I said, "I don't see what's so wrong about helping people. It's not a big deal. We'll leave on time. We'll leave as soon as we find a way out. I'll solve the other problem before then."

"Promise." Brijit spit in her hand and reached out. "Space cookie or not, we leave as soon as we find the way out."

I hated to do it – I was potentially dooming the Muffincake Kingdom to total disaster – but Brijit made sense.

I spit in my hand and shook, sealing the deal.

Birthday Cake asked, "Did you say we're all going to die?"

Party Waffle pulled on my socks to get my attention. "What is die?"

"Party Waffle, go dance on the balcony," I said. He ran off. "Birthday Cake, no one's dying. Not as far as we know. There is *potentially* a problem that *might* mean everyone in the Muffincake Kingdom will need to move someplace else. But no one is going to die."

"What's the problem?" she asked.

"Space cookie," Brijit said.

"It's a big cookie chunk way up in the sky," I told her. "Past the clouds."

"Higher than the balloons?' she asked.

"Way higher than the balloons," I said. "And when it lands, it's going to break stuff. So you and your sisters just need to figure out where to go... *if* that happens."

"Oh." Birthday Cake watched my face for a moment, then reached up and put her hands over her eyes.

237

I moved aside and pulled Brijit with me to give Birthday Cake space to pray.

She paced in circles.

"Hey Butter Pad? Sugar Cube? It's Princess Birthday Cake. I hate to bother you. I know you guys probably think I'm a burden and I'm pretty sure I am and I know I ask you guys for help all the time, but this time it's not just about my stupid sadness. This time there's a thing in the sky. It's a..." She peeked out at us.

Brijit said, "Space cookie."

Birthday Cake went back to praying. "Space cookie. And it's going to make us all die. I don't care if I die, but I don't want anyone else to die. If you just have it kill me, would that be okay? I don't mind. Not if it means everyone else gets to live. I just don't want anyone to be mad at me. And I hope you're not mad at me for asking. I'm sorry. I'm sorry I went on so long. I'm sorry. If you want to help me, you can. I'll leave you alone now. I'm sorry. Goodbye."

Listening to her go on like that made me feel bad for her. I know what it's like to have a god that doesn't help you when you really need it.

Birthday Cake took her hands away and gave me a shrug. "Maybe that'll help? I dunno. I bother Butter Pad and Sugar Cube all the time. I don't think they listen to me anymore."

"They listen to you," I said. "They like you very much."

She frowned. "I doubt that."

"No," I said. "They told me."

Her face lit up. "They told you? You actually saw them?"

"I did," I said. "I've been traveling through all sorts of different worlds and I've been to a lot of places. I saw Butter Pad and Sugar Cube myself and they specifically said they listen to you every time you call them. And they also said they like you. They said every time you're sad, they watch over you to cheer you up."

Birthday Cake's eyes filled with tears. One dripped down her cheek. "They said that?"

I nodded. "Every word."

5

Two things were possible when it came to the citizens of the Birthday Cake Kingdom. One, they had no idea that their princess struggled with depression. Or two, they knew and no

238

one cared enough to do anything about it.

If it was possibility number two, that would have been fucked up. Everyone was so wrapped up in themselves for their birthday. And since every day is everyone's birthday, they're never going to think about anyone else.

If it was possibility one where they just didn't know, it was still kind of fucked up. Don't they notice that their princess isn't around? When the end of the parade comes and there's no royalty there waving at her adoring subjects, why don't they stop and wonder, "huh, where is she?" Why don't they go looking for her and find her in bed and get her some help.

Because it's everyone's birthday.

I was getting real sick of the Birthday Cake Kingdom.

Look, I get it. The Muffincake Kingdom is weird in its own way. There are two suns. Time works differently, if it works at all. Inanimate objects are alive. I mean, hell, I'd spent the last few weeks traveling on foot with a dancing waffle. But I couldn't make excuses for the Birthday Cake Kingdom. Their culture, their morality, was inexcusable.

We had to elbow our way through the crowded streets to make our way out of the city. Party Waffle rode on my shoulders so he wouldn't get trampled. This lady came up to us and tried to give us gifts.

"I'm good," I said, pushing mine away.

The lady looked *real* confused.

"I'll take one," Brijit said.

"I want one!" Party Waffle shouted. "Gimmie, gimmie!"

So they took their gifts. The lady lowered her eyebrows at me and asked, "You're sure?"

"I don't want it," I said.

That got her to go away. We resumed pushing our way through the crowd.

Party Waffle asked Brijit, "What did you get?"

Brijit had torn open the paper and threw it on the ground. Who was going to pick that up? No clue. The janitors had the day off for their birthday. She opened an extra large shoebox and threw the lid on the ground. Yeah, sure, fuck it. If those people didn't care, why should we? Inside the box were a pair of bright yellow rain boots.

"Oh, wow," she said. She immediately kicked off her old, worn wedding flats.

"Tradesies?" Party Waffle asked her.

"Depends. What did you get?" Despite the potential trade, Brijit pulled one of the boots on.

"Markers!" he said. He held out a plastic pack of 10 brightly colored markers. "You use them to write or dance with."

"No deal," Brijit said.

Party Waffle popped open some of the markers and drew on the back of my neck. I didn't mind. It was just marker and he was going to draw on something.

After the rain boots, it occurred to Brijit that she could get endless stuff just by asking for it. That's when she started stopping random people and demanding gifts because it was her birthday.

Everyone gave her one.

She got a box of checkers which she tucked under her arm. Someone else gave her a birdcage with no bird in it, so she carried that around in her cigar hand. Another person gave her a necktie that she tossed over her shoulder. Then came the blank journal (which she stored in the birdcage), the stuffed bear (that she tucked under her arm with the checkers), and a brand new stew pot.

"Carry this for me," she said to me, holding out the pot.

"Look at all this junk," I said. "You need to stop. You have plenty enough already."

"It's all free," she said. "These rubes are just giving it away."

"What are you going to do with any of this stuff, you fucking hoarder? A birdcage? Seriously? You need a birdcage?"

She looked in it and said, "I use it to carry the journal."

I took the stew pot from her. "And this? You need this?"

"For gumbo," she said. "I'll use it when I get home."

"You don't already have a pot to make gumbo?"

"I do," she said. "And now I have another one."

She stopped another random person and demanded a gift. They gave it to her. Unbelievable. Brijit was now the proud owner of a mens extra-large swimsuit that read HAPPY BIRTHDAY right across the ass.

"You need that?" I said. "You need a fat man's swimsuit?"

"Maybe," she said. She stopped so she could put the swimsuit inside the birdcage, but she couldn't really use her arms, not while trying to keep the checkers and the stuffed bear tucked under her elbow. She tried to balance the birdcage with her knee, but dropped her package of water balloons. The necktie slipped off her shoulder.

I watched her drop all her stuff. "You're all over the map."

When she leaned forward to pick up her water balloons, her rum bottle rolled out of her dress and clinked on the stone roads.

I rolled my eyes.

She was really struggling. She said, "I've just got to... here. Here. I'll set this down." She put down the birdcage. "Here. Okay, now this goes in here." She put the swimsuit in the birdcage. She picked up her rum bottle and the checker box slipped loose from her arm. The box opened and checkers spilled everywhere. "Shit."

I said, "Oh my god."

She set everything on the ground and got on her knees to scoop up the checkers. "Fucking help me."

"I fucking helped you when I told you to stop."

Party Waffle climbed down off my shoulders and landed on the ground next to Brijit. I thought he was going to help her pick up the checkers. I was wrong. He just started dancing right in front of her.

"Do the Jelly Bones!" he shouted, waving his arms all around, wobbling his legs and dancing right through her checkers. "Oh yeah! Jelly 'em up!"

Brijit picked up the checker pieces from between Party Waffle's moving feet. "Move it, food monster! You're right in my goddam way!"

Chapter 13

1

We crossed out of the Birthday Cake Kingdom and into one of my most anticipated destinations: The Wedding Cake Kingdom.

I never got to see Princess Parcel in her true form of Princess Wedding Cake. And I never saw Princess Cardboard as Princess Coffeecake. It was going to be a real trip to see them again. Princess Parcel was a colossal drunk and as we entered the Wedding Cake Kingdom I could start to see why. The rivers and lakes were gold in color and when we crossed our first stream I realized they were made of champagne. Of course the water would be champagne in the Wedding Cake Kingdom. I scooped some up in my hands and slurped it down. It was bubbly and sweet-tasting.

"Is it good?" Brijit asked.

I shrugged. "If you like champagne."

Once in junior year, Ilana Rittenberg took me to her cousins wedding, who I also knew from around the way. Jewish weddings can get a little crazy and after a while the adults got drunk and didn't keep a very close eye on us. When no one was looking, Ilana swiped two bottles of champagne and we went to go drink them in the temple parking lot.

We got O-bliterated. That was my only experience with champagne, so I wouldn't know good champagne from bad champagne.

Brijit knelt down at the riverbank and dunked her cupped hands into the river, too. She put them to her lips and drank some.

"What do you think?" I asked her.

"It's different," she said. "I think I like it."

"Me next!" Party Waffle shouted. He jumped off my shoulders and splashed his flat waffle face right into the stream. I could hear him gulping.

"Don't drink too much," I said.

"Don't let him get drunk," Brijit said.

Party Waffle kept gulping.

Brijit said, "Stop him!"

"Okay, dude," I said. "That's enough."

I grabbed his head and pulled him out of the stream. I turned him to face me. He licked his lips and said, "Delicious."

"You shouldn't drink that much," I told him.

"Why not?" he asked.

"You'll get drunk," I said.

"What is drunk?"

"It's when you can't walk straight and you can't talk right and you forget everything."

Party Waffle pointed at Brijit. "Like Bat Face."

"Exactly," I said. "Like Bat Face."

Most everything in the Wedding Cake Kingdom was white. The ground was white wedding cake. The mountains were three or four or five-tiered wedding cakes that rose high into the atmosphere, each topped with those little wedding figurines. The trees were flutes of champagne and wine. Bushes of silver tinsel sprouted pink and blue and yellow buttermint candies.

When the breeze came, it didn't blow like wind. It sounded faintly like soft, romantic dance floor music.

The birds of the Wedding Cake Kingdom were black ravens and they wore tiny tuxedos. Some of them had top hats. Some of them wore little bird monocles. White rabbits bounced around, each one wearing a rabbit-sized wedding veil.

Strangest thing of all were the doves. The doves could talk, but they said the strangest things. We only found this out after several hours of walking. This one dove landed on the rim of a champagne glass and looked down at us. At first I thought it was just like a regular bird, but then it flapped its wings and said:

"Okay, everybody! Let's get the bridesmaids out on the dance floor!"

"Whoa," I said. "You talk."

Party Waffle looked around and said, "Dance floor?"

The dove said, "Lovey is going to toss that bouquet so let's get all the single ladies lined up behind her!"

"I don't think it's listening to you," Brijit said.

I looked at the dove. "Are you listening to me?"

It said, "It's time for the dollar dance! Come on everybody, we want Casanova and Juliet to have a good time in Coo-Coo Bananas, don't we? Let's tip them a dollar for a dance!"

Then the dove flew away. That was it.

An hour or so later we passed by this tall wine glass that had a whole flock of doves up there. They were all talking at once and I could only make out a few things they were all saying.

"...and then after the father daughter dance we're going to..."

"...the buffet line starts back there by the bar and goes..."

"...getting a speech from the best man before anyone..."

Brijit asked me, "What are they talking about?"

"They're like wedding DJ birds or something," I said.

"They're annoying," she said.

"Yeah, I'm not going to argue with you on that one."

With rivers and lakes and streams of champagne, of course Princess Wedding Cake would be drunk all the time. And I bet in this magical world, she could get as drunk as she wanted and never get hung over. In New York City, Princess Parcel consumed a remarkable amount of alcohol and was constantly drunk, but she never got alcohol poisoning and died. She was just in a perpetual state of being trashed.

"You're going to love Princess Wedding Cake," I told Brijit. "You two have a lot in common."

"Hm." Brijit took a drink of rum. "I've met her once. She tried to steal Semedi away from me. She's the reason I want to destroy this place."

"She didn't try to steal Semedi away from you," I said. "Look, I know we don't always see eye to eye, but let me tell you, from my personal experience, Semedi is the one who flirts with girls and tries to marry them. He did the same thing to me. He wanted to marry me and I kept telling him no, but he just kept bugging me about it."

Brijit crossed her arms and kept her eyes dead ahead. She didn't argue. Maybe deep down she knew I was right. She just didn't want to admit it.

I went on. "I'm not even saying it's his fault. He's a Voodoo spirit of love, too. It's just in him. He just falls in love really easy."

Brijit didn't look at me, but said, "We've been seeing Baron Kriminel once a week, talking about our marriage. We've been very honest with each other. And you're exactly right. Everything you just said, Semedi said that about himself at the meetings. He's made a lot of changes. He's doing so much better."

"Well, that's good," I said. "I can't imagine any two people better suited for one another than you and Semedi."

"Thank you," she said.

"You're welcome."

2

The capital city of the Wedding Cake Kingdom was built out of bright white ivory. Silver sashes swept from one building to the next like power lines, each one saying things like CONGRATULATIONS SWEETHEART AND BABE. Another one said A NEW LIFE TOGETHER. The doors of every house and shop had flower arrangements out front as well as wedding gifts wrapped in white and silver and gold.

We walked into the city and passed every kind of store you'd need to plan a wedding: bridal shops with wedding gowns in the window, colorful flower shops, and tons and tons of bakeries with signs that read TRY OUR WEDDING CAKES or BEST WEDDING CAKES IN TOWN. There were tuxedo shops and caterers and travel agencies that advertised discount trips to the Ice Cream Cake Kingdom for all newlyweds.

Everything in the city was very organized and precise. The buildings were perfect white squares. The roads were meticulously arranged in a grid. And the citizens were dressed so nice, either in tuxedos or wedding gowns or colorful bridesmaids dresses.

Standing above the ivory buildings were bell towers and the bells would ring from time to time, almost certainly celebrating whatever wedding just got finished.

"Do you want to marry me?" Party Waffle asked me.

"No, thank you," I said.

He turned to Brijit. "Do *you* want to marry me?"

She said, "I'm already married."

"Oh," Party Waffle said. "Congrakkalashuns."

I couldn't tell if everyone in the Wedding Cake Kingdom was already married or not. I saw one bride walking around alone, but she had a bouquet and a huge smile on her face, so maybe she was on her way to her ceremony. Then there would be a group of five men in suits standing in a circle, smoking cigarettes. Ah, the groomsmen taking a break from the reception dance floor.

I recognized people from all the other kingdoms. There were a couple of people from the Pancake Kingdom wearing the white aprons of their people. They probably traveled here to get married. And I saw a group of parka-ed people from the Ice Cream Cake Kingdom funneling into a nearby chapel.

The Chapel of Butter Pad, to be precise.

We passed by a gleaming jewelry story that had all manner of diamond rings in the front window. I took a moment to peer inside. There were a bunch of men and women in there trying on rings, searching for the perfect one.

"This place has a certain charm about it," Brijit said.

I said, "We should get you a new wedding gown since we're here."

"What's wrong with the one I've got?" she asked.

"Dude, seriously? We've been here for weeks. You've been soaked in chocolate and milkshakes and two pints of my blood. Your dress looks like hot garbage."

She looked down at her wrecked dress. "What? This?"

She closed her eyes and took a moment to focus. Just like that, her dress was restored to showroom perfection. It was as white as anything on display at the bridal shops. Her torn up sleeves and hems turned into flawless and delicate lace patterns.

Party Waffle's eyes went wide and he took a step back. "Wowie zowie!"

Brijit opened her eyes. "There. Happy?"

"You could do that this whole time?" I asked.

"Yes."

"Well, why didn't you?"

"Didn't occur to me." She used her two cigar fingers to tap me on the chest. "I'm not attached to material things."

"Not attached to material things?" I repeated. "Do you not remember the Birthday Cake Kingdom? You couldn't even carry all the things you took."

"They were being generous," she said. "It would have been rude to decline."

"You are really something."

"Thank you."

After walking a couple more blocks, I decided to interrupt a group of chatting bridesmaids to ask them for directions. They were all dressed in the same yellow dresses and had fantastic makeup and nails.

I, however, was dressed in a t-shirt and shorts and I had on different color baseball socks. I did not look like I was going to a wedding. I was definitely from out of town.

"Hey, do you ladies know where I could find Princess Wedding Cake?"

All five of them in unison answered without thinking. "The Heart Gallery."

"It's a reception hall," one of them said. "In the Celebration District."

"Where's that?" I asked.

And thanks to the grid work layout of the city, the directions were simple. Eleven blocks that way, twenty-one blocks that way. Bing, bang, boom. Super easy.

So we were off again. We passed by so many churches for Butter Pad or Sugar Cube. Brides and grooms fled out the church doors, showered in rice thrown by the rest of the wedding party. Ravens in tuxedos were in attendance, too, along with the white rabbits wearing wedding veils.

More churches, more rice throwing. There were weddings everywhere. One thing I liked about the Wedding Cake Kingdom was that people were actually working. Apparently you didn't get married every day in the Wedding Cake Kingdom, so there were plenty of people to work in the jewelry stores and the bridal shops and the bakeries.

Closer to the city center sat Princess Wedding Cake's castle. If Butter Pad and Sugar Cube had churches all around town, and if the occasional cathedral that made those churches look small, then her castle was the freaking Vatican. It was a sprawling fairytale castle that had a lot of "church" elements going on: lots of pointy towers, lots of ringing wedding bells, stuff like that.

And just a few blocks before the castle walls, we came to the "Celebration District" with all the reception halls and bars and outdoor gardens. Each one of them was packed with a wedding reception, filled with catered food and gift tables and tons of best men and bridesmaids and ravens and rabbits.

And, of course, a group of doves crowded around the DJ equipment going on about "Let's get Je Taime and Romeo out here on the dance floor for their first dance as Mister and Misses Goodheart!"

3

Party Waffle was going to explode if he didn't get into one of these wedding receptions and soon. We could hear music blast out of each different event space – dance music or disco or slow dancing – the tell-tale sounds of partying. Party Waffle did his best to keep himself under control, but he was losing it. He reminded me of a little kid who needed to go pee, the way he was shuffling his feet back and forth and making anxious noises.

Sometimes he would start to wander just *slightly* away from me and Brijit and I would have to use my mom voice and say, "Party Waffle..." and he would straighten up.

But then we found the Heart Gallery, a modest building with glass walls that let you see right inside. Whatever reception we were about to crash was in full-swing. People walked around with plates of wedding cake and flutes of champagne. There were at least a hundred people in there (and another dozen or so ravens and rabbits) so it made it difficult to spot Wedding Cake.

"Come on," I said as I headed to the entrance. "Let's go."

I opened the glass door and we walked in. Party Waffle looked up at me with cartoonishly sad eyes.

"Go ahead," I told him.

He was gone in a flash. He danced into the crowd and disappeared in their legs.

I looked around for Wedding Cake. Or, to be fair, I looked around for the bar knowing that if I found the bar, I would find Wedding Cake. Sure as shit, the bar was in the back corner and there was Princess Parcel, dressed in a white, backless wedding gown and full length white gloves that came up past her elbows.

She leaned cock-eyed at the bar, undoubtedly drunk. Her brown hair was a mess and her tiara was on backwards.

"Come on!" I headed for the bar. Brijit followed me, but not fast enough. "Come on!"

Whatever. Brijit wasn't going anywhere. She'd be around. I wasn't going to wait on her slow ass. I bobbed and weaved through the wandering party guests that got in my way.

248

The bar was the real deal; wooden table top, bar stools, and a well-lit stock of liquor bottles. There was a trough of ice stocked with dozens and dozens of bottles of champagne. The bartender was some silver fox looking dude who was entertaining the princess at large. I came up and stood right behind Wedding Cake. She had no idea I was there. I was close enough to overhear her conversation with the bartender.

"Do you have any idea how much I pay for this shit?" Wedding Cake said, totally shitfaced. "D'any idea?"

"No, I know," the bartender said. "I know."

Wedding Cake had two empty champagne glasses in front of her. She clinked them both together. "Refills. Refills. I got a couple fallen soldiers here."

The bartender laughed politely, popped open a bottle of champagne and refilled her glasses to the brim. He looked up at me and Brijit.

"Can I get you ladies anything?" he asked.

"I'm good," Brijit said, swishing her magical bottle of rum in the air.

"I'll have whatever she's having," I said as I took a seat next to Wedding Cake. I turned so I was half pointed at her. I was also grinning like an idiot.

Wedding Cake looked up and gave me a passing glance. She took a drink of her champagne, then froze. She turned her head with the most bewildered look on her face. We made eye contact and I just kept smiling.

I laughed a little bit. "Hi."

"What the *fuck*!?" She spun in place and knocked over her two glasses of champagne with her elbow. They spilled across the bar, not that she cared. She jumped off her bar stool and repeated it. "What the fuck!?"

I said, "I know, right?"

"What the fuck!?" she said one more time, then threw her arms around me in the biggest hug I'd had in years. I hugged her back. She squeezed me tight and tried to swing me back and forth, but I was too heavy so I swung her around. She leaned back and held my face in her hands. "Is it really you?"

"It's really me!"

She stared at me, then shook her head. "What the fuck? How did you get here?"

"That's a long story," I said. "I've kind of been all over the place and then I ended up here."

"Well... how long are you staying?" she asked.

"Not long," I said. "I've got a lot of stuff going on right now, but I definitely wanted to pop in and say hey."

"Uh, yeah! I'm so glad you did! This is crazy."

"I know, right?"

"Does Coffeecake know you're here?"

"No, she's the only one of your sisters I haven't seen yet."

Wedding Cake got even more excited, as if that were possible. "You met my sisters!?"

"All of them," I said. "They're all awesome."

Her excitement faded. She did a skeptical "hmph" and said, "You just met them. Believe me, they can all be a pain."

"I bet," I said. "Speaking of pains, this here is my friend Madam Brijit."

Wedding Cake turned. Brijit sat on her bar stool facing us, manspreading and puffing on her cigar. She raised her bottle of rum at Wedding Cake. "Hey."

"You look weird," Wedding Cake said.

Brijit didn't react. "*You* look weird."

"Okay, okay, okay, okay, okay." I got between them. I could see that going south real fast. "Brijit is from the Guinee. She's a Voodoo spirit. She's looking for her husband."

"I'm sure you remember him," Brijit said with a snotty tone in her voice. "You were flirting with him a few years ago."

"That old Voodoo wizard?" Wedding Cake said. She looked disgusted. "That guy was terrible. He wanted to marry me."

Brijit jumped off her stool. "What you did was-"

I interrupted her. "Let's not get into all that. It's old news. No need to bring it up." I turned my attention to Wedding Cake. "See, Baron Semedi is missing and Brijit is looking for him. I don't suppose you've seen him."

"No," Wedding Cake said. "And I would remember if I had, no matter how black out drunk I got."

Brijit looked real disappointed. Defeated, almost. She took a long, four bubble pull from her rum.

"Hey." I gave her a pat on the shoulder. "Don't give up. We'll find him."

She hung her head. "I'm starting to worry."

"Well, don't. We'll think of something."

"Will we?" She looked up at me. "Just like how we'll think of something to fix..." She slowly mouthed the words *space cookie.*

"Look, look, look." I turned to Wedding Cake to see if she read Brijit's lips. No. No, she had her head tilted back, downing one of her replacement champagne glasses. I looked back at Brijit and used my hands to stress my point. "Look. Everything's going to work out somehow. Don't get all stressed out on me. If you get stressed out, it's going to stress me out and then we'll really get nothing done."

She said, "Kay."

"You sure? You going to be okay?"

She looked at the butt of her cigar. "I'll give it a shot."

"Here," Wedding Cake said. "You know what we need? Shots." She turned and slammed her open hand on the bar a couple times to get the bartender's attention, which was unnecessary because he was literally right there. "Chris! We need shots!"

The bartender said, "My name's Mark."

Wedding Cake stared at him, then slammed the bar again. "Shots! Shots! Shots! Shots!"

The patient bartender just smiled. "Okay, what are we shooting?"

Wedding Cake looked at Brijit. "What do you like?"

"Rum," Brijit said.

Wedding Cake waved a finger at her. "I know what that is, but we don't have it here."

"Then whiskey," Brijit said.

Wedding Cake replied, "We don't have that either."

"Vodka?"

Wedding Cake smiled and patted Brijit on the shoulder. "I like you, but no." She turned to the bartender. "Let's do Watermelon Slammers." She pointed at Brijit and then me. "Watermelon Slammers? Watermelon Slammers?"

I shrugged. "Sure."

"What is a Watermelon Slammer?" Brijit asked.

"You're going to love it," Wedding Cake said. "Trust me."

Mark lined up three shot glasses and poured various liquors into a metal shaker with ice. He shook it up and poured the bright red mixture into the three shot glasses.

Wedding Cake glared at him.

Mark said, "What?"

Wedding Cake looked at him, looked at the shot glasses, then looked back at him. "My friends want some, too."

Mark looked confused. "There's three right here."

Wedding Cake reached out and pulled all three shot glasses towards her. "These are mine."

4

Brijit didn't like the Watermelon Slammers. "Too sweet," she said. "Not spicy enough." Wedding Cake didn't seem to mind the criticism. She asked Brijit what she did like to drink and Brijit offered her the rum bottle with floating red peppers inside. Wedding Cake didn't hesitate to take the bottle and try it.

"Wedding Cake," I said, trying to warn her. "You might not want to-"

Wedding Cake lurched forward and sprayed the rum out of her mouth. She coughed and coughed and waved the bottle at Brijit to take it away.

"It's like drinking fire!" Wedding Cake said.

Brijit swiped the bottle back and took a quick swig. She laughed and said, "Yes, it is."

Seeing Wedding Cake was one of the best things to ever happen to me, but I knew we couldn't get caught up staying too long. We had a lot of other things we had to do. Wedding Cake didn't want me to leave and somehow kept finding ways to get us to stay. First she wanted us to meet the "happy couple" and that only seemed fair. So Wedding Cake led me and Brijit through the crowded dance floor to meet them.

There were a couple DJ doves working the DJ table. One of them saw Wedding Cake walking by and hopped up to the microphone. "Ladies and gentlemen, our esteemed guest of honor, Princess Wedding Cake!"

The crowd parted, formed a circle around the three of us and started an applause. Wedding Cake waved at her people, stumbled around drunk for a second, then caught her balance. After a few moments of adoration, Wedding Cake spotted the newlyweds and led us over to meet them. She took us right up to two ladies wearing matching wedding dresses.

"Penelope. Brijit." Wedding Cake said. "This is Joy and Gloria."

Joy and Gloria. Two brides.

"Oh, this is like a..." I trailed off. I pointed at the two of them. "You're..." I trailed off.

"We're what?" Joy asked.

"Well, you know, you're..."

252

"We're *what?*" Gloria asked, sincerely confused.

"You're... progressive."

Joy looked at Gloria. Gloria looked at Joy. They both looked back at me. Gloria said, "I don't follow you."

"Hey, never mind, not the point." I reached out to shake their hands. "Congratulations."

Handshakes all around. Me and Joy, Brijit and Gloria. Wedding Cake shook my hand for some reason. Handshake city. And after we'd met the bride and bride, it was time to go. But yet again Wedding Cake stalled up, insisting that we try a piece of Joy and Gloria's wedding cake. "One of the best in the kingdom," she told us. I couldn't eat food like that, so Brijit was the one who needed convincing.

Brijit shrugged. "I'll try some."

The wedding cake was on a nearby table along with plates of buttermints, a variety of mixed nuts, and a giant punchbowl with bright pink punch. Brijit ate a square piece of wedding cake with idle curiosity, lost in her own thoughts.

That gave me a moment to talk to Wedding Cake.

"Hey, you know what space is, right?" I asked her.

"Yeah, I know what space is," she said. "I'm not stupid."

"Okay, well, have you ever heard of an asteroid?"

"No."

"Or a meteor?"

"No."

"Or a comet?"

She took a drink of champagne. "Is this going somewhere?"

"There's a space cookie up in space," I said. "Pancake found it with her telescope. And I'm kind of concerned that it's coming this way."

"To the reception hall?" Wedding Cake asked.

"I mean, it might be bigger that that. A lot bigger. When you were on Earth, did you ever learn about dinosaurs?"

"No."

"Ugh. Okay. Just listen. There's this big rock coming this way from space and if it hits the Muffincake Kingdom, there is going to be a lot of death and destruction."

"Okay." She downed her whole champagne glass. "And?"

"Well, *and*... I think you and your sisters should do something about it."

Wedding Cake inspected her flawless silver fingernails. "Eh. That's more of a Pancake thing. She's the smart one."

I pointed two fingers at her. "I think that is the wrong attitude to have in this kind of situation."

"Oh, you do?" Wedding Cake swiped a champagne glass off of a passing waiter's tray. "And what kind of attitude should I have?"

"I don't know, someone that cares? Maybe act like a leader and keep your people safe."

"Penelope, I don't know if you've noticed this about me." She threw her arm around my shoulders and drunkenly pulled me close. "But I am selfish. And I am drunk."

"Yes, I can see that."

"Someone's going to fix it and it's not going to be me."

"Someone like Butter Pad and Sugar Cube?"

Wedding Cake scoffed. "Who told you about them?"

"All your other sisters have been praying to them."

Wedding Cake scoffed again. "Those idiots. Here's a secret, Penelope." She stuck her mouth right up against my ear and whispered, "Butter Pad and Sugar Cube aren't real."

I said, "I wondered."

"Yeah, well, now you know! It won't be them that saves us." She poked me in the chest. "Hey. You do it."

"Dude, believe me, I've been racking my brain trying to think of an idea and I got nothing. That cookie is in space and we're down here and that's a pretty big obstacle to overcome."

She shrugged. "Then we're doomed."

"You have the magic to leave this world," I told her. "You and your sisters escaped to Manhattan. You could do something like that. Evacuate the Muffincake Kingdom."

"Pfft. D'you have any idea how long that would take? Evacuate everyone? And where would we go? New York City? The place was crowded enough as it was."

"You haven't even tried anything and you're just giving up."

She swung her arms out wide. "I don't know what you want me to do, Penelope. I haven't seen you in two years and then you come and tell me my kingdom is doomed by a big space cookie. Okay. Great. Then you want me to do something about it, but you said yourself you can't think of anything to do. I don't know anything about space. I don't know anything about mass evacuations into a new dimension. I drink champagne twenty-four seven three-sixty-five, so excuse me for giving up, but believe it or not, this kind of problem isn't in my wheelhouse!"

I sighed. "You're right."

She took a sip of champagne. "Now if there's ever a tsunami of liquor coming to wipe us out, call me and we'll talk."

"I just..." I paused. "I want to help you. I don't want to lose you. You guys are my friends."

"Yeah." Wedding Cake gave me a pat on the back. "You're good people. Come on. Let's go do shots."

5

Me and Wedding Cake stood around by the bar drinking champagne. Five of the bridesmaids had kicked off their shoes and were line dancing to some song played by the DJ doves. They moved in perfect sync, stepping and kicking and tapping their feet together. Party Waffle came running out of the crowd, took his place at the end of the dance line and joined them. Unsurprisingly, he learned the dance moves after watching for just a few seconds and fit right in.

Brijit stood off by herself, mesmerized by the whole thing.

"We've got to go soon," I told Wedding Cake.

She said, "Yeah."

"Do you want to come with us? We're going to see Coffeecake."

"I think I'll stay here," she said. "I'm wasted. I'll just slow you down."

"Gotcha."

She set her glass down on the bar and gave me a big hug. I set my glass down and hugged her back. "It was so nice to see you again. Come back again sometime."

"I'll try."

"If the kingdom is still here, that is."

"Oh, come on. Don't talk like that."

We hugged it out for a minute. When we broke off, I could see Wedding Cake was crying. Her mascara was running.

"You okay?" I asked.

"I'm just drunk," she said. "And seeing you and thinking about dying and everything else. And it's been such a beautiful wedding. It's just everything."

"Here." I grabbed a cocktail napkin and handed it to her. "Clean yourself up. You got makeup all over your face."

Wedding Cake dabbed at her eyes. She did a pretty poor job of fixing her makeup. You could tell she'd been crying.

"How's that?" she asked me.

"It's... fine."

Convincing Brijit to leave wasn't going to be the hard part. She was having an okay time as best I could tell. The real challenge was going to be rounding up Party Waffle. He was going crazy out of the dance floor, whirling and twirling to some upbeat disco song.

I went over to get him.

"Party Waffle, come on," I said. "Time to go."

"One more song!" he shouted.

"No, not one more song. We already stayed way longer than we should have. Come on."

"Ten more songs!"

"No more songs," I said. "We're leaving. Let's go."

"No!" Party Waffle sprinted away from me.

Didn't see that coming.

"Party Waffle, goddammit, get back here!" I chased Party Waffle in circles around the dance floor. He made a mad dash for the food table, jumped up on top, and threw a handful of peanuts at me. "Party Waffle, what is your deal!?"

"Stay back!" he shouted. He armed himself with a handful of buttermints. "I don't want to hurt you, Pencil, but I will."

I stood in front of him. I didn't reach out for him. Not yet. I didn't want to spook him into running. At least in this position, he was standing still.

"Party Waffle, we need to go."

"But I'm partying!"

"I can see that. But Brijit and I are leaving and we need you to show us the way to Princess Coffeecake."

"Go without me!"

I crossed my arms. "You're being a brat."

Party Waffle said, "*You're* being a brat."

"That's it." I swiped my hand out and caught him before he could run. He swung his arms and kicked his legs and shouted for help. He was making a huge scene. People in the wedding reception gave us concerned looks. "It's okay," I said. "He's my waffle. He just doesn't want to go home. He's cranky."

Wedding Cake saw us to the front exit. She shared a hug with Brijit, which Brijit wasn't ready for, but Wedding Cake was plastered and would have hugged anyone. Then she hugged me one more time.

"I've missed you," she said.

"I missed you, too."

"You come back soon."

"I will."

"Tell my sister I said hi."

"Okay."

"Come back soon though."

"You already said that. I will."

"I love you, you know that, right?"

"I love you, too, man."

She hugged me in silence for a bit, then let go. She was crying again.

It was night by the time we left the Heart Gallery. Party Waffle was out like a light. He partied way too hard. I carried him in my arms. We usually needed him to lead the way, but the Wedding Cake Kingdom was laid out so well, so organized, that I was able to figure our way out of town on my own.

"Did you have a good time?" I asked Brijit.

"I suppose."

"Still worried about Semedi?"

"Yeah."

I didn't have any good advice to give her. I don't know what it's like to deal with a missing person case. I'm the type of person who just goes "hey, don't worry" and "I'm sure everything will be fine" and those things aren't very helpful. I wished I had something to say to cheer her up, but I didn't.

Chapter 14

1

Princess Cardboard – sorry, Princess *Coffeecake* – was my first real supernatural friend after I swallowed Impossible Red. We met when she delivered a letter from the Westland Corporation to me and we were fast friends after that. She was a bit of an airhead, but super nice.

Brijit and me and a sleeping Party Waffle traveled all night and reached the Coffeecake Kingdom just around double-sunrise. The morning air smelled like East Village coffee shops: roasted espresso, microwaved scones, steamed milk. The smell was amazing, but just came as another reminder that I would never be able to eat or drink regular food again.

The ground of the Coffeecake Kingdom was all hardwood floors, like what you'd expect from a locally-owned and operated coffee shop. Even still, there were hills and deep river banks and rising slopes, they were just made of hardwood flooring. There was grass in places, confined to acre-sized squares in the floor.

Off in the distance wandered these giant metal elephant-looking things. Princess Cardboard told me about them once. They're called, like, buffaroasters or roaster-phants or something. I just know their name had something to do with roasters because they roast coffee beans inside their bodies. She described them as a kind of metallic elephant and their trunks are the cranks used to rotate their cylindrical torsos.

The roaster-phants wandered in herds and used their long handle-trunks to pick and eat coffee beans off of the trees that grew out of the hardwood ground. Another herd of them were further out, hanging out near the bank of a milk river.

"Woo, yeah, espresso!" Party Waffle shouted. He strutted across the hardwood and pointed at all the trees. "Dark roast, French roast, breakfast roast, premium roast, roast beef!"

I checked Athena.

22 kilometers.

God. Had we really walked thousands of kilometers? And how long did that take us? It felt like weeks. Maybe a month.

I looked up to where space cookie was supposed to be. Even in the morning daylight of two suns, space cookie twinkled like a star in the blue sky.

Not good. Not good at all.

Party Waffle led us to a sign post with three different names pointing in three different directions.

North, dead ahead, was HAZELNUT COUNTRY.

East was MOCHA ACRES.

West was LAND OF SCONES.

Party Waffle stared up at the sign, silently swaying his hips back and forth.

"Well?" I said to him.

"Uhm." He looked east. Then he looked west. "Uhm."

"Are you lost?" I asked him.

"No!" He marched confidently forward. "This way! Oh yeah! Follow me to party town, Jack!"

Me and Brijit exchanged glances.

"He doesn't know where he's going," she said.

I looked at Athena. The arrow was *kind of* telling us to go north, but it was also kind of telling us to go east. We needed to get out of the Muffincake Kingdom, but I definitely wanted to see Coffeecake before I left. I decided to ignore Athena and put my trust in Party Waffle with his fast-and-loose directions.

"Are you sure you know where you're going?" I asked him as Brijit and I caught up.

"Of course I'm sure!" he said as he did a cartwheel.

"Because you hesitated back there at the sign."

"I was just remembering!" he said.

Hazelnut Country was beautiful. We passed by this giant mocha waterfall that flowed over this tall hardwood cliff. It splashed down into a mocha lake and drained into a river that twisted and turned off to the horizon.

After hours of walking through the barren coffee shop wasteland, we finally came across people. There were just a few at first, mostly twenty-something hipsters sitting alone at their single table, reading books or drawing. They looked like the regular, everyday people you'd find sitting at the coffee shops in Queens. The only difference was that none of these people had laptops or phones.

They didn't notice us. Or what's more likely is that they did notice us, but didn't want to be disturbed. That's typically the case at coffee shops. People just want to be left alone.

There was some free-standing coffee counter with a barista. It wasn't even indoors, it was just out there alone. Behind the barista guy were shelves of flavored syrup and paper cups and a display case of pastries. His espresso machine hissed as he cleaned the steam wand. A line of three people had formed in front of him.

It was a free-range coffee shop. I don't know how it got power or water, but everything seemed to work just fine.

Party Waffle ran to get in line. "Coffee!"

The last thing Party Waffle needed was caffeine, but I figured one coffee wouldn't hurt. Plus, he was from the Pancake Kingdom; coffee was probably a part of his regular diet. So Brijit and I stood in line with Party Waffle, who shimmied excitedly while he waited.

We got to the front of the line and Party Waffle was too short to see over the counter. He stuck his arms in the air and waved them around. I picked him up and held him to where he could see the barista.

"And what can I get started for you?" the barista asked.

"Coffee!" Party Waffle shouted. "Extra strong! Black! Two sugars! Extra cream!"

The barista looked frustrated. "So you don't want it black."

Party Waffle shouted, "No!"

Brijit asked the guy, "Do you sell ears of corn?"

To which the barista replied, "No."

Then Brijit asked, "Do you have beef liver and plantains?"

"No," the barista said. "Just coffee and cookies and scones and egg sandwiches."

"Do you have sausages or blackened chicken?" Brijit asked.

"No." The barista was starting to get an attitude. "I just told you. I have coffee and cookies and scones and egg sandwiches."

"Do you have-" Brijit began.

I jumped in. "We'll just take the coffee, man. Thank you."

The barista was more than happy to give us our order and get us out of there. He grabbed a cup and poured Party Waffle's coffee by pumping it out of a big silver air pot. He handed the drink over. Party Waffle chugged the whole thing with both hands. He finished, stuck the cup out, and said, "More!"

"No." I set Party Waffle back down on the ground. "That's enough coffee for right now. I don't want you getting too crazy."

"Okay, then a juice!" Party Waffle said.

I sighed. What the hell did he want a juice for? He was a waffle. I wasn't even convinced he had a stomach, so what was a juice going to do for him? But since juice wasn't caffeinated, I didn't figure it would matter.

I pointed at the ice well behind the barista where the bottles of juice were sticking out. "Can I get an orange juice, please?"

"Grape!" Party Waffle shouted. "Grape juice!"

"Grape juice," I said to the barista. He reached back and gave me a bottle of grape juice. I handed it down to Party Waffle. He popped it open and leaned backwards so he could guzzle it down.

He looked up at me with his empty bottle in hand. "More?"

"That's plenty," I said. "Time to rock and roll."

"Yes!" Party Waffle smashed the bottle on the ground. "Yes, I can't wait! Let's go!"

Party Waffle went sprinting across the wooden floors. I looked down at the broken glass, then at the barista, and I slowly backed away. Brijit walked away, drinking.

"Sorry," I said. The barista looked furious. "Sorry."

2

After another couple hours of travel, we came across a biscotti sign that said CAPPUCCINO CITY: JUST A LITTLE FURTHER.

"Just a little further"? That was vague. But I wasn't surprised. And I didn't ask Party Waffle what "a little further" meant because I was sure he didn't know.

"That's where the princess lives," Party Waffle said. "Cappuccino City!"

"A little further" ended up meaning less than an hour of walking. Cappuccino City was built around a colossal espresso machine the size of Midtown Manhattan. The top of it was nearly up into the clouds. The sides were made of dark brown metal and the front had everything you'd expect from an espresso machine: two spouts where the espresso would drip out, temperature control knobs, and a massive steam wand that occasionally blasted a cloud of steam into the drainage tray.

Aside from the giant espresso machine that blocked out both suns in the sky, the Coffeecake Kingdom looked the most "Earth-like" of all the other kingdoms. Built around the base of the machine were neighborhoods of normal-looking houses, brick storefronts and even a few parks with jittery, super-hopped up squirrel. There were coffee shops on the corner of every intersection, as well as at the bottom of every apartment complex. The coffee-shop-to-citizen ratio had to be something crazy, like one coffee shop for every five citizens.

Pedestrians walked through the streets with a coffee in one hand and a pastry in the other. The people all seemed normal, very similar to Earth. They wore jeans and button up shirts and some of them even wore ballcaps.

Deeper into the city, we found ourselves walking through the shadow of the Great Espresso Machine, which darkened half the city. After some muffled clanking that came from deep inside the machine, it blasted steam into a ten-second cloud that quickly dissipated.

Walking beneath the Great Espresso Machine made it feel like we had been hit by some kind of shrink ray. On the opposite side of the road was a fairy tale castle built from dark and light brown bricks. The castle grounds were well-manicured gardens of coffee bean trees and coffeecake flowers. There were decorative ponds of milk and coffee and mochas. Teabags splashed in the ponds like school of fish.

Aside from the espresso machine, the castle was the largest thing in the city. It stood stories and stories tall, with dozens of individual towers and offshoot additions, including a small chapel for Butter Pad and Sugar Cube. We stood right out front where there was a drawbridge that led over a flowing latte river. The bridge was down.

Me and Brijit and Party Waffle crossed the bridge and headed for the main gate, which was sealed off by a grid of metal bars. Two guards stood there at the gate, each one dressed like a barista and armed with spear-length spoons and a forks.

As we came closer, the guard with the fork pounded the end of his utensil on the wood floors. "In the name of Princess Coffeecake, daughter of King Muffincake, identify yourselves."

"I'm Penelope Salvo," I said.

"Madam Brijit."

"Jabby-jabs!" Party Waffle exclaimed. "Jab jabbin' jabby jabs just jabbin' and babbin'!"

I nudged him with my foot and scolded him. "Party Waffle."

He looked at me for half a second, then turned back to the guards. "My name is Party Waffle." He did a little breakdance. "Oh, yeah! Do the shim-sham!"

The guard with the spoon stepped forward. "We know where the waffle comes from. But you two are strangers."

"Yeah, I'm from Earth," I said.

"I'm from the Guinee," Brijit said. "I'm looking for my husband."

"I'm old friends with Princess Coffeecake. If you tell her Penelope Salvo is here, I guarantee she'll let me in."

Spoon looked at Fork. Fork nodded in approval. Spoon opened a small door next to the main gate and went inside the castle.

"We'll see what she says," Fork said.

"It's going to fine, man," I said. "I promise you. When she finds out I'm here, she's going to flip her shit."

"And then we can leave, right?" Brijit said to me.

I sighed. "Yeah." I looked at Athena. We were only 4 kilometers away from the exit, which was somewhere off to the left. And while I intended to keep my promise to Brijit that we would leave as soon as we found the exit, I hated to think that we never figured out what to do about space cookie. It was damn near time to leave and I didn't even have anything close to a solution. I looked up to the sky. Space cookie was still there, glowing as bright as a star in the daylight.

The metal bars of the main gate raised up to the sound of clanking gears and squeaking chains. Just beyond the gate was a dark corridor. Out of the darkness came Spoon, as well as Princess Coffeecake in a mocha brown princess gown.

She had a nervous, anxious look on her face that faded away the moment we locked eyes. Immediately she stopped and held her hands up to her mouth. Tears came down her cheeks. She ran through the gate and threw her arms around me.

I picked her up and swung her around. Party Waffle loved all the excitement. He clapped and jumped in place.

"It's really you!" Coffeecake cried.

"It's really *you!*" I said.

"I never thought I'd ever see you again!" she said. I set the princess down and she leaned back to look at my face, but kept a hold of my shoulders. "How did you get here?"

"I walked," I said. "All the way from the Ice Cream Cake Kingdom."

Her eyes went wide. "You walked here from Ice Cream Cake? That's the whole entire world!" she said.

I laughed. "Believe me, I know."

God, how I missed that girl. We barely got to know each other or spent any time together before she had to leave. I had almost forgotten what she looked like, but in that moment it was as if nothing had ever changed. She had the same brown eyes, the same pert nose, and a delightful smile that showed off her perfect teeth.

Her crown wasn't a cardboard box like it was on Earth. Here, it was a silver tiara in the shape of a coffee mug. She had cut (or magically changed) her golden hair down to shoulder length. It was still straight on one side, wavy on the other. Whether that was how she liked it, or if that's just how it was naturally, I never knew.

"What happened to your arm?" Coffeecake asked. She had taken my left arm and held it delicately in her hands. The glowing red mechanics of my forearm amazed her.

"Oh, do you like it?" I asked. "It's new. My friend from Japan gave it to me."

Coffeecake looked up at me. "What's it do?"

"Well, it's complicated. There are these portals that connect different dimensions together. This arm helps me find them."

She laughed. "What?"

"It's helped me get here from Earth," I said.

"Oh." She turned her attention to my head and ran her fingers through my hair. "And you have pokey stuff in your hair."

"It's barbed wire," I said. "I killed a demon and got her powers and this was part of the deal."

"And this?" she said, touching her thumb to my chin. "This scar is new."

"An angel cut me." I traced my finger over the scar. "Hurt like a son of a bitch."

Coffeecake just gleamed with joy. "You are so cool."

I smiled. "Thanks."

Brijit pushed her way between us. "Yeah, she's cool, you're cool. Have you seen my husband? Voodoo guy, about this tall? Smokes cigars. Smells like dirt?"

Coffeecake looked at Brijit, stunned. She shook her head. "No."

Brijit walked away. "Of course not."

Coffeecake muttered to me, "Who's that?"

"That's Madam Brijit," I said softly. "Baron Semedi's wife. She's been looking for him everywhere and we haven't been having much luck."

"And I'm Party Waffle!" Party Waffle said as he turned around and rubbed his waffle butt on Coffeecake's shin. "Boogie time! Come on. Boogie. Boogie! What are you waiting for?" He raised his voice and screamed it. "What are you waiting for!?"

"Party Waffle!" I snapped. "Calm down." He got quiet, but kept dancing up against Coffeecake's leg. I said to her, "Sorry. He's been drinking coffee the whole way here and he's pretty amped up."

"I think he's cute!" Coffeecake said. "Look at him dancing! We get a lot of people from the Pancake Kingdom that come to visit. We have a lot in common. We're both very breakfasty people."

3

Princess Coffeecake took us to her favorite coffee shop – *Brew Haha!* – just a few blocks away from her castle. It was in a cute little neighborhood that kind of reminded me of Queens. We were walking up to the door when Coffeecake leaned over to me and whispered, "Will you tell your friend there's no smoking inside?"

I looked over. Brijit was absent-mindedly puffing away on her cigar. "Yeah," I said. "I'll tell her."

We stood there at the door and I said to Brijit, "So... smoking isn't allowed inside."

Brijit just deadfaced me as if I wasn't serious. Then she sat down right there on the concrete and puffed away. "I'll wait here then. Party Waffle, stay out here with me."

"Okay!" Party Waffle danced ballerina circles around her.

I gave Brijit a curious look. She *wanted* Party Waffle to stay? Brijit saw the confused look on my face and said, "You're going to talk about the thing, right?" She gestured to the sky with her cigar. "You don't want him to hear the 'D' word, right?"

"You're right," I said. "Thank you."

"Whatever." She looked away and waved me off. "Just hurry it up."

Inside, Coffeecake and I sat at one of the tables. She had ordered a lavender latte with extra whipped cream as well as a piece of coffee cake. I just asked for silverware.

"So tell me everything!" Coffeecake said. She drank her latte and asked, "How's the old man? What's his name?"

"Xin." Damn. That wasn't an easy question to answer. "He died a little more than a year ago."

Coffeecake covered her mouth with her hands. "Oh, no. What happened? Did he explode?"

That was also not easy to answer. "He was murdered by this lady, Isobella Westland."

"Oh, no," Coffeecake said.

I didn't like the direction this conversation was taking.

"So tell me about you," I said. "What have you been doing since I saw you last?"

Coffeecake shrugged. "Not a lot. Coffee in the morning. Coffee in the evening. I took a trip to Funnel Cake Island a while ago. That was really fun."

"I've been to Funnel Cake Island," I said. "I met your sister."

"She is so much fun. It makes me tired trying to keep up with her. She has so much energy."

"Yeah. She really does." Time to segue the conversation to the bad news. "And I met your sister Pancake, too."

"Oh, isn't she smart? She's the smartest person in the world."

"That's also true," I said. "She showed me her telescope."

"The telly-scope. I never understood that thing. Pancake says it's because I can't wink. See?"

Coffeecake squeezed both eyes shut. Then she tried to close one eye and not the other, but she really struggled with that. She kept making ridiculous faces trying to wink.

Through the coffee shop walls, I could hear the hiss of the Great Espresso Machine blasting its steam wand.

"Well, I looked through her telescope," I told her. "And I saw something bad."

"Oh, no," she said. "What?"

"It's a big chunk of cookie floating out there in space. And I think it's coming this way."

"To Brew Haha?"

"No, to the Muffincake Kingdom. It's going to hit the ground really hard. I don't know how big it is, but if it's really big, it could mean a lot of trouble for everyone."

Princess Coffeecake stared at me as she tried to process everything. "I'm sorry. I guess I don't understand."

"See, when something falls from space, it's traveling at like a million miles an hour."

"A million what a what?"

"It's traveling faster than anything. And when it hits the ground, it's going to explode. And the explosion will be so big, it will set everything on fire."

Coffeecake leaned back from the table with a horrified look on her face. "That's not possible."

"It's super possible."

"But that wouldn't happen here," she said as she looked around. "Everything's perfect here."

"Well, for one I don't think things are as perfect as they seem. Your sister Birthday Cake is wicked depressed so it's not perfect for her. And for two, I've looked through Pancake's telescope and seen space cookie with my own eyes. Hell, we can go outside and look at it now. It's so close now, you can see it in the daylight."

Coffeecake stood up. "Show me."

So I got up and took Coffeecake outside. Brijit was still sitting out there, drinking. Party Waffle danced in circles around her, careful to jump over her left leg, then her right leg, so he didn't trip and fall.

I looked to the sky, found the twinkling star, and pointed.

"There," I said. "That's space cookie."

Coffeecake looked up. I knew she saw it. You couldn't miss it. It was as bright as the North Star.

"It looks like a star," Coffeecake said breathlessly.

"I know," I said. "That's how it looks now, but believe me, it's going to get a lot bigger."

She turned to me. "Who else knows about this?"

"Only your sisters," I said. "Well, and me and Brijit. Party Waffle still doesn't really know."

Party Waffle stopped dancing and looked up at me. "Party Waffle still doesn't know what?"

"Nothing," Brijit said. "Resume dancing."

"Okay."

Coffeecake, just like her other sisters, was overwhelmed with the news. I could see the worry on her face. She looked up at the star for a while, then turned to me.

"You're going to fix it, right?" she asked.

I knew that was coming. "Ah. Man. I've been thinking about it this whole time walking here and I just don't know. I'd need to get up to space, but that's just impossible. You guys don't have the technology."

Coffeecake put her hands over her eyes. Before she could get going and build up a false sense of hope, I took her hands and pulled them away from her face.

"Your sisters already tried that. Pancake, Funnel Cake, Birthday Cake. They all tried to pray. It didn't work. It's still there."

"But." She looked like she was on the verge of tears. "We have to do something."

"I don't know what," I said. "Like I said, I can't get to space."

The Great Espresso Machine hissed its steam wand. The sound echoed up and down through the streets.

Brijit finished a long drink from her bottle of run and said, "What if you could?"

4

Brijit strolled down the main street of Cappuccino City, right through the shadow of the giant espresso machine. Me and Coffeecake followed behind her with Party Waffle trying to give me a flat fire by stepping on the heel of my shoe. Brijit chomped her cigar tight between her teeth and gestured at the city around us with her sloshing rum bottle.

"I had this idea," she told us. "I was thinking about when I used to cook Joumou. It's a Haitian soup. And when I cooked it with the lid on, it would rattle around because the hot air is trapped inside and needs out."

"Okay," I said. "What does that have to do with going to space?"

"We'll use that." Brijit pointed up above us, to the steam wand of the Great Espresso Machine. The metal tube was easily the length of the Empire State Building. She said, "We'll point it at space cooking and you crawl inside. When the steam goes off, it'll blast you into the sky."

I looked up at the steam wand. Her idea wasn't the worst, but there were all sorts of problems with it. For one, even if we could point the steam wand at the sky – which I wasn't even sure if *that* were possible – how could we possibly aim the steam wand in such a way that I would actually be pointed at space cookie? That involved shit like calculus and physics and all kinds of complicated math that none of us knew.

"There's no way, dude. Do you have any idea how precise you'd need to be to pull that off? Off by a fraction of a degree and I'm just going to fly through space for the rest of my life."

Brijit stared me down and puffed on her cigar. "Then don't do it. I want to leave anyway."

I looked back up at the steam wand. Her idea was cool *in theory*. But there was no way to actually pull it off.

Unless...

I turned to Coffeecake. "How smart is Princess Pancake?"

"She's the smartest person in the world," Coffeecake said.

"Is she good at math?"

She shrugged. "Pretty good."

"Could she figure all this out?" I pointed up at the steam wand. "Could she aim that thing at space cookie?"

Her eyes went wide. "You're not really thinking about doing this, are you?"

I took a deep breath and looked up at the twinking space cooking star in the sky. "I kind of am."

"Penelope, no. You're going to fly up past the clouds? What if you get lost in space? What if you die?"

"I don't think I'll die." And I really didn't. "As long as Pancake can actually aim the stupid thing."

"Ohh." Coffeecake nervously wrung her hands together. "I don't know."

"Dude, I'm not going to let your whole world get destroyed. If there's a chance I can save you and everything else, I'm going to try. It's philanthropic."

"Philanthropic?" she asked.

"You know, generous for humanity's sake or whatever. It means being nice."

She bit her bottom lip. "I still don't know."

"Look," I said. "It can't hurt to at least bring Pancake down here and have her take a look at it. If she thinks she can do it, I'll do it. And if she can't do it, then we'll think of something else."

"It's going to take a while for her to travel all that way," Coffeecake said.

"That's okay. We can wait." I looked at Brijit for approval. "We *can* wait, can't we?"

Brijit gave me an annoyed sigh. "Fine."

I looked back at Coffeecake. "We can wait."

Coffeecake hesitated, but she said, "I guess we could ask..."

"Okay." I knelt down to Party Waffle. "Party Waffle, I have a special mission for you."

"Yeah, you do!" he said. He spun in place, snapped his fingers and pointed at me. "Lay it on me, sister."

"Go back to the Pancake Kingdom as fast as you can. Find Princess Pancake and tell her we need her help here in Cappuccino City. Tell her to come as fast as she can."

He leaned in close to me. "Is this a secret?"

"Do you want it to be?"

He whispered, and his eyes were filled with intensity. "I do."

"Okay," I said. "It's a secret then. Top secret."

He winked at me. "Do you want me to leave now?"

"Go for it, buddy."

Party Waffle gave me a salute, spun around and broke into a sprint. He ran down the middle of the street as fast as his short legs could carry him.

I looked up the sky. The star was brighter than I remembered it. I wondered how much time we had. I wondered if Pancake would show up before it was too late.

5

Coffeecake invited me and Brijit to stay as her distinguished guests in her mocha-colored castle. The two of us were each given our own room and while I'd never stayed in a five-star hotel before, this was what I imagined penthouse suites looked like. My room was fit for a queen with a giant four-post bed surrounded on all sides by lace curtains. There was a supply of clothes hanging in a tall antique cabinet, but they were all full-length medieval dresses and gowns. There were six big windows with an excellent view over the castle gardens and all the rest of Cappuccino City, and by the window was a fully functional espresso machine and coffee bean grinder.

The castle hallways smelled of coffee, of course, and were decorated with oil paintings of Coffeecake, her sisters, and old man Muffincake.

Brijit was a remarkably patient guest. I was fully prepared for her to spend every moment of every day bugging me to leave, but she didn't. I think she had started to come around to my way of thinking and realized that the Muffincake Kingdom was worth saving. She spent most of her days wandering the streets of the city searching for Baron Semedi.

I got to spend some quality time with Princess Coffeecake. We posted up in her bedroom, which was ten times bigger than my room. She had dozens of wardrobes filled with gowns, treasure chests filled with trinkets from around her world. She had candles from the Birthday Cake Kingdom, a picture of her and Funnel Cake riding front seat on a roller coaster in Coo-Coo Bananas, and even a stuffed owl from the Ice Cream Cake Kingdom with an ice cream scoop for a head.

After she gave me the grand tour of her room, she asked me what I wanted to do. More than anything, I needed a bath.

Her castle had a pretty swanky bathhouse set up with two rows of bathtubs. They weren't private bathtubs, unfortunately; they were all just lined up in two facing rows. The place was steamy like a sauna and dimly lit by a couple high-up windows that let in the sunlight. There were these attendants posted up just outside in the hallway ready to bring you towels or soap or anything you needed. They filled a bathtub with steaming water for me and told me to shout if the water got cold.

They gave me a bar of soap and a towel and cut me loose.

The bathhouse was empty when I walked in, which was cool because I kind of didn't feel comfortable getting naked around a bunch of strangers. I got out of my clothes and my shoes and socks and submerged myself in the hot bath.

Some attendant came in after a moment and offered to wash my clothes. I was like, "hella dope, yes, please." So they did.

I soaked there in the tub and mentally processed everything I'd been through. Things had been so go-go-go lately that I rarely got a chance to just kick back and think.

"Everything okay?" Coffeecake asked as she walked into the room. She was barefoot and carrying a towel.

I lowered myself just a little bit more underwater. "Oh, yeah. This place is killer, dude."

"I'm glad you like it!" she said. She reached up behind her back and pulled the bow loose on her princess gown.

Was she going to get into a bath, too? I mean, hey, they put all the bathtubs together, just like how they did it in Rome. And you know that old Italian saying, "When in Rome." A lot of cultures don't have the same hang ups about nudity that Americans have. You know, in some countries it's customary for dudes to kiss each other when they meet. You don't see that in America because everyone-

Aaand she's naked. Trying to not look. But also not making it obvious that I'm trying to not look. Just looking somewhere else. Once she's in the bathtub, I won't see anything but her head, so that's when I'll look.

Coffeecake got in the water and dunked her head under. When she came back up, her wet hair clung to her face and she let it stay there. She blew air out of her mouth and sprayed the water away.

She asked me, "Did you get to see Wedding Cake?"

"I did. I saw her a couple days ago."

"How is she?"

"She's fine," I said. "Shit faced on champagne, but that was no surprise."

Coffeecake laughed. "Yeah."

"This whole place is weird," I told her. "I never in a million years imagined I would end up in the Muffincake Kingdom, but let me tell you. This place is bananas."

She laughed again. "It's not like New York."

"It's nothing like New York."

"I miss New York sometimes."

"You do?"

"Sometimes," she said. Her face brightened. "Hey, you want to see something cool?"

"Sure."

"Okay!" She raised her voice and hollered for one of the bathhouse attendants. Two of them came in, one with a bucket of steaming water and another carrying fluffy towels. Coffeecake gestured to one of them to come closer. She whispered something to them and they left.

"What's going on?" I asked.

She grinned at me. "You'll see."

The attendant came back with a heavy bucket. She poised it over my bathtub and dumped it out. It was full of ice.

My indestructible body doesn't register hot or cold temperatures unless they're at their extremes, so that bucket full of ice did nothing. I looked up at Coffeecake. She was grinning like an idiot.

"Is that it?" I asked.

She nodded vigorously, quite pleased with herself.

"This was the cool thing?" I asked.

She nodded again and laughed. "It's funny."

I laughed politely. "You got me good."

I forgot what it felt like to feel clean. Since my clothes were being washed, Coffeecake insisted I follow her up to her room and wear something of hers. We padded barefoot through the castle hallways wrapped in towels.

It felt really bizarre.

I stood in front of a full length mirror and looked down at myself in a formal ballgown. It was backless, came down low in the front to show off just how big my boobs aren't and hung down as far as my ankles. Coffeecake had put a necklace of coffee beans around my neck and insisted I put on the matching gloves.

I slouched and looked at myself in the mirror. I didn't have the poise or posture necessary to wear something so regal and fancy. "I look ridiculous."

"You look fine." Coffeecake handed me a pair of strappy shoes. "Here, put these on."

"Dude."

She gave me a pleading look. "Just try them on. They all go together. It's called an ensemble."

I sighed and rolled my eyes and stepped into the shoes. They had a wedge heel and I was suddenly two inches taller. "Nah, man, this isn't my look at all. I look stupid."

"No, come on. Come on." She took my hand and tried to pull me to the door. "We're going to dinner! You look nice!"

I pulled my hand free from her grip. "Oh, no. No way. I am not going anywhere dressed like this."

"Come on," she whined as she pulled on me again. "It's a banquet at a castle with a princess. You have to look nice!"

I sighed. I couldn't believe I was even entertaining the idea.

6

With each day that passed, the space cookie star glowed just a little brighter. That worried me. Brijit noticed and pointed it

273

out to me, too. The citizens of Cappuccino City who had no idea what that star truly was, even they noticed it and it became quite the topic of conversation.

Sometimes at night when I would wander alone through the castle, I would hear Coffeecake in her bedroom praying to Butter Pad and Sugar Cube. I couldn't make out what she was saying exactly, and I know it's rude to eavesdrop like that.

One day over breakfast I asked her what she prays for.

She looked embarrassed and poked at her scrambled eggs. "You know. Stuff."

I was eating a metal candle stick holder. Gold. Fucking tits. "You don't have to tell me if you don't want to."

"I just..." She hesitated. "I've been asking them to watch out for you."

"For me?"

She looked up. "You're going to ride the steam wand up past the clouds to save us. Because you're phlan... phlan..."

"Philanthropic."

"Yeah, that. And I just..." She looked down at her food. "Don't want you to die."

"I'm not going to die," I said.

She softly said, "I hope not."

Me and Coffeecake did all sorts of things while we waited for Party Waffle to return from the Pancake Kingdom. We went to the coffee shop every day, of course. We also did some shopping. She showed me this coffee mug design that she adapted from the "I heart NY" shirts she had seen in Manhattan, except hers said, "I heart CC." Cappuccino City. She said everyone from all over the Muffincake Kingdom loved it and every tourist who came to visit wanted one.

Sometimes we would just sit at the dock overlooking the mocha lake and the coffee bean trees and talk about stupid shit.

"Can I ask you a question?" I said. We each had a bagful of coffee beans and we were using them to feed the whipped cream ducks.

"Of course." She threw a few beans into the lake. The ducks gobbled them right up.

"Your dad's that Muffincake guy, huh?"

"Yeah."

"Is he, like, around?"

She didn't meet my eyes. She was quiet for a while and she threw more beans in the lake. "He's sleeping."

"Oh."

"He's been sleeping for a long, long time."

"Oh." I threw in a few beans of my own. "Is he... dead?"

She kept her eyes straight ahead. "He's sleeping."

I nodded silently and let it go. It had steadily become apparent that death was a rare experience in the Muffincake Kingdom and not a well received topic of conversation. I went back to feeding the ducks.

"What's your dad like?" Coffeecake asked me.

"He's not my dad. His name is Michael. And he's a prick."

She looked at me confused. "Prick?"

"An asshole. A real piece of shit. A prick."

"Ooh." She nodded. "Right."

"The dude walked out on me and my mom when I was twelve. And you know what? Good fucking riddance. He wasn't worth a shit when he was around anyway."

"He sucked?" she asked me.

"He sucked big time."

She nodded. "I'm sorry."

"Eh, it's whatever."

"My dad kept me locked up," she said. "I was the youngest. I wasn't allowed to leave my room."

"I remember you telling me something about that."

"I was so bored. For years."

"Yeah." I nudged her. "But look at you now. Out and about, doing shit, feeding the ducks."

"Yeah." She rattled some beans around in her hand and then said, "If you were around then, you would have rescued me." She turned to me. "Wouldn't you?"

"Dude, are you serious? Of course I would."

She smiled and looked at the sky. "Of course you would."

The suns were starting to set. The first star visible was the one star that never went away. It was visible in the daylight, but at night it glowed twice as bright. You couldn't miss it. Space cookie was close. How close? No one could say.

But Party Waffle needed to hurry.

Me and Coffeecake didn't talk about space cookie or the destruction of the Muffincake Kingdom. I don't think that was anything Coffeecake wanted to deal with. She'd put her faith in me and Butter Pad and Sugar Cube to save the day.

And that was going to have to be good enough.

275

Chapter 15

1

The day Party Waffle returned to the Coffeecake Kingdom, the space cookie star not only glowed brighter than ever before, but it had changed colors from white to yellow. It really spoke to how close, and how hot, that thing was getting.

Princess Pancake arrived up the main thoroughfare of Cappuccino City escorted by a small contingent of her egg yolk guards armed with whisks and spatulas. Her dress looked worse for wear. Their journey across the Muffincake Kingdom was, if not dangerous, at least messy as hell.

Coffeecake and I met up with them at the castle entrance.

"I did it, Pencil!" Party Waffle said as he came cartwheeling up to me. He stopped at my feet and kicked me in the shin. "You owe me a dance!"

Princess Pancake and Princess Coffeecake hugged and exchanged pleasantries. "It's been too long" and "it feels like it's been forever."

Pancake held Coffeecake's hands and said, "Party Waffle says you've thought of some way to stop this space rock?"

Coffeecake said, "We're going to use that steam wand..." she pointed overhead, "...to blow Penelope into space."

I chimed in. "Pancake, I need you to do whatever kind of math wizardry you do to figure out how me at space cookie."

Pancake looked up at the steam wand, then turned her attention to the space cookie star. Then she turned back to us.

"You're serious?" she asked.

Coffeecake said, "We're serious."

I told her, "It's the only thing I can think of."

Pancake turned to the sky and scrunched her face as she calculated the math in her head. "I don't see how that's even possible. You have to account for things like wind resistance and... and... and if you're off by even a single degree you're going to miss space cookie entirely and then what?"

I didn't want to focus on the negatives. I asked her point blank, "Do you think you can do it?"

She made her eyes go wide as if I was asking the impossible, but she looked at the sky again. "It's going to be the most math I've ever done." She yawned. Her guards yawned. "But I can try."

Princess Pancake spent the rest of the day doing her calculations. She climbed the ladder system on the side of the Great Espresso Machine to get a better vantage point at the sky. She didn't have a calculator, or even a pen and paper. She did all the math in her head and on her fingers.

That didn't make me feel any better.

In the evening, she got down on her hands and knees and drew calculus on the streets in chalk, sketching out dotted arches and numbers and variables. We tried our best not to bother her – she needed to concentrate – but I would check in on her from time to time. I was putting my life on the line, after all.

"How's things coming?" I asked as I stood over her shoulder.

Pancake focused on her chalk drawings. "This is really... unpredictable." She stood up, dusted herself off, and looked down at her math. "I could be spot on or way off the mark. I don't really know."

"You don't know?" I asked.

"I don't know how much you weigh. I don't know the pressure of the steam when it comes out. And we won't know the wind speeds will be the day of launch. And I don't have the tools I would need to figure all of that out. All I can be sure of is..." She looked at the steam wand. It wasn't facing down at the espresso machine tray anymore. She had adjusted it so it pointed out over the horizon. "...That..." She pointed at the steam wand. "...Is pointed at that." And she pointed at the star.

"You're sure?" I asked.

"I'm certain."

I pointed at her chalk drawings on the street. "And the rest of this math?"

"Unsolvable." She yawned long and loud and then said, "I don't think I'll ever figure it out."

"So this is as good as it's going to get?" I asked.

"I'm afraid so."

While we did our best to keep Operation: Penelope Rocket a secret from the citizens of Cappuccino City, any idiot could figure out that something strange was going on. The steam wand on the giant espresso machine was pointed diagonally into the sky. As if that weren't already strange enough, it just so happened to be pointed right at that mysterious star that wouldn't go away.

I weighed the future events out in my head.

What would it mean if I missed? My life would be over. Theodore would stay in Hell forever. I'd never see Corolla again. He would spend the rest of his life wondering if I was alive or dead, and he would stay up every night wondering if that was the day that I would come home. He would have no idea that I was drifting off alone in space for all eternity.

And Ilana would worry just the same.

And no one would be there to take care of the flower shop. All the wisdom that Xin had passed down to me would be lost. No one else on Earth was qualified to take care of those plants or watch over the dangerous collection in the basement.

Or, I guess Ilana and Corolla would take care of it. The plants might die in their care, sure, but the collection would be safe. They would figure things out.

If I missed space cookie I would spend the rest of my life floating alone in the cold of space. But isn't that what good people do? Risk their lives for the sake of others? It's philanthropic. And if I didn't do it, who would?

But let's say - one in a hundred - Pancake's aim was spot on. Then what? I land on space cookie and punch it until it shatters into smaller, harmless pieces that burn up in the atmosphere. I'd fall back down to the Muffincake Kingdom. Maybe I'd die. Maybe that would be the thing that finally killed me.

I'd be saving an entire world of people. Everyone riding roller coasters on Funnel Cake Island, everyone celebrating their birthday in the Birthday Cake Kingdom and, most importantly, Princess Coffeecake and Princess Wedding Cake, my dearest of friends; they would all be safe.

My friends all gathered around me before launch, Coffeecake, Pancake, and Madam Brijit. Party Waffle danced pirouettes around us. Oh, how I envied him. Ignorance truly can be bliss.

Before I set off on my suicide mission, I wanted to say my goodbyes. You know. Just in case.

I knelt down on the ground and held Party Waffle still. "Thanks for showing us around, little buddy. You be good while I'm gone."

In a moment of lucid calm, he looked up at me with big, sad eyes. "Where are you going?"

"I'm going to space."

"Can I go, too?"

"No," I said. "You have to stay here and keep an eye on Brijit. Don't let her get into any trouble."

"Oh, yeah! You can count on me!" He kicked me in the shin. "Bye bye, Pencil!"

I stood and faced Brijit. She was a million dimensions away from the Voodoo world.

"What about you?" I asked her.

"What about me?" she replied.

"How are you going to get home?"

She shrugged. "I'll think of something."

"You could be stuck here."

She looked around. "There are death simulators here. And that one place had good champagne."

I smiled at her. "You're sure?"

She gave me a stern look and poked me in the chest. "Don't get confused. I don't *want* to stay here. I'm counting on you to stop space cookie and make it back alive."

"I'll do my best."

I gave Brijit a friendly pat on the shoulder. She had only the slightest grin and, for old times sake, said, "Don't touch me."

No sooner had I turned to Princess Coffeecake than she had her arms around me and pulled me close. She was already crying.

"You just got here," she said.

"I know," I said. "But it's time."

"You'll be back, right?"

True answer? No idea. But I wasn't going to say that. I wasn't going to answer her at all.

I said to her, "You take care of yourself, okay? Look out for Brijit and Party Waffle."

"I will." She leaned back from the hug and looked me right in the eyes. Her mascara was all smeared. "Penelope?"

"Yeah?"

She asked me, "Can I kiss you?"

Whoa. Strange turn. "Kiss me?"

She looked down at her feet and said, "If that's okay."

"Uh." I looked at Brijit. Brijit shrugged. I looked back at Coffeecake. "You mean, like, on the lips?"

Coffeecake nodded.

Never thought about that before. Did Coffeecake have feelings for me? Or was what we considered "feelings" back on Earth the same as what "feelings" were in the Muffincake Kingdom? What the hell. I was about to shoot myself to space. If all she wanted was a kiss goodbye...

"I mean, I guess," I said to her. "If you want to."

Coffeecake lunged at me and pressed her lips to mine. I stood there stunned and let it happen, but then I figured that was rude and ruining the moment, so I kissed her back. It felt weird to kiss a girl. Not super weird, but kind of weird. Weird only because it was new.

And then she backed away and it was over.

"Thanks," she said.

"Anytime," I said.

And then I kind of processed what I said. "Anytime." That makes it sound like "anytime you want to kiss me again, that would be okay." "Do you feel like kissing me? Kiss me *anytime*." And then I thought maybe I should have been more careful with my words.

But that was the word I used. Anytime. Did I mean anytime?

The powerful steam wand hissed. A cloud of steam darkened the sky, then evaporated away. The sound of it snapped me back to reality. I backed away from Brijit, Coffeecake and Party Waffle, ready to climb the espresso machine.

Party Waffle waved at me. I waved back.

Brijit raised her rum bottle at me, then took a long drink.

Coffeecake shouted out, "You're my hero!"

I gave her double thumbs up.

Pancake escorted me to the base of the espresso machine, giving me directions the whole way. "Get inside the steam wand, about halfway. You'll build up more speed from there," she said.

"Right."

"Fan out your arms and your legs before the blast hits you, so you have more surface area."

"Okay."

"Then when you go flying, make your body as straight as you can. Like an arrow."

I laughed and pointed at Pancake. "I'll be *arrow*-dynamic."

She just blinked at me.

"Arrow. Dynamic. Because aerodynamic is-"

She cut me off. "You're going to experience a great deal of friction as you leave our atmosphere. Try not to burn to death."

"I'll try."

"Okay," she said. We had reached the base of the espresso machine and stood by the ladder system that led up the side. "Good luck." She hugged me. "Thank you for this."

"Hey, anytime."

There was a normal-sized ladder attached to the side of the machine that climbed up the legs, then up the sides, and ultimately to the very very top. It was there for maintenance, although I couldn't imagine anyone actually working on a machine that large, not with gears the size of castles and water hoses as big as the Lincoln Tunnel.

Hand over hand, rung after rung, I scaled the side of the espresso machine. It took me half an hour to reach the drainage tray. By the time I got to that part of the machine I could look down and see the rooftops of Coffeecake's castle.

Higher and higher I went. Cappuccino City was nothing more than a bunch of tiny, colorful shapes below me. Somewhere down there were Coffeecake and Party Waffle and Brijit watching me climb and fade into the clouds.

The air was so much colder up there and condensation formed on the ladder rungs. A flock of pancake birds flew past.

I climbed for probably an hour. The twin suns almost set, but then they didn't. They kissed the horizon, then climbed back into the sky. Thanks, suns. It would have been a lot harder to pull off this dumbass stunt in the dark.

"Stupid," I said to myself. "This is so stupid."

The steam wand didn't point straight up at the sky. It was more diagonal, like at a 45-degree angle. I had to climb it on my hands and knees. Gusts of cold wind tried to push me over the side. Any normal person would have fallen to their death, but not me. I kept a good grip on things, even if it meant leaving dented finger marks in the metal.

On my entire climb up the steam wand, I muttered to myself. "This is so stupid, Penelope. What the fuck are you doing?" I looked at the star in the sky. "If this thing is off by a fraction of a degree, you're dead. This is how you die. This is how you fucking die."

But I kept climbing.

I crawled my way out to the very tip of the steam wand and peered inside. Darkness. The steam hadn't come in a while. It was overdue.

I turned and lowered myself feet-first down to the nozzle of the wand. I moved deeper into the dark tunnel just like Pancake suggested. I positioned myself right in the middle, legs spread, arms spread, ready to take the full blast of steam to the back.

I waited patiently in the humid darkness.

Not knowing when it would come drove me crazy.

"Come on!" I shouted. I pounded my fist against the inside of the tunnel. "Come on, you mother fucker! Do it!"

Metallic clanking echoed from deeper inside the wand. Then came the sound of rushing water. A gust of hot air blew past me.

And then...

3

I was blasted out of the dark tunnel and into the blue sky. I was flying. My cheeks ballooned with air. Tears formed in my eyes and were immediately whisked off my face. The wind shear burned my skin. The sky lost its blue color and slowly faded to black. I could see millions of stars.

I was in space.

So stupid. So so stupid.

I drifted through the void, helpless to steer myself. Impossible Red increased my body heat to compensate for the extreme cold. I could only hope the nanites were protecting me from the solar radiation and whatever else can kill you in space.

God, this was stupid. Why did I think this was a good idea? Mathematically speaking, there was simply no way that I was going to hit space cookie. I couldn't hope to be that lucky. I would have to be, like, powerball lottery lucky.

So there I was, floating weightlessly through space, doing nothing, stuck with nothing but my own thoughts. Get used to it, Salvo. This is your life now. Floating, thinking, doing nothing for all eternity. You'll never see anyone again, not Corolla, not Coffeecake, not anyone. At least if you were human you would suffocate or burn up in the solar winds and it would end. But you're not human. You're a god and you'll probably live forever, so this is really, really, really going to suck.

Space cookie was more than a twinkling star up in space. It was a radiant, trembling asteroid of chocolate chip destruction, 1,000 times more powerful than the cookie we dropped on Japan.

I was actually headed right for it.

Maybe this was going to work.

I would land on space cookie and punch the shit out of it, break it into pieces, then ride whatever was left back to the Muffincake Kingdom.

Space cookie grew bigger and bigger. As I flew closer, I could start to gauge the size of it. It was bigger than a city bus. It was bigger than a house. It was bigger than a city block. The chocolate chips were like mountains. Caverns and caves were cut deep into the cookie crust. You could build a research stations on space cookie and have plenty of room to drive around.

Closer and closer I came. And then I realized.

I was going to miss.

Off by a fraction of a degree, the craggly edges of space cookie were just barely out of reach. My fingertips briefly swept across the mountain peaks of the asteroid, sending weightless cookie dust floating in space. I swung my arms out to grab any part of it, but couldn't. I just wasn't close enough. I tried to swim for it, but you can't swim in space. That's not how it works.

I whisked right past space cookie. I went one way and it went the other. I plunged deeper into space and space cookie tumbled in slow-motion towards the Muffincake Kingdom.

I missed. I had one shot at this and I missed. I couldn't do anything but hang there, weightless, and watch everything slip away. My life. My friends. And poor everyone back down on the surface. I let them down. They were all going to die.

I done fucked up.

4

I was suspended limp in space with my arms and legs dangling there and my untied shoelaces drifting softly behind me. There was no way to turn myself around. I had no music. I didn't have anyone to talk to. There were no sounds. In that moment, I would have killed for some Chicago, or some Phil Collins, or some Journey. The only thing I could hear was the voice in my head repeating the same word over and over.

Stupid. Stupid. Stupid.

The twin suns of the Muffincake Kingdom, white and yellow, were dead ahead. Cool. Maybe instead of spending eternity alone with my thoughts, I'd fall into one of those stars and burn up in its white-hot plasma. I had always called myself indestructible, but even I had limits. I'm pretty sure falling into a star would kill me. And just like how those two suns moved strangely through the skies of the Muffincake Kingdom, they moved just as weird in space. They orbited directly into my field of vision, one on my right and one on my left.

The yellow sun pulsed with energy. "Hello, Penelope," it said. It had a man's voice.

At first I thought I was hallucinating. I hadn't been alone for all that long and I had already lost my mind.

"We are very proud of you," the white sun said, brightening with each word. It had a woman's voice.

I couldn't speak. You can't speak in space.

"You are probably wondering who we are," the yellow sun said. "I am the one called Butter Pad."

"And I am Sugar Cube," said the white sun.

Oh, snap.

Butter Pad said, "We have been watching you."

"And we have heard the prayers of your friends," said Sugar Cube.

I wanted to speak. I wanted to ask them, if they heard the princesses prayers, why didn't they bother to respond to any of them. I wanted to know why they didn't do anything about space cookie. I wanted to know why they let everyone get so stressed out about dying.

"Sugar Cube and I made a wager," said Butter Pad. "I believed that doing nothing in the face of total obliteration would have made the people of the Muffincake Kingdom turn their backs on us. They would hate us for our silence."

"And I believed the opposite," Sugar Cube said. "I believed that even in the face of certain death, the people of the Muffincake Kingdom would still love us for giving them life."

Since I was unable to talk, all I could do was stare at them dumbfounded. All of this was over some kind of *bet*? They were willing to terrorize an entire planet just to see how far they could push the simple people of the Muffincake Kingdom before they didn't love them anymore? What selfish, inconsiderate gods.

"We didn't account interference from another world," Butter Pad said. "You were willing to sacrifice yourself if it meant saving our people."

"You tried your best," added Sugar Cube. "You failed, but your efforts were most admirable."

Some magical force turned my body around so I faced away from them. Space cookie, still silently drifting through space, came to a stop. It hung there, motionless and harmless.

"You are a good god, Penelope," Butter Pad said.

"A better god than us," said Sugar Cube. "Because of you, we have learned what it means to be philanthropic."

"For that," said Butter Pad, "we are grateful. And we will be philanthropic, as well. We will send you back."

"Tell Princess Birthday Cake that we are always listening to her when she's sad," Sugar Cube said. "And tell her she's never bothering us. She can call on us any time she wants."

That same magical force that turned me around flicked my body and shot me through space. I spiraled and tumbled, completely out of control. Every few rotations I would catch a glimpse of the Muffincake Kingdom coming closer and closer.

The black space faded to blue. The twinkling stars gave way to white, fluffy clouds. I was falling out of the Muffincake sky. My body became a mass of dead weight tearing a line of smoke across the sky. I smacked into the wood floors of the Coffeecake countryside and blew a cloud of wooden planks high into the air.

I was strangely starting to get used to hitting the ground at terminal velocity.

I slowly crawled out of my pile of broken floorboards. I brushed myself clean of splintered wood. I looked up at the sky. The space cookie star was there in the clouds, still glowing bright in the daytime. At least it wasn't a threat anymore. Space cookie was now just a harmless moon hanging out up there with Butter Pad and Sugar Cube.

Thing didn't go quite according to plan, but mission accomplished. I gave myself a satisfied nod and hoofed it back towards Cappuccino City.

The coffee-going citizens had no idea that crisis had been averted. Sure, they were mildly curious about the new glowing star in the sky, but it didn't disrupt their lives. They went about like normal, crowding the streets, shopping, drinking coffee, and eating pastries.

I was barely back to Coffeecake's castle when my whole group of friends came running towards me. They had apparently seen me fall from space and crash land outside of town and were waiting for me to get back.

"Did you do it?" Coffeecake asked, half excited, half nervous. She pointed at the star. "It's still there. Did you fix it?"

Man, it felt good to actually have good news. "Yeah. I did."

"Goodness!" Coffeecake threw her arms around me and pulled me close. She started to cry. "I thought you were lost and gone forever."

I laughed to myself. "I almost was."

Pancake came up and joined the hug. "You're the greatest!"

Brijit stood behind them. "It *was* my idea, you know."

Party Waffle ran up and started stomping on my foot. "Squish them tootsies! No take-backs!"

Coffeecake kept crying. I had two people attached to me and a waffle attacking my feet. I was quickly reaching the acceptable levels of physical contact.

"Okay," I said, trying to get loose. "Hugging time is over."

Pancake let go. Coffeecake let go. They were both crying.

Brijit stared at me with crossed arms. "How'd you do it?" she asked. "Punch it to death?"

"Oddly enough, no," I said. "I never even got to it. I missed." I looked at Pancake. "You were close though. Real close."

Pancake asked me, "Then how'd you stop it?"

In that moment, I debated whether or not to tell them the truth. They believed so much in Butter Pad and Sugar Cube, but what would it do to them to just straight up tell them their gods are real?

Eh, you know what? Fuck it. They already think they're real. And they are real. I was just confirming it.

"I met Butter Pad and Sugar Cube," I said.

Coffeecake and Pancake's eyes went wide. Even Party Waffle leaned back to stare up at me with his mouth hanging open.

Finally Pancake whispered, "What?"

"You met them?" Coffeecake asked. "What were they like?"

"Uh," I said. "They're not... great. The whole space cookie thing was, like, a *test*. But they said they learned something by watching us, so I think they're going to try and get better."

Coffeecake looked at Pancake. "I'm going to tell them thank you right now!"

Pancake said, "Me too!"

They both covered their eyes and took to walking in circles. They both prayed at once, thanking their gods for saving them from death and destruction.

Party Waffle pulled on my sock. I looked down. He asked, "What is death and destruction?"

I said, "Nothing you need to worry about, Party Waffle. Not anymore."

5

I heard this saying one time that goes like, "It's been real and it's been fun, but it hasn't been real fun." And I used to just think that was some play on words, up until I went to the Muffincake Kingdom.

It *was* real. We dealt with some real shit. Me and Brijit had it out in the Ice Cream Cake Kingdom. We dealt with Birthday Cake's depression. And we figured out a way to stop space cookie from killing everyone.

And it *was* fun. Roller coasters, wedding receptions, dancing. I had my first girl kiss in the Muffincake Kingdom.

But it hadn't been *real fun*. Because the shit that's "real" balances out the stuff that's "fun." Things can't be "real fun" if things are "real," because things that are "real" are inherently not "fun."

God, I was high.

Me and Coffeecake sat on the edge of her castle walls while the two suns set. The sky had turned a purplish-pink. Space cookie twinkled in the sunset. I smoked a spliff and kicked my legs back and forth, letting the rubber heels of my sneakers bounce off the bricks of her castle walls. Party Waffle danced across the walkways that connected all the walls.

I heard him singing softly to himself. "Happy, happy birthday, from Applebee's to you..."

"We gotta go soon," I told Coffeecake.

She hung her head. Her crown slumped down. "I know."

"But it was really awesome seeing you again."

"It was great seeing you, too," she said. "I think about you all the time."

"Well." I didn't know what to say to that. I was flattered of course. I never considered myself worth thinking about. At least not all the time.

She turned to me. "I'll see you again, won't I?"

"Yeah!" I didn't know if that was true, but I wanted to think it was. "I mean, who knows? I ended up here on total accident. It just kind of worked out."

Coffeecake looked pretty bummed out. She looked down at her strappy, open-toed shoes and said, "Yeah."

"Hey, can I ask you a question?"

She turned back to me. "Yeah."

Okay, we were about to delve into some tough conversation stuff, but I really wanted to talk it out.

I said, "When you kissed me before... Uhm. What was that all about?"

She shrugged and said, "I wanted to kiss you."

"Sure," I said. "I just don't know if kissing means the same thing here in the Muffincake Kingdom as it does on Earth. Did you kiss me because you... *like* me?"

"*Like* you?" She repeated as if I were crazy. "Penelope, I love you."

Long pause. Processing. "You mean 'love' as a friend?"

"As a friend. As my hero. As one of the greatest people to ever live."

I was still somewhat uncertain what that answer really meant, or what she wanted our relationship to be, or what. But maybe that wasn't important. The Muffincake Kingdom had a different culture and society than Earth. Maybe it had a different definition of what love meant. Maybe the type of relationship Coffeecake had with me wasn't anything that even exists on Earth. A fairy tale world has three kinds of people: heroes, villains, and people who need saving. And sometimes the people who need saving fall in love with the heroes who save them.

And I had saved her twice.

"Are you mad at me?" Coffeecake asked.

"What? No!"

"You got quiet," she said.

"Oh. Sorry. Just..." I pointed at my head. "Lost in my own thoughts up here."

"So you're not mad at me for kissing you?"

"I'm not mad at you for kissing me."

"Not even a little bit?" she asked.

"Not even a little bit."

"Because if you're mad, just say so now so I can-"

I kissed her to shut her up. She was just going to keep going and going, on and on, convinced that I was mad at her for kissing me. The only way to show her that I wasn't mad at her for kissing me was for *me* to kiss *her*, so I did.

Our first kiss was weird and out of left field, so I didn't really get to process what had happened. This time I did. My heart was pounding.

The moment was ruined when I opened one eye to see Party Waffle standing there, just staring at us. Kiss over.

I said to Party Waffle, "What?"

"Are you eating her face?" he asked.

I laughed. "No."

He looked at Coffeecake, "Are *you* eating *her* face?"

Coffeecake looked disgusted. "No."

He stared at us skeptically for a moment, then said, "Okay. Carry on."

6

That next morning, we made the final four kilometer walk to the exit from the Muffincake Kingdom. It was me, Brijit, Party Waffle, and Coffeecake. Coffeecake led us out across the floorboard hills of her kingdom and to our destination: A full-length mirror with a single, long crack in the glass that split the mirror diagonally in half.

"We used this to escape to Earth," Coffeecake said. "It took me and all five of my sisters to do it and even then it wasn't easy. If you're looking for something that leads to other worlds, this would be it."

I looked in the mirror. I saw my reflection. I touched the glass. It felt cold. The glass of the mirror stuck to my fingertip and stretched like glue when I took my hand away, then it snapped back into place.

I looked at Brijit and gave her an approving nod. "This looks like it."

"Great," she said. "Who knows what horrors await on the other side this time."

I went over to Coffeecake. Her brown eyes were already filled with tears, but she kept her head up and tried to stay composed.

"I guess this is goodbye," she said. Her voice was so sad.

I hugged her. "You know where to find me."

"And you know where to find me," she said.

Party Waffle looked up at Brijit. "And you know where to find me, Bat Face!"

Brijit glared at him and said, "We will never have to worry about that happening."

Coffeecake would have hugged me for forever if I would have let her – and I would have let her if I could – but we had to get moving. I ended the hug, held her by both shoulders and said, "I'm going to miss you."

"I'm going to miss you, too."

I thought about kissing her, but Party Waffle and Brijit were standing right there and I'm not much of a PDA sort of person in the first place, so it was just best to save that for some other day.

I went up to the mirror and looked at myself. Brijit followed. I offered her my hand. Again, just best to travel safely. You never know what could happen when you move across dimensions. One of the worst things we could do was get separated.

Party Waffle stood at our feet and marveled at his reflection in the mirror. "What's it do?"

I told him, "It's a doorway to another world."

"Another world?" he asked. "Like Funnel Cake Island?"

"No," I said. "A much, much different world."

"Ooh," he said. "I wanna see!"

And Party Waffle jumped through the mirror.

"Party Waffle, no!" I shouted.

Shit. Before I could grab him, he was already through the glass and vanished. No time to lose. We had to follow up fast.

I took a half second to turn back to Coffeecake. "Gotta go! See ya!"

Coffeecake clutched her hands to her chest, still crying. "Good luck!"

I jumped through the mirror and yanked Brijit along behind me.

HAVOK

Many words can be used to describe angels. Stubborn. Proud. Single minded. As soldiers in the army of the self-proclaimed "perfect" God, angels cannot even fathom the concept of failure.

In the case of Metatron and Zophiel, neither one was ready to admit failure in the case of Penelope Salvo. The bothersome Daughter of Eve was no longer a mere nuisance. She was now, categorically, a problem. Not only had she disobeyed the ruling of Heaven, not only did she violate the boundaries of creation by trying to enter Hell, she was making Metatron and Zophiel look incompetent as they chased her across worlds.

That type of embarrassment would infuriate any angel. But these were not just any angels. This was Metatron, Knower of the End Days, and Zophiel, the Spy of God. Their inability to locate Penelope Salvo was particularly humiliating.

"How do you know she even came this way?" Zophiel asked Metatron as they walked down the yellow brick road.

"I can't sense the girl," Metatron said, "but I am still the archangel of boundaries. Someone crossed into this world recently. I can feel it. They went this way."

Together they stood at the gates to the Emerald City. Something had blown them right off their hinges. Massive slabs of cracked emerald laid in the streets.

There was blood on the emerald cobblestones.

Together they walked into the Emerald City. The people of Oz watched dumbfounded as the two angels marched confidently through the city. The humble people had never seen armor of platinum and white gold. They had never seen wings so white and majestic. They had never seen a man so large, or a woman with such piercing eyes.

Piercing, of course, because Zophiel was using direct eye contact to read people's minds.

"What do you see, sister?" Metatron asked.

"The mudblob had been here," Zophiel said. "She travels in the company of a Voodoo loa."

"No surprise," Metatron said. "Cavorting with dark magic."

Zophiel looked into another citizens eyes and read their minds for additional details. This one knew more. This one had seen a fight. "The Daughter of Eve has toppled this world's government. She reduced their leader to a rusted lump of metal."

The two angels turned a corner and found the complete aftermath of Penelope's fight with Steelia. Entire skyscrapers of emerald had shattered like glass. Citizens worked, throwing shards of emerald into wooden wagons to be carted away. Opposite of them stood the broken remains of Steelia's castle; the great walls had shattered like a mirror and entire portions of the ceilings had collapsed.

The people of the Emerald City had long been at work cleaning up after Penelope Salvo. There was still so much more to do.

Metatron huffed. "Witness her wake of destruction."

"An anathema," Zophiel said. She knelt down, picked up a loose shard of emerald and examined it from all sides. "She must be stopped."

"She must be killed," Metatron said.

They headed for the castle.

"Perhaps we should ask the Heavenly Host for help," Zophiel said. "Before events come to-"

"I will pretend you did not say that," Metatron interrupted. "We do not need assistance. Penelope Salvo is *mudblob*, Zophiel. We will find her on our own and deal with her ourselves."

"But if she reaches Hell-"

Metatron stopped and leveled Zophiel with a finger in her face. "She will not reach Hell."

Zophiel shook her head. "Pride goes before a fall, Metatron. If yours leads us to failure, I will be most unhappy."

Metatron stared her down, then turned towards the castle. "So will I."

The interior of the castle had been ground zero for a devastating fight. The stained glass windows were destroyed. The walls were cracked. In the main throne room, the ceiling had caved in. Impact craters could be found on the emerald floors and walls, most of them humanoid in shape.

"Anything?" Zophiel asked Metatron.

Metatron looked around the room, feeling for a weakness between worlds. It was close by. He could feel the tingling in his fingertips. It was coming from the metallic throne sitting in the middle of the room.

"This way," he said.

He led Zophiel over to a set of footprints set in a concrete plaque. They were Dorothy's footprints and Penelope's way out of Oz.

"There." Metatron pointed. "She went that way."

Zophiel nodded, then drew her sword. Leaning back, she got into strike position, then lunged. The blade of her sword disappeared as it sank into the very reality of things, piercing the boundaries between that world and the next. With all her strength, she pulled down on the sword, dragging it through reality, cutting it open.

Satisfied with her work, she put her sword on her back and stepped forward. She drove her fingers into the cut she had made in thin air and pulled. Worlds divided. On the other side was the swirling, electric world of CONAN-6.

She pulled the curtains open and stepped through. Metatron followed. Behind them, the open wound in reality sealed shut and they were gone.

Chapter 16

1

Brijit and I tumbled over one another and fell through the door of a tall grandfather clock. We ate shit and spilled out onto the tile floor of a grand banquet hall with wooden arched ceilings and dozens of crystal and gold chandeliers. The walls were lined with thousands of grandfather clocks, all of them exactly the same as the one we fell out of. It was a museum of clocks, with cuckoo clocks mounted high up on the walls. They all ticked and tocked in perfect unison.

Party Waffle had a head start on us. He sprinted into the middle of the room with his hands in the air. He busted a move and started singing, "One, two, three o'clock, four o'clock rock!"

I scrambled to my feet and ran after him. "Party Waffle, get back here!"

"But look at all the clocks!" he said, pointing. "Look at that one! And look at that one! It's Clock City. Is this Clock City? Are we in Clock City?"

"I don't know Clock City." I reached Party Waffle and scooped him up. "You're going back home, you little shit."

"I don't know if that's how it works," Brijit said. She was investigating the interior of the grandfather clock we fell out of. She ran her hands along the inside of the clock and touched solid wood. "I don't think these doors go both ways."

"What?" I said. "Tell me you're not serious."

I carried Party Waffle over to the clock and felt for myself. Sure enough, it was solid. There was no going back.

I held Party Waffle up to my face. "Dammit, Party Waffle! Look what you've done!"

"Dammit, Pencil," he said back, parroting my tone. "Look what *you've* done!"

I set him down and got on one knee in front of him to scold him good. "Do you have any idea what you've done? Do you have any idea how much trouble you're in? You can't go back home. You're stuck here with us."

Brijit muttered, "More like we're stuck here with him."

I continued. "The dimensions we're going to are going to be really dangerous. You're in a whole lot of danger."

He stared up at me. I wondered if I was getting through to him or not. Slowly but surely, he started moving his hips in a circle. Very softly, he went, "Woo."

I got up to pace in circles and massage my temples. "Oh, goddammit, Party Waffle."

Party Waffle looked up at me. "I did a bad thing?"

I waved my finger at him. "You did a very bad thing, Party Waffle! Bad Party Waffle! Bad!"

Party Waffle stopped his dance. His bottom lip quivered. His eyes welled up with maple syrup tears. And then, right in the middle of this mysterious clock room, Party Waffle cried.

I rolled my eyes and threw up my hands. Party Waffle held out his arms and wandered around, helpless, until he found Madam Brijit's leg. He grabbed her and cried into the hem of her wedding gown.

Brijit crossed her arms and glared at me.

"Oh, don't give me that look," I said. I pointed at Party Waffle. "I didn't cause any of this shit."

She said, "You made him cry."

"He shouldn't fucking be here!" I said, nearly yelling. "He needs to go back home! He comes from a world where pancakes are birds and rivers are candy! The moment we come across anything worse than that... like a monster... or a *shark*... he's gunna fucking die!"

Party Waffle wailed. "What is die?"

"It's something you *do* have to worry about now!" I yelled.

Brijit threw her cigar at me. "Stop yelling at him!"

I slapped the ashes off of me. "Oh my god, am I the only one here who's not fucking stupid?" I stormed away from them. "I'm going to go figure out where we are. Come find me when you're done with therapy. Fuck!"

Party Waffle's crying echoed throughout the whole hall. I had to get outside. I was so fucking pissed off. It sucked that I had to yell at Party Waffle and make him cry, but that was only because I was scared for him. He wasn't cut out for the adventure we were on. He was going to get eaten alive.

Huh. Party Waffle. "Eaten alive."

That'd be funny if I wasn't so fucking pissed.

There were a set of wooden double doors that led out of the hall of clocks. They were big doors, like something you might push open to get onto the floor of the senate. They didn't have any windows, but there were golden handles to push them open.

So I pushed them open.

Outside was a swirling metropolis of activity. Wooden boats decorated with brass pipes zipped effortlessly through the air. I couldn't tell what made them fly. Some of them had wings made of canvas, some didn't. Mixed in with those flying boats were space craft looking things made of reflective silver, and I could have sworn I saw a floating bathtub.

The city was filled with skyscrapers, except they all seemed to come from different centuries. Some of them were hammered together out of wood. Others looked like the glass and concrete ones you'd find in Times Square. Still others were made of liquid green metal that stood eighty stories tall, but moved like water. Each one of the skyscrapers – of which there were thousands – had a big clock built into the side of it. Funny thing was, each clock showed a different time. None of them agreed.

Between me and the skyscrapers was a sprawling plaza of black and white bricks. This is where people gathered, each one standing close to some type of vehicle. And when I say vehicle, I don't mean car. Some of them were as simple as a metal cube, others were elaborate Rube Goldberg machines of copper tubes, whirling wooden wheels and clickity-clackity glass blocks that stacked and unstacked themselves all on their own. Each "car" was like something from a fever dream, or something you'd find in an absurdist painting, and the courtyard was filled with them.

The people were dressed from all throughout the ages. I saw men and women decked out in top hats, velvet vests and corsets, and leather belts that held all kinds of oddly-shaped brass tools designed by Dr. Seuss. There were people in white jumpsuits with futuristic helmets and technologically advanced bracelets. All of them kept checking the time, some of them on golden pocket watches, others on holographic displays broadcasts from their helmets.

An old wizard rushed through the crowd, focused intently on how much sand was draining out of his hourglass.

I spotted a guy closest to me, all alone. He wore a bright red jumpsuit and had crazy, wild hair. He rooted through a curved vehicle that looked like an upside down football helmet, big enough that he could sit inside it.

I came up behind him. "Hey," I said. "What is this place?"

His head poked up and he turned around. "Who are you?"

"I'm Penelope Salvo," I said. "Nice car thing you have here. Would you mind telling me where I am?"

"You don't know where you are?" he asked.

"Nope." I looked all around. "First time."

"If you don't know where you are, then you shouldn't be here," he said. "How did you find us?"

"I fell out of a clock. My Voodoo friend and a talking waffle are with me, too. We're not looking for any trouble. We're just passing through."

"So you're not a time traveler?" he asked.

I rubbed my nose. "A time traveler?"

His face turned to panic. He grabbed my arm, pulled himself in close, and whispered, "Are you serious?"

I yanked my arm free. "Serious about what, dude?"

"This is Chronopolis," he said. "The City of Time. Only time travelers are supposed to be here. If the Conclave finds out you're here, you could be in a lot of trouble."

"Trouble like how?"

"Trouble like they'll erase you from the timeline."

I didn't like the sound of that. "Well, then we just need to be sure that the Conclave doesn't find out."

He looked around anxiously, then pointed at me. "Wait right here," he said. He jumped into his red football helmet looking thing. He pulled some thick, red goggles down over his eyes, pulled some levers on the dashboard of his contraption and said, "You're lucky you ran into me first. I'm one of the good ones."

His red machine pulsed and glowed, brighter and brighter, then in a blinding flash it vanished.

The city was filled with skyscrapers, except they all seemed to come from different centuries. Some of them were hammered together out of wood. Others looked like the glass and concrete ones you'd find in Times Square. Still others were made of liquid green metal that stood eighty stories tall, but moved like water. Each one of the skyscrapers – of which there were thousands – had a big clock built into the side of it. Funny thing was, each clock showed a different time. None of them agreed.

Between me and the skyscrapers was a sprawling plaza of black and white bricks. This is where people gathered, each one standing close to some type of vehicle. And when I say vehicle, I don't mean car. Some of them were as simple as a metal cube, others were elaborate Rube Goldberg machines of copper tubes, whirling wooden wheels and clickity-clackity glass blocks that stacked and unstacked themselves all on their own. Each "car" was like something from a fever dream, or something you'd find in an absurdist painting, and the courtyard was filled with them.

The people were dressed from all throughout the ages. I saw men and women decked out in top hats, velvet vests and corsets, and leather belts that held all kinds of oddly-shaped brass tools designed by Dr. Seuss. There were people in white jumpsuits with futuristic helmets and technologically advanced bracelets. All of them kept checking the time, some of them on golden pocket watches, others on holographic displays broadcasts from their helmets.

An old wizard rushed through the crowd, focused intently on how much sand was draining out of his hourglass.

I hadn't been outside the grandfather clock building for a few seconds when this guy in a red jumpsuit came waking up to me.

"Are you Penelope Salvo?" he asked.

Uh. Bad sign. It's always a bad sign when someone knows your name and you don't know theirs.

"Maybe I am," I said. "What's it to you?"

"Don't you remember me?" he asked.

I didn't recognize this guy at all. "No."

"From..." He stalled. "Paris."

"I never been to Paris."

"I thought you were from Paris."

"I'm from New York, dude. What is your deal? I don't know you. What is this place?"

"Oh, I know New York," the guy said. "I've been to Newark."

"Newark's in fucking Jersey." I backed away from the guy. He was strange enough, talking to me all weird, but then talking about how Newark is in New York? No way. Stranger danger. "Get away from me."

"Right," he said. "Newark is in New Jersey." Then he just walked off. Good thing, too, because he was about to get his world totally rocked.

3

Between me and the skyscrapers was a sprawling plaza of black and white bricks. This is where people gathered, each one standing close to some type of vehicle. And when I say vehicle, I don't mean car. Some of them were as simple as a metal cube, others were elaborate Rube Goldberg machines of copper tubes, whirling wooden wheels and clickity-clackity glass blocks that stacked and unstacked themselves all on their own. Each "car" was like something from a fever dream, or something you'd find in an absurdist painting, and the courtyard was filled with them.

The people were dressed from all throughout the ages. I saw men and women decked out in top hats, velvet vests and corsets, and leather belts that held all kinds of oddly-shaped brass tools designed by Dr. Seuss. There were people in white jumpsuits with futuristic helmets and technologically advanced bracelets. All of them kept checking the time, some of them on golden pocket watches, others on holographic displays broadcasts from their helmets.

An old wizard rushed through the crowd, focused intently on how much sand was draining out of his hourglass.

This guy in a red jumpsuit came walking up to me.

"Hello," he said.

"Hi." Okay. Lucky break. I needed to know where we were and this guy was making conversation easy. He seemed normal. Normal enough, at least. "What is this place?"

"It's like New York," he said. "But different."

"I'm from New York," I said.

He said, "I've never been to Paris."

Okay. Random. "Me either. And I've never been to Moscow."

"I have been to Moscow."

"Cool," I said. "What am I supposed to do with that information?"

I checked Athena to see how far I had to go to get to the next world.

59 kilometers.

Oh, that wasn't bad at all. I asked the weird jumpsuit dude, "So any idea what's 59 kilometers that way?" I pointed in the direction of Athena's arrow.

"What do you need that's 59 kilometers that way?" he asked.

"I got this thing," I showed him my Athena arm. "It tells me where these portals to other worlds exist. I've been using them to travel back and forth. I'm trying to get to Hell."

He said, "Fascinating."

"Yeah. It's not all it's cracked up to be. I just made a waffle cry."

He scratched his head and tilted his head. "A waffle?"

"He's from another world," I said. "He's not supposed to be here. So if you see a singing, dancing waffle, don't freak out. He's harmless."

"Penelope," he said. "You are one of the most interesting people I have ever met."

I backed away from him. "How do you know my name?"

He suddenly looked nervous and fumbled over his words. "Uh, you told me."

I glared at him. "No, I didn't."

"Oh no."

Red Jumpsuit ran away from me. That guy somehow knew my name and then when I called him out on it, he goes "oh no" and runs off? Something seriously fucking weird was going on. I ran after him, but he ducked around the corner of the clock museum. By the time I caught up to him, he was gone.

4

The people were dressed from all throughout the ages. I saw men and women decked out in top hats, velvet vests and corsets, and leather belts that held all kinds of oddly-shaped brass tools designed by Dr. Seuss. There were people in white jumpsuits with futuristic helmets and technologically advanced bracelets. All of them kept checking the time, some of them on golden pocket watches, others on holographic displays broadcasts from their helmets.

An old wizard rushed through the crowd, focused intently on how much sand was draining out of his hourglass.

This guy in a red jumpsuit came walking up to me.

"Hello," he said.

"Hi." Okay. Lucky break. I needed to know where we were and this guy was making conversation easy. He seemed normal. Normal enough, at least. "What is this place?"

"It's like New York," he said. "But different."

"I'm from New York," I said.

He said, "I've never been to Paris."

Okay. Random. "Me either. And I've never been to-"

"Moscow," he said, interrupting me, but totally guessing the city I was going to say.

"How'd you know I was going to say that?" I asked.

"Psychic," he said, pointing to his temple.

Oh shit. Was I in a land of psychics? That would be sick.

"You're straight up a psychic?" I asked.

He smiled and nodded. "Sure am."

"Prove it," I said. "What am I thinking?"

I started thinking about something totally random. Ice cream soup. No, Party Waffle. Let's see if this jabroni can guess that I'm thinking about a fucking Party Waffle.

He pointed. "You need to go 59 kilometers that way."

Okay, weird, that wasn't what I was thinking, but it was worth checking. I looked at Athena.

59 kilometers.

Sure as shit, the arrow pointed in the same direction as what the guy said. He didn't guess what I was thinking, but he was right.

"Holy shit, dude, that's amazing."

"And you made a waffle cry."

Okay, now, what the fuck? How could he possibly know that?

The dude was psychic.

"You're totally nailing it," I said. "Look, when you said I need to go 59 kilometers that way, you're totally right. Me and my friends are trying to get out of here and we don't want any trouble. I don't suppose you could help me with that?"

"A lot of people here don't like outsiders," he said. "They're going to know you're strangers just by looking. If they see you, you're going to be in big trouble."

"Ah, shit," I said. "Can we put on disguises or something?"

"That won't work," he said. "They'll see right through you."

"Hell, I ain't afraid of psychics," I said. "If they cause any shit, I'll bust their heads open. Let's see how psychic they are when their brains are all spilled out on the concrete."

"Look, I can help you," he said. "But first you have to answer a question for me."

"Shoot."

"Let's say you didn't know me."

"I *don't* know you."

"What could I say to get you and your friends to follow me right away with as little conversation as possible?"

"I'm ready to do that now."

"No," he said. "Less conversation. Less interaction. If I wanted you to follow me in one sentence, what would it be?"

I thought about it for a moment. Only one thing came to mind. I gave him my answer: "Come with me if you want to live."

He gave me a weird look. "That would work?"

I shrugged. "Of course it would. When someone comes up to you and says 'come with me if you want to live,' you go with them. *If* you want to live."

He thought about that for a moment. "It makes sense."

"It makes perfect sense."

Red Jumpsuit turned and ran away from me, headed towards some upside down football helmet car. He didn't look back.

"Hey!" I shouted. "I thought you were going to help me!"

"I am!" he said back.

But what the hell? He wasn't helping me at all. He jumped into the football helmet thing and it started to glow. It pulsed and glowed brighter and brighter, until it vanished in a flash.

5

An old wizard rushed through the crowd, focused intently on how much sand was draining out of his hourglass.

Out of nowhere, this guy in a red jumpsuit came walking up and planted his feet right in front of me.

"Hello," I said.

The guy said, "Come with me if you want to live."

I sized the guy up. He had a normal looking face. He didn't have that serial killer look in his eyes. His hair was a wild and untamed, but that doesn't mean anything; I have barbed wire in my hair, so what does that matter?

And he legit said "come with me if you want to live." How do you say no to that?

So I shrugged and said, "Okay."

"Get your friends," he said.

I thought about that for a second, too. "Okay."

I went back into the banquet hall with all the grandfather clocks. Brijit was carrying Party Waffle around at arms length. Party Waffle was still crying, just not as hard.

I poked my head back in through the door. "Okay, Brijit, let's go. There's a guy out here who said 'come with me if you want to live,' so we're going to do that."

"Just some guy?" Brijit asked.

"Yep."

"You don't know him?"

"Uh. No."

"Do you have any idea where he's taking us."

"No."

"And you think this is a good idea?"

I cleared my throat. "Dude, he said 'come with me if you want to live.' When someone says that to you, you go with them. If you want to live."

Brijit carried Party Waffle to the front doors. "You better be right."

I held the door open for her. "I got us this far, haven't I?"

Red Jumpsuit had this red floating vehicle that kind of looked like an upside down football helmet. There were these red suede seats inside. It was a single bench seat, designed for two people, so me and Brijit and Red Jumpsuit had to squeeze in together.

"Here," Brijit said, handing me Party Waffle. "Take him. Tell him you're sorry."

I took Party Waffle. He looked at me with sad eyes. "I'm sorry, Party Waffle."

His mood immediately changed. "All is forgiven!" Party Waffle threw his hands in the air and kicked the air with a new dance I hadn't yet seen. "Oh, baby. Get down and do the Boat Legs! Whoooa! Man overboard!"

The controls on this red football thingy were out of this world. There were colorful, plexiglass levers and tons of small computer screens and buttons galore.

"What kind of car is this?" I asked. I looked all around. "What is this place?"

"Best you don't know," he said. "Try to sit low."
Brijit and I slumped down in our seat.
I checked Athena.

59 kilometers.

"Hey," I said. "I don't know where you're taking us, but-"
"I'm taking you 59 kilometers," he pointed, "that way."
He pointed in the exact direction of Athena's arrow.
"How did you know that-" I started.
He cut me off. "Don't ask any questions."
I didn't get to see much of whatever city we were in, not between slouching low in my seat and the high walls of the flying machine. Flying overhead were all sorts of cars and machines and strange steampunk-looking boats.
And then, swear to god, I saw Corolla.
I shot up out of my seat and looked back. It was fucking Corolla! I would recognize those hubcaps anywhere!
"Corolla!" I screamed as I stood on the red suede seat. Corolla kept going. He was too high up to hear me. I waved my hands and screamed his name again. He still didn't stop, *and* he was getting away. I looked down and shouted at Red Jumpsuit. "Go back!"
"Get down!" Red Jumpsuit said, swatting at me. "Someone will see you."
Corolla was already shrinking out of view. "Go back!"
"If the Conclave sees you-"
I put my foot up over the edge of the car, ready to jump out. If this guy wasn't going to stop, I was going to bail out. I wasn't going to let Corolla get away. Absolutely nothing was going to stop me from-

6

"All is forgiven!" Party Waffle threw his hands in the air and kicked the air with a new dance I hadn't yet seen. "Oh, baby. Get down and do the Boat Legs! Whoooa! Man overboard!"
The controls on this red football thingy were out of this world. There were colorful, plexiglass levers and tons of small computer screens and buttons galore.
"What kind of car is this?" I asked. I looked all around. "What is this place?"
"Best you don't know," he said. "Try to sit low."

Brijit and I slumped down in our seat.
I checked Athena.

59 kilometers.

"Hey," I said. "I don't know where you're taking us, but-"
"I'm taking you 59 kilometers," he pointed, "that way."
He pointed in the exact direction of Athena's arrow.
"How did you know that-" I started.
He cut me off. "Don't ask any questions."
I didn't get to see much of whatever city we were in, not between slouching low in my seat and the high walls of the flying machine. Flying overhead were all sorts of cars and machines and strange steampunk-looking boats.
"Look at this," Red Jumpsuit blurted out. He tapped an inscription across the dashboard of his weird machine. It read:

SOMETIME, ANYTIME, ALWAYS, AND NEVER

"What's that mean?" I asked.
"Whatever you want it to mean," he said.
Sometime. Anytime. Always. Never. It seemed... familiar. It reminded me of those signs at the crossroads in the Guinee. Somewhere. Anywhere. Everywhere. Nowhere.
And even back then, that reminded me of something else. Something from a dream.
Something. Anything. Everything. Nothing.
It seemed so god damned familiar, like it was important, but I couldn't remember where I knew it from.
"Have you seen a guy dressed like me?" Brijit asked Red Jumpsuit. "He wears a tux. Has similar face paint? Sound familiar?"
"Not around here," he said. "And I know everyone here."
Brijit slumped further down in her seat, "I didn't think so."
Red Jumpsuit drove us through the city streets of Wherever We Were and eventually parked in front of some sort of marble museum looking building. It had a dome for a roof and in the middle of the dome was a huge clock. The clock hands moved ten-times normal speed. Athena pointed us at the building.
"Whatever you're looking for is in there," Red Jumpsuit said. "Go quick before anyone sees you."
"Yeah," I said. "Hey, thanks for the ride."

"You're welcome," he said. "Just happy to help."

Me and Brijit jumped out of Red Jumpsuit's strange floating machine. Party Waffle crawled up the inside of the car and jumped onto my back. I took the helpful guy's advice and tried to lay low. I jogged to the front doors of the museum.

Brijit strolled along like nothing was wrong, moving at a normal pace, smoking her cigar.

"Come on," I whispered at her from the museum entrance. "Before someone sees."

"Let them see," she said.

"You're going to get us in trouble," I said.

"I'm fine."

She reached the entrance eventually, and lucky for her no one spotted her. We went inside and found an art museum. The place was a maze of hallways, all of them decorated with paintings. Some of them I recognized. The Mona Lisa. The Garden of Earthly Delights. And there were other famous ones there, too, just ones I didn't know the names of.

There were paintings of different countries of Earth, and different periods of history. There was a painting of the invasion of Normandy. There was a painting of old Roman times. There was a painting of dinosaurs. There were paintings of space, and of space ships, and of alien worlds. There were paintings of dreams, and of angels, and even a painting of Alice In Wonderland.

Party Waffle jumped off my back and wandered around, amazed at all the artwork.

"Party Waffle, you stay where I can see you," I said.

He didn't respond. He saw a painting of Dogs Playing Poker and it blew his mind. Dogs can't play poker! He stood directly in front of it, pointed, and laughed and laughed.

"Hey," I said to Brijit as I pointed out one of the paintings. "Look. Last Supper."

It was the real deal Last Supper by old Leo DaVinnies. I'd never seen it with my own eyes before. Now, how did this museum have all these super rare paintings when they're supposed to be on Earth? Who knows.

"I've seen this before," Brijit said, looking at the Last Supper.

"I mean, yeah," I said. "It's, like, one of the most famous paintings in the world."

Brijit walked away, disinterested. "It's fine."

We'd spent enough time sight seeing. I looked at Athena to see where we were supposed to go. It led us on a twisting, turning venture through the interconnected hallways of the museum. I kept Party Waffle by my side. Brijit trailed behind us.

After following the arrow around for a while, it pointed me at a specific painting:

A painting of Hell.

There were demons and fire and smoke. Was this like the mirror in the Muffincake Kingdom? Did Athena want me to go *through* the painting? I reached out and touched the canvas. It wasn't entirely solid. With just a slight bit of pressure, my fingertip passed right through.

So all of these paintings – the dinosaurs, the Last Supper, the Alice In Wonderland – they weren't just paintings. They were portals to other worlds.

And this painting of Hell was everything I'd been looking for. I'd traveled down through all those random dimensions and finally made it. Theodore was on the other side waiting for me to set him free.

But was it fair to lead Madam Brijit and Party Waffle into Hell? It was dangerous to take them with me, but I also couldn't leave them behind. I didn't know what to do.

I turned around to talk it out. Brijit was right there. Party Waffle was off looking at a psychedelic painting of the Beatles.

"Oooh," he said.

I snapped my fingers to get his attention. "Party Waffle."

Party Waffle put his hands on the Beatles painting. He made a louder, even more interested, "Oooh!" His hands started to pass through the canvas.

"Party Waffle! No!"

Party Waffle hooked his leg over the painting frame and crawled in. I made a break for him, but I didn't get there in time. He passed with through the canvas and vanished.

I threw my hands up. "Oh, god dammit!"

Brijit strolled up behind me. "He is nothing but a liability."

I sighed. "He's so dumb."

"So do we go in after him?"

I looked at Athena. The arrow was pointing me towards Hell. But Party Waffle was all alone in whatever Beatles world he went to. And then I thought about what Tengoku told me when she gave me Athena. She said, "Don't stray from whatever path Athena gives you." She made it sound like if I got off track, I might never come back.

I pointed at the Hell painting. "Athena says to go this way."

She pointed at the Beatles. "Party Waffle went this way."

"I can't keep chasing Party Waffle, man," I said. "That guy's a loose cannon. He's all over the map."

We locked eyes for a moment, then she pointed at me and said, "You're the one who brought him along in the first place."

"I didn't bring him *here*."

"You brought him with us the whole way through the Muffincake Kingdom."

"I fucking had to, dude. Do you remember how lost we were before he came along?"

"Right," she said. "He was useful then, but he's not useful now. So now he doesn't matter. You're going to leave him lost in whatever dimension he's in because it's inconvenient to you."

"Oh, like you wouldn't bail on Party Waffle if you knew Semedi was behind one of these paintings?"

She didn't have an answer for that.

"Exactly," I said. "Don't go acting like you're fucking Mother Teresa all of a sudden."

She took a step towards the painting of the Beatles. "I'm going to go after Party Waffle."

"You *hate* Party Waffle," I said.

"*You* hate Party Waffle," she said.

"I don't hate Party Waffle!"

"Then why am I the only one worried about him?"

"Whatever," I said. "You want to go after him? Go after him."

"I will. And if you don't come with me and bring your fancy arm, me and Party Waffle are going to be lost for forever."

I sighed. God dammit. "Brijit..."

She turned her back on me, said, "It's up to you," and stepped through the painting.

Chapter 17

1

Once we crossed through the painting of the Beatles, there was no going back. Whatever supernatural door connected one world to the next was sort of a one way trip. Crossing over, I found myself standing on a green hill overlooking a very Earth-like small town down in the valley.

Brijit was already headed down the hill after Party Waffle. Party Waffle rolled down the grass, laughing his ass off.

"Party Waffle," Brijit said. "Come here."

But Party Waffle was a circle rolling down a hill. He couldn't stop himself even if he wanted to.

There was an odd sound in the air. Something high pitched that would come and go, depending on the wind. Somewhere off in the distance, way beyond the town, I saw smoke. Black smoke. Something was burning.

I walked down the hill after the two of them.

"I hope you're happy," I hollered down.

"Are you talking to me or him?" Brijit asked.

"Either one of you," I said. "I hope you're both happy."

Brijit gave me a disgusted look and kept going after Party Waffle. Party Waffle kept building up speed. We both just walked after him. There was no hurry. He was going to be so dizzy when he reached the bottom of the hill, we'd have all the time in the world to catch up.

As we went further down the hill, that high pitched noise got louder. It was strange. I couldn't quite figure out what it was. It sounded like an animal, maybe like a dragon or something? It wasn't mechanical, I could tell that much.

The town looked very Earth-like, except from decades ago. A sign for one of the gas stations said gas was 23 cents a gallon. The abandoned cars looked like they were from the '50s.

And the high pitch sound was screaming. Not one person screaming, but thousands of people screaming. All girls. Thousands of screaming girls that sounded like they were getting murdered.

Party Waffle stumbled in place, dizzy from his roll down the hill.

"It's loud here," he said.

"Is that screaming?" Brijit asked.

I looked all around, but I didn't see any actual girls getting murdered. I did, however, see a big billboard sign welcoming us to town.

WELCOME
TO NEW BEATLEMANIA

That wasn't good. That wasn't good at all. I didn't know the first thing about New Beatlemania, except that every time anyone mentioned it, they didn't have anything good to say. They never said why, but they never had anything good to say.

"This isn't a good place," I said as I looked up at the sign.

"Have any of the places been good places?" Brijit asked.

"I think this one's really bad news, though."

"You *think*?"

"Yeah," I said. "I think."

A rushing, jet engine sound came from the sky. A jet liner flew overhead all cock-eyed and weird. It was practically sideways, careening towards the ground.

"Oh, shit," I said. "That plane's going to-"

The plane struck the ground and exploded into a fireball. There's no way anyone survived. The burning fireball faded into a bulging plume of black smoke that slowly rose up into the sky.

"That's a strange looking party," Party Waffle said.

Party Waffle had never seen a plane crash before. He didn't know what "die" meant. This was not the world for him.

"Here," I said to Party Waffle. I picked him up. "Come here. You stay with me."

"Oh, yeah!" He crawled up my body and posted up on my shoulders. "Baby on the dance floor!"

I checked Athena.

ErrorG. +-167../FFr72=+"begin:@go" 225:17
Calibrating...

Dammit. I smacked Athena with my free hand to get it to work. No such luck.

"What does it say?" Brijit asked me.

"It's broken," I said. "We went the wrong way and now it doesn't know where we are. Tengoku warned me about this."

"So how do we get out of here," she asked.

"No idea," I said.

We walked into the nearby town, past an auto body shop, a hairstylist, and a used bookstore. Almost immediately, I pieced together what all the screaming was about. We came across was an old '50s-looking diner and I could hear girls screaming inside. Cautiously, I climbed the front steps of the diner and looked in through the glass front door.

I saw two things inside. One, I saw the Beatles performing on a black and white television. We're talking the old mop-top Beatles during their British Invasion or whatever.

The other thing I saw was the entire diner filled with teenage girls straight up losing their shit over the Beatles. That's what all the screaming was. They were watching the TV, jumping in place, screaming so loud you couldn't hear the music.

Even the waitresses in the diner were screaming and jumping around. They were trying to serve milkshakes, but they couldn't keep their composure, not with the boys on the TV. The girls all spazzed out and lost their minds. Trays of chocolate milkshakes hit the tile floor. Broken glass went everywhere.

One girl looked at a menu like a sane person. Another girl stood there, trying to take her order. But when one of the girls sitting at the booth saw the Beatles on TV, she started screaming and pointing. Once she screamed and pointed, the two relatively sane girls turned to look. The moment they saw the Beatles bopping their stupid haircuts around, they also started screaming.

The waitress threw her notepad on the ground so she could run closer to the TV.

"What are they doing?" Brijit asked as she peered over my shoulder.

"They're in love with the Beatles," I said.

"Those men on the television?" she asked.

"Yeah. This really happened, but different. Where are the adults? Where are all the men?"

I turned to look at the rest of the town. An out of control car came screaming down main street. The girl in the driver seat screamed hysterically at whatever Beatles song played on her radio. There were two other girls in the car, one in the passenger seat, one in the back. Both of them were just as insane. The hyperventilating driver wasn't paying attention to where she was going. I doubted she could see through the tears in her eyes.

The car suddenly jerked hard to the left and smashed straight into a telephone pole. The girls in the front seats exploded head-first through the windshield and smacked the concrete. The driver split her skull wide open and her brains splattered everywhere. The other girl shoulder checked the telephone pole at top speed and it sent her body spinning sideways. She hit the ground hard and rolled around like a rag doll.

The girl in the back seat smashed her face on the seat in front of her and died.

I grabbed Party Waffle and turned him away.

Another plane sputtered out of control overhead. It passed right over the town, swerving left and right, doomed to come crashing down. I could just imagine some girl flying a jet when a Beatles song came over her headset and she lost control.

The plane was going to crash, it was going to kill every girl on board and none of them were even going to notice.

Brijit got out her shovel and walked over to the car wreck with the three dead girls. God, if she was going to bury all the girls in New Beatlemania, we were going to be here for a very long time.

But there was no talking her out of it, of course. It was a thing she had to do.

"I'm going to go look around," I told her.

"Okay," Brijit said. She grabbed the girl with the spilled brains by her armpits and dragged her body over to a grassy part of the sidewalk.

"I'll come back for you," I said.

"I'll be here," she said. She started digging.

2

There was a television shop with a dozen black and white TVs in the display window. They were all showing a broadcast of the Beatles on the Ed Sullivan show. A crowd of twenty girls had gathered in front of the store window, screaming and jumping and crying.

"Party!" Party Waffle said. He jumped off my shoulder and went running.

"Party Waffle, stop!" I shouted.

He didn't stop. He ran to go join the girls. He jumped in place and screamed, even though he couldn't see the TVs and didn't know who the Beatles were.

I needed to get him a leash.

I reached the group of screaming girls. They totally ignored me and Party Waffle. I snatched him up off the ground.

"Party Waffle," I said. "You can't keep running off like that."

"But party," he said.

"This is not a party," I said. "It looks like a party, but it's not. These girls are very sick."

"What is sick?" he asked.

"Sick means they have no idea what they're doing."

I kept a tight grip on Party Waffle and kept walking. Once we got a block away from the TV store, I heard the distinct sound of screaming tires. I turned just in time to see a speeding car plow through that group of girls and smash into the front windows of the TV store. Blood and guts and glass went everywhere.

"God, this place is mayhem," I said.

Was the whole world like this? Why hadn't this city already burned to the ground? Destruction lurked behind every corner. Every intersection was a pile-up of burning cars. The burnt remains of an airplane stuck out of the top of a library. Smashed bodies of teeny-bopper girls were strewn all across the sidewalks, all of them dead, some of them decomposing.

Was there not a single adult in New Beatlemania? Was this whole place nothing but mindless teenage girls?

No, there was a man. Just one. He stood in the middle of the street in front of us. He wore a black suit, like a record label executive. He wasn't screaming his head off like all the girls, so I kept walking towards him.

"Hey!" I called out. "Hey, buddy!"

He stood there and faced me. He didn't respond, he didn't wave, he didn't do much of anything but stand there.

"Hey," I said as I reached him. "Hey, what's going on?"

He tilted his head and stared through me with vacant eyes. "Have you come for the concert?"

"The concert?" I asked. "No. I'm not here for any concert. I'm trying to get the hell out of this place."

"The concert is starting soon," he said. "You should go to the concert." His voice was plain. Monotone. Emotionless. It put me on edge.

I took a careful step away from him. "We don't really want to go to any concert. We're just trying to leave."

"Everyone is going to the concert."

"Everyone but us."

"You should go to the concert."

This guy was really wrapped up in this concert. I wasn't going to go to any concert, not in New Beatlemania, but this was my one chance to maybe figure out what was going on.

"Alright," I said. "What's this concert?"

"Haven't you heard the big news?" he asked, plainly. "The Beatles are playing a concert at the gazebo in Abbey Park. You should go."

"The Beatles are playing *here*?" I asked. "Oh, man. This place is going to go nuclear."

"You should go to the concert," he said.

"I don't want to go to the concert."

"Everyone is going."

"Well, good for everyone," I said. "Nice talking to you. Thanks for nothing. I'm going to go this way now."

I walked away from him. Curious, I glanced back over my shoulder. The guy was still standing there, stock still. He stared me down. Chills ran down my spine.

We walked another block and when I turned to look behind me one more time, the man was gone.

I hugged Party Waffle a little closer to me.

Eventually we came across Lady Madonna's Memorial Hospital. The noise from inside was terrifying. Hundreds and hundreds of girls were screaming. The parking lot was a mess of overturned and smashed cars. Bodies of dead girls were scattered everywhere. A renegade bulldozer had crushed a hole into the hospital wall.

Somewhere in the distance came the deafening crack of a powerful explosion. The street shook beneath my shoes. I couldn't see what exploded, but another rising plume of black smoke floated up in the distance. Who knew what that was. A gas station? A fertilizer factory?

Past the hospital was a massive twelve car pile up. Most of the cars were on fire. Dead and burned bodies laid all around. A car full of hysterical girls came speeding towards us; I just barely heard it coming and jumped out of the way. It barreled straight into the pile up. The girls smashed right through the front windshield and disappeared into the wreck of mangled cars.

Their screams went silent.

Wherever I went, all I could hear were Beatles songs being drowned out by screaming girls.

We needed a way out of New Beatlemania and bad.

I whacked Athena again to get it to work.

Calibrating...

Still "calibrating"? Fucking thing.

3

New Beatlemania was a humble little Midwestern town with a single hospital, only one high school and no major highways. I'd explored a vast majority of the major streets by the time evening came. Just before sunset, all the girls came flooding out into the streets like a mass evacuation. They all funneled onto Main Street and started moving in the same direction, screaming and crying and running as fast as they could.

Party Waffle and I would have been trampled if I didn't dip into the front alcove of a clothing store and watch them flood past us like the running of the bulls. Party Waffle watched them go by with wide eyes and a huge smile.

The girls must have heard the news that the Beatles were playing a surprise concert at the gazebo in the park. The only thing these girls cared about were the Beatles, so what else could have possibly dragged them away from their TVs and radios?

When the mob had mostly passed, I decided to follow them. For lack of any better leads to follow, the concert was the one thing that stood out as something important. Maybe that's where

I would find our way out.

I trailed behind the riot of girls, safely out of harms way. They pushed and elbowed against one another in a desperate bid to get to the front of the crowd. They eventually led me to a big park of walnut and pecan trees with a white octagon gazebo built in the middle. The gazebo was a pretty good size, big enough for a full band and raised up off the ground so that when the Beatles did take the stage, they would be just out of reach.

Every girl in New Beatlemania was there in the park, pressed up against all sides of the gazebo and filling the park all the way back to the streets that surrounded it. Since the Beatles weren't actually there yet, the girls managed to keep themselves under control. But just barely. They were still squealing and bouncing in place and most of them had tears running down their faces. They were wound up tight, ready to explode at the first sight of their British crushes.

It was my one chance to talk to one of them and maybe get some answers.

Me and Party Waffle were tucked safely in the very back of the crowd. I grabbed one of the girls as she came running up, arriving late. She was some teenie-bopper in a pink '60s skirt and cute shoes. She was about to blaze right past me, but I managed to grab her by the arm and hook her back around.

"Hey," I said to her. "Can I ask you-"

"Which one's your favorite?" she nearly screamed, already crying. "I love Paul so much."

"I don't really have a favorite," I said.

"I know! It's so hard to decide! I love Paul!" She covered her face with her hands and cried harder. "I just love him so much."

I leg go her arm. "Ugh. Okay, never mind. You can leave."

None of these girls were going to be of any help. They couldn't think straight. They were all one big hysterical mess. All of New Beatlemania was one big hysterical mess.

I kept my distance from the back of the crowd. Keeping out of the way was easy. None of the girls wanted to be in the back. They all pushed their way closer to the front.

One thing was for sure: when the Beatles did show up, this place was going to go bananas.

"I want to go party," Party Waffle said. He tried to struggle free from my grasp.

"Absolutely not," I said, tightening him against me in a hug. "This is not a party. This is dangerous."

"It's a party!" he said.

"It's not. Trust me."

He pouted, but I wasn't going to cave. This was for his own good. Party Waffle had no idea what was really going on. I mean, I didn't know what was going on either, but I did know one thing: whatever was going on was super bizarre and it wasn't safe for Party Waffle to go off dancing.

A man in a suit climbed the steps to the gazebo. It was the same dude in the black suit from before, the creepy one who wanted me to go to the concert. He got up in front of everyone and took a microphone off one of the microphone stands, ready to address the crowd. He didn't seem the least bit excited. He just stood still and looked out over the sea of girls with emotionless eyes.

In a dull, monotone voice, he asked, "Are you ready to begin the concert?"

The girls didn't notice his lack of enthusiasm. They weren't there for some soulless thing in a suit. They were there for the Beatles. When he asked the girls if they were ready to start the concert, they all flipped their collective shit. The screaming doubled in volume. The black suit guy kept talking, but I couldn't hear a word he was saying over the crowd.

Four men crawled out of holes in the gazebo floor and stood. They were the Beatles, alright. But these couldn't be the real Beatles. I mean, that was impossible. For one, not all the Beatles are dead. Johnny Lennon and Georgey-Boy Harrison were dead, but old man Ringus and Pauly McCarts were skin-and-bones music zombies still living on Earth. The four boys in front of us strapping on guitars and setting up behind the drum kit were in their mid-twenties.

So who were they? Some type of clone? Some kind of spiritual reincarnation? Or who knows what. They were real enough for the girls, because the moment they hit the stage the crowd screamed with such intensity that they started to hyperventilate. Some of them even passed out and fell down to the grass.

The Fab Four started playing their instruments, but I couldn't hear what song they were doing. Things were too loud. Impostors or not, not four really got into their performance, bouncing in place and flopping their mop-top hairstyles around.

I hated to admit it, but in that moment, I did feel like I was having fun. I mean, come on, this was an experience I would never get in real life, to see the OG Beatles do their thing. I inched a little bit closer to hear what song they were playing.

Oh, how could I dance with another?

Ooh.

When I saw her stand-ing there.

I caught myself smiling. Now, I wasn't fan-girling out like everyone else – no, no, that would be crazy – but I'd be a liar if I said I didn't start feeling the vibe.

"I want to dance!" Party Waffle whined. "You get to dance! I want to dance!"

I didn't even notice I was dancing. Ha. I don't know if it was dancing, necessarily, but I was shaking my hips back and forth. Alright, well, fair was fair. If I was going to dance, I couldn't rightfully tell Party Waffle that he couldn't.

"Okay." I set him down. "Let's dance."

I boogied at Party Waffle. He boogied at me, swinging his arms and shaking his waffle hips.

The band finished their song and started in with "I Wanna Hold Your Hand." I was really feeling the energy, so when I heard the first line I excitedly jumped in place.

Oh, yeah I'll

tell you something.

I think you'll understand.

Ooh, I knew that song! I jumped up and cheered and...

I stopped. I froze. What in the hell was I doing?

Oh my god, I was getting sucked in.

I shouted at party Waffle, "Stop dancing!"

"What?" He looked up at me. "No!"

"Party Waffle, stop!" I swiped him up off the ground. "Cover your ears!"

I had no idea what was causing it, but the music was somehow turning me into one of those idiot girls. Once the realization set it, I looked around the park and saw things for what they really were.

The gazebo wasn't really a gazebo. It *looked* like a gazebo, but each one of the eight sides opened up with a long, narrow mouth. Inside were needle-sharp teeth of rusty nails and cracked wood. As the crowd pushed closer and closer to the Beatles, the girls up close were pushed off balance and fell into waiting mouths of the monster. Once a few girls toppled inside, the mouths chomped closed and chewed their bodies into a bloody pulp. Blood and guts and bones and clothes were all mashed up, then swallowed down in a pulpy mess.

The monster opened its mouths again, hungry for more.

None of the girls noticed. They were too wrapped up in the Beatles on stage. They were hypnotized.

Those men weren't the Beatles. I didn't notice it before, but those impostors had sunken black eyes. Instead of feet, they had a mass of black octopus tentacles wriggling out of the bottoms of their pants. Those "Beatles" were just an extension of the same terrible monster that chewed up human bodies.

I couldn't bring myself to look away as another round of human girls were unwittingly pushed inside the monsters open jaws. I slowly stated walking backwards.

"I wanna go back!" Party Waffle cried. "I wanna dance!"

The dancing *was* fun. And the Beatles were playing one of their most iconic songs. It wouldn't hurt to go back for just a little longer...

No. I tried to shake the cobwebs out of my brain, trying to break whatever spell that music had over me. I had to get us away from the park. I had to get us to safety.

The nightmare mouths were making an absolute mess of the human cattle gathered all around them. Thin, metal teeth shredded the flesh from the girls' bones. Hair and flesh and strips of skin were caught in the monster's teeth. The many mouths seemed to almost smile as they devoured more of the hypnotized victims. Once the girls closest to the stage were devoured and gone, the next round of girls pushed their way to the front.

The continued force of the shoving crowd pushed them against the gazebo and into the gnashing teeth.

"I like this song," Party Waffle said.

"I said cover your ears!"

Party Waffle hummed along.

I tightened my grip on him. I wasn't going to let him get away from me. Not now. Him running off and jumping through a portal was one thing. Getting devoured by this terrifying gazebo-type Pokemon was another.

The grass in front of the gazebo was soaked in blood. Crushed bits of skulls and femurs and rib cages were scattered all around. The hysterical girls slipped around on the wet gore as they pressed closer to the stage. More than anything, they wanted to be closer to the Beatles.

"This is fucked." I turned to run.

I was about to break into a sprint when I came face to face with the man in the black suit. He stood a foot taller than me and glanced down with wet, black eyes.

"You came to the concert," he said.

I looked down. His feet were a wormy mess of black tentacles.

"What are you?" I said.

He tasted the air with his tongue, licking and smacking. The saliva coating the inside of his mouth was the sick color of lead.

"Impossible Red," he said. "You taste of Impossible Red."

I took a step back and balled up my fists.

"What do you know about that?" I said. "What *are* you?"

"Don't you recognize me, cousin?" He tilted his head and pointed his black eyes at the gazebo. "I am Unthinkable Black."

Unthinkable Black. I hadn't heard anyone use that name in years. Just like how Impossible Red made me the god of war, and Untouchable Orange made Theodore the god of fire, Unthinkable Black would make it's host body the god of destruction. It had already destroyed an entire dimension, the place where the god spheres had first been created.

But Unthinkable Black hadn't been activated. No one had swallowed it. It existed as a tiny black marble hidden in New York City and only I knew where it was.

"You're not Unthinkable Black," I said.

"Unthinkable Black was always the most powerful god," he said. "I cannot be contained for long. My power has been leaking out. What I have done to this world is only a glimmer a what I can do. This is only a shadow of what I can become."

I shook my head. "Unthinkable Black hasn't been activated."

He said, "I am powerful, even when I am asleep."

Black Suit took a step towards me. Panic welled up inside me and Impossible Red responded by injecting an entire pint of adrenaline directly into my bloodstream. My face flushed red and my hands started to shake. Impossible Red expected me to fight, but I couldn't. I had Party Waffle in my arms and I couldn't let him go. If I let him go, he'd get sucked into the music and run straight for those terrible mouths.

I pointed at Black Suit. "You stay away from me."

In that some monotone voice, he said, "Or you'll what."

"Or I'll this."

I threw a Back Hand of a Thousand Dump Trucks.

The creepy dude's head caved in like a busted jack-o-lantern. The bottom half of his jaw hung limp from his skin and muscles.

Black sludge gushed down over my hand and all down the front of his suit. It smelled like shit and sulfur and wet trash. He stood there for half a second, then slumped to the ground.

4

I wasn't going to hang around and see how much worse things were going to get. I tucked Party Waffle into my arms like a football and made a mad dash back into the city streets.

Behind us, I heard a roar that shook the ground and knocked me to the ground. I tried to get back to my feet, but the streets were shaking so bad, it felt like trying to walk on a trampoline. I looked back at the park and saw the gazebo shudder in place. It cracked loose from its foundation and rose up from the ground, supported by thousands of unfolding granddaddy spider legs. It rose higher and higher into the air until it towered high above the treetops.

The gazebo monster wasn't interested in eating girls any more. I had killed its suit monster. Now it wanted revenge.

I sprinted through the streets of New Beatlemania as fast as my scrawny legs could carry me. The eight-mouthed gazebo monster chased after us, walking taller than the stores and houses. The Beatles were still on stage, but they weren't playing music anymore. I saw them in their true form; slimy black creatures with white tentacles wriggling out of their eye holes and mouths. Instead of singing, they howled with ungodly noise.

A thin spider leg came down right in front of us and spiked a hole in the street. I juked around it and kept running.

I had to get to Madam Brijit.

"Is this fun?" Party Waffle shouted.

"Absolutely not!"

I didn't know the streets of New Beatlemania that well, but you don't live in New York your whole life without getting good at directions. I recognized my landmarks, like the intersection filled with burning cars and the TV store with the dead bodies scattered all around, and I used them to work my way back to where I had last seen Brijit.

I hooked around a corner of the bank just as one of the spider legs smashed through the wall. I cradled my body around Party Waffle to protect him and felt chunks of brick and mortar crunch against the back of my head.

I kept running and didn't look back.

The gazebo monster stepped right over entire buildings and could cross city blocks in no time flat. It shadows loomed over me and I knew it was on my ass pretty good. I kicked my pace into overdrive and crunched footprints in the concrete. I started to put distance between us and the monster, but it wasn't giving up. It kept coming, skittering up and over anything that got in its way.

Brijit was dead ahead. She had finished a dozen graves and was waist-deep in the ground digging another.

"Brijit!" I shouted. She looked up at me. "Run!"

Her eyes moved from me up into the sky where she saw the gazebo monster.

With her eyes locked on the freaky thing, she dropped her shovel and slowly backed out of the grave. "What did you do!?"

We reached her and I grabbed her arm to pull her along. "Just run!"

She sprinted alongside me. "What in the hell is that thing?"

"Unthinkable Black," I said. "Bad news!"

We ran aimlessly through town. We passed the empty record store. We passed a bunch of burned down homes. We passed an abandoned high school. It quickly became obvious that there was no way out of New Beatlemania.

We had to do things the old fashioned way.

"We're going to have to kill it!" I shouted at her.

"Kill it?" she said. "How?"

"I don't know!"

"You're the god of war," she said. "You don't know how?"

What the hell? I'm the god of war, not General Fucking Eisenhower leading the charge on D-Day. I had no idea how to fight a spider gazebo. What's more, my hands were full with Party Waffle. He was quiet and confused and scared.

Spider Gazebo used its front legs legs to uproot a five story apartment building and lift it into the air. Water lines popped and sprayed into the air. The concrete foundation crumbled into pieces and crushed the cars below. The iron fire escapes twisted loose and clattered to the ground.

Spider Gazebo swung its arms back and and threw the entire building at us. Almost immediately, we were swallowed up in its dark shadow.

I called out, "Brace for impact!"

Five stories of brick and steel crashed down on us. Brijit was running next to me one moment, then suddenly she vanished in the rubble. A steel girder whacked me across the head and knocked me to the ground. T thousand tons of bricks piled on top of my body and pinned me to the ground. Concrete dust got in my eyes and blinded me. Somewhere in all of that I lost my grip on Party Waffle and dropped him.

I was deafened by the sound of the world ending, then everything went quiet. I coughed the dust out of my lungs. I tried to push myself free, but I was trapped beneath three stories of brick.

Come on, I thought to Impossible Red. *Give me more juice.*

I put all my strength into my arms and legs and pushed up. Brick walls and steel beams shifted and clattered off of me. I got the upper half of my body free. Things were dark, but a little sunlight shone through the gaps in the debris. Oil dripped from my mouth and nose.

I coughed and spit the taste of concrete out of my mouth. "Brijit?" I called out. "Party Waffle?" No answer. Their silence freaked me out. I worried that they were dead. I shouted again, even louder. "Brijit! Party Waffle!"

Nothing.

Finally I heard the sifting of broken glass and the sound of Brijit coughing. "I'm good," she called out. She pulled herself loose from underneath a pile of bricks and wooden rafters. Blood drizzled from a deep cut on her cheek and her wedding gown was all torn up. She dusted herself off and said, "Party Waffle?"

He didn't answer.

I shouted louder. "Party Waffle!?"

We both called his name. Still nothing.

That's when we started searching. In a panic, I sifted through the bricks and threw steel girders out of my way.

"Over here," Brijit said.

I crawled over to Brijit. There beneath a pile of cinder blocks were the golden edges of his waffle body. I swiped the bricks out of my way like a woman possessed. Party Waffle laid there flat on his face. I flipped him over. He wasn't moving.

He didn't open his eyes.

"Party Waffle," I said. He didn't respond. I shook him, just enough to get him back to his senses. "Party Waffle!"

"Penelope," Brijit said, softly. I looked up at her. "He's dead."

"No." I looked back at Party Waffle. "You don't know that."

"Yes. I do."

I was already crying. "He can't fucking be dead." I shook him harder and shouted. "Party Waffle! Wake up!"

Brijit didn't say anything.

Party Waffle laid there limp in my arms. His little hands and feet didn't move. He used to point into the air with those fingers. He used to kick me in the shins with those feet. All Party Waffle ever wanted to do was party.

And now he was dead.

I fought back my tears, tightened my lips and told Brijit, "Bring him back."

A single tear dripped down her cheek. "I can't."

5

Party Waffle's death was all my fault. Before I came along, his life was everything he wanted it to be: he could dance his way through the Muffincake Kingdom and deliver messages back and forth between the princesses. Then I came along and changed everything. I made him act as our guide and that led us here. Now he was dead. No more singing. No more dancing. No more happy, happy birthday from Applebee's to you.

I'm no good with death. I put my face in my hands and sobbed like a baby, then I looked up at Brijit and said, "I want to kill that fucking gazebo."

Brijit nodded. She spit in her hand and reached out.

I spit in my hand. We shook on it.

We came crawling out of the rubble. I had so much rage inside me, my clothes started to smoke. Madam Brijit's rain boots lifted up off the ground. Her red dreadlocks floated weightlessly around her head. I don't know if the Unthinkable Black Spider Gazebo could see the fury in our eyes.

I hoped it could. I hoped it was scared.

I planted my feet on the concrete and clenched my fists.

I asked Brijit, "You got any special moves?"

"Besides flying?"

"Can you get me up there?" I pointed at Spider Gazebo, suspended far overhead by its countless spider legs.

"I can give you a lift." She held out her hand. "Grab on."

We gripped forearms.

"Alright, Bat Face," I said. "Let's do this."

"You got it," she said. "Pencil."

She lifted off and whisked me up into the air.

Spider Gazebo raised dozens of its spider legs into attack position and swiped at us, trying to knock us out of the sky. Brijit swerved and dodged like a fighter pilot dodging anti-aircraft fire. One leg almost scored a direct hit, but I swung my arm out and knocked it away.

Once we were in range of the gazebo body, Brijit spun me around and threw me into the air. I flew with my arms and legs flailing, then landed with a thud on the slanted floor of the gazebo. My arrival was anything but graceful and I tumbled right in front of the four black sludge monsters.

I wiped the blood off my face. "You killed Party Waffle."

Their deformed mouths opened and howled four dissonant nightmare noises.

I got to my feet. "I don't accept your apology."

I ran into the mix of all four of them. I punched one in the head with such tremendous force, the floorboards of the gazebo cracked.

Brijit flew into one of the gazebo mouths. It bit down, but she held it open with her arms and legs. It tried to bite down harder, but she pushed against it. She pushed so hard, in fact, the wood exploded and the bottom jaw burst loose. It crashed down to the city below.

The other seven mouths howled in pain.

I don't know which fake Beatle I was fighting, but I punched him right in the chest. All of his rotten black organs exploded out of his back. The creature collapsed to the floor.

Spider Gazebo stumbled around, racked with pain.

Brijit took out her magic shovel and used it to bash planks of wood off the outside of the gazebo. The monster lurched forward, trying to swallow her up.

The sudden movements of the gazebo threw me off balance and I wiped out, sprawling all across the floor. I nearly slid over the edge, but I grabbed two of the rail posts and dangled there.

Brijit came flying up, grabbed me by the waist of my shorts and boosted me back onto the gazebo floor. She created a solid beam of blue moonlight in her hands and chucked it like a spear, impaling one of the sludge monsters right through the chest.

I dashed for her moonlight bar and yanked it free. I used it to bash another one of the sludge monsters head open.

The last Beatle impostor monster used its face tentacles to gore me right through the guts. I cried out and doubled over in pain. Hot oils gushed out of my stomach and spilled all down the fronts of my legs.

No time to wimp out now.

I grit my teeth and karate chopped the black tentacles into pieces. With the spikes still stuck in my stomach, I dashed forward and gave the monster a solid SWAT Team kick to the chest. Its torso caved in. Black goo came gushing out.

Brijit flew beneath the Spider Gazebo, then rocketed straight up. She exploded through the wood floors like a missile and smashed through the ceiling beams.

Spider Gazebo began to lose its balance. It tilted hard and this time I couldn't hang on. I slipped right over the edge, fell out of the sky and smacked down on the concrete street.

The gazebo toppled over and crashed down on top of me.

I laid there, bleeding and wondering if I was dead. Since I was *wondering* if I was dead, I obviously wasn't dead. I literally clawed my way out of the wreckage. Twitching spider legs were draped across the town for blocks. The wooden gazebo body was destroyed. Slowly the wooden planks of it melted into black tar.

I limped to the sidewalk. There, I pulled the two wriggling tentacles out of my guts. More oil poured out. It soaked the front of my shirt and squished in my shoes when I walked.

"You alright?" Brijit asked as she descended out of the sky.

"I think so." I pressed my hands to the holes in my body and then looked at my palms. They were coated in oil. "I'm losing a lot of blood."

"Are you going to die?"

"I don't think so," I said. "Impossible Red is pretty good about..." Whoa. I suddenly felt dizzy. "It's pretty good about..." I was going to fall over. "I just need to sit down."

I plopped down there on the curb. I felt so light headed.

I kept telling myself, *Don't pass out. Don't pass out. Don't-*

6

When I came to, it was night in New Beatlemania. The pain in my guts throbbed in time with my heartbeat. I wrapped my arms around my stomach and found that the holes were gone. Impossible Red had healed me up on the outside. Now it was just working on my insides.

I was starving. Impossible Red had used up all the raw materials in my stomach. I needed more.

I rolled my head to the right. Brijit sat there on the curb, legs spread, her bottle in one hand and her cigar in the other. She was staring off into space.

"You okay?" I asked.

She looked over, surprised to see I was awake. "I should be the one asking you that."

I winced in pain as I sat up. "I think I'm good."

"You've been out for hours. I got you some food." She slid a restaurant bus tray full of clean silverware towards me. "Figured you'd be hungry after all that."

I reached into the tray and pulled out a fork and spoon. "Thanks."

I ate the fork. Brijit puffed on her cigar and looked up at the stars. "I buried Party Waffle while you were out."

"Oh."

"I figured you'd want to be there, but I couldn't wait."

"It's okay."

She pointed at a small flower garden out in front of a nearby shoe store. "He's over there if you want to go say something."

I growled in pain, but managed to get to my feet. "Yeah." I limped towards the garden, then turned back. "You coming?"

"No." She didn't look at me. She took a swig of rum. "I already said my peace."

I nodded.

I could see where Brijit buried Party Waffle. There was a small square of recently tended dirt. She had put a stick of butter and sugar cube there to mark the spot.

What do you say to a Party Waffle?

"Hey, buddy. I know I didn't know you very long, but you were always pretty cool. I'm sorry I yelled at you that one time."

I'm not very good with words when it comes to emotions. I didn't know what else to say. I felt tears coming. I slowly moved my hips back and forth. I did the slightest dance while I cried.

"Baby on the dance floor."

PERTINACITY

Metatron and Zophiel marched through the crowded walkways of Funnel Cake Island. All around them were creatures that resembled the Sons of Adam and the Daughters of Eve, but they were something else entirely. They were creatures of flour and water and sugar and eggs. They weren't anything of God's creation and, therefore, absolutely no interest to the archangels.

They were surrounded by flashing lights and clattering bells. Their noses were bombarded with offensive smells of buttered popcorn and hot dogs and cotton candy.

Zophiel's eyes perked up as one smell in particular caught her attention. It came from something called a "BBQ stand."

"Do you smell this?" Zophiel said to Metatron.

"I do," he said. "It is the smell of burning sacrifice."

"Scorched oxen," Zophiel said.

The front side of the "BBQ stand" had an open window with a serving counter. There were three people working inside, placing mysterious food stuffs inside paper bags and boxes. Zophiel moved closer for a better look.

"What can I get you?" the smiling young flour-creature said from inside the stand. It wore a uniform of red and white stripes.

"This smell," Zophiel said. "Is it oxen?"

"It's beef," the boy said. "Beef ribs."

Zophiel did not respond.

The boy added, "And we make our own sauce. Do you want to try it?"

Zophiel was confused. "Try it?"

"Here." The boy took some small plastic container and filled it with a thick liquid that reminded Zophiel of human blood. He put the container down on the counter between them and smiled. Zophiel looked at the sauce, then at the boy. The boy mimed putting his fingertip to his tongue. "Try it."

Zophiel recreated his action. She put her gleaming platinum finger into the sauce, then placed her fingertip on her tongue.

The sauce was vile. She spat it out.

"Poison," she said. She stepped back and drew her sword.

"Poison?" Metatron asked.

Zophiel pointed. "This one tried to poison me."

"It's not poison," the creature said. "It's-"

Zophiel brought her colossal sword down with an overhand swing and demolished the front of the BBQ stand. The creatures inside the stand panicked and dashed out the door to safety. The angel raised her sword and swung again, crushing what was left of the countertop.

Metatron was quick to act. He swung his battle ax and smashed the side wall of the stand into toothpicks. Zophiel spotted the large metal pot of poison inside. She gave it a solid kick, spilling the contents all across the concrete walkway.

They did not stop there. The desecrated stand had to be completely destroyed. Together, driven by holy justice, the two of them reduced the BBQ stand to trash. The people of Funnel Cake Island – a humble and simple people – backed away with confused and terrified looks.

"Let's not stay here any longer than required," Zophiel said. "This is a place of depravity."

Metatron nodded in agreement. "All these people know is sloth and gluttony. There is no discipline here."

The two angels continued down the path. This time they did not put their weapons away. Zophiel turned to address the gathered crowds.

"Had we the time or the inclination, we would eradicate this entire conurbation!"

"And you sinners along with it!" Metatron added.

They stormed through the rest of Funnel Cake Island.

"The longer she evades us," Metatron said, "the more infuriated I become."

"We are close," Zophiel said. "The memories of Penelope Salvo grow stronger with each new world. We are gaining on her. She can't hide much longer."

Chapter 18

1

"Tell me we're not stuck here for forever," Brijit said.
We sat on the curb of Lucy Avenue in New Beatlemania.
"I don't know," I said. "I hope not."
I looked at Athena.

6Y://00004bB JjKLM0+..+
Calibrating...

Stupid thing. It was trying to rectify where I was supposed to be with where I actually was, which was the wrong dimension. It never meant for me to go to New Beatlemania. It was searching for a new path to Hell and having a hard time finding it.

Tengoku warned me about this.

But Tengoku knows everything. She knew this was going to happen. If she knew this was going to happen, then she should have programmed this part into Athena. But I guess there are a lot of possible worlds for her to keep straight. Knowing literally everything out of all possible possibilities can't be easy.

We sat there in the dark night, Brijit and I. She drank her rum. I drank a can of motor oil I found at the gas station around the corner. The night air was filled with the shrieking of girls watching the Beatles on TV. We'd killed the monster, but not New Beatlemania.

I felt so bad for Party Waffle. I couldn't stop blaming myself. If I never would have gone on this trip, if I never would have met Party Waffle, he'd still be alive. He was dead because of me.

I would never be able to forgive myself for that.

And, oh god, what would Princess Coffeecake or Princess Pancake say? Party Waffle was in my care and he died? They think of me as their hero. I really let them down.

Brijit didn't seem to be in any higher spirits than me. She just sat there, shoulders slumped, taking occasional drinks of rum.

Silence.

Brijit said, "I blame myself."

I nodded. "I do, too."

More silence.

I asked her, "Do you know any jokes?"

"I don't feel like joking," she said.

Fair. We stayed quiet.

"It might make you feel better," I said.

"Doubt it." She drank more rum.

I nodded. She was right.

I dug out my cigarette box and pulled out a spliff. I didn't think the hysterical girls of New Beatlemania would mind. I lit it up, took a puff, then held it out to Brijit. She took it and hit it.

Things went on like that for a while, silently puffing and passing.

Eventually she spoke up. "Why don't you ever see elephants hiding in trees?"

Was this a joke? Did she change her mind? "Why?" I asked.

She took a hit and said, "Because they're really good at it."

I made a stupid laugh. Stupid laugh for a stupid joke.

Was this going to be us for all eternity? Sitting around New Beatlemania as the world burned all around us? I didn't have enough weed for that.

"How much do you really know about Earth?" I asked her.

"Some," she said. "Caribbean stuff, mostly. I don't go to Earth very often. When I do, I mostly go to Haiti." She looked at me. "They love me in Haiti."

"I've never been to Haiti."

"You'd fit right in," she said.

"Really?"

She shook her head. "No."

I reflected on my relationship with Madam Brijit. It had changed a lot in the months we'd been traveling. I didn't hate

331

her anymore. And it didn't seem like she hated me. She wasn't all that bad, really, just a little moody. And it's not like I'm not moody, too, so we were just a bad combination. She's alright once you get to know her and-

Athena flashed at me.

Calibrated.
Searching...

"Whoa." I jumped to my feet and didn't dare look away from my arm. I raised Athena closer to the sky, because that's what you do when you need a stronger signal.

Brijit got up. "What?"

"We might have something here."

Searching...

"Come on," I said, coaxing it to work. I bumped it lightly. "Come on. Come on. Come on."

5 kilometers.

And the arrow popped up, pointing east.

"Oh my fucking god, it's working!" I threw my arms around Brijit and hugged her. "It's working!"

"Okay." She tried to get free from the hug. "Okay."

"This way!" I moved in the direction of the arrow. "Let's go!"

She picked her rum bottle up off the sidewalk. "I'm coming."

I jogged through the streets of New Beatlemania, but that quickly turned into a full sprint. Just when I was convinced we were going to spend eternity in the worst place ever, things turned around for us.

Brijit ran alongside me. She was just as eager to get out of New Beatlemania as I was. The endless screaming was driving me insane.

Athena led us to the middle of an intersection. We were at very little risk of getting hit by cars since it was the middle of the night. We stood there in the intersection and looked around.

"Now what?" Brijit asked.

"Uh." I took stock of everything around me. A blinking red traffic light hung overhead, suspended on a wire. We were at the intersection of White and Revolver. There was no supernatural door. There was no mysterious portal.

I threw up my arms. "Well, what the hell."

Brijit looked around. She bent over and said, "This?" She stuck her finger in the hole of a manhole cover.

"Is that it?" I asked.

She lifted the manhole cover and dragged it away. It scraped loud across the concrete.

A white light glowed from inside. Fog drifted out like dry ice.

"Do street holes usually look like this?" she asked.

I said, "Nope."

"Then I think this is it," she said.

"Definitely."

"You first," she offered.

"After you."

She stared down into the hole. It was impossible to tell what was on the other side. It was obscured by a bright white fog.

"Okay." She pulled up the hem of her dress. She looked at me. "See you on the other side."

She jumped in and vanished.

My turn. I took a moment to flip New Beatlemania both birds. "Fuck you, New Beatlemania!" I shouted. Then I looked up the lonely streets and said, "See ya, Party Waffle."

And I jumped in after her.

2

"Penelope?" Brijit called out.

I couldn't see her. We were in a big white nothing. Fog filled the air.

"I'm right here," I said.

"Where?" she asked.

"I don't know," I said. "I can't see you."

"I can't see you."

I swept my arms through the fog in hopes I might touch her.

"I'm feeling around for you," I said.

"I'm feeling around for *you*," she replied

"Follow my voice."

"I *am* following your voice."

The ground was soft and fluffy, like walking on foam. There was no color to the sky. It was just a world of white fog. Eventually I saw the dark shape of a person. I went towards it.

It was Brijit. She saw me, too. We found each other, but even standing face to face, it was hard to see one another. The fog was that dense. It wasn't wet like fog, but it didn't smell like smoke. It was just... swirling whiteness.

"You don't know where we are," she said. "Do you."

"Nope."

She asked, "What's your arm say?"

I looked down to check.

1,000,000,000,000,000,000,000,000,000,000,000,000 kilometers.

What in the actual fuck. That can't be real. I smacked it. The number stayed the same. That was a lot of zeroes.

"What?" she asked. "What's wrong? What's it say?"

I sighed. "You don't want to know."

"What? Why?"

Athena did have an arrow, for what that was worth. It pointed... well, *that* way. There was no east or west in this place, no left or right.

"It's a really big number," I said.

"How big?" she asked.

"Pretty god damn big."

"Like a million?"

"Oh, waaaaaay more than a million."

"Let me see." She took my arm and held it close to her face so she could read it in the fog. She processed the number, then looked at me. "Is this a joke?"

"I don't think this thing jokes around, man."

"Well, maybe it's broken." She had an accusatory tone to her voice.

"Maybe it is," I said. "I don't know."

There were no sounds except for our voices. No smells. Nothing to see. Just me and Brijit.

"Welp," I said. "Let's start walking."

I headed in the direction of Athena's arrow.

"You actually want to walk a million, billion, trillion, miles?"

I said, "I'm just going to follow the arrow, dude. Who knows how distance works here. Maybe it's not really that far. Or, like you said, maybe Athena's broken. It's probably all out of whack because we're way off track and lost in a bunch of worlds we're not supposed to be in. Either way, we gotta go somewhere, so we might as well go this way."

I headed off in the direction Athena told me to go. Brijit didn't follow. If I took one more step, I would lose her in the fog.

"Brijit, come on."

"Wait." She held her finger in the air and looked all around.

"What?"

"He's here," she said. She whipped around to me. "He's here!"

"Semedi?"

"He's this way!"

She bolted into the swirling fog. I immediately lost her. "Brijit!" I shouted. I ran after her, but I couldn't see her.

I could *hear* her. "This way!" she called out.

"That's not helpful, dude! I can't see you!" She didn't answer. "Brijit, come back!" Still no answer. I shouted at the top of my lungs. "Brijit, god dammit!"

She was gone. Lost in her excitement, she left me all alone. Now I had my choices: keep following Athena to the end of eternity in one direction, or get even more lost hoping to stumble ass-backwards in Madam Brijit going the other.

Screw it. I was already lost. What did it matter?

I did my best to determine which way Brijit went and started walking.

3

I kept getting this strange feeling that I wasn't alone in this place. I didn't see any signs of life and I didn't hear any voices, but I had this strange feeling that someone – or some*thing* – was out there.

I had a lot of time to think as I walked through the nothingness. Something about the endless fog seemed familiar to me. Not because I had been here before, but because someone had once described a place that looked and felt exactly like this.

It was Voel, the painter demon who lived in New York, the one who ended up being Theodore's mom. She told me once about how she escaped from Hell and traveled to Earth through a blank world of white fog.

If I was right, this was Limbo.

Growing up Catholic, I heard a lot of crazy stories. The one about Limbo was particularly nuts. The idea was this: if you were a sinner and died, you went to Hell. If you were a good person and baptized, then you went to Heaven. That part was important;

you had to be baptized because God really needs you to have magic H2O molecules touch your forehead or else it doesn't count.

So what happened to the people who weren't baptized, but weren't sinners? What happened to the little babies who died three days after being born? The Catholic Church couldn't possibly say that little three-day-old babies were burning in Hell, but they couldn't go back on their hard and fast rule that you had to be baptized to go to Heaven.

So that's when they came up with Limbo. Unbaptized babies went to Limbo.

Oh god. I started to panic. Was I in a dimension filled with dead babies? I had fucking better not be.

Limbo was so totally made up. Or, at least, I used to think it was. But there I stood confronted with the physical evidence. I was physically in Limbo.

Could it be possible that Limbo didn't exist before the Catholic Church made it up? Is it possible that the moment they wrote their idea down in doctrine and people started believing it that Limbo just, *poof*, came into existence?

What if that's how it worked for Madam Brijit and the Voodoo spirits? What if believing in them made them real? That might also explain how we ended up in the Land of Oz. Oz isn't real. Oz shouldn't be real, but I had been there. I had touched it. So when old man What's-His-Giblets wrote about Oz, did he make Oz poof into existence, too?

I heard something, but it wasn't a sound. It was as if my eardrums were picking up sound *waves*, but no actual sound. I knew something behind me was moving. I turned and saw the fog shifting. Something big was out there, stirring things up.

That nothing sound got louder.

Voel had once described another thing she found in Limbo. The Great Nothing. "As tall as the sky and as wide as the ocean and it rolls like an egg," she said. She never said why it was so dangerous, but she did say that she ran away from it. And she was a demon. If demons run from something, you should run from it, too.

Now I don't know if the thing behind me was the Great Nothing or not, but I wasn't going to stick around and find out.

So I ran.

I hoped there weren't walls in Limbo, because I was so blinded by the fog that I would have run smack into one of them.

I couldn't see anything more than a few inches away from my face.

That sound, that rolling sound, kept coming. The Great Nothing was in hot pursuit. What did the Great Nothing want? I supposed nothing. Nothing is all that exists in Limbo. And I was something. The Great Nothing didn't want something in Limbo.

Even as I ran, the idea of "being something" felt so familiar. *I am something.*

There's four states of being: nothing, something, anything, and everything.

Who told me that? Someone told me that, but it was so hard to remember, like trying to remember details of a fading dream.

There was a girl. A bald girl in an orange robe. She said I was something. She said she was nothing. She said someday I could be anything, whatever that meant.

Well, in that moment, I wished I was nothing like the girl in the orange robes. If I could be nothing, the Great Nothing would leave me alone.

The rolling sound got louder. The Great Nothing was going to roll right over me. And what then? Was it going to roll right over me and squash me into nothing? I ran as fast as I could, which is pretty damn fast, but in the infinite fog of nothing, what did it matter? I could run for ten years, or a hundred, or a thousand. I would never know where I was going and the Great Nothing would never give up.

I could feel it behind me. It whipped the fog into a swirling frenzy. It was going to roll over me.

The edges of it just barely brushed the back of my sneakers as I ran.

And then I ran over a hole and plunged into the ground.

4

The Great Nothing rolled right over me and kept going. I stood upside down on the bottom-side of Limbo. On this side, gravity was reversed, but I was still consciously aware of being upside down. On this side of the world, everything was black with black fog, but it wasn't dark. It was just black. I could see just as well as I could on the light side of Limbo, which wasn't saying much.

Two people stood in front of me.

337

There was a blond woman in a white robe. She had a disc of gold over her head, except it looked old and tarnished and rusted. Beside her was a man with stitches all over his face, as if it were pieced together from a dozen other face. His left eye didn't match his right eye. His nose was a different color from his cheek. His top lip was bigger than his bottom lip. He tried to hide his face with the hood of an ash gray cloak, but it didn't quite get the job done.

"Hey," I said. I pointed at the hole in the floor that led back to the light side of Limbo. "Cool trick."

The girl in the robe stepped forward and asked, "What are you?" She did not sound happy.

"I'm a human," I said. "I mean, kind of. I'm half-human, half-robot. Technically I'm a god."

"A god?" she asked.

"Well. An artificial one."

The girl sniffed the air. "You smell like a demon."

"Oh." Uh oh. I hoped that wasn't going to be a problem. Time to explain. "Yeah, I got a demon soul in me, too. I killed a demon and drank her bottle and I got her powers."

"How did you come to find this place?" Jigsaw Face asked.

"Okay, so that's a crazy story," I said. "I've been traveling through these, like, doorways between worlds. I just came from New Beatlemania and I'm trying to get to Hell."

"You?" The girl sounded surprised. "Are *trying* to go to Hell?"

"Exactly."

She shook her head. "I suggest you countermand that idea."

I tilted my head. She had a white robe and a metal disc above her head and she used the word countermand. I asked her, "Are you an angel?"

She gave me an impressed look. "Very astute."

Astute - adj. Keen in perception. Clever. Cunning.

"Thank you," I said.

"I am, indeed, an angel," she said. "Or I once was. What name do they call you, Daughter of Eve?" she asked.

"Penelope Salvo," I said.

"I am Harmozey, the Liberation of Want. This is my partner, Bazath, the Endless Calm."

Bazath didn't look like an angel. He looked more like a demon. His face was all cut up and pieced back together. And

338

Harmozey wasn't all that angel looking, either. Her halo was in terrible shape. Something fishy was going on here. They could read the confusion on my face.

"I am a demon," Bazath said.

"Yeah, no shit," I said. I pointed at Harmozey. "And what's your story? If you're an angel, where's your armor? And where are your wings? And what's up with your halo?"

"I fled Heaven." She reached over and held Bazath's stitched-up hand. "I abandoned my post to be with Bazath."

I gave her a skeptical look. "You quit Heaven to live with a demon?"

"We were in love before the War For Heaven," Bazath said. "We were a type of angel called the Archilem. We were builder angels. The Old Man sent us down here to build Limbo, which we did. But as construction went on, I started to grow more and more suspicious... of *him*." He pointed up. "There was something he wasn't telling us. I knew it. So after I built the floor of Limbo and Harmozey built the white fog, we built this place as well."

He gestured at the dark haze that surrounded us.

"Obmil," Harmozey said. "Our home. A place we could hide from *him*, should we ever need it."

Bazath said, "When the War For Heaven began, we didn't realize it was a war until it was too late. At first we just had questions about Hell. What did Yahweh need with an entire dimension of torture? It was just sitting down there, unused, so why build it? We asked him why and asked him what for, but he never told us. He just told us it was all a part of his "plan." That wasn't good enough. What "plan" required endless torture? We demanded answers. Very quickly, that led to rebellion."

"Some of us rebelled, and some of us remained loyal to the Father," said Harmozey.

Bazath said, "Only after the war started did we realize what his sadistic plan really was. He took all the angels who rebelled and cast them down into Hell."

I said, "He had you build Hell, didn't tell you what it was for, and then when you demanded to know, he sent you to go live in it?"

Harmozey tightened her grip on Bazath's hand. "I know the books on your world paint a different picture, but believe me, he is a terrible, terrible monster. Imagine building your own prison and then being sentenced there when your only crime is asking why the prison exists in the first place. He rules with unbelievable cruelty. When the rebellion began to slip through the clouds and plummet into the stinking pit, mass hysteria set in. Even the angels who weren't banished we struck with fear and tribulation. In all the confusion, I took Bazath and secreted him away to this place. Unfortunately, not before he had been transmogrified into the form that stands before you now."

"We have lived here for eons," Bazath said. "He has never found us, because the idiot doesn't know Obmil exists."

"And the Great Nothing," I said. "You built that, too?"

"No," Harmozey said. "The Great Nothing was created by the Father himself. Its purpose is unclear, but it is unstoppable."

"We are safe from it on this side of Limbo," Bazath said.

"I have friends still trapped up there," I said, pointing at the floor. "Madam Brijit and Baron Semedi. They're Voodoo loa. We can't just leave them up there. We need to-"

"We have already found them," Harmozey said. "In fact, the female sent us to find you."

"She's here?" I asked, relieved. "Brijit's here?"

"Come." Bazath turned around. "Follow us."

So I did. Bazath and Harmozey led me through the black fog. They were careful to walk slow enough that I wouldn't lose them.

"This isn't the first time I heard about the War For Heaven," I told them. "Shit sounds pretty fucked up."

Harmozey scoffed. "You do not know the entirety of it."

"No one can escape from Hell," Bazath said. "But no one can escape from Heaven, either."

"Honestly," Harmozey said, "the ones in Hell are better off."

5

Bazath and Harmozey led me through the smoke and to Madam Brijit. My Voodoo friend knelt there on the ground and held Baron Semedi's head in her lap. Baron Semedi was laid out on his back, eyes closed, not moving. Brijit wore his top hat on her head and slowly ran her fingers through his dreadlocks.

I was afraid to ask. "Is he...?"

"He's alive," she said. She was crying. She stared down at his face. "He just needs to go home."

Harmozey came up behind me. "He came here lost some time ago. He was weak and unable to remember who he was."

Bazath said, "We rescued him from the Great Nothing. He's been sleeping ever since."

"Thank you," Brijit whispered. "Thank you."

I watched Brijit hold Semedi. There we no two people better suited for one another than those two: her in her wedding dress and red dreadlocks, him in his dusty tuxedo. Watching them together suddenly made me feel incredibly sad. Not because Madam Brijit had finally found her husband – that was great and also a total relief – but because their reunion meant this was the end of our journey together. Brijit only came along with me to find Baron Semedi and she had succeeded. Now it was time for the two of them to go home.

When I first set out for Hell, I told Brijit that I wanted to do things on my own. I was a wolf pack of one. But in that moment, I realized how arrogant that was. I did need help. I needed *her* help. I wouldn't have made it this far without her, and she wouldn't have made it this far without me.

We went from trying to kill each other to... well... this.

She looked up at me with tears in her eyes. "Thank you."

"Thank *you*," I said.

She stroked his face. "I need to get him home."

"But how?" I asked. "We're a bajillion miles from anything."

She reached inside Baron Semedi's jacket pocket and pulled out a bundle of cigars. "His cigars are infused with magic. He uses them to travel to all the different worlds." She offered one up to me. "Want one?"

"Could it... take me to Hell?" I asked.

She nodded. "It can take you anywhere."

I took one of them. "Wow. This is super nice of you."

"I know."

She stuck one of Semedi's cigars in her teeth and flicked her fingernail across the head of a matchstick, popping the little flame to life. She held the fire to the end and puffed on it. The tip of the cigar caught fire and turned bright red.

Satisfied that it was lit, she took it away from her mouth and looked back up at me. "Good luck in Hell."

"Thanks. And, you know..." I briefly contemplated not saying it. But I did. "Thanks for coming along. You're not all that bad."

She nodded in consideration. She spit in her hand and reached up for a handshake. "See ya around, Pencil."

Hearing my nickname brought a bittersweet smile to my face. No one was ever going to call me Pencil, no one but Madam Brijit. I spat in my hand and shook hers. "See ya, Bat Face."

She smiled at me. She stroked Semedi's cheek with one hand and puffed her cigar with the other. A cloud of smoke formed around them, thicker and thicker until all I could see was smoke. Then, as the cloud drifted away, they were gone.

6

I was left alone with Harmozey and Bazath.

"You really want to go to Hell, huh?" Bazath asked.

I turned to face the pair of angel-demons. "I have to. Last year a friend of mine sacrificed himself to save Earth from Legion. I'm going there to set him free."

"It is a perilous place for humans," said Harmozey.

"You forget." I waved a finger at her. "I'm part demon."

I stuck Semedi's cigar in my mouth and dug out my lighter. I told the two of them, "It sucks that you have to live here in hiding like this. Maybe someday I could figure out a way for you two to go free."

They smiled politely.

"Thank you, Daughter of Eve." Harmozey bowed.

"Thanks, mudblob." Bazath gave me a pat on the shoulder.

"You guys saved my ass," I said. "I'll never forget that."

I sparked up my lighter and puffed away on the cigar. It was robust and sweet-tasting. A cloud of smoke gathered around me, obscuring my vision of the former angel and her demon lover.

I wasn't really sure how Semedi's magic cigars worked. Maybe I should have asked Brijit for a crash course. As I puffed more smoke into the air, I thought about how Semedi always showed up wherever he wanted, whenever he wanted. I could be doing something as normal as sweeping up the flower shop and all of a sudden, poof, there was Semedi. How did he have that much control? Voodoo magic, I guess. So I decided to give that a try.

I told the cigar what I wanted.

"I want to go to Hell. I want to find my friend Theodore. Send me to Theodore in Hell, little cigar."

Chapter 19

1

When the cigar smoke cleared, I found myself standing in ramshackled city of wooden lighthouses. The streets were coated in a layer of ash that blew in on the wind. The skies were sick-looking bands of tans and browns, each swirling like milk mixing in coffee but never combining. It felt like looking at Jupiter from the inside.

There was no sun. The city was shrouded in twilight, lit only by the dozens of lighthouses that loomed high overhead and by the flickering torch-posts that lined the streets.

I checked Athena.

Destination achieved.

The distance was gone, but I still had an arrow that pointed... south? Who knows. And I wasn't surprised about the distance. I had reached Hell and my journey was over.

The streets were crowded with demons: some of them were skeletons with just the final scraps of rotting flesh clinging on, others were sexy seductresses dressed in slinky dresses, but with acid-scarred skin, and so many other species. There were tiny yellow ones that squeaked a funny little language, huge red ones that shook the ground when they walked, and some that resembled humans except they had snake arms or goat legs.

A guy with fire for hair crossed the street. It was Theodore. He made his way through a dark farmer's market of the damned. All around me were the sights and sounds of commerce. Merchant demons attended wooden booths of blackened wood nailed together with spikes. They sold rusted weapons and smoldering rocks, and some traded strips of human flesh. Some of the booths were reinforced with twisted steel and rusted iron. Whoever built those booths had no care for symmetry or evenness; they were all lopsided and unbalanced.

One of the booths was attended by a fanged goat-man selling lumps of burning coal. The next booth was slightly bigger and was run by a human-looking demon with a missing face that revealed a deeply scratched up skull. He was selling all kinds of bones – human and animal and otherwise – with big femurs dangling from his display sign and with bowls of finger bones laid out on the counter.

I followed as Theodore approached one of the booths. He had no clue I was behind him. I expected to find him wasting away or being tortured, but he looked perfectly healthy and in good shape. He still had on his old Westland suit, but it had seen better days. The shoulder was torn open, the hem of his pants were all shredded up, and he was covered in ash. Every time he took a step, a cloud of dust kicked off of him.

His hair burned with bright orange fire and cast a powerful light in the dim marketplace. It made it really easy to follow.

He went up to this booth that had two big obsidian barrels filled with lava. This little pipsqueak lizard demon was standing on a stool, scooping lava out of the barrels with a ladle and selling cups of it to passing customers.

Theodore pointed at one of the barrels behind the counter. "Is this lava made from granite?"

"Granite!" the lizard demon said. "Granite! Fresh!"

"Yeah, that's what you said last time and I broke out in hives because there was limestone in it. You know I have a limestone allergy, so if there's any limestone in this, you better tell me."

"Five bones!" Lizard Demon said as he poured Theodore a pewter mug of lava. The mixture smoked and bubbled. "Five bones! Fresh granite! No limestone!"

Theodore put five small finger bones on the counter and took the cup. He pointed at the demon. "If there's limestone in this, I'm going to be able to tell."

"No limestone! Fresh granite!"

"Better be. I'd hate to have to raise your rent." Theodore raised his eyebrows at the demon and put the mug to his lips.

"No!" Lizard Demon waved his arms and gestured for Theodore to hand him the mug. "Gimme back."

"What?" Theodore looked at the cup. "So there *is* limestone in this. You little liar."

"Just gimme back. Make you fresh one."

"You said this *was* fresh!"

Lizard Demon was all flustered, caught in a lie. "Fresh, not fresh. Make yesterday. Fresh enough. Gimme back."

Theodore handed the demon the mug. Lizard demon dumped the lava back into the first barrel and scooped Theodore a new cup from the second barrel.

"Fresh granite," it said. "Real deal."

"See." Theodore waved a finger at the little thief. "This is why people don't shop here anymore. You're always pulling this shit and you're not very good at it."

"Me not pull shit."

"And by the way," Theodore said, "your marketing sucks. You have no brand recognition outside of Krussplot. If you really want to move up in the world and open that storefront you're always talking about, then you need to start working on your visibility."

"Move!" the demon said, waving him off. "Make bye bye!"

"Alright," Theodore said. "I'm just saying that a little optimization would do you a lot of good."

Lizard Demon leaned over the counter and pointed further up the street. "Make go bye bye! Mudblob!"

"Whoa," Theodore said. "No need for that kind of language. I'm leaving."

Ha. Theodore is definitely his father's son.

He continued his stroll through the market place. The streets echoed with tinny sounds of demons hammering weapons into shape. Other demons stood by their open storefront doors shouting infernal advertisements, trying to coax customers into their dark shops. A muscle-bound demon walked down the middle of the street, twenty foot tall with a face like a bull.

Theodore passed with by him and didn't bat an eye. All of this was normal to him.

One of the demons stood in the front stoop of his store - he was thin like an elderly man and covered in wasps - and he shouted at me to get my attention.

"Listen!" he called out. "Listen to what I can offer you!"

I was curious. I stopped and looked at him. "What?"

"I'll cut your head off, fifty bones." He gestured at his open door. It was dark inside and smelled like rotting meat.

"No, thank you," I said.

"Forty bones!" he said.

"Nah." I walked away.

"Thirty-five bones!" Even after I was gone, he kept shouting lower prices. "Thirty bones!"

Walking away, I realized the demons weren't speaking English. They were speaking in some kind of demon language that sounded all guttural and gross, with lots of hard K sounds. Strangely, I could understand every word they were saying, despite never studying a word of demon.

I ran my fingers through my hair and felt the barbed wire poking out of my scalp. I wondered if having a demon soul inside me had something to do with it.

Hell had a culture that I didn't understand and it was just a matter of time before I started trouble, that much was for sure, so before that happened I decided to make the big reveal to Theodore.

I ran to catch up to him and jumped on his back, throwing my arms around his neck.

"Hey!" I said. "Guess who?"

Theodore struggled to see who was riding him, looking over both shoulders. I moved my head to put my face right in view. He did a double take and said, "Penelope!?"

I jumped off him and he turned to face me. I held out my arms for the big presentation and smiled. "Look who it is!"

"What the hell!" He hugged me. I hugged back. "Haha. Hell. No pun intended."

"Oh yeah, I hate puns."

Theodore smelled like a campfire and burned like hot sand. The color in his eyes were bright orange. He stepped back and shook his head at me in disbelief. "What are you doing here?"

"I'm here to rescue you!"

"Rescue me?" He sounded surprised.

"Yeah, dude."I grabbed his sleeve to pull him along. "Come on. Let's go."

"Whoa, whoa, whoa," he said. "Penelope, slow down. What do you mean you're here to rescue me?"

"What do you think I mean?" I said. "I'm getting you out of here, dummy."

"Penelope." He paused. "I don't want to be rescued."

"*What?*"

He hesitated. "I like it here."

"You like it here... in Hell?"

He looked all around. "Well, it took some getting used to, but I'm half-demon you know? This place kind of feels like home. Plus, I have Untouchable Orange in me now. I like the heat."

None of this made sense to me. "Dude, fuck this place. This is your one chance to come back to Earth. I specifically came down here to get you."

He laughed and gave me a playful punch on the arm. "Well, it's the idea that counts."

"Dude, what is your deal? I've spent the last year doing this for you! You're seriously telling me you don't want to go home?"

"I can't leave, Penelope. I have responsibilities here."

"*Responsibilities?* What do you mean responsibilities? What fucking responsibilities could you possibly have in Hell?"

"Penelope," he said. "Calm down."

I shoved him. "Don't tell me to calm down!"

He spilled his mug of lava. "Hey, that cost me five bones!"

"I came all this way, I did all this shit just to rescue you, and now you don't want to go because you have 'responsibilities'!? Party Waffle died for this!"

"Party Waffle?" he repeated. "Penelope, are you on drugs?"

"No!" I said. "Well, yes, but that's not the point!"

"I don't even know what a Party Waffle is."

"Well, it doesn't matter cuz he's dead now!"

"Penelope, I appreciate that you came down here to get me. I really do. I can only imagine it was really difficult to get this far. But I can't just up and leave."

"Well, why the fuck not?"

"Because of Isobella Westland. She's slowly been taking control of Hell ever since we got here. I'm one of the few demons still standing in her way. She thinks like a human, I think like a human. The rebellion here needs me, otherwise she's going to take control of everything. Like I said, I have responsibilities."

"Well... Well..." I was at a total loss. For a year I had this all planned out. This is not how I expected things to go. I was starting to feel really stupid. "Well, what the fuck, man? What about Earth?"

"I'm doing this *for* Earth," he said. "If Isobella takes control of Hell, we're all going to be in big trouble. Earth. Hell. Everyone."

"Well, what am I supposed to do now? Just go home?"

"Don't go!" he said. "You just got here. I've missed your face! Hang out here. I'll show you around."

"Show me around? *Show me around?* I didn't come down here to fuck off sight-seeing, Theodore. I came down here to get you and bring you home."

"I don't know what to tell you, lady. I'm not going."

I fumed and gave him the angriest face possible.

He said, "If you knew what I knew about this place, you'd see things my way." He put his hand on my shoulder and turned to coax me down the street. "Come on. I'll tell you all about it while we fuck off sight-seeing."

2

Theodore lived in Krussplot, the City of Lighthouses. Dozens and dozens of lighthouses towered over the city, despite there not being a single drop of water. The lighthouses were thin and rickety, built from beams of charred wood. They swayed like jenga towers in the hot breeze. If the wind were any stronger, they would snap and crash to the ground, but they never did.

Each lighthouse was topped with a giant chamber of glass. Some of the glass chambers were round, others were cylindrical or square. The walls were pieced together from big sheets of broken glass, held in place by a haphazard metal framework. Rotating lights shone from inside and swept across the city streets like spotlights at a prison break.

Krussplot wasn't entirely lighthouses. There were homes and shops and even an infernal library, some built from charred wood and others from black bricks of obsidian. Demons lived here in a little society where they would craft weapons, mend clothes, and sell food like coal or lava or blood.

"Krussplot is on the furthest edges of Hell," Theodore said. "The only thing beyond us are the Shattered Mountains and going out there is a death sentence."

"Why do you live so far away?" I asked.

He laughed as if to say *oh, you're going to love this*.

"Isobella Westland's been hunting me and my mother down. She knows we're somewhere in Hell and she blames us for being here. Her first week in Hell..." He leaned in closer. "And I'm using the word 'week' here very loosely, you know, because time doesn't work the same here as it does on Earth." He returned to normal walking. "Her first week here she found one of the biggest, baddest demons in all of Hell, this thing called Gag, the Only Mouth, and she kicked its ass for no reason. She used her magic spellbook to rip him to shreds and destroyed his bottle."

I said, "Kind of like beating the shit out of someone on your first night in prison."

"Exactly," he said. "She's been looking for me and Voel so we had to hide someplace safe. If she found us here, she'd level this whole city to kill us."

"She won't find you out here?" I asked.

"Hell's pretty big," he said. "And Krussplot is about as far away from New Chernobyl as you can get."

"New Chernobyl is..."

"It's the capital city of Hell," he said. "Well, the *new* capital city of Hell. That's where she lives."

I looked at Athena and considered where my potential exit from Hell might be. I made a wild guess and pointed in the same direction as Athena's arrow.

I asked Theodore, "Is New Chernobyl that way?"

"Yup. Did your techno-arm tell you that?"

I grumbled, "Not in so many words."

"Isobella Westland is shrewd, I'll give her that much. She's been taking control of Hell, little by little. Lucifer barely has any power left anymore. Almost all the demon generals follow her orders. There aren't very many people left in the rebellion."

I slapped him on the shoulder. "Why don't you just go kick her ass?"

He laughed. "What dreamworld are you living in."

"You don't think you could take her?" I cracked my knuckles and did a little shadow boxing. "I could take her."

"Think so?" he asked. "I fought her once. It did *not* go well."

"Oh yeah? What happened?"

He unbuttoned his jacket to show me the white button-up shirt he had on underneath. It was torn open and scorched across the left side of his stomach. His skin underneath had a gnarly scar about the size of a softball. He traced his fingers over it. "She blew a hole right through me. I should have died. This was meant for my head. I just barely got out of the way."

"But you got away."

Very plainly he said, "I got away because my body exploded."

"Exploded?"

"Yeah!" He looked excited. "Penelope, it's so awesome. My blood is like napalm. When something cuts me open, I explode like a bomb. The bigger the wound, the bigger I explode."

"Did that do anything to her?" I asked.

Theo buttoned his jacket back up. "Not a damn thing. She was totally fine. She has all kinds of angel magic at her disposal. Now she's learning demon magic, so there you go. Have that, too. It's going to take a lot more than you or me to bring her down."

After walked across town, we reached the base of a twelve-story lighthouse. The wood creaked and moaned as it rocked back and forth in the wind. It wasn't put together very well and there were wide gaps between the boards. Bats used them to fly in and out. The lighthousey part at the very top was a lopsided cube of tea-stained glass that swept an orbiting beam of light through the neighborhood and then off into the distant parts of the city.

"So this is where I live," Theodore said as he looked proudly up at the swaying lighthouse. "Home sweet home."

"You live here?" The place looked like it was thrown together in an afternoon and was on the verge of total collapse.

"Yeah. Why're you looking at it like that?"

"You live in a haunted lighthouse?"

"It's not haunted." He unlocked the front door with a key that looked more like a knife. "It's cursed. There's a difference."

Theodore led me into the main entrance of his cursed lighthouse. There were hundreds of flickering candles set in bent, rusted stands for light. A candle chandelier hung from the ceiling, slowly swinging back and forth. Cracked mirrors hung on the wall, busted windows let in the hot air, and the floor was wet with blood. The walls creaked like the inside of a pirate ship.

There was a piano at the other end of the room with some of the white keys missing. There was a coat rack that was home to spider webs and no coats. Open doorways led off in different directions and a spiral staircase went up to the higher floors.

"Voel!" Theodore shouted. "I'm home! We have a visitor!"

I whispered at him, "You live with your mom?"

"Of course I live with my mom. You think I can afford a place like this on my own?" He laughed. "In this economy?"

The wooden stairs creaked as someone came down. Lime green feet came into view, followed by the bottom half of a paint-covered apron. Voel, the Deranged Painter, walked down the stairs with paintbrush in hand.

"Who is-?" She made eye contact with me and temporarily froze. "Oh. It's the mudblob."

I waved my hand. "Sup."

She resumed her descent down the stairs. "Strange to see you here. You're a long way from home."

I laughed. "That ain't no shit."

She came over to stand in front of me and used her free hand to tilt my head and smoosh my face with her fingers.

"It really is you," she said.

"Of course it's me," I said.

"Such an impossible journey for a mudblob." She ruffled my hair. "Good to see you again, Salvo."

"You're looking good," I said. "You seem more... composed."

"As terrible as it is in Hell, it does satisfy my twisted nature." She looked me up and down. "What could have possibly brought you all the way down here?"

"I... uh..."

The truth was, I came to rescue Theodore, but Theodore didn't want or need rescuing. Saying it out loud was just going to make me feel more stupid than I already did.

Theodore spoke up for me. "She came to check on us. And to check on Westland."

"Westland. That deplorable cunt," Voel said. "Every day more and more demons buy into her nonsensical plan."

I looked at Theodore. "Plan?"

"Oh, Westland has a plan," he said. "Come on, I'll show you the rest of the city and tell you all about it."

"Okay." I turned to Voel. "Nice to see you again."

Voel made the sign of the devil. "Hail Satan."

3

At the edge of Krussplot stood a humble wooden train depot, open-air, with nothing more than stairs and benches to decorate the place. Cobwebs collected in the ceiling beams. The tracks were bent and rusted. If a train came down those tracks, the whole thing would derail in a massive fireball. Everything about the train station looked long abandoned, but Theodore assured me that the trains were still running.

We sat on the bench and looked out past the city limits. Beyond the train station were the coal fields, which were literally what they sounded like: fields and fields of smoking, smoldering coal. Giant black snails the size of elephants slithered across the fields, tending to the crops.

"Those are tar snails," Theodore said. "Freaky, right? They're not demons. They're indigenous to this place. I think they evolved from something that lived here billions of years ago. They don't have brains at all and the only thing they know how to do is eat coal. They eat as much as they can, then they come to town and puke it back up. It ain't pretty, but it's convenient."

"They're gross as fuck."

He nodded. "They sure are." He took some coal out of his pocket and showed it to me. "Here. You ever tried coal before?"

"No."

He waved it at me. "Try it."

"I'll pass. I'm on a diet."

"Come on. Try it."

I took the coal from him. "Why are you always pushing food on me?"

"Try new things. Push your horizons."

"Push my horizons? Dude, I eat chain link fencing."

He nudged my arm holding the coal. "Try it."

The piece of coal was the size of a charcoal briquette, hot and glowing red in places. I bit off a piece and chewed it up. It wasn't bad, but it wasn't good. Impossible Red probably had a use for coal molecules, but I still preferred raw metal.

"Like it?" he asked.

I made a sour face. "Not really."

"I think it's great." He tossed a lump of it into his mouth. Smoke drifted out as he chewed. "Spicy."

"So Westland has a plan..." I said.

"Right!" He adjusted himself on the bench. "So let me lead off with some quick background stuff. The main thing to keep in mind is that the demons are miserable in Hell."

"They don't seem miserable," I said.

"They're don't look it, but they are. It's just that after billions of years, they've given up hope that their situation will ever get better, so they try to make the best of what they've got. But believe me, ask any demon if they'd rather live here or on Earth, they'd pick Earth. And it's not like they particularly like Earth all that much. They'd go to the moon or Mars or anywhere if it wasn't Hell. Problem is, their inner nature is just as dark and twisted as their body. If they try to suppress their nature to stay hidden on Earth, it drives them nuts. Take my mom for example. She escaped to Earth and went crazy." He paused. "Well, crazy-er."

"So what's this got to do with Isobella?"

"Well, anyone who's ever been in charge of Hell has been promising to take over Earth entirely since day one. Lucifer, Mephistopheles, Beelzebub, every century or so someone comes along to get everyone all riled up with this 'take over Earth' talk. Most of the demons know it's a lost cause, but they can't help but try."

"They almost took over Earth," I said. "Twice."

"Yeah, *almost*. It's always *almost*. Morale in Hell is lower than it's ever been. But then here comes Isobella Westland, a homeless mudblob who starts shouting her crazy ideas from the street corners."

"What ideas?"

"Isobella doesn't promise the demons Earth. She promises them Heaven."

"Heaven? How's she going to promise them Heaven? That fight didn't go so well for the the last time. Have they had a look around?"

"The demons said the same thing. But Westland never gave in. She kept shouting about knowing a secret way into Heaven. She said she was smarter than any angel." He looked me in the eyes and said, "She says she knows how to kill God."

I made a skeptical face. "Does she really?"

"I mean, I doubt it, but who knows what kind of magic she found in that book of angel talk. Plus, if you stack demon magic on top of that, who knows what she can do."

"I seriously doubt she could kill God."

"Maybe she can and maybe she can't. Either way, she sounded convincing. All the demons believed her. It made Lucifer look like Captain Small Potatoes. The demons were all like, hey, why hasn't anyone said anything like this before? Look at this mudblob with new ideas. She's crazy, but what if she's right?

"For months she spread these ideas around New Chernobyl. At first she only had a few followers, but then she got a few more, then a few more. Mostly dumb ones at first, but smarter ones came after. Someone confronted Lucifer about it and Lucifer said she was crazy and told everyone to ignore her."

I said, "But they apparently didn't."

"Nope. Isobella called Lucifer out on his same old failed ideas. Corrupt the humans. Infect Earth with sin. The same old boring stuff he'd been doing for the past two-thousand years. More time passed and more demons started agreeing with her. Before long, everyone in New Chernobyl knew all about her. Lucifer finally had no choice but to cave in and say... you know what, her ideas might be far-fetched, but they're not *impossible*. I don't think Lucifer really believed that, but he could see the way the wind was blowing. If he didn't change with the times, the times were going to leave him behind. After that, after Lucifer 'endorsed' her ideas, that things really went haywire."

"What happened?"

"Isobella picked her most devoted followers and named them prophets. She sent them out to the other cities in Hell to preach her good word. Her ideas spread like wildfire. Demons started visiting New Chernobyl just to hear her speak."

"It sounds like Jesus," I said.

Theodore nodded eagerly. "It's exactly the kind of story that appeals to a bunch of fallen angels. A messiah story."

"Damn."

"So get this," he said. "Lucifer got fed up and tried to make a move on her."

"Like... he tried to bang her?"

"What?" He looked at me and laughed. "No, he tried to *kill* her. Not bang her."

I said, "Ohh. You said 'make a move' so I thought-"

"No, I know what you thought."

"Sorry. Go on."

He said, "No, Lucifer tried to *kill* her. He sent one of his loyalists out to go slit her throat. She's only a mudblob after all, with a physical body."

"But if she died, her soul would just come right back to Hell."

"As a soul," he said. "And souls don't get to walk around like you and me and her. Souls get tortured."

"Oh."

"So this assassin comes out to kill Westland. Problem is, the assassin screws it up and slits her throat when she's preaching in front of a crowd of demons. That just made her a martyr. And Westland's no slouch. She knows angel magic. So right there in front of all of those demons, with her hand at her neck gushing blood, she summons the power of God to close her wounds and heal herself. She stands up and goes right back to preaching."

"The demons weren't pissed at her for using God magic?"

"Pissed? No way! They were mind blown. Up until then, they thought this 'take over Heaven' stuff was just a wonderful pipe dream. But after a lowly mudblob used holy magic to save her own life, everything changed. Lucifer was humiliated for his pathetic attempt on her life. People started looking to Westland for new leadership. Real leadership. Not the billions of years of 'someday this' or 'someday that.' Westland was going to actually do something."

I sat there and tried to process the story he had told me. Theodore got quiet and ate some coal.

"You wanna know what's really crazy?" he asked.

"Sure."

"I think Westland *knew* that assassin was coming. I think she wanted to almost die in front of all those demons. She's *the* Westland in the Westland Corporation. That's exactly the kind of trick you'd expect her to play."

"I doubt she can actually take over Heaven," I said. "Angels are impossible to kill. Believe me, I've fought a couple of them. Demons might be powerful, but there are three angels for every one demon. I don't see how it's possible."

Theodore made a sour face and threw his coal for distance. "She doesn't give a damn about Heaven. She's just saying that stuff to get the demons all riled up. No, Isobella Westland only wants the one thing she's ever wanted: her corporation back. She wants to rule Earth from the top floors of her HQ building in Manhattan. She needs the demons to pull that off. After that, maybe she'll send them off to Heaven."

"Where they'll get massacred."

"Big time," he said. "But once she has Earth, it won't matter anymore."

Isobella Westland was one of the most shrewd, most evil people I had ever heard of. I mean, Carl is bad, but Carl isn't *that* bad. Isobella murdered Xin. She murdered Baron Kriminel. She tried to kill me and Theodore and Carl. Hell, twice she almost set the armies of Hell free on Earth just so she could play god.

"I see it now," I said to Theodore.

He looked at me. "See what?"

"Why you can't leave Hell. You have to stay. You have to stop her."

"Alright." I hopped off the bench. "Show me what you got."

"Got?"

"With Untouchable Orange. I haven't seen it in action. You're the god of fire now. Let's see what you can do."

"Alright. Hope you brought your welding goggles, because this can get a little bright."

We left the train depot and walked out into the scorched coal fields. Theodore made an over-exaggerated "tah-dah" pose and lit his skin on fire. Not his suit, but his head and hands went up in flames.

I'd seen that once before, in that moment a year ago when Theodore first fell into hell, seconds before the doorway closed behind him. Still, it was cool to see it up close.

"Dope." I took his hand in mine so I could feel the fire.

He said, "I can also be lighter than air." He lifted up off the ground by a couple feet.

"Wow, dude, you get to fly? That's not fair. I don't get to fly."

"Have you ever tried it?"

Disappointed, I said, "Oh yeah. Of course. No dice."

"Well, we all get different powers," he said. "Check this out."

He flew higher up into the sky, putting a safe distance between us. He tightened his face and flexed his muscles tight. His burning body intensified, glowing orange, then yellow, then bright white. I couldn't even see him anymore; he was a white-hot thing burning in the sky. A dark shadow stretched away from my feet.

Theodore exploded in a shock wave of fire that thundered through the ground. Hot air washed over me and blew through my clothes. The tar snails recoiled into their shells for safety.

The fire cleared. Theodore floated in midair, perfectly fine. He floated back down to the ground.

"That was the fucking tits," I said.

"It's cool alright, but it makes me so hungry." He pulled a handful of coal out of his pocket and munched it down. "A move like that isn't particularly useful down here in Hell anyway. Demons eat fire for food. It would be like being on Earth and your body exploded in donuts."

"Yeah, but if you ever ended up back on Earth for some reason, you could seriously wreck some shit."

"I could blow up a whole *hospital*."

I wrinkled my eyebrows at him. "Weird that that's the first thing that comes to you mind."

"I mean, it doesn't have to be a hospital."

"Why is that the first thing you thought about blowing up?"

He shrugged. "Gotta blow up something."

"I... guess?" Moving on. "So do you have lava for guts?"

"Penelope. Think," he said.

"What?"

"When it's inside me, it's magma. It's only lava when it comes out."

I huffed. "Wow."

"Does Carl know you're here?" he asked.

"Kinda sorta," I said. "I told him I was coming to save you. He just didn't know when. Hell, I didn't know when."

"What did he say to that?"

I had to think back and remember. "What was that he called me?" Thinking. Thinking. "He said I was being a Silly Stephanie and a Careless Carolina."

"He didn't think you could pull it off?" he asked.

"You can never tell with that guy. But I don't think so."

Theodore put his arm around my shoulder and pulled me close. "I knew you could do it."

I laughed. "Well, that makes one of us."

On our walk back to Krussplot, I told Theodore all about my journey to Hell. I showed him Athena and explained how it worked. I told him about Madam Brijit and how she went searching for Baron Semedi. I told him about the Princesses. And I told him all about Party Waffle.

My trip had a lot of highs and lows, a lot of ups and downs.

Theodore told me about living in Hell and leading a small resistance against the rise of Isobella Westland. Not every demon was thrilled with the promises of Isobella Westland. Westland was a mudblob, through and through, and for some, the thought of deferring to a mudblob for leadership was like giving up their last shred of dignity.

For that reason, Theodore – who was at least half-demon – was able to organize a respectable underground rebellion.

He told me about the other cities that refused to fall under Westland's control: Isico, the City on the Lake of Fire; Puspool, the Diseased Realm; Akagina, the Collection of Alleys. Leaders in those cities straight up refused to work under the banner of a mudblob, no matter what she was offering.

When we were back under the paroling lights of the Krussplot lighthouses, I told Theodore:

"I have to go to New Chernobyl."

"Oh, do you?" he asked. "You know, if you're looking to die, I know a guy who will chop your head off for ten bones."

"Hardy har har, Theodore. I'm serious."

"Have you not heard a word I've been saying? Isobella Westland runs New Chernobyl, top to bottom."

"Well, first and foremost, I'm pretty sure that's my way out of here. But for two, I think it's time for you and me go kick Westland's ass, tag team style."

Theodore shook his head. "So you *haven't* been listening."

"Yes, I have!"

Theodore sounded exasperated, trying to talk some sense into me. "Penelope, you've fought demons before. You know how hard they are to kill. One of them is bad enough. If you go to New Chernobyl, you're not just fighting Isobella Westland. You're fighting all the demons she has working for her. We're talking millions of them. We'd be dead before we even saw her face." He shook his head again. "New Chernobyl is sealed up like a bank vault. You can't just run up and slap her to death. We need to bring her down politically."

"So you're giving up?"

"I'm not giving up," he said. "You ever heard that phrase that goes 'when you're a hammer, every problem looks like a nail'? Well, you're a hammer and you're thinking this problem is a nail. But this problem is not a nail. This problem is a screw. And I'm a screwdriver."

I frowned. Theodore was probably right. "Fine." I took a breath. "Okay, I promise no fighting, but I still need to get into New Chernobyl if I want to get back to Earth."

"Now getting you *in* to New Chernobyl, that I can do."

"How?"

"I've got connections."

"You have connections?"

"I might live in Hell, but I was raised in the Westland Corporation. Of course I have connections."

5

The cities of Hell were connected by a network of train tracks called the Nightmare Rail. Theodore described the trains as thunderous black locomotives that howled like ghouls and belched columns of black smog into the air. Trade was an important part of the Hell economy. Shipments to and from Krussplot came once a week. The city imported things like raw iron and lava and blocks of obsidian. In exchange, they would export carloads of coal collected by the tar snails.

Theodore said he could smuggle us into one of the coal cars and stow away to New Chernobyl. Once there, he could sneak me around the city until I found my portal out.

It felt weird to just cut and run from Hell without giving Isobella Westland the smackdown she so sorely deserved. Kick-punching my way to victory was much more my speed, but Theodore consistently reminded me how that wouldn't end well.

The next train on the Nightmare Rail wasn't scheduled to arrive until tomorrow. Until then, I had a day to spend in Krussplot. Theodore showed me all around. We saw a fight break out in the marketplace between a gangly thin-armed, thin-legged demon and a group of chattering little red devils. He showed me the view of the city from the top of his lighthouse. I got to check out a desecrated library filled with books written in a blood-soaked language I had never seen before.

"Here." Theodore led me down a narrow side street. "I want you to show you something. You hungry?"

"Yes. I haven't eaten since New Beatlemania."

He led me down a dark alley, lit by a few dwindling torches. The buildings of the alley were crammed in together, built at random angles, creating dozens and dozens of dark alcoves and corners where any murderer could come jumping out.

Theodore didn't seem the least bit intimidated. He walked right up the alley and pounded on some oversized wooden door.

"Open up, god dammit!" he yelled. He looked at me and whispered, "You gotta know how to talk to demons. Just follow my lead."

Someone stomped closer to the door. After the sound of a few unlatching locks, the door swung open. In the doorway stood a blood-soaked gorilla, ten feet tall.

"What!?" the gorilla shouted, showing off its powerful fangs.

"Gorko!" Theodore shouted back. He pointed at me. "Greet Penelope Salvo! Now!"

"No!" the gorilla replied.

Theodore slapped the gorilla across the face. "Now!"

Gorko huffed and puffed at Theodore. I thought the bloody gorilla was going to rip Theodore's arms off. He certainly looked strong enough to do it.

Gorko turned his bloodshot eyes to me. "I hope you die!"

I jumped right in and yelled, "I hope you die, too, Gorko!"

"You're both bothering me!" Gorko said.

Theodore shouted, "Feed us!"

Gorko replied, "No! Go starve in the streets! Die alone!"

I see how this game is played. I wanted in on the fun. I walked up to Gorko and gave him a smack in the mouth, half-strength. It was still enough to spin his head and send slobber flying. "Gorko, feed us, now!"

Gorko stomped out of the doorway and pointed us inside. "Get in here before someone else sees!"

We went inside. Gorko screamed at us to "hurry!"

Inside was a sort of restaurant with tables and chairs. The place was dark, lit by two fireplaces burning charred up animal bodies. The air smelled of toxic chemicals and burning wood. A few demons sat at the random tables, another few loitered at the bar drinking cups of lava. Gorko kicked over one of the chairs at an empty table.

"Sit here!" he told us. "Or die!"

I picked up the chair and sat down. Theodore sat on the opposite side. Gorko stormed back to the kitchen.

"This place has *the* most amazing sulfur," Theodore said. "I don't know how Gorko's wife does it, but she's a miracle worker in the kitchen."

I heard Gorko yelling at his wife in the kitchen. An equally loud woman yelled back. A whole rack of pots and pans came crashing down. I was pretty sure they were fighting back there.

I asked Theodore, "Do they serve metal here?"

Theodore eagerly nodded. "That's why I thought of it. I don't eat metal, but I've had other people tell me it's good. And if it's anything like the sulfur, you're going to love it."

"Do they have gold, you think?" I asked.

Theodore frowned a little bit. "You don't get a lot of gold in hell. That's more of a Heaven sort of thing. Down here you mostly get inert stuff like iron and aluminum and zinc. They do have plutonium here, but I don't know if you should eat that."

"I've never had plutonium before," I said.

"The radioactivity might screw up your insides," he said.

"I'm not about to find out the hard way."

Growing up poor, I never had enough money to experience a high class restaurant, but this must be what it feels like to travel to another country and find out they can cook you something exotic like kangaroo. There I sat with a chance to try plutonium, but I didn't want to turn into a walking radioactive meltdown, so I chickened out.

Gorko leaned his giant gorilla torso out the swinging kitchen door, getting his bloody hand prints all over everything.

"Mudblobs! Tell Treenka what to feed you!"

"Sulfur!" Theodore yelled.

"Uh." I was put on the spot. I had to decide and quick. "Zinc!"

Gorko disappeared back into the kitchen and shouted, "Cook them sulfur and zinc, you bog witch!"

6

Theodore was halfway through his block of yellow, smoking sulfur when he asked, "Remember that diner in Utah?"

I was working through a bowl of raw, freshly mined chunks of zinc. "Of course I remember. I had a dream we were at that diner."

"Oh, yeah?" Theodore said. "What happened?"

"Not a lot," I said. "We were just talking. Your hair was on fire. I don't remember much else."

"When did you dream?" he asked me. "You don't sleep."

"It was magic sleep. From when we left the Land of Oz."

"Ooh." He accepted that as a perfectly normal answer. "How's your zinc?"

I raised my eyebrows and looked down at the lumps of silver metal. "It's not bad. I didn't know about all this coal stuck to it at first, but the two go together really well, like bacon on donuts."

Theodore nodded with his mouth full, but covered it to say, "This place is amazing."

It wasn't bad in all honesty. Never in a million years did I think I would be eating at a little hole-in-the-wall diner in Hell.

Halfway through our meal, Gorko came to stand at our table and shout, "Twenty bones!"

Theodore stood up and dug into his front pocket. "Dammit, Gorko. Here are your bones!" He pulled out a handful of finger and toe bones and threw them across the restaurant. They bounced across the tabletops and went scattering underneath the seats. "Go fetch!"

Gorko fumed and pointed at the door. "Get out!"

"Fine!" Theodore said. He picked up the last of his sulfur.

"Fine!" I said. I slammed my hands on the table – one-quarter strength so I didn't break it – and scooped up the rest of my zinc. I added, "We're never coming back!"

"I don't want you to come back!" Gorko said.

Gorko's wife Treenka came out from the kitchen. She was also a bloody gorilla. "You're banned for life!" she yelled at us.

"Your food sucks!" Theodore replied.

"Yeah, fuck you, silverback!" I yelled at Treenka. I mimicked how gorillas do sign language. "Koko want raindrop drink!"

Gorko and his wife yelled at us the whole way out of the restaurant. Theodore and I yelled back. Once we were outside, Gorko slammed the door in our faces and latched it shut.

"That place is so good," Theodore said.

"That whole experience was bizarre," I said.

"If you think that was crazy, imagine trying to get fitted for a suit."

7

That next morning, a locomotive came screaming across the train tracks that crossed the coal fields. It rattled at break-neck speeds, threatening to jump loose of the tracks and tumble into a pile of wreckage. There was an ear-piercing shriek that I thought came from the metal wheels grinding on the girders, but then realized, no, it wasn't coming from the metal. It was coming from the locomotive itself.

Black smoke gushed out of the smoke stack. The train pulled a row of thirteen coal cars behind it.

I couldn't decide what was more likely to happen: was the train going to wreck off the tracks? Or was it just going to straight up explode?

Theodore and I waited at the humble train depot for its arrival. The tar snails were lured to the station by their Pavlovian response to the sound of the approaching train. Hundreds of the slimy things gathered around the tracks, waiting to deposit their weekly crop of burning coal.

Fifty yards out from the station, the train showed no signs of slowing down. It barreled towards us at top speed. It looked like it *wanted* to derail, the way it bucked its weight back and forth on the tracks.

I took a step back. "Are you sure this is safe?"

"Of course it's safe," Theodore said. "These trains have been running for eons."

The locomotive was nearly to the station when it slammed on the brakes. Orange sparks sprayed out of the wheels as they froze up and slid across the tracks. I slapped my hands over my ears to keep from going deaf at the piercing sound of metal-on-metal.

The train screeched to a grinding halt just barely inside the ramshackled train depot. For all of its reckless speed and dangerous maneuvering, it managed to stop precisely next to the station platform. The heavy doors of the cargo cars slid opened and a variety of worker demons piled out. Small red imps scurried around, oiling the train wheels with blood, tightening bolts with rusty tools, and shoveling more coal into the boiler. Taller brutes with zombie white skin began mindlessly unloading blocks of granite, barrels of lava, and armloads of twisted metal.

Theodore pulled one of the red imps aside and talked to him for a moment. Their conversation was brief and ended with Theodore pushing a whole skeleton foot into the little creature's hand. The creature seemed delighted and nodded vigorously.

Theodore turned and gave me a double thumbs up. We were clear to stow away on the murder train.

We were officially on our way to New Chernobyl.

Chapter 20

1

The tar snails gathered silently around the recently emptied train. They used their sticky, slimy bodies to crawl up the sides of the cars and perch their heads over the open tops. There, they began puking up smoking, smoldering coal. They came from all over the fields, dozens and dozens at a time, vomiting their stomachs into the cars until they were slowly filled to capacity.

All the cars, that is, except for one. Theodore had paid off one of the imps to stop loading the thirteenth car when it was half full. That one was going to be ours. Sneaking on board involved hiding in the middle of the swarm of snails, obscured by their massive obsidian shells. No one saw us approach and no one saw us sneak on board through the rear doors.

It wasn't comfortable inside the coal car. This wasn't going to be no luxury cruise. It was hot and the air tasted toxic. Our main source of light was Theodore's fiery hair.

The demons outside locked the train doors and prepared for our outbound trip. The train screamed like a tortured person and lurched forward. We were going to circle around on a closed loop and then head out of Krussplot the same way it came in.

We had a long journey ahead of us, even at the dangerous speeds reached by the death-wish express.

"Can I ask you something?" Theodore said.

"Shoot."

"You know more about Impossible Red than I know about Untouchable Orange. This thing isn't going to give me cancer or something, is it?"

"I highly doubt it."

He gave me a funny look. "Because I don't want cancer."

I laughed. "I really don't think it's going to give you cancer, dude. In fact, it's far more likely that we're going to end up living forever or something. I dunno."

"Forever?" Theodore almost looked terrified of the idea. "Is there any way to get these things out of us?"

"I don't think so."

"You don't know very much."

I nodded. "You're not wrong there. But I know some."

I told him the story of the god spheres as best I knew it. There was once this Earth-like planet who had lost their gods. Maybe their gods were dead or maybe they never existed, I couldn't quite remember that part. But in any case the people of that world built an underground facility called the Pantheon Project. They were going to scientifically recreate the powers of their gods and compact them into these little colorful marbles.

Unobtainable Pink, the god of love.

Impossible Red, the god of war.

Untouchable Orange, the god of fire.

Unknowable Yellow, the god of knowledge.

Incorruptible Green, the god of nature.

Unsinkable Blue, the god of the ocean.

Unreachable Indigo, the god of the sky.

Intoxicated Violet, the god of wine.

And, lastly, Unthinkable Black, the god of destruction.

I told him how, after those people successfully created seven of these "god spheres," the experiment went south at number eight, when they tried to contain Unthinkable Black. The destructive power of black broke loose in a swarm of animal legs that destroyed the facility, destroyed the city, destroyed the planet, destroyed the solar system, then destroyed the universe.

How did these god spheres end up on Earth after that? That was anyone's guess.

I told Theodore that since Unthinkable Black's containment marble was flawed from the very beginning, its power was leeching out. I told him about New Beatlemania.

I didn't tell him that I had Unthinkable Black and only I knew where it was hidden. Theodore didn't need to know that.

Honestly, Theodore was probably safer by not knowing.

As far as I knew, only four of the god spheres had been activated; pink in Baron Kriminel, red in me, orange in Theodore, and yellow in Tengoku. I told him all about Tengoku, how she was half-robot and half-human just like me, although she was much less in touch with her humanity.

"Have you gone looking for the others marbles?" he asked.

"From time to time," I told him. "It's easier said than done. They're the size of marbles. They look totally normal. They could be in a kids toy box in Pakistan for all I know."

"Carl's probably looking for them," he said.

I scoffed. "Oh, I can guarantee that. He found Untouchable Orange and didn't tell me about it until it was already too late. Westland's not interested in finding them for safety. They want them for power or money or weapons."

He laughed a little bit. "That sounds about right."

I said, "That's how I first met Carl. He was trying to kill me for Unthinkable Black."

"Carl wouldn't kill anyone."

I rolled my eyes. "Okay, technically he wasn't the one trying to kill me. He was ordering other people to kill me, but, yeah, that's basically it."

"He has a strange way of twisting things around so he's never responsible for anything bad and gets to take all the credit for everything good."

I grumbled at the sound of that. "You got that right."

The train hit some sort of hard bump and our dark coal car bounced us around. The coal shifted and resettled.

I asked him, "How much further, you think?"

"We have four major stops to go through, but we should be in New Chernobyl in a couple days."

"What four stops?" I asked.

"We'll pass through Sheol first," he said. "It's this hell city ruled by Ereshkigal. It's mostly Old Testament people who live there as shadows. The whole place is a huge bummer."

"Sounds like."

"Then there's Tit ha-Yaven, Tzoah Rotachat, then Qliphoth. But trust me, you don't want to see any of those places."

"Why not?"

"Too dangerous."

"Psh. *Dangerous.*"

"No, I'm serious, Penelope. Krussplot might not seem that bad with the restaurants and the marketplace and everything, but that's Krussplot. Not every place is like that.

"Tit ha-Yaven is the City of Clinging Mud. In the old Heaven days, there was this sparkling lake of diamond-white water. When God sent all the angels to Hell, some of them hid in the lake. God drained the whole thing and it splashed down in Hell. When the water from Heaven mixed with the ash and soot from Hell, it made clinging mud. If you get it on you, it's never coming off. If even a drop touches your skin, it will stick there until you cut that part of your flesh off."

I made a disgusted face. "Okay. Gross. Also, the place has the word 'tit' in it, so haha to that."

Theodore rolled his eyes and laughed. "Oh my god."

I laughed.

"After that comes Tzoah Rotachat. It literally means 'Boiling Excrement.' I don't know if you want more details than that."

"Nah." The name gave me a pretty good idea what that place was about. "I'm good."

"Then there's Qliphoth, home of the shapeless evils, all ruled by the impure forces from the Kabbalah. That's where you find a lot of your demonic possession demons. If they see you or me, they'll try to possess our bodies."

"Alright, fine. No getting out. No sightseeing."

"Trust me," he said. "You're not missing much."

2

One year ago, Theodore found out he was half-demon. Minutes after that, he was sucked down to Hell. He told me how lost he was when he first showed up. Sure, he wouldn't die, not between Untouchable Orange and his half-demon heritage, but he was afraid being stuck in some torture world for all eternity.

A couple days later, Voel tracked him down. Voel knew Hell, of course. She knew it quite well; she had helped build it, painting the Shattered Mountains that served as the boundaries of the world on the infinite edges. Voel and Theodore moved to to Krussplot, the City of Lighthouses, where their capitalist culture would come as less of a shock to her son.

Krussplot was intriguing enough. The idea that the other cities of Hell were stranger and more dangerous just made me all the more curious. But I knew Theodore was right; going out to

367

explore was needlessly reckless. Still, I can't say that I wasn't tempted.

Our screaming locomotive rattled against the tracks as we approached Tit ha-Yaven, the City of Clinging Mud, at full velocity. Theodore and I were thrown against the back wall. Any other train would have slowed down as it approached the station, but not Murder Train. Murder Train screamed like a tortured animal and the bolts holding everything together clattered in place.

No sooner had we hit the back wall, Murder Train slammed on the brakes. The train dropped half its speed. Our coal car lurched and Theodore and I were thrown forward. We crashed into the front wall along with our payload of coal. Metal screeched on metal as the wheels of the train shredded against the rails.

The train slid into the station in a spray of bright orange sparks, then came to a stop. Theodore and I were lost under the coal like free prizes inside a box of cereal. I had to dig my way out. Moments later, Theodore sifted to the surface as well.

I heard squeaking and pounding from outside, as well as demons barking orders in their demon language. One-by-one they slid open the doors to the train cars, loading and unloading cargo, and unlatching locks.

I shot Theodore a concerned look. If some demon opened our door and saw us inside -

"Don't worry," he said. "Our cargo is for New Chernobyl. No one is going to open it until we-"

The door to our car slid open.

I had just enough time to dive down into the coal and hide. Theodore did the same. Someone came into our car, crunching their way across the top level of coal. It sounded like two someones.

"This is better than I hoped," some low-voiced demon said. "I thought we'd need to clear out coal to make room, but this one is only half full."

Some other demon with a wet, gross voice called out, "Okay! Bring it in!"

Then I heard a dozen of those little red imp worker demons squeak as they also crunched their way across the coal. The were loading something new into our train car. Whatever it was came down heavy. Each new load made the car sag a little deeper.

I tried to peek through the piled up coal and steal a glance at the intruding demons.

"You don't think anyone is going to notice?" Low Voice asked. He was the same kind of demon as Gorko, a bloody gorilla.

"Not until it gets to New Chernobyl," Gross Voice replied. She was some type of ghoul with her throat ripped open and her voice bubbled out of her blood-soaked throat. "By then, it's in Isobella's hands. She can handle it."

"She's going to be upset," Low Voice said. "This isn't anywhere near as much as she asked for."

Gross Voice said, "Let the mudblob be upset. I'm shorting her on purpose. She's been getting bossy. I want her to remember who's really in charge over here."

Low Voice laughed. Gross Voice laughed, too. The imp demons fled the car and scattered back out onto the station platform. Low Voice and Gross Voice followed them out, slid the door closed, and latched it.

I poked my head out of the coal and looked around. These demons had loaded up twenty barrels of something. I wanted to check them out, but it was too risky. We were still in the station. What if they came back? I decided to wait until we were back on the tracks and the coast was clear.

After thirty impatient minutes of waiting in the station, Murder Train was back on the road. The risk of someone opening the doors and catching me and Theodore were back to zero. I crawled out of the coal entirely and went to one of the barrels.

Theodore came and stood over my shoulder.

I popped the lid off. Inside was mud. It was full of mud.

"Is this that clinging mud you were talking about?" I asked.

"Yes," Theodore said.

I smacked the lid back down on the barrel as fast as I could. I said, "Isobella wants twenty barrels of this shit?"

"She's probably going to use it as a weapon. Or as some kind of torture."

The train hit a bump and made everything bounce. In my mind, I imagined the lids of those barrels popping off and mud going everywhere. I was surrounded by twenty mud bombs that could go off at any second.

"I don't want to be on this car anymore," I said.

"It's going to be fine," Theodore said. "Just try not to think about it."

I laughed sarcastically. "Try to not think about how we're stuck in a train car with cursed mud that makes you cut your skin off to get rid of it?"

"Yeah." He sat down on the coal and leaned back against the wall. "Try not to think about *that*."

I sat down next to Theodore, nervously eyeing the barrels that surrounded us. The train hit another bump and everything in the coal car – specifically the barrels of mud – bounced in place with a loud thud.

3

Somewhere along the line, the air turned rank. And I mean rank like the East River. It wasn't very strong at first, just a whiff of something foul, but that quickly changed. With each passing moment the stench just grew stronger. It smelled horrible.

It smelled like shit.

We were approaching Tzoah Rotachat, the City of Boiling Excrement. Theodore had pulled up the front of his shirt and used it to cover his nose and mouth. I did the same thing.

It didn't help. Not at all.

Curiosity got the better of me. I just had to see what this part of Hell looked like. I crawled up on my knees and pressed my eyes to the crooked gaps in the wooden walls. Outside, everything was brown and hazy, covered by a swirling orange-brown sky. There were charred and blackened trees. A flat, barren wasteland stretched as far as I could see.

And then there were the ponds of boiling shit. It made me sick just to look at it. Brown steam rolled off the bubbling ponds, contributing to that god-awful smell in the air.

I put my hand over my nose and mouth, adding another layer of filtration to my shirt. Didn't help.

"Oh my fucking god." I turned back around and sat next to Theodore. "This place is terrible."

He also covered his mouth and nose with his hands. "I know. Still feel like getting out and having a look around?"

"No." I coughed. "But I will tell you one thing. I'm not letting any smugglers put twenty barrels of boiling shit in this car, that's a goddam promise."

Theodore nodded and said, "That's a deal."

Just like our last stop, Psycho Train cranked itself into top speed just as we approached the station. That's when panic set in. Last time we went into a station, the train kept going faster and faster, and then it slammed on the brakes.

When that happened, we were all going to go flying; me, Theodore, and twenty barrels of clinging mud.

"Nope." I got to my feet and went for the sliding train door. "Not doing it."

"Not doing what?" Theodore asked.

I tried to open the train door. It was locked shut. I pulled hard, popped the lock, and the door slid open. Hot wind blew in and the smell of shit got a million times worse. It blasted me right in the face and I couldn't help but gag.

I fought back my need to puke my guts out and said, "I'm not going to be in here with this mud when everything gets tossed around like like a slap chop. Isobella and her mystery shipment can go to straight to Hell." I turned to Theodore and shrugged. "Figuratively, of course."

I grabbed one of the barrels and chucked it overboard. Then another. Then another. One, two, three, they all hit the ground and burst open. A wash of thick mud spilled across the heat-baked ground. There. Now Tzoah Rotachat has boiling shit and sticky mud. Best of both worlds.

Theodore ran to help me ditch the illegal cargo.

Down at the end of the tracks, I could see the shape of a city. We were coming in to Tzoah Rotachat at mach two. Psycho Train was moments away from slamming on the emergency brakes. If that happened with the loading door open and barrels on board, we were going to be in all kinds of trouble. We had to finish and quick.

Theodore hauled barrels across the car and closer to me. I pitched them out the sliding door as fast as I could. With the last barrel overboard, Theodore slid the door shut with a solid bang. Just in time, too. Metal screeched on metal. We dropped half our speed in less than a second. Everything launched forward. Me and Theodore smacked into the far wall along with the coal.

At least we were safe from the mud.

I crawled out of the coal just as we slowed to a stop inside the station of Tzoah Rotachat. This station sounded bigger. The echoes were more distant, like how it sounds inside Grand Central Station. Outside I heard far more voices than before. I could hear other screaming trains coming and going around us.

This was like some sort of major hub. And it smelled horrible.

371

Now, I'm no stranger to bad smells in small, enclosed spaces. I am from New York after all. I was in the kid in the early 2000's, when New York City had been mostly "cleaned up." And "cleaned up" is subjective, of course. The city was full of rats and garbage, but it wasn't like New York City in the '70s and '80s when it was basically a fucked-to-death post-apocalyptic cyberpunk world. Anyway, point is, even after New York City was cleaned up in the mid-2000s, people would still shit their pants on the subway. Sometimes they would even drop their pants and just shit right there on the seat. Very often, the subways smelled like shit.

That did not hold a candle – not a little tiny baby birthday candle – to the smell of Tzoah Rotachat. There in the thick of the city, the air was so thick with shit fumes, it clouded everything like a brown fog.

I didn't peek outside. I didn't want to see what kind of god awful demons lived in a city of shit. I didn't want to see what they were loading onto the train. I didn't want to know anything about Tzoah Rotachat. The smell was bad enough.

I longed for the comparatively fresher smells of sulfur and burning coal for elsewhere in Hell.

We sat quietly in our car for forever. I didn't know if those demons were taking their sweet ass time, or if it just felt longer because of the olfactory torture we were being subjected to, but it took them hours to get everything situated.

That smell was not a smell you eventually got used to.

"I don't know how much longer I can put up with this, dude."

"I hear you," Theodore replied. "It can't be much longer."

"Hell *sucks*," I said.

"Yeah. That's kind of the point."

4

Eventually – and not quickly enough for my tastes – the train screamed to life and rolled out of the station. We still had to ride out a city's worth of sick air, but I felt a twinge of relief just knowing we were on our way out. It took us an hour of high speed racing to get away from the smell and even then, when the wind shifted or changed, I would occasionally get a waft of it.

In time, even that passed. I could breathe normal sulfur air again and it was so nice.

Our next stop was Qliphoth, the place where possession demons lived. Theodore suggested I stay away from the gaps in the wall. If a single one of those formless, swirling demons caught even a glimpse of my eyes, it would come right for me.

The demons of Qliphoth used to be guardian angels, designed specifically for protection. When the guardian angels joined the rebellion in Heaven, their crime was seen as particularly offensive. How could angels whose sole purpose was to protect, rebel against the Heavenly Host? For that, God took away their bodies. Maybe they were better off, spared from being twisted or deformed, but they were still formless. Their whole existence was consumed with the dream that they might someday have a body again. They didn't care what kind of body, just any body. Even if it meant inhabiting a Son of Adam or Daughter of Eve.

When the train approached the station at Qliphoth, Theodore told me, "Try not to make any sounds."

"Okay."

"And try not to breathe."

"I don't need to breathe."

"Then why are you breathing?"

"Makes me feel normal," I said.

"Well, stop breathing for a while."

"Okay."

Not breathing makes me panic. Sure, me breathing isn't necessary. I don't have human blood, so I don't need to oxygenate it. I have some kind of oil chemical and Impossible Red cleans it with my mechanical liver, which functions more like a pool filter, I guess. But even in knowing all that, there's this deep-down caveman part of my brain that instinctively, animalistically knows I need to breathe. It was just like how I still got that rush of adrenaline whenever I fell out of the sky, even though I know the landing won't kill me.

So I sat there on the coal, trying to focus on anything other than the fact that I wasn't breathing. We weren't supposed to make any noise, so I couldn't distract myself by talking.

Once again, stuck with my own thoughts. Not one of my personal favorite past times.

Qliphoth was a literal ghost town. I sat there on the coal with my head between my knees and squeezed my eyes shut. While I wasn't going to look outside and risk a possession, I could still hear things. There was a rushing wind. There were creepy, hollow church bells. The demons outside moaned like zombies. Others wailed and cried, like something out of a ghost story where a mom drowns her own kids in a murky river.

I peeked one eye open to look at Theodore. He sat there, legs out, with his eyes closed. His face looked peaceful, like maybe he was meditating. Slowly, he picked up a piece of coal and put it in his mouth.

Something banged against our train door.

I shut my eyes and put my head back between my knees.

I whispered to Theodore, "Maybe we should get under the coal?"

"Shh," he said.

Getting under the coal would make way too much noise. I should have thought of that before now.

Something rattled the handle to our loading door. There used to be a lock on it, but I broke that when I pitched those barrels of mud. Now it was super easy to open. Just grab the latch and pull.

Don't open the door, I thought to myself. *Don't open that door. Do not open that door.*

The demon passed. It didn't open the door.

Our door stayed shut for our entire stop at the station. The demons unloaded whatever supplies they needed and loaded up their exports. I wondered what a city like Qliphoth could possibly trade to other cities in Hell.

After an hour, we pulled out of the station.

Next stop, New Chernobyl.

5

On our way there, Theodore filled the time with a little Hell history.

Ugh. History. I hate history. But information like that could end up being important, so I did my best to pay attention.

I did, however, light up one of my funny cigarettes.

The capital city of Hell used to be Pandemonium, or at least that was the English word for it. It was a mash up of old Greek words; Pan, which meant "all." Demon, which means "demon." And -Ium, which I guess meant "place."

Pandemonium. The All Demon Place.

There, Lucifer used to hold court in front of the other high ranking demons, where he would come up with his idiot plans to convince people to drink too much beer or skip church on Sundays or whatever stupid things he wanted to try that week.

When Isobella Westland started taking over, she moved the capital city to New Chernobyl as a demonstration of power.

Whoa. Demonstration. Demon-stration. I never thought about that word before, but it has "demon" right in it.

I thought about other funny words. Lollygag. That's a good one. "Stop lollygagging." I wonder if that word came from someone gagging on a lollipop, so they stop to cough. And then someone goes, "Stop your lollygagging."

Malarkey is another good one. "That's a bunch of malarkey." No idea where that word comes from.

One you don't hear too often anymore is nincompoop. Just thinking about it made me giggle. "Nincompoop." I need to start using that word more.

"Are you listening to me?" Theodore asked.

"What?" I looked up. I realized he was talking to me. "Yeah."

"You were spaced out laughing at something."

I smiled at him. "Nincompoop."

He looked confused. "What?"

The look on his face made me laugh. I repeated it. "Nincompoop."

He looked even more confused. "Why are you saying that?"

"Lollygaggin' nincompoop." I busted up laughing.

"What in the world?" he said.

Still laughing, I held out my spliff and said, "Here. Here. Smoke this."

"I've never smoked before," he said.

I gave him a look like he was from another planet. "What?"

He shrugged. "Westland does random drug testing. Corporate policy."

"Well, here." It was my turn to push something onto Theodore. "I doubt they have drug testing kits down here in Shitsville. You're fine."

He looked at it. "I don't know."

"This isn't some Lifetime movie," I said. "You don't have to smoke it if you don't want to. But unless there's a field of Winnipeg Kush around here I don't know about, this is probably going to be your one and only chance."

He considered that for a moment. "Okay."

He took it, put it to his lips, and inhaled. I saw the end turn bright red.

"Not too much at first," I said.

Theodore sputtered and coughed. I took the spliff back.

"See," I said. "You did it wrong."

He coughed more. "Well, how am I supposed to do it?"

"Like this." I took a drag and showed him.

"I did that," he said.

"Well, apparently not, because you coughed it up like a little bitch."

"I've never smoked before," he said. "I have to get used to it."

"You're the god of fire. You can't handle a little smoke?" I held it over to him. "Here. Get used to it. Try again."

He took it and tried again. He didn't inhale as deep, or as much. I could see him strain, like he *wanted* to cough, but he didn't. Then he exhaled.

"Nice work," I said.

We smoked together. Theodore told me more about New Chernobyl.

New Chernobyl was exactly what it sounded like: a one-to-one recreation of the actual Chernobyl nuclear power plant in a perpetual, endless state of melting down. There were no cleaning crews, no scientists there to make things safer. The radioactive material just crackled and burned as it melted down deeper into the ground.

The mushroom cloud that rose out of the reactor stood as a permanent fixture in the sky, always moving and rolling, but never fading away in the winds.

The reactor was built by a bunch of Archilem demons, commissioned by Lucifer as a monument to their efforts to reach Earth through the actual Chernobyl nuclear facility in the Ukraine. The recreation of the nuclear plant was a popular site that attracted new businesses and neighborhoods. After a time, larger structures were built: a gladiator arena where demons could fight and train, a strip mining facility looking for raw iron, and even a school where demons could study things like metallurgy, military strategy, and infernal literature.

With the school came dorms. With the mining facility came storage silos and weapon smiths. With the arena came restaurants and lava bars and places that would cut your head off for eight bones instead of ten, which is a pretty good deal.

New Chernobyl expanded outwards and upwards. Within half a century, it was one of the largest cities in Hell.

Isobella Westland truly wanted to reforge Hell with her new vision. One of the most symbolic ways to do that was to move the capital city. Pandemonium was still a giant metropolis where Lucifer and the other demonic elites lived, but New Chernobyl became the true seat of power. Lucifer already looked weak in the eyes of the demons and moving to New Chernobyl would have made him look weaker, so he stayed in Pandemonium.

But in a damned-if-you-do, damned-if-you-don't sort of thing, not moving to New Chernobyl was just as bad for Lucifer. Isobella took command of the demon armies with no one to oppose her. In time, the demons of New Chernobyl kind of forgot Lucifer was supposed to be in power in the first place.

It was the next day on the train when I saw the mushroom cloud of New Chernobyl in the distance. We were on a fast approach. Athena, who still didn't know how far I was supposed to go, pointed me in that direction.

My way out of Hell was somewhere in the capital city.

Chapter 21

1

The demons working the cargo station of New Chernobyl began sliding open all the doors. Before they reached the last car and exposed me and Theodore, we quietly dipped out the rear access door and jumped down to the tracks. All of the demons – muscular things with dragon wings and demolished faces – were more focused on unloading the cargo than looking for potential stowaways. They shoveled the delivery of coal out into piles and unloaded the boxes from all our other stops.

We kept our heads down and snuck along the opposite side of the train.

"There were supposed to be barrels of clinging mud in one of these cars," a demon said.

"Check again," another one responded.

"I've checked three times. Twenty barrels are hard to miss. They're not here."

After a pause, one of them said, "Tit ha-Yaven promised they would smuggle it out on this shipment. Isobella will not be pleased."

Haha. Oops.

We crept along the entire length of the locomotive. See ya, Danger Train. Thanks for the trip. Theodore led me past the platform of the station and around to a quiet corner.

He checked all around to see if anyone had spotted us. "I think we're going to be fine now."

I stressed the word. "Think?"

"You smell like a demon, I smell like a demon. My head's on fire, you have barbed wire in your hair. We might look like mudblobs, but I don't think we'll stick out as long as we both act like demons."

"Right. Demons. Got it." I bared my teeth and growled at him.

He gave me a weird look. "Okay, not like that."

I growled louder and opened my eyes up wide. "Like this?"

"Uh. No."

I slumped my shoulders and glared at him. "Well, I give up."

"Just follow me lead." He poked his head around the corner and scouted things out again. "Now, do you know where we're going?"

I checked Athena for an arrow. It pointed deeper into the city, straight at the mushroom cloud rising out of the meltdown reactor.

Theodore looked at the arrow over my shoulder and followed its direction with his eyes. "Inside Chernobyl?"

"I think so," I said. "Is that bad? That's bad, isn't it?"

He nodded. "That's where Isobella lives."

"Of course it is."

A patrolling demonic soldier came up behind us. He looked human enough, except his eyes were missing and squirmed with maggots. He wore some burned up military uniform that was too damaged to really make out any details. His voice boomed when he spoke.

He loomed over us and asked, "What are you two doing hiding back here?"

"We're-" Theodore began.

"What's it to you, nincompoop?" I shouted, then backhanded the demon across the face.

He looked at me, then nodded as if I just showed him legal identification. "Carry on," he said and walked away.

"There," I said to Theodore. "Acting like demons."

We made our way through New Chernobyl, sticking mostly to side streets and alleyways, anything that would draw the least amount of attention. The last thing we wanted was attention.

New Chernobyl had everything. There was no time to stop and poke around, but I saw at least five places that served human blood, a couple restaurants that smelled like burning tires, and three places that would cut your head off.

I have no idea why you would want someone to cut your head off, let alone why you'd pay someone else to do it, but there were a lot of people going in for it. Is it better when you get your head cut off by a professional? And then what? Do you die?

What is the point?

This one place offered to cut your head off for 20 bones. That was a really good deal, considering it starts at 50 bucks back in Krussplot. You're really saving bones that way.

I pointed it out to Theodore.

"See that?" I said. "Cut your head off, 20 bones."

Theodore made a face. "That's gotta be some sort of scam."

"Right?"

"You're not going to find someone to cut your head off for anything less than 35 bones."

I shook my head. "Not in this economy."

New Chernobyl had pictures of Isobella Westland hung up all across the storefronts. Sometimes entire walls were painted (poorly) to look like her: a blond, pixie-cut mudblob striking a triumphant pose in her black Westland suit that had to, at this point, be over 50 years old.

She hadn't aged a day since Theodore and I first saw her in that vision Abraham Lincoln gave us from Mount Rushmore. It was either her magic or her exile from Earth that locked her age in that early-thirties range.

Isobella's demon guards patrolled the streets of New Chernobyl in pairs. They came from all species of demon – everything from little red imps to towering lizard behemoths with pecs and abs and swollen arms – each dressed in burnt up uniforms that looked like they were pulled out of a house fire. They watched the citizenry move and trade and shop with careful, suspicious eyes.

Everywhere, demons were brandishing swords carved from spinal columns or rusted iron or smoky shards of pure darkness. If I didn't know any better, I would have guessed they were preparing for war.

The racket filling the street was a mix of the high-pitched, tinny hammering of cold iron weapons and shouting, fighting demons. But above it all, I heard a voice shout after us.

"Theodore!?" the voice rang out.

I turned to look. I didn't see anyone. I nudged Theodore to get his attention. "Someone back there is calling for you."

He turned to look, but also couldn't see who it was. "Who?"

380

"I don't know."

Whoever it was called out his name again. "Theodore!? Is that you?" Someone came pushing their way through the packed crowd of monsters.

Theodore squinted in that direction and said, "No one should know I'm here."

Eventually the guy wedged his way through the crowd and came out to where we could see him. He looked strangely familiar. Human. He wore a Westland suit. Blood drained out of his nose and mouth.

Whoever it was, he did not look happy.

"Shit." Theodore grabbed my arm and pulled me forward. "Run."

I followed after him and within seconds, we were sprinting further up the street. "Who is that guy? Why are we running? I feel like I've seen him somewhere before."

"You have," Theodore said. "That's Frederick Kruger."

2

Frederick Kruger worked as a saboteur for Isobella Westland. He sabotaged the Westland Corporation from the inside in an effort to get her body and soul out of Hell. In the end, he killed himself by throwing himself off the 37th floor of the Westland Corporation headquarters in Manhattan. He smacked the concrete and splattered his guts halfway to Jersey.

Kruger was a real piece of shit and there was no way his traitorous ass didn't go straight to Hell. Convenient for him, because now Isobella was running the show and he could be rewarded for his loyalty.

But in that moment, he shoved his way through the demon crowds and followed after us in hot pursuit.

Theodore yanked me sideways and we disappeared down a narrow alley just barely wide enough for us to squeeze through. "We have to get out of here."

"Get out of here how?" I asked. "We're balls deep in New Chernobyl. There's nowhere to go."

He whipped around with panic in his eyes. "Kruger's spotted us. It's just a matter of time before he tells Isobella. If Isobella finds out we're here, we're going to have every single demon in the entire city hunting us down."

"I get that, dude. But where else do you want to go?"

He looked confused and worried. "I don't know."

I balled up my fists. It looked like we were going to fight an entire metropolis of demons.

Our spot down that narrow alley didn't buy us as much time as I thought it might have. Kruger sprinted up at slid to a stop at the end of the alley. He spotted us both, then shouted for backup.

"Spies!" Kruger shouted. He waved his arms to get attention and pointed down the alley. "Spies from Earth!"

"Gotta go." Theodore started running. I followed right after him. "Run faster."

I went faster.

Two guard demons joined Kruger at the mouth of the alley. One was a baphomet goat demon like you'd see on a death metal album cover. The other one was a malnourished old woman dressed in rags, propped up on a gnarled wooden cane.

Honestly, I was more scared of the old woman.

The baphomet goat demon was too muscular and thick to fit down the alleyway. The old crone, however, she was thin like a scarecrow. She skittered after us, shuffling after us like a jittery elderly woman hopped up on caffeine and cocaine.

"Go, go, go," I said, pushing Theodore to go faster. "There's a creepy old witch after us."

Kruger shouted at the goat demon, "Go around! Stop them!"

The shuffling old woman reached out for us with her twisted, arthritic old fingers and she came within inches of touching us when we shot out of the other side of the alley. Theodore slid in our shoes into the middle of the weapon crafting district, suddenly surrounded by demons hammering on iron swords, or plunging red hot armor into hissing pools of radioactive water.

"Get to the reactor!" Theodore said as he pushed me away. "I'll lead them off in a different direction!"

"Bullshit, dude! I'm not going to let you die!"

He shoved me hard. "Just go! If you don't get out of here-"

The old witch woman dropped out of the air and landed hard on Theodore's back. She cackled like a crazy person and sank her black fangs into his neck.

Theodore cried out in pain, then I went blind as his body exploded in a supernova of fire.

The entire street was swept with fire like from an open air fuel bomb. I crashed through a stone forge and blasted red hot coals into a cloud behind me. Theodore stood alone in an epicenter of fire. The old witch had took the brunt of the explosion; her body laid on the ground engulfed in flames.

I was like, shit, did Theodore kill her? Did he just one-shot a demon with his exploding blood trick? But no such luck. The witch sprang to her feet and cackled with laughter.

Demons are notoriously hard to kill. I did a 360 and realized that as a crowd of them slowly closed in all around us, we were about to find out exactly how tough.

Kruger came hooking around the corner with that giant baphomet goat demon dude, along with two more soldiers he picked up on the way: bloody gorilla armed with a dinosaur femur and little tiny child whose head was mostly chopped off, but just barely hanging on by a strip of skin.

Again, I was more scared of the headless child than the bloody gorilla.

"Run!" Theodore yelled at me. "Now!"

I hesitated. A part of me knew he was right. We were fucked if we stayed. If I ran, I could get to the portal and get out. Theodore would keep them busy. But this other part of me, the *philanthropic* part, couldn't let him sacrifice himself. Not again. Not twice.

Old Witch shrieked like a widowed ghost from Russian folklore. She broke into a supernatural sprint and exposed her claws, ready to slice Theodore wide open. Theodore lit his fists on fire. That wasn't going to help him much against a demon.

It was time to show those demons what I could do. I flash-dashed in front of the witch and used the momentum of a runaway semi-truck to deck her fucking lights out. I heard neck bones crack as he head spun around backwards. Her body whipped circles in the air and she crashed to the ground, arms and legs all splayed out.

She wasn't dead. No way. That's not how you kill a demon.

This is how you kill a demon.

I threw myself down on top of her and punched the shit out of her chest. Boom, boom, boom, one, two, three, I heard her rib cage crunching to bits. Last punch, full force, I drove my fist deep into her squishy guts. I fished around until I felt her bottle.

I yanked it out. It was a tall and thin bottle with a wide base. The glass was black and looked like melted candle wax.

"Say goodnight, bitch."

I smashed her bottle on the cobblestone street. It burst open and black goop splattered everywhere. The Old Witch's eye shot open, she gasped once like a deflating gas bag, then died.

Problem solved. I stood up, quite satisfied with how much my demon-killing speed had improved. I got to my feet and saw every demon on Forge Street staring me down. Kruger and his guards stood there with front row seats for my little display. I killed a demon in front of hundreds of demon witnesses. They did not look happy.

"Well, well, well," I said as I backed away. "If it isn't the consequences of my own actions."

3

I backed right into Theodore. With demons surrounding us on all sides, I had no choice but to put my fists up.

"Well," he said. "This was fun."

"I don't like that attitude."

"On three, grab on to me," he muttered softly. "I'm going to try to fly you the rest of the way."

"Can you even lift me off the ground?" I muttered back.

"We're about to find out."

Metallic caterpillar demons and red imps and growling death metal devils closed in on us, armed with axes and swords and spears. Theodore silently counted down. Three. Two.

On one, I spun around and threw my arms around his shoulders. The demons swarmed us, but Theodore launched like a patriot missile and flew us high above the rooftops.

It was a good idea in theory, but Theodore wasn't the only demon who could fly. Half of the mob came flying after us, some of them on leathery wings, others just floating on their own supernatural power. Now it was a race to the Chernobyl reactor.

Arrows of sharpened bones came zipping past us. We were too high up and the scorching wind was too strong for any of them to even come close.

"Stuff like this must happen to you a lot," Theodore said.

"Oh yeah," I said. "All the time."

The Chernobyl reactor was dead ahead. A raging blaze of green fire crackled from inside, glowing as bright as the sun. A mushroom cloud of smoke rose up out of the radiation.

In the midst of the brightness, I saw a dark figure floating in midair. A person. She came into view.

Isobella Westland.

Her angelic spell book floated in front of her. By the time I realized who it was, she was already singing one of her angelic spells. Theodore tried to reverse course, but it was too late; Westland finished her spell and Theodore dropped out of the sky.

We crashed into the middle of a major intersection of town. Armies of demons flooded down the five connecting roads, blocking our escape in all directions. We were cornered.

Isobella Westland descended from the sky and hovered in front of us. She had a smug, satisfied grin on her face.

She said, "Well, isn't this serendipitous."

I stuck my hand in my pocket.

Serendipitous - adj. To luckily come upon or find by accident

"Theodore Carl *and* Penelope Salvo?" she said. "I don't know what you two are doing here, but I'm so glad you came." Her face changed from pleased to infuriated. "I'm going to enjoy watching you both die."

I closed my eyes and did my best to focus. Sometimes I'm easily distracted, but in that moment, whatever shreds of concentration I could muster were more important than ever. I squeezed my eyes shut tight and reached out with my mind.

Can you hear me? I thought. *Please, tell me you can hear me.*

"You'll suffer first," Isobella said. "Oh yes, you will suffer for a very long time as I let my demons torture your mortal bodies."

Are you listening?

Isobella kept blabbing. That was always her flaw. Her ego wouldn't let her shut up. "You will come to beg for death instead of freedom. And then you will die."

The barbed wire in my hair tingled and I finally got my reply.

We hear you, Our Queen.

I couldn't help but grin. I had a trump card and Isobella had no idea it was coming.

I looked up at her with a glimmer in my eyes.

"What?" she asked. "Why are you smiling?"

Are you guys ready? I asked.

Simply give the word, Majesty.

No one was coming to save me? Oh, Isobella couldn't have been more wrong.

"Behold!" I shouted as I threw my arms into the air. My voice echoed down the streets of New Chernobyl like a demon's. "The Army of Arms!"

The obsidian street beneath Isobella Westland shattered. Thousands and thousands of black tar arms erupted like a geyser.

They followed my fingertips and engulfed Isobella Westland. She recoiled, but not in time. The darkness swallowed her up and she was lost in the Army of Arms.

We have missed you, Our Queen.

I've missed you guys, too.

I whipped around and pointed down the street. The rush of demon arms changed directions, following my silent commands. They swept through the street like flood waters and crashed into the approaching demons like a wave, pulling the monsters off balance and knocking away their weapons.

The demon armies coming down the four remaining streets broke into a riot and barreled right for us. Theodore charged up his hands and sprayed one of the streets with fire. It didn't burn the monsters, but the force pushed them back like a fire hose.

I spun around and pointed down the third street, directing the Army of Arms to protect me at all costs. Some of the arms were crushed underfoot or smashed with hammers or shields. I could feel each one of them that died.

Still, this was a war of attrition. There was no individuality in the Army of Arms. They were a hive, eager to obey and ready to die to protect the queen.

Up above us, a bunch of my arms clung to Isobella and did their best to pull the book free from its orbit around her body. It wasn't happening. Her bond with that book wasn't going to be easy to break. She summoned holy magic that made her burst with sunshine like an angel. It melted my poor arms and sent them splattering to the ground. Their little bottles came down shortly after, cracking like eggs on the obsidian cobblestones.

The Army of Arms had numbers, but they were a stalling force. They weren't all that useful when it came to killing demons. Eventually even the ocean waves of my black army were pushed back by the advancing demon crowds.

I could hear the demons coming. They were pissed.

"Mudblobs!" they shouted.

"Eat them!" others screamed.

And above them all, Isobella called out her commands.

"Break their bones!" she said. "Crush them!"

The Army of Arms was a good ploy, but it wasn't going to pan out like how I hoped. They did their best to slow the advancing horrors, and Theodore did a bang up job keeping everyone at bay, but it was just a matter of time before were were overtaken.

But then something happened that brought all the fighting to a standstill.

Two burning people flashed across the sky in smoke and fire. They shuddered like twin jumbo jets flying too low and about to crash. The buildings around us shook in place.

The twin objects struck the street behind us like a couple of tactical missiles. Their impact brought a three-story chapel crumbling to the ground. Debris and a cloud of sulfur smoke swept over us so I couldn't see what exactly had struck the city.

Our questions were quickly answered when two gleaming metal figures stepped out of the dust cloud.

"Shit," I said.

Now the party was really over.

It was Metatron and Zophiel.

4

"Penelope Salvo!" Metatron belted out. You could tell by the power in his voice that he had command over the very laws of creation. The fallen angels recognized the voice of the Daylight of Enoch and instinctively, they retreated a few steps. I had to admit, hearing his voice sent a rush of panic through my veins.

The Army of Arms turned their attention to the angels. Through our psychic link, they were suddenly hyper-aware of this new threat, tense and ready to strike. I put my hand out and told them to hold their positions. Sending my minions to fight two archangels was sending them on a suicide mission.

Metatron and Zophiel stepped closer towards me and Theodore. Their metal boots clanged on the obsidian street. They looked really pissed off because there I was in Hell, the one place they told me not to go. Because of me, they personally had to come down to the stinking pit to kick my ass. Angels and demons have such a strong sense of smell, I could only imagine how much the archangels despised the air. The only scents on the hot winds were demons, black magic, and – for their sensitive noses – the boiling excrement of Tzoah Rotachat days away.

Metatron gripped his ax tight in his platinum gauntlets. Zophiel dragged her oversized sword lazily behind her, carving a deep gouge in the black road.

"Stay thy hand, foul traitors," Metatron said to the demons of New Chernobyl, never taking his hateful eyes off me. He used his ax to single me out. "This mudblob is our quarry."

Theodore leaned closer to my ear. "Who are these guys?"

"Angels," I said.

"Friends of yours?"

I laughed. "No."

Metatron raised his right arm. Clutched tight in his hand was Armstrong, the only arm from the Army of Arms that stayed on Earth. I left him alone to watch the shop in New York, but those angel pricks must have kidnapped him.

Armstrong wriggle in his tight grip. I didn't like the way Metatron was holding him. It was too hard.

"Armstrong," I said.

I am sorry, my Queen. I have failed you.

"You have trifled with unspeakable evils, mudblob," Zophiel said to me. "You have laid waste to your very soul. And you have violated the natural order of things by coming here."

"We warned you," Metatron said. "Now we bring oblivion."

I pointed at Armstrong. "Let him go."

They weren't going to let him go just because I told him to. I knew that much. I was in no position to negotiate.

The demons of Hell could have kicked the shit out of Zophiel and Metatron if they worked together. They outnumbered the angels a thousand to one. The idea that those two jabronies could petrify an entire city of demons was absurd. If Legion had it in their heads that they were going to retake Heaven someday, well, they weren't going to get very far if two angels brought them to a screeching halt.

But these weren't just any two angels. This was Metatron and Zophiel, the Anchor of the Jubilation and the Spy of God, two of the most powerful angels to ever exist.

Isobella Westland didn't have the same innate fear that the demons did.

She shouted down at them, "You think you can come down here to Hell and make commands!?" Metatron and Zophiel looked up at her. She went on, "This is my domain! Do you hear me? Mine! And she-" Westland pointed at me, "-is mine to do with as I please!"

The angels stared blankly up at her.

"Zophiel," Metatron said. "Who is this chattering mudblob?"

Westland repeated it, stunned. "Chattering mudblob?"

Zophiel locked eyes on Isobella to read her mind. She furrowed her brow and said, "This one is called Isobella Westland. She has somehow learned our celestial language. She uses the power for her own means, not to glorify the Lord."

Metatron flexed his jaw. "Has every Daughter of Eve lost their faculties of mind? Do they all so crave annihilation?"

"Annihilation!?" Westland said. She laughed briefly then said, "Do you have any idea what I can do?"

Metatron and Zophiel readied their weapons. Zophiel said, "Nothing we cannot do seven times seven, Daughter of Eve."

I looked around. The demon crowds were awe-struck by the radiant angels. Half of them were turned away to shield their eyes from their angelic glory. Metatron and Zophiel were concentrated on their tiff with Westland. And Isobella Westland had turned her attention to her book, readying some type of magic to throw at the heavenly intruders.

No one, at least for the moment, was looking at us.

I elbowed Theodore and whispered, "Hey, let's blow this popsicle stand."

Theodore leaned over. "Oh. I was going to suggest we run."

I rolled my eyes. "Okay. Yeah. Let's do that."

We didn't move. We didn't have to. Slowly... *very* slowly... I had the Army of Arms shift under our feet and conveyor belt us out of the middle of the street. It was just slow enough that no one noticed. Once off the road, we found a store – one of those "cut your feet off" operations – and we disappeared through the front door with plans to go out the back.

As we crouched and hurried past wicker baskets filled with bloodied feet, I could still hear Isobella and the angels out there, shouting at each other.

"You test our patience, mudblob!" Metatron called up to Westland. "I suggest you fall silent before we bring the force of a dozen plagues down upon your entire realm!"

"Are you dense?" Westland shouted back. "This realm is nothing but plagues! There's literally a city built around a lake of boiling shit! You can't possibly make things any worse!"

"I beg to-" Zophiel stopped, then her voice got louder. "Where is she!?"

Metatron looked all around. I wasn't there. I was ducking out the back door of Cut Off Your Feet and fleeing down the crooked alleyway with Theodore.

Metatron's voice shook the city like an overdue volcano blowing its top off. "*Where did she go!?*"

Run.

Run.

Gotta run.

Theodore couldn't fly. And that was fine. His fiery hair would have been a beacon in the sky and tipped everyone off.

We had angels after us. We had demons after us.

Neither group knew where we had gone, but that was a limited time offer. They were going to track us down eventually, just hopefully not before we got to the reactor.

Create a distraction, I told my army.

In what way? they asked.

I dunno, I said. *Tear this whole city down if you have to.*

Good move. The Army of Arms lacked onto the walls of the shops and storefronts and pried the boards loose. They smashed out the windows. They pulled up the floorboards of the homes and walkways until buildings started to collapse.

Theodore and I sprinted through the alleyways. Every few blocks we had to cross a wide open street, then duck back into the alleys. We weaved our way through the disorganized, haphazard town. With each passing break in the rooftops, the billowing mushroom cloud of Chernobyl got closer and closer.

I didn't know if radiation worked the same way in Hell. If it did, I had to hope that me and Theodore would be fine. Only parts of us were human. He was half-demon and I had a demon soul. He was half-god of fire and I was half-god of war. If Impossible Red and Untouchable Orange couldn't handle a little radiation, then, well, we were dead.

All I could do was hope.

Behind us, the howl of a million demons cried out like sweeping alarms, enraged, on the hunt for Penelope Salvo.

The shadows of Metatron and Zophiel swept over us as they passed overhead on glorious wings of the purest white. And they would have caught up to me and cut my head off if Isobella Westland wasn't in hot pursuit right behind them. She cast a spell – the same one she used on Theodore earlier – and the two angels lost their ability to fly. Their wings could no longer carry the weight of their bodies and they crashed down into the city.

Haha. These idiots. Everyone wanted to kill me so bad, they were fighting over who had the right to do it and it was literally making it easier for me to get away.

Theodore hurdled over a short obsidian wall. I smashed right through it because fuck your wall. Chernobyl was dead ahead, right in front of us.

I stole a quick glance at Athena. It still had a distance of ???, but it directed me ever forward, coaxing me to go *into* the radioactive glow.

I looked behind me. The sounds of chaos grew louder and louder. The Army of Arms infested the city like ants, tearing it apart little by little. The demons came storming through the streets, screaming and shouting and banging their weapons together.

And somewhere out there were two *really* pissed off angels who were out for blood.

Theodore and I reached the base of the reactor. There wasn't much time for long goodbyes.

Theodore pushed me forward, but kept his attention on the alleyways behind us. The sound of rioting demons grew louder and louder.

"Looks like this is goodbye," he said. "Next time call before you come over."

I shuffled away from him. "You going to be okay?"

He still had his attention on the alleyways. He nodded, but sounded nervous. "Sure. Probably. Maybe."

I kept moving away. "You're positive you can get out of here in one piece?"

He turned and smiled at me. Not a nervous smile like I would have expected. A confident one. He said, "Eh... sixty-forty."

I laughed, but I worried that he was being too conservative with his odds. In any case, time was running out.

"I'm going to miss you!" I called out as I backed away.

"I'm going to miss you, too," he replied. "Now go!"

I wanted to stay. I wanted to help. But I couldn't. I turned and made a mad dash for the Chernobyl reactor.

"Good luck, Penelope!" Theodore increased the intensity of his fire body until he was a shapeless, white-hot flare of light.

A mountain of rubble stood between me and the burning reactor. Chunks of smoking concrete and scorched pieces of lead were piled up everywhere. I scrambled over the debris on my hands and feet, climbing, climbing.

Demons came flooding out of the alleys. They spotted me right away and howled for additional troops. Isobella Westland came drifting over the rooftops. She had a spell on her tongue, undoubtedly one that would freeze me in place and keep me from running, but she didn't get to finish it.

A giant broadsword of platinum came looping up from ground level and thumped diagonally across her body. It chopped lengthwise in her chest and stuck there. Isobella floated still for a moment and then, as if someone cut the strings on a dangling puppet, she dropped out of the sky.

Good. I hoped that bitch was dead.

I wasn't putting too much stock in that, though.

"Time to go," I said to myself. I finished my scramble up radioactive mountain. Just on the other side of the peak was a giant pit of crackling green and yellow fire. If I had a Geiger counter in my head, I'm confident it would have been clicking like crazy. And if I had any other options available, I might have countermanded my jump into certain death, but Athena really wanted me to do it. The arrow was blinking.

Options, limited.

With a running start, I sprung up off the bricks, kicking my legs through the air.

I plunged into the irradiated light and became nothing more than a fading black shadow.

Just like that, I was gone.

Chapter 22

1

My body tumbled weightlessly through a world of increasing brightness. I squeezed my eyes shut and covered them with my hands. After a time, I got the sense that I wasn't falling anymore. I was standing. I took my hands away from my face and opened my eyes.

I could see again. Hell was gone. I was somewhere else. I was standing on clouds.

The ground beneath me was solid, but it felt like walking on pillows. Swirling white fog covered my shoes and came up as high as my ankles. The sky above me was the brightest blue with a glorious sun. The air smelled like flowers and the temperature was perfect.

In front of me was a city of gleaming ivory buildings, some of them topped with solid gold domes. They were tall and narrow with archways and columns, like something from ancient Greece or Rome, but showroom perfect. The windows were colorful stained glass, the planters out from were polished gold and platinum, and they grew some of the strangest plants I had ever seen, and believe me, I know strange plants.

Three people came out of a sprawling five-story museum and marched down the front forty steps. They reached street level and turned away from me, headed deeper into the city. They wore armor of silver and platinum and gold. On their backs were white bird wings, big enough to lift a person.

They were angels.

I was in Heaven.

So I panicked.

I was standing right out in the open where anyone could see me, so I sprinted through the clouds and ducked into an empty alcove of a nearby cathedral. Once I was safely out of view, I had to stop and consider why I was hiding. This was Heaven. Ever since I was a kid, Heaven had always been described as a paradise, the one place you wanted to go when you died.

I wasn't convinced that story was true anymore.

I was able to watch the society of Heaven from my super secret hiding spot. Angels wore full-plate armor. Human souls wore white robes with rope tied around their waists like belts. Flat discs of gold hovered just inches above their heads. Halos.

When I left Earth, Tengoku was very clear about how to use Athena to get to Hell. One thing we did not cover was how to get back home. I smacked my forehead with the palm of my hand. "Stupid, stupid, stupid." Why didn't I ask her about that?

I stayed hidden and watched with increasing curiosity as the people of Heaven went about their day.

I heard singing from blocks away. It sounded like a million people singing all at once.

Holy holy holy
is the Lord God almighty
who was, and is, and is to come.

They sang it again. Then again. They sang it over and over. They never stopped singing it.

Fuck me, I was really in Heaven. What was I supposed to do? Just walk out and introduce myself to some angels? Ask for help? You'd think that of all the places to go and feel welcome, Heaven would be it, but somehow I just really doubted that. I decided to just stay hidden.

I checked Athena.

???

There wasn't even an arrow. No surprise there. If Athena couldn't get a gauge of distance in Hell, it certainly wasn't going to figure anything out in Heaven. You're on your own, Penelope.

Sneaking around was going to be impossible. Heaven was as white as a laundry commercial and I was in a black shirt and black shorts with black hair. I stuck out like an ink blot on a sheet of computer paper.

I wondered if I could just knock someone out and steal their robe and their halo. Unlikely. This was Heaven. These people were souls. You can't bop a soul on the head and knock them out because they don't have brains.

But those robes and halos had to come from somewhere, right? If there were enough robes and halos for everyone in Heaven, they had to be kept in some huge warehouse. I just had to find that warehouse.

I didn't have the first clue where to start, so I dipped inside the cathedral I was hiding in front of. The front doors were solid gold and twenty feet tall. They were set in a facade of white marble. They had Greek letters on the door, and while I can't read Greek, I recognized those two symbols from Catholic school.

They were the symbols for alpha and omega, one of the many names God used in the Bible.

I put my hands on the doors and pushed them open.

Inside was a sprawling church filled with rows and rows of pews. The windows were stained glass artwork of saints and angels. Candles hung on the walls and from the arched ceilings. The pews were packed full with people, like Christmas mass. Angels sat on one side. Human souls sat on the other.

At the front of the church was a statue of Jesus dead on the cross hanging over a golden altar. On the altar was the body of a lamb with its throat slit open. It's blood pooled on top and drizzled down the sides.

The angels and souls sang the same song over and over.
Christ has died.
Christ has risen.
Christ will come again.

It reminded me of when I went to church, everyone singing the same monotone, brainwashed songs over and over with no emotion. I remember in eight grade being struck by the irony of singing the words "joyful, joyful, joyful," in the most monotone, bored way, because it was the millionth time I had to sing them.

I needed information, so I took a gamble on talking to someone. Not the angels, of course. Angels are dicks. I was going to hit up one of the human souls. I skirted along the back wall squeezed in at the end of the back pew. The person next to me was an old man with a full white beard. If he was in heaven, he must have died of old age. Just like everyone else, he wore a white robe and had a floating disc of gold over his head.

I leaned over, gave him a little nudge, and whispered, "Hey."

His eyes darted at me for half a second, then turned his attention forward. He was singing along with everyone else.

Christ has died.

Christ has risen.

Christ will come again.

I nudged him again. "Hey, dude. Is it cool if I sit here? I'm not taking anyone's spot, I hope."

The old guy shifted nervously, kept his eyes forward and repeated his song louder than before.

Christ has died.

Christ has risen.

Christ will come again.

Okay. Old dude doesn't feel like talking. I leaned forward and tapped a different soul on the shoulder. It was some teenage girl, younger looking than me. Poor girl. It sucks when someone dies so young.

"Yo, what's up, homie," I whispered at her. "Can I ask you a question?"

She glanced back at me, almost terrified that I would dare talk to her. She immediately turned forward as if I were poison. She sang:

Christ has died.

Christ has risen.

Christ will come again.

I sat back in my seat, crossed my arms and slouched. These people were no help. I got out of the pew and slowly, quietly let myself out of the cathedral through those solid gold doors.

Outside, six angels came walking up the cloudy walkway, each one armed with a flaming sword. They looked all around, as if they were on patrol for something. My policemen radar went crazy and I ducked down behind a marble bench there in front of the cathedral.

I watched them from under the bench. The angels marched past me in strict formation, clattering in all their armor. They came across two humble looking human souls, maybe man and wife who died together in a plane crash. The two souls stopped in the presence of the angels, stood perfectly upright, and sang:

Here I am to worship

And although I am not worthy

I beg for your forgiveness

And offer my life to you.

"Not worthy?" Not worthy of *what*? They're already dead and in Heaven, why are they still begging for forgiveness? Where's the paradise? Where are the fun and games? Forgive the pun, but Jesus Christ.

The platoon of angels passed right by those two souls without so much as a word. Once they were gone, the humans scurried away. The street was empty for the time being, so I dipped out of my hiding spot and chased after those two souls.

"Hey," I called out as I came running up behind them. "Hey guys, can I ask you something real quick?"

They turned, looked me up and down and backed away from me like I had goddam leprosy. I took another step closer, they backed away even more.

"I won't hurt you," I said. "Can you tell me where-"

They hurried away from me without looking back. They left me all alone in the middle of the street. I threw my arms out in frustration.

"Well, fuck me, I guess."

The longer I stayed out in the open, the more likely it was that I'd be spotted. I looked all around, picked a *new* church to hide behind and made a break for it. There were a lot of churches to choose from.

I didn't think I liked Heaven all that much.

2

I felt very alone. I felt more alone in Heaven than I did in Hell. I guess maybe I wasn't perfect enough for Heaven. I'm a flawed person, a person who makes mistakes, big ones sometimes, and I fit in better with people who get punished for stuff like that.

I wouldn't have made it this far without so many people's help. I wouldn't have started without Corolla. I wouldn't have made it out of Oz without Brijit. I never would have found my way through the Muffincake Kingdom without Party Waffle. I would have been dead for sure in Hell without Theodore.

Now, in Heaven, I was completely alone. No friends, no one to help me.

And I was terrified. I was terrified of being alone. I was scared because no matter how much I thought I wanted to be a lone wolf, deep down, I wasn't certain I could do it by myself.

397

I poked my head out from behind the pedestal of a thirty-foot statue of Jesus. A squadron of angels marched past me, oblivious to the fact that I was hiding nearby. I waited for them to pass me by and turn a corner before I darted to the next hiding spot I had picked out. Twenty feet away was a lush little park with green grass, white flowers and towering fruit trees. A marble gazebo sat in the middle. The columns of the gazebo were lambs and lions standing on their hind legs, propping up the roof with their heads.

If I see one more gazebo on this god damned trip...

I ran in a crouched position to the edge of the park and dove behind the trunk of an apple tree.

In the middle of the park, gathered on the gazebo, stood a dozen human souls. They were arranged like a choir and sang yet another song praising Jesus. Was this all Heaven was? Standing around, singing praises to Jesus Christ for all eternity? Jeez, guys, you sure do know how to throw a party.

From the safety behind my Tree of Good and Evil, I could scout around for my next tactical move. There was a Colosseum-looking arena on the opposite side of the garden. Surely there would be tons of places to hide in a Colosseum. Colosseums are huge.

I nearly jumped out of my socks when I heard a voice behind me.

"Hello, my child."

I spun around and fell on my ass to see Jesus Christ standing in front me, in the flesh. Instinctively, I crawled backwards away from him and butted up right against the tree.

Jesus stood there in a white robe and a red sash. He had long curly hair and a beard. A crown of thorns had been jammed deep into his head. A single trickle of blood dripped down his cheek. He held out his arms and I could see the holes in his hands. A beam of sunlight illuminated his head.

"You're..." I could barely spit it out. "You're Jesus."

"And you are Penelope Salvo."

"Yeah." I couldn't say why, but I wanted to get away. I looked all around for an escape route. "I'm, uh..." I didn't know what to say. "I'm lost."

Blood dripped from the holes in his palms. "You are all lost. Only through me will you be found."

"Yeah," I said. "That's not what I meant. I mean I'm physically lost. I don't want to be here. I want to go home."

Jesus stared down at me with vacant eyes. He smiled in a creepy way, as if he were looking right through me. He sat down on a nearby rock and kept pointing his eyes at me.

I had a laundry list of things I want to say to Jesus if I ever met him, but now that he was right there in front of me, I drew a complete blank.

I stood up. "I'm gunna go."

"You should stay," he said. "You and I need to talk."

"Oh, do we?" I said. "About what?"

"About your faith. About how you don't follow me anymore."

"Follow you *where*?" I said. "Where the hell you've been all this time. There's a lot of people on Earth looking for you."

"I am everywhere," he said, plainly.

"Are you? I don't know if you've been keeping up with current events on Earth, but there's a lot of bad shit going on down there. War. Homeless. Climate change."

"I know. I see everything."

"Well?" I held out my arms. "Why don't you do something?"

"I did do something," he said. "I died on the cross."

"You know, this might come as a shock, but that hasn't all that helpful. In fact, all it's done is cause a shitload of problems."

"I have given you all the help you will ever need," he said. He stared down at his bloody hands. "I died for your sins."

"Maybe you should have died for our cancer. Or died for our arsenal of nuclear bombs. Or died for starvation. Those things would have been helpful."

Jesus turned his eyes and smiled at me. I realized then what was so creepy about the way he was looking at me. Jesus never blinked.

"I'm not buying this 'died for our sins' bullshit," I said. "Look at you. You're not dead. You were dead for three days and then you came back to life to be king of the Universe. I'd hardly call that a sacrifice. At least when Kurt Cobain died for grunge, he stayed dead."

"You are so angry," said Jesus.

"I'm not angry. I'm the opposite of angry. I'm *very* angry. You know, I used to pray to you when I was a little kid. My dad used to beat the shit out of me and I asked you for help – I *begged* you for help – like a million times. Where were you for all of that?"

"I was right there beside you."

"Right there beside me while a fully grown man beat me up? Real cool, Jesus. Real cool."

"My father created humanity with free will because-"

"Look, I'm going to stop you right there," I said. "You can take your free will and shove it right back your ass because I'm not buying it for a second."

"There's nothing to buy."

"Bullshit there's not. You made the rules of the universe. It's impossible to fly by flapping your arms. It's impossible to breathe underwater by taking a deep breath. You could have, *if you wanted to*, made it impossible to hit a little kid. But you decided not to."

In a calm voice, he asked, "Have you ever heard the story of Job?"

"Yeah, I have. And you know what? Fuck Job and fuck you, too. Just look at this place, Jesus. You have everyone up here singing your praises and you don't do shit for nobody. Where were you on 9/11? Where were you in World War 2? Your only claim to fame is that you took a three day nap two-thousand years ago and now everyone has to worship you for all eternity? You need to get your priorities straight."

Jesus had a tranquil look on his face. "I forgive you."

"Forgive me? *Forgive* me? News flash, Jesus, I'm not asking for fucking forgiveness. I didn't do anything wrong. I'm a god, too, you know. And you want to know the big difference you and me? I do more shit helping people in one day than you've done in the last two thousand years, stacked one on top of the other. I've saved Earth like five times and I saved the Muffincake Kingdom twice, because when I see bad shit going down, I get off my ass and do something about it."

Jesus didn't have anything to say to that.

"And someday, when I die, I'll do everyone the fucking favor and stay dead. I won't wake up after three days and be king of the universe."

He didn't have anything to say to that either. I got right in his face and poked him in the chest.

"I'm ten times the god you'll ever be."

I jinxed it.

I heard thunder in the distance and felt two shock waves sweep through the ground. Pillars of clouds puffed up among the bell towers of the cathedrals. Something had landed over there – *two* somethings to be exact – and they had landed hard.

Who else could it have been. Metatron and Zophiel.

Fine. Let them come. I was tired of running. My ragu was already boiling over from reading Jesus the riot act. If I ran from the angels again, I'd be running for the rest of my life. If they were going to kill me, then let them kill me.

There's an old Italian saying. "Don't run from death, you'll only die tired."

Metatron and Zophiel came walking up the streets side by side. Their armor gleamed in the daylight of Heaven. Metatron had his ax slung over his shoulder. Zophiel drug her sword across the ground. They sifted through the ankle-deep clouds and approached the park.

"You're in for a real treat, Jeezo," I said to Jesus as I cracked my knuckles. "I'm about to give your two lackeys the old razzle-dazzle and you've got front row seats."

3

"Penelope Marie Salvo!" Metatron boomed as he came forward. Zophiel walked close beside him. Furious lightning flickered in their eyes.

I wasn't afraid to talk a big game, but I knew the reality of things. No one in Vegas would put money down on me in this fight. It was a million-to-one shot. Those two had wiped the floor with me countless times, and they were holding back. This was the final showdown. I'd be lucky if I even got a punch in.

Jesus stood up and held out his hands. "I am a precious lamb, meek and mild."

Meek and mild? Tell that to the babies in Egypt. Or tell it to everyone who drowned in the great flood. Directly in front of me are two angels ready to kill me. Yeah, Jesus is meek and mild only because he has someone else do the killing for him. You know who else pulls that kind of shit?

Carl.

Zophiel said, "Lay down your life without contest, bothersome mudblob. Die with one last shred of dignity."

I put up my dukes. "I don't want to die with dignity, thank you very much."

I squared up with the two of them, face to face, Metatron, Zophiel and I. I was about to get the oblivion they promised me so many months ago. It wasn't just anger in their eyes; there was also eager anticipation. They were going to pull me apart and they were going to enjoy doing it.

401

I said to them, "Before we knuckle up, I just want you to know..." I pointed at Jesus. "This guy is a total nincompoop."

Metatron flared his nostrils. Zophiel tightened her lips. I don't think they knew what that word meant, but they really didn't like it. Zophiel hefted her sword into combat position. Metatron readied his ax.

Jesus paced around in aimless circles, arms out, face pointed up at the sky. "I am the beginning and the end. Whoever shall eat of my flesh and drink of my blood shall find everlasting life."

I gave Metatron the stink eye. He bared his teeth. I moved my eyes over to Zophiel. She squinted at me and adjusted her stance. Someone had to make the first move. Who was it going to be?

Welp. I was the one who wanted to at least get one punch in.

I threw a sucker punch at Metatron's stupid face. With a clang, he caught my fist without even flinching. I threw a quick left jab and pounded him right in the gut. His armor rang like a gong. I didn't even make a dent.

There was a slight grin on his face when he brought his right hook around and decked me across the face. My ears rang when his gauntlet struck my tungsten carbide skull. My body spun in place and I hit the ground like a sack of mail.

I went to sit up, but Zophiel stomped her boot down on my chest. I was pinned. Both her and Metatron loomed over me.

Zophiel said one word. "Oblivion."

She dropped to her knees and decked me across the face. A glob of oily blood whipped out of my mouth. The impact echoed through the buildings. She leaned back with her fist and pounded my face again. Then again. Then again.

My vision flickered like a black and white television. Oil spilled out of my nose and coated the bottom half of my face. I could taste it in my mouth.

She stopped hitting me and stood. I blinked to get my eyes to work and looked up at them. Metatron held out his arm. Armstrong was clutched in his fist.

He said, "Bid farewell to your infernal pet."

I reached my hand out for Armstrong. It hurt to move. I spit blood and said, "Let him go. He doesn't have anything to do with this. He's just a-"

I feel fear, my Queen.

Don't worry, little buddy. I'll-

Metatron clenched his fist and crushed Armstrong's wrist. His bottle shatter. I knew it had, I felt it in my heart. Our psychic connection vanished. I couldn't hear his thoughts. Armstrong's hand went limp. His fingers stopped moving. Metatron carelessly threw his limp body to the ground.

I rolled my head and stared at his dead body. His body hissed and slowly dissolved into a puddle of tar.

I laughed, only because I was so pissed. "You're really going to wish you hadn't done that."

Metatron stomped his foot down square in my gut. I bent in half, then laid back out, arms and legs spread. He followed that up with a swift kick across my face. My vision scrambled. I heard static in my ears.

I sent thoughts to Impossible Red. *Come on, Red. Give me something to work with. Give me more juice.*

My vision slowly returned. Everything was blocky and pixelated, as if I were streaming a video on the lowest possible settings.

I tried to sit up again, but Zophiel kicked me in the ribs and rolled me over onto my hands and knees. Blood drizzled out of my mouth and nose and formed a puddle in the clouds.

I never did get that punch in.

Metatron grabbed me by the back of the neck and stood me up. He turned me to face him and backhanded me. My ears rang. My vision sizzled with brief, flickering images.

I fell back to the ground.

Metatron and Zophiel didn't just want to kill me. They wanted to beat me to death. No weapons. This wasn't about justice. This was about revenge.

Jesus wandered around behind them, his arms outstretched and his head leaned back in ecstasy. "You know not the day, nor the hour..."

Metatron held my eyelids open with his thumbs so I could see him and he shouted in my face, "Repent!" He gave me a right hook that broke my nose. He pointed at Jesus and demanded, "Beg him for forgiveness!"

I was really scared because I felt pain inside my skull. They had done something bad to my brain. Strange new chemicals filled my eyes. Something was broken inside me.

"Beg!" he commanded again.

I did my best to focus my eyes on Metatron. With the last reserves of energy, I raised my arm and made the sign of the devil with my fingers.

"Hail Satan."

Metatron had blown past the red line of all possible rage. He clenched his teeth and brought down the full glory of God. The metal around my eye socket fractured. I lost vision in that eye. The other one worked, black and white only.

I caught glimpses of gleaming metal coming right for me.

Zophiel hit me. My head jerked left. More warm blood spilled out of my mouth.

I had a vision of Corolla. I was in the passenger seat. We were arguing about music. Or... no... I was feeding him egg rolls. Shrimp. I think he likes shrimp egg rolls. We sat on the beaches of some island and listened to music. I loved Corolla. I wondered if he would be okay without-

Metatron hit me. My head jerked right. Nausea cramped my stomach. I puked up globs of molten hot metal.

I saw Ilana. She was sitting in front of me in literature class. It was freshman year. It was the first time we met. She turned around to borrow a pen because she didn't bring any. I didn't bring any either. Underachievers right out of the gate. We were the best of friends. I was so proud of her, even if she was working for the-

Zophiel hit me. I couldn't move my head. Out of power. The angels were killing me. Blood came out of my ears. Everything sounded underwater.

Princess Cardboard. No, Princess Coffeecake. Help me.

Metatron hit me. Need to crawl to safety. Body won't work.

Zophiel hit me. Need help. Carl. Xin. Someone help me.

Red. Help.

My body shut down.

4

I stood in some strange plot of grass situated in the middle of a sprawling Tibetan temple. I was at the top of some snow capped mountain, one in an entire range of snow capped mountains. This mountain, however, was basked in warmth and sunlight while all the others were frozen and cold.

Inside that grass area were stones and boulders of all different sizes. And there, among the stones, was this bald girl in an orange robe. She looked like one of those monks you might see in a Kung Fu movie.

Something about her seemed familiar. Everything about that place seemed familiar.

The girl turned around. She was Korean.

Io. Her name was Io.

But how did I know that?

"I haven't seen you in a while," she said. "Did you get hit by lightning again?"

"No," I said. I couldn't quite remember. "At least, I don't think so. I think I'm dead."

She smirked and nodded. "Yep. That'll do it."

I had no idea what she was talking about. "What'll do it?"

She walked through the grass and perched up on one of the larger boulders. She gestured for me to sit on one of the smaller ones, as if she were going to impart some ancient wisdom on me. I took her up on her offer and sat in front of her.

She asked, "Do you remember the last time you were here?"

"Uh. Not really. Kinda. I know your name's Io."

"Good!" She looked pleased. "You're getting better at this."

"At what!?" I said, standing up. "What's going on?"

"You are having an out of body experience," she said. "It happens to you sometimes. I have no idea why. But when it does, you come here. And before you ask, I have no idea why that is, either."

"Am I really dead?" I asked.

She shrugged. "Search me. It wouldn't be that bad." She looked around at the empty temple grounds. "It gets boring here. I sure could use the company."

I looked up at the sky as if that was where I might find my answers. "I'm dying. I don't know how I know it, I just know it. I'm dying. Something is killing me."

I paced back and forth in the grass. Io stuck her hands between her knees and smiled at me, like I was seriously entertaining. "Well, then you should get back to your body ASAP before you slip away for good."

"How do I do that?"

She shrugged again. "No idea."

Great. Super helpful.

"Here." She hopped off her boulder and came over to me. "Do you remember when I told you about the four states of being?"

"No."

"There's Nothing, Something, Anything and Everything."

I snapped my fingers in realization. "Oh my god, I *do* remember that. I couldn't remember where I heard it from."

"Yeah." She smiled. "It's a bunch of philosophical mumbo-jumbo, but it's the easiest way to explain how existence works. Don't forget, you heard it here first. The last time you were here, I told you that you were something."

I pointed at her. "And you're nothing."

"And I told you that someday you could become anything."

"I don't know what that means, though."

She laughed to herself. "I don't either, really."

"Why tell me stuff if you don't know what it means?"

She looked at me long and hard, really pondering her answer. After a moment, she pressed two fingers to my chest. "You have so much potential inside you that you haven't unlocked. Your ability to stop being something – Penelope Salvo – and become anything."

I shook my head. "I don't understand. What potential? Are you talking about my soul or something?"

"Hmm." She thought about that. "No. Something else. Something red. Sorry, I'm not good at this enlightenment shit."

"Something red?" I repeated. "You mean Impossible Red?"

"I wouldn't know. I guess it's possible? I've never heard of Impossible Red. What is that?"

"That's what's in me," I told her. "It's what makes me a god."

She grinned and gave me a condescending look. "Oh, you're a god, huh?"

"An artificial one," I said. "Of war."

She peered into my eyes as if they were windows to the control center of my brain. "You don't look like a god of war."

I crossed my arms. "Well, what do you think a god of war looks like?"

"I don't know," she said. "Not you."

"Well, I am."

"Yeah?" She put her open hand on my chest. "Then why don't you start acting like it?" She pushed me. I'm strong enough to be totally immobile, but she pushed me over like a feather. "Go be anything."

I fell backwards, but I didn't hit the ground. I slipped right through the grass and fell into darkness.

5

My brain restarted.

I could barely open my eyes. My vision was still black and

white. I was in Heaven. On the ground in front of me was a black puddle that used to be Armstrong.

I heard Zophiel's voice. "She's alive."

Metatron said, "You assured me she was dead."

"She *was* dead. Her soul was gone. But now it's back."

Be the god of war, Penelope. Come on. You're a god. Time to fucking act like it.

Metatron picked me up by the neck and lifted me off the ground. I dangled there, broken and helpless. He pulled my face close and looked deep into my eyes.

I made a fist.

I made a fist like I'd never made a fist before. Every time I made a fist before, I made a fist as Penelope Salvo. This time I made a fist as the god of war.

My pointer finger was a fleet of bombers dropping their payload across the streets of Berlin.

My middle finger was the invasion of D-day, with artillery that rained down from the sky and exploded in the sand.

My ring finger was a fleet of battleships off the coast of Italy, firing off their cannons in an 18 hour bombardment.

My pinky finger was the Russian front, driving back the Nazis. If the man in front of you dies, you pick up his gun and take his place.

My thumb was a month long campaign in the Pacific, down to the last kamikaze fighter pilot.

Metatron said, "This ends now."

I said, "Yes, it does."

I swung my fist and punched Metatron with World War Two.

Metatron launched backwards. He crashed through the front wall of a cathedral. The building crumbled. The golden dome collapsed down on top of him.

There at my feet, clattering in the clouds, were the shattered chest pieces of his plate mail armor.

I looked down at my hand. It was smoking. My metal finger bones glowed bright red, so bright that I could see them through my skin. It felt hot, like the inside of a jet engine.

Curious.

I raised my eyebrows and glanced over at Zophiel. She stared confused at Metatron's broken armor.

I had to get her while she was still off guard.

I gave her the Back Hand of Every Abrams Tank Hauling Total Ass Across the Hot Deserts of Afghanistan right to the face,

"Ka-*boom*, bitch!"

I nearly took her head off. Her head whipped around and golden honey blood sprayed in ribbons from her mouth and nose. She spun in place and dropped to the clouds. I thought maybe I had killed her.

I stumbled in place. I had suffered a lot of damage to the head. I almost certainly had the mechanical equivalent of a concussion. Now I was pushing myself beyond power limits I ever thought possible. My legs felt all wobbly, but I managed to stay upright.

The rubble of the collapsed cathedral shifted. Metatron pushed 100-ton columns of marble off of him as he crawled his way free. He sifted through the wreckage and walked out in the street. He took a moment to size me up – he was understandably caught off guard by what had just happened – and he wanted to plan his next move carefully.

He unfurled his wings and took to the sky. Higher and higher he went, putting more distance between us.

Then he came streaking down in full meteor mode.

Come on, Red. Let's god of war this asshole

Metatron came at me with shuddering speed. His body smoked and burned and burst into flames. He was going to hit me at supersonic speeds.

I squeezed my fist as tight as I could, ready to take a swing the nano-second he came into reach.

I could see the fire in his eyes. I could see the wrinkles on his unhappy face.

I threw a haymaker that connected with the side of his head.

My fist detonated like Hiroshima.

A mushroom cloud exploded up from my body. A shockwave of fire trashed all the cathedrals around us. Entire cathedrals crumbled to the ground. Statues were ripped out of the clouds and throw off into the distance. I stood in the epicenter of the blast where even the clouds at my feet were scorched black and burning.

No one died, of course. This was Heaven and everyone was already dead. They were, however, terrified by the destruction.

Metatron and Zophiel had been blasted away from me. Their armor was blackened and pitted. Metatron's face was badly burned. His hair was gone. Zophiel had lost a leg, blown clean off in the explosion.

I couldn't give them a second to recover.

I speed dashed for Metatron. He was already dragging himself to his feet, using his ax for balance. He saw me coming and swung his weapon at me in an exhausted attempt. I side-stepped it and gave him an uppercut that exploded like a field of landmines.

My punch lifted him up off the ground and he crashed down flat on his back. I jumped on his chest. "You killed Armstrong!" I rained blows down against Metatron's head, left and right, left and right. Pound, pound, pound, I vented a year's worth of pent-up frustration. I screamed caveman nonsense as I beat his face in. His bottom lit split open and golden blood came out.

Zophiel grabbed me and threw me off of him. This wasn't Zophiel in her human-form. This was Zophiel in her true form: a beam of sunlight with a million wings. The column of light moved wobbly, like a dangling noodle.

Beams of light came out of Zophiel, God's Light Spaghetti, and whapped me across the face. Another one hit me in the stomach. A third one looped around my ankle.

"Hands off the merchandise!" I shouted. I picked up a shattered piece of marble and threw it at her new body with the power of a battleship-mounted magnetized rail gun. It burst the column of light like glass and the attacking spaghetti noodles fell dead to the clouds.

My attack was just a set back for Zophiel. The shattered pieces of her body drifted back together to reform.

Laying in the clouds near me was Zophiel's human body. It laid there, comatose. Going full soul-mode had left her physical body behind. I ran for it.

Metatron left his body and took his true form, too. He loomed behind me as a swirling ball of fire with four faces on each side, an eagle, a lion, a ram, and a human. Each of his faces had a thousand eyes. Time gushed from their four mouths.

I couldn't beat those archangels in their human-form. Having the power of war was useful, but their Revelations-style power was seriously going to fuck me up.

Unless my gamble paid off.

With all the power of the Vietnam War, I punched my fist into Zophiel's human torso. Gloopy honey bubbled out around my wrist. I felt around as best I could and pulled out a bottle.

Zophiel, the beam of light, and Metatron, the fiery ball of faces, advanced on me. They stopped, however, when I spun around and held Zophiel's bottle up above my head.

"Alright, back up!" I shouted. "Back up!" I tightened my grip on the bottle and gave them my most dead serious face. "Unless you want me and the entire Holy Roman Empire to crush Zophiel's soul, I suggest you back the fuck up."

The beam of light and ball of faces hesitated, then backed off.

"Yeah, that's right." I spat out a mouthful of oil. "What up now?"

Jesus wandered aimlessly through the scorched, blood-soaked clouds of our fight. He was stuck in some kind of trance. "Hosanna," he said. "Hosanna. Hosanna."

"Both of you stay back," I told the angels. "I just want to go home. I'm leaving. If you stay out of my way, I'll leave this bottle behind and you can have your soul back. But if either one of you do anything to stop me..." I mimed a fake punch at the porcelain container. "It's bed time for bonzo."

6

With Zophiel's bottle as my hostage, I was able to walk worry-free through the streets of Heaven. No more hiding for me. I was beaten and bruised. I had blood all over my face and soaked into my clothes, right down to my socks. I looked terrible. I would have been a better fit in Hell. I was sick of Heaven. I was sick of traveling. Adventure over. All I wanted to do was go home.

No one bothered me, not the angels and not the souls. I got weird looks from both of them, of course, but none of them dared mess with me. They just stood there, eyeing me cautiously, singing their stupid songs.

I considered staying. My mom was a good Catholic woman, so she had to be in Heaven somewhere, but Heaven is literally populated with billions of dead people going all the way back to the beginning of time. It would have been impossible to track down one person in a dimension that big. Plus, no one in Heaven wanted to help me at all and the longer I hung around, the more trouble I was going to get into.

Ma was out there somewhere. I stared off over the clouds and softly said, "I love you, Ma. I miss you."

I wandered through the churches and cathedrals of Heaven, searching for anything that was going to lead me home. I eventually found the edges of whatever city I was in. Beyond that was a wasteland of clouds.

Forward I went.

I wandered aimlessly for who knows how long before I came across a throne of white ivory, accented with silver and gold. It was a throne for a giant, something you could set on the top of the moon and rule everything as King of the Galaxy. Sitting on the throne was a humble burning bush, engulfed in flames, but never burning down. The bush wasn't all that large, and the fire wasn't all that bright, but it was the only thing around. And I knew enough of my Bible to recognize one of God's forms when I saw it.

He spoke. His voice came from everywhere: the sky, the clouds, from inside my own body.

"Hello, Penelope."

"Hey," I said to the bush. "So you're God, huh?"

He replied, "I am... who am."

"So that's a yes," I said. God did not answer. "Look, I'm not going to apologize for setting off that nuke back there. Your guys started it."

"You have sinned against me," he said. "You have broken the boundaries of the worlds I have made. You have injured the angels in my army. You cause dissent in Hell. You are a bothersome creature."

"That's funny coming from you," I said. "I never drowned a whole planet."

"I am the Lord of Earth," he said. "There shall be no other gods besides me."

I laughed. "I got bad news for you there, coach. There's all kinds of gods all over the place. You're looking at one."

"You are a false god," he told me.

"Oh, I didn't create the Universe, but believe me, I am a god. And I'm a demon. And I'm a robot. And I'm a mudblob."

"You are not worthy to be here in the presence of my glory."

"Well, you know what, God, that fucking works out for the both of us because I didn't want to be here in the first place."

A white door appeared in front of me. Its door frame stood there, not connected to anything. The doorknob was solid gold.

God said, "I want you to go."

"Thank you so much," I said sarcastically. I went for the door. "Hey, you know you screwed over all those demons with that whole War For Heaven trick, right?"

"I am perfect in all things."

411

"Yeah, perfect. You had the angels building their own before they even committed any crimes. You totally knew that shit was coming. It's almost like you did it on purpose."

"Those angels craved power."

"Oh, I'm sorry, *who's* ruling the Universe? Who's the one sitting on a throne, making everyone sing songs about how great he is? Who does that? Oh, right. It's *you*."

"I am the Lord thy God," God said.

"You're not *my* god."

"Then your portion will be the lake that burns with fire and sulfur, prepared for the devil and his angels."

I scoffed. "I got bad news for you, bucko. I busted out of your jank-ass Hell prison not six hours ago. It wouldn't break my heart to rub it in your face and go for a two-fer."

"Then yours will be a different punishment."

"Oh, yeah? Lay it on me, Yahweh."

I really wished I hadn't said that.

Visions hit my brain. Visions so real that I could see a city on Earth, smell the exhaust and feel the mist in the air. I was looking down on some city in England. London, maybe? There was a house there, two-stories tall with a third story that could have been a renovated attic. The tree out front had a tire swing.

And sitting on the couch inside was Michael. Next to him was a woman. They had wedding bands. Was this woman the reason why he left me and Ma? And there were kids sitting on the floor in front of them. Two boys and a girl. None of them were yet teenagers. The three of them looked... similar to me.

That whole family sat with rapt attention and watched their TV. The events of 9/11 were unfolding on the screen. The World Trade Center was burning. The lady next to Michael had tears on her face. Michael leaned forward with his elbows on his knees.

I was looking into the past. 9/11 happened fourteen years ago. Michael was at a dig site during 9/11. Or... he was supposed to be. And that little girl was probably seven or eight years old, nearly the same age as me at the time.

But how was Michael watching 9/11 with his new family when he didn't walk out on me and Ma until 2006? When 9/11 happened, Michael was at a dig site in Egypt. Or, at least, he was *supposed* to be.

Wait. Did that mean...

Michael had other kids that weren't me. And he had them with some woman who wasn't mom.

He had two families.

I tried to shut my eyes, I tried to look away, but it was impossible. I wasn't just seeing it, I was *experiencing* it. Whatever God was doing, he was putting these visions straight into my brain and there was nothing I could do about it.

"Alright, stop!" I shouted. My physical body in Heaven dropped to my knees and I slapped my hands over my eyes. "Don't show me this shit, you asshole! I don't want to see it!"

The girl turned away from the TV and went up to Michael.

"Daddy, why is everyone sad?" she asked.

"Something happened in New York," he told her.

Something *happened*? That's putting it mildly.

Me and Ma were in New York City *living* 9/11, stuck underground in the Lexington Avenue and 63rd street subway station. People all around us were screaming and crying and talking on their cell phones. There was a dust cloud up there on the surface that made it impossible to see. Occasionally groups of firemen or cops or EMTs would come running through the crowds with gas masks on and no explanation as to why. No one had any clue what was going on. No one knew what to do. I remember Ma waiting in line for thirty minutes to get to a pay phone to call Michael.

In my vision, Michael's cell phone rang. He looked at the caller ID and saw the area code for Manhattan. During 9/11. Who else could it possibly be? Your *other* wife and your *other* daughter.

He silenced his phone and put it on the end table.

Michael didn't ignore me because I was a girl. Michael didn't beat me because I was bad at history. Michael hated me because I was the inconvenient byproduct of a marriage he didn't want.

All of those missed birthdays. All of those summer vacations where he was MIA. The physical and emotional abuse. Walking out on an eight year old kid and leaving a single mother behind.

It was all because...

I felt sick. I puked up molten steel.

"There is your penance," God said. "Now you may go."

"Fuck you," I said, crouched there on my hands and knees. I spat battery acid out of my mouth. "Just... fuck you."

The magical white door slammed open. My body was invisibly jerked off the ground and dragged through the air. Zophiel's bottle rolled from my fingers and landed in a puff on the clouds.

God threw me out of Heaven and slammed the door shut.

Chapter 23

1

I splashed down in the East River and plunged deep. I let myself sink. I didn't swim for the surface. I didn't have any fight left in me. I hit the bottom and laid there in the cold, muddy darkness.

The Lord had tested me, and I forgot to study.

I thought I hated Michael before. I didn't realize how much deeper that hatred could go.

My vision explained so much. Michael never loved me or Ma. He had to've loved Ma at first - why else would they get married? - but then I came along. The charm wore off and the troubles cropped up. He never cared about my grades. He just hated hearing Ma nag about it. His solution was to put the fear of God into me so I would straighten up and that would be the end of it.

He would literally say that. "I'm going to put the fear of God into you."

Well, you know what, Michael? I met God and I'm not scared of him anymore.

I laid underwater for hours processing my emotions. Eventually I became more aware of the world around me. I was squishing into the bottom of the East River. Disgusting. There's nothing down there but hypodermic needles and cut up dead bodies dumped by the Mafia. I pushed myself off the muddy river floor and swam for the surface.

It was the middle of the night when I crawled out of the water and reached shore. I was coated in mud from the East River. It smelled as bad as Tzoah Rotachat. Well, maybe not quite that bad, but close.

I looked up at the glimmering skyline of New York City. Home sweet home, back in the city that never sleeps. God, how long had I been gone? Months? A year?

I hoofed it through the city streets, soaking wet and splattering water everywhere. I found a recycling bin in Yorkville and dug through it until I found a newspaper.

MARCH 13, 2015

2015!? I left in *May* of 2014. I'd been gone for almost a whole year! Everyone probably thought I was dead. My birthday was in, like, 17 days. The whole thing was fucking nuts.

I ran through the streets of the Upper East Side headed for Central Park. I needed to find out what happened to Corolla. I had no idea where to find him.

I decided to start with Ilana. If Corolla was okay, she would know where he was. But after a year, she wouldn't be easy to find. She might have moved. She almost certainly wasn't still training at Ithaca Gym, not after this much time. It was late night, but I knew one place that she might be and I was already headed that way.

I got to the Westland Corporation headquarters just a little after midnight. Their HQ never closed. The supernatural doesn't sleep so neither do they. I let myself in through the revolving doors, speed-walked through the terrarium lobby and walked right up to the round wooden receptionist hub. I was still wet from the East River and I'm sure I smelled just fantastic.

I went up to one of the receptionists, some middle-age lady, and asked her if she had a listing for Ilana Rittenberg.

"Who?" the lady asked.

"Ilana Rittenberg," I said. "She used to be personal security for some middle manager dude."

The lady looked at me. "I'm sorry, this is a private firm. You shouldn't even be in here. I can't just give out-"

"Oh, I know exactly what this place is," I told her. "In fact, I probably have a better idea what's going on here than you do. Will you just look up the name Ilana Rittenberg and see if-"

"Penelope?" said someone behind me.

It was Ilana. She came out of an elevator with a tablet computer in one hand and a briefcase in the other. She wore the traditional black Westland suit. She had a blacked-out laminate ID card on her chest and a gun strapped to her hip.

"Ilana!" I ran over to her with my arms out.

She dropped her briefcase and tablet right there on the floor and ran to hug me. We wrapped our arms around each other and I pulled her close.

"Oh my fucking God, Penelope, I thought you were dead!" she said. "Where the hell have you been?"

"Heaven," I said. "And Hell. And all over the place."

She pulled back to look at me. "You finally made it to Hell?"

"I did."

"Did you rescue Theodore?"

"I did not."

Her face fell. "What?"

I smiled and gave her a pat on the shoulder. "It's okay. He didn't want to be saved. He's fighting the good fight."

She held me by the shoulders, looked me up and down and started to cry. "I just can't believe it. I was so sure you were dead. You've been gone for a year."

"Eleven months," I said, "But yeah, basically a year. I didn't feel like that long."

She pulled me close and stuck her face into my shoulder. She cried for a moment, then said, "You smell terrible."

"I was in the East River."

"You need to stop."

"Believe me, I know."

"Come on." She let me go and went to gather up her briefcase and tablet. "Come with me back to my place. You can use my shower and we'll get you something clean to wear."

"Thanks," I said. "But I really need to go find Corolla and-"

"Oh, well, that works." She gave me a big smile. "Corolla's at my place. He's is going to literally flip shit when he sees you."

"You're serious!? Corolla's okay?"

"He's fine," she said. "He's been worried sick, but he's fine."

Ilana got us a ride from a talking Westland SUV named Blazer. Blazer wasn't her car-partner - she wasn't high enough up the corporate food chain to get her own car yet - but the cars all knew Denali and Denali knew Ilana, so all the SUVs were nice enough to give her a ride home sometimes.

416

"A lot's changed since you've been gone," Ilana told me on the ride to her apartment in Queens. "Just last month I got promoted to second in command of Zulu team. I'm on track to be the Westland Corporation's youngest team leader ever."

"That's awesome," I said. "Was that because of Carl or...?"

"No way, dude. I did it on my own. I'm really great at security. You wouldn't believe the training I put myself through. I'm still learning Krav Maga, but I'm really good at shooting and I can be a bossy bitch when I need to be. It's like the perfect job."

I elbowed her and said, "Someday you're going to be running the place."

She rolled her eyes. "Yeah, right. And someday the Jets will win the Super Bowl."

2

Blazer pulled up in front of Ilana's apartment building just on the other side of the RFK Bridge. There parked out front was Corolla. He looked exactly the same as I remembered him. I had every intention of thanking Blazer for the ride and I meant to wait for Ilana to get out of the car so I could follow her up to her apartment, but all of that went to the wayside once I saw Corolla.

I threw open the car door and ran up the sidewalk.

"Corolla!" I shouted.

His headlights popped on. I heard his sleepy voice come from inside the car. "Penelope?"

I held out my arms, laughed and cried. "Oh my god, Corolla!"

"Penelope!"

It's not easy to hug a car. I've tried to hug him a ton of times before, but never quite figured out the best way to do it. I leaned against his passenger side and draped my arms across his roof.

Corolla didn't have eyes, so it was difficult to wrap my mind around the idea of him crying, but in that moment he was crying.

I cried, too.

I ran my hands across his roof. "I missed you so much."

"I wish I had arms so I could hug you!" he said. "I thought you were dead!"

"No way, man. I don't die! And I told you I'd be back."

"You did. And I wanted to believe you, but so much time passed and I started to worry. Then I started thinking the worst-"

He broke down, sobbing, unable to talk.

We hugged it out for a while.

417

Ilana came strolling up behind us. "One year ago, Corolla washed up on the shores of the Bahamas. The local government started emailing people about him and someone in Information Collection picked up on it. When Carl heard about a Toyota Corolla mysteriously washing up out of the ocean, he immediately knew who it was. He sent my team to go check it out. A week later, we had him back in our garage."

"Saved by the Westland Corporation," Corolla said. "Can you believe it?"

A pathetic, sad laugh escaped me. "I'm just glad you're okay."

We hugged more. There wasn't much to say. I was just so relieved to be back home and have Corolla back in my life.

"Penelope," he said.

"Corolla?"

"You stink."

I laughed. "I was in the East River."

"If I had a mouth, I'd be throwing up."

"How can you smell me if you don't have a nose?"

"That's literally how bad you smell."

Ilana nudged me and said, "Come on. Let's get you a shower and some new clothes."

"Okay." I stepped back from Corolla. "I'm going to go get cleaned up. After that, let's go fly around and listen to Journey."

"And get egg rolls?"

"Sure, man," I said. "All the egg rolls you want."

He said softly, "Egg rolls *and* Journey? *And* you're back? This has been a really good day."

Ilana lived in a pretty killer apartment building. It was all paid for by the Westland Corporation. The corporation took care of everything she needed, she said. Bills, groceries, clothes. She didn't even really get a paycheck. Well, she got a paycheck, she explained, but it wasn't a normal paycheck. It showed up in all black, so she technically didn't know how much money she made.

Bizarre stuff. But I wouldn't expect anything less from the Westland Corporation.

We walked into her apartment and she flipped the lights on. Her place was a wreck. Clothes were all over the floor and dirty dishes overflowed in the sink.

"Do not sit on my couch," she said. "I will never get that smell out."

"Okay."

"And don't touch anything."

"I won't."

She gave me a disgusted look. "You reek."

"Yeah, dude, I'm very aware."

It's strange to think about what a Westland employee does when they're off the clock, but there I was hanging out with one. Ilana pulled off her work jacket and threw it on the floor as she stepped into her bedroom. She talked me while she changed.

"I brought Corolla home with me the day he was all fixed," she said. "We get lunch at least twice a week. Sometimes more."

I told her, "I was worried that he was dead."

Seeing Corolla alive was the best thing to ever happen to me. I felt knots being untied in my stomach that I didn't even realize were there. It didn't even occur to me how much his fate had been bothering me until the weight was lifted off.

Ilana came out of her bedroom dressed in a black T-shirt and torn up jeans. She tossed me a towel and a bunch of clothes.

She pointed at Athena. "Is that robot arm waterproof?"

I held my arm up to look at it. "Yeah."

"Because I don't want that thing going off like a bomb."

"It won't."

"Then go wash that stink off your body. Bathroom's down that way."

Ilana had decorated her bathroom with all kinds of weird shit. Her shower curtain was clear, but had a silhouette of a knife murderer on it. On one wall was a life-sized cardboard cutout of Captain Kirk. On the floor of her bathtub were three rubber duckies. They could have been there ironically or Ilana might legit take bubble baths with rubber duckies. Either one was possible.

I stripped naked, got in the shower and washed off that film of East River. Letting the water pour over me was like a baptism or a rebirth or something. I don't know, I'm not a philosopher. All I knew was that once that smell was gone, my journey had ended and I was officially home.

Chapter 24

1

In the days that followed my return to Earth, I tried to get my life back to normal. One of the hardest things to deal with was Xin's shop. Left unattended for a year, the plants had all died. The Looping Bandis, the Fire Crocus, the Lemon Lime Suckles, everything was dead. Walking into the shop and seeing all of my little plants all brown and shriveled up literally broke my heart. I did my best to keep from crying and I managed to maintain my composure for a while, but when the time came to actually throw them in a trash bag and carry them out to the dumpster, that's when the tears came.

I had let Xin down. When he was alive, I made all kinds of overconfident promises about how I could take over the business someday. I told him the shop would be in good hands.

I started to wonder if that was true.

Losing the plants was devastating, but that wasn't necessarily the end. There was a road to recovery. After having to replace all the plants once before, forward-thinking Penelope created an emergency bank of seeds. Carefully sorted and painstakingly cared for, I had a tackle box in the back with a collection of seeds from every plant and spores from every fungus. I'd have to start from scratch and raise them as sprouts, but if that's what I had to do, then that's what I had to do.

I worked all alone in the shop for a whole week. At first it was nice to have some me time, but I eventually grew bored. I missed

Armstrong. He was always a welcome distraction. I thought a lot about him while tilling soil and reseeding everything. It would take a month for my plants to sprout, some of them even longer.

It was around noon on that Friday when Ilana walked through the screen door with a THANK YOU THANK YOU THANK YOU plastic bag of Chinese food and two rolls of silverware. She must have come on her lunch break, because she showed up in her Westland uniform. A laminated ID card hung from her breast pocket, solid black with only the cursive Westland "W" on it. I was kneeling on the floor of the shop, wrist deep in a large ceramic pot, prepping it for the Kowanda Acorn I had yet to plant. We exchanged hello's and she sat a styrofoam container of lo mein on the counter. She handed me some silverware and said she came to help me plan my birthday on that Wednesday of next week.

I kept gardening, occasionally taking bites off the spoon and fork she stole off the front patio of some brewery in Midtown.

"I don't do birthdays," I told her.

"No, I know," she said. "But you're turning twenty-one. You can't *not* celebrate your twenty-first birthday."

"Oh, I can't?" I said. "Watch me. What am I supposed to do? Get trashed?"

"Uh, yeah? That's the point."

"I don't get drunk, dude. It's impossible."

"Well, I'll get drunk then," she said.

"I'd rather not. I like to let my birthday come and go."

"Okay, how about this," she said. "Let's just go out like normal. We won't make it about your birthday and I won't tell anyone it's your birthday. We'll just go out, I'll get destroyed, and we'll treat it like a regular night."

I sighed. This was Ilana's round-about, loop-holing way of celebrating my birthday, but whatever. She seemed really psyched to go out. Admittedly, after the adventure I'd been on, it would have been nice to go do regular human things. "Where do you want to go?"

"Gold Mine," she said.

I glanced up at her. "You still go there?"

"Of course I still go there. They never charge me for anything."

"I just figured you would have quit drinking after getting your big britches job at Westland."

"Quit drinking?" She gave me a crazy look. "I got a job, Penelope. I didn't convert to Islam."

"So you go out and get trashed at some bar that smells like piss and then you go work for a corporation where you're second in command over a bunch of people with guns?"

She looked me right in the eyes as she chewed her lo mein. "Exactly," she said, as if it were no big deal.

"Okay." I turned back to my gardening.

"So we'll go out?" she asked.

"I guess," I said. "Just don't make it about my birthday."

"I won't. Promise."

Ilana hung out with me for the rest of the afternoon. We listened to music on Xin's old boxy radio. I told her about my drinking contest in the Guinee, about Peepee and Dori and Tonganoxie, and about the Muffincake Kingdom. I asked her if she should be at work, shouldn't she be leading a team somewhere, but she said she had the next three days off. There was going to be a big operation in Transylvania coming up. A bunch of cultists were trying to resurrect a vampire and they were sending a field agent out there to "deal with it."

"The field agent specifically requested Team Zulu," Ilana said with a big smile on her face. "Can you believe it? I mean, okay, admittedly they're calling in three different teams for the whole operation, but my team is one of them."

"So you're going to Transylvania to, what, shoot a bunch of people?" I asked.

"Cultists," she said.

"But you're murdering them."

"It's not *murder*, Penelope. Jeez."

"What do you call it then?"

"It's..." She stalled by eating a corner of her crab rangoon. With her mouth full, she said, "Okay, whatever. It's not murder. It's for world safety. We're doing the world a favor."

"Uh huh." I said. "Spoken like a true Westland employee. What flavor Kool-aid did they give you?"

"Oh, ha ha," she said. "Do you think the world would be safer with a bunch of cultists running around the woods of Romania, picking off tourists and draining their blood?"

I mean, the obvious answer was "no." But it was time to change the subject.

"Come find me that Wednesday when you get back," I said. "We'll go get food and then we'll go to the Gold Mine."

"Cool." She hopped off the bar stool "And maybe we can go spray paint some shit."

"Oh, is that stupid water bar still there on 8th?" I said. "We should go tag that."

She gave me a face like, yeah, duh, that's obvious. "Oh, totally. Fucking hipster bullshit. Water for, like, eight bucks? What kind of gentrified capitalist bullshit it that?"

"I fucking know."

"Okay." She went for the door. "We'll tag the water bar, then go get, like, tacos or something."

"Tacos?"

"Yeah," she said. "Believe it or not, I'm actually starting to get sick of Chinese."

2

That weekend, Corolla drove me to the garden center up in SoHo. I needed to get a couple different things for the shop: some nitrogen fertilizer, a fresh bag of soil, and some sticks to stab in the dirt so the sprouts had something to help them grow straight and tall.

As we drove, I told Corolla about all the places I visited when I was traveling through the different worlds. I told him that Madam Brijit wasn't that much of a bitch once you got to know her. I told him all about Party Waffle, how he loved to dance, and how he ultimately died when some Unthinkable Black monster threw a building at us.

I told him about how I got to see Princess Wedding Cake and Princess Coffeecake again.

"You mean Parcel and Cardboard?" he asked. "That's crazy! Were they surprised?"

"Oh yeah, " I said. "They were stoked."

"Aw. I'm sorry I missed that."

Corolla's like my best friend and I usually tell him everything, so I just came right out and said it:

"I also kissed Princess Coffeecake."

He laughed. "What?"

"Well, technically she kissed me the first time. I just kissed her back."

"What do you mean the first time?"

"We kissed again after that."

"So you kissed twice."

"Well, the second time was different. She was worried that I was mad at her for kissing me the first time, so the only way to show her that I wasn't mad was for *me* to kiss *her*."

"Uh, that was the *only* way?" he asked.

Defensively, I said, "Yes."

He paused, then said, "How did it feel to kiss a girl?"

"It was..." Fine? Weird? Nice? "It was new."

Some bike courier suddenly swerved in front of us to dodge a panicked squirrel scrambling around in the middle of the road. Corolla slammed on his brakes and screeched to a stop, just barely avoiding vehicular manslaughter. He laid on the horn, rolled down the window and yelled, "Get off the damn road!"

The bike guy looked over, but since Corolla was just a disembodied voice coming out of the speakers, the guy assumed it was me yelling at him instead.

He flipped me off. "Fuck you!"

"Man, fuck *you*," I yelled back. I didn't really have a dog in that fight, but you can't just let a "fuck you" go unanswered.

Funny thing was, I was in the passenger seat. The driver's seat was empty, but the guy was so pissed he didn't even notice.

Corolla yelled, "Go ride your bike in the park, you hippie!"

"Capitalist!" the guy shouted back.

Corolla floored it and left the guy in our dust. I sat back and smiled. Man, it was nice to be back in New York where everything made sense.

I smoke some weed before I went into the shopping center, so what should have been a twenty minute in-and-out trip ended up taking me an hour and a half as I stared at every plant and flower. Eventually I came back out and loaded all my supplies into Corolla's trunk. On top of the stuff I needed, I also picked up this cool little pineapple plant. It was only a foot tall, but it already had a little baby pineapple budding out of the top. I named him Pokey.

"Did you hit Jesus when you went to Heaven?" Corolla asked me on the ride home.

"No."

"Did you chicken out?"

"No," I said. "He was acting all weird. I don't think he's all there, if you know what I mean. But I did tell him to fuck off."

"You said 'fuck off' to Jesus?"

"Hell yes, I did. That guy sucks."

424

"There's this guy on Canal Street with those signs? He says Jesus is the reason for the season."

I rolled my eyes. "Whatever."

3

That following Wednesday evening, Ilana came rolling up to the shop. I was out on the porch tending to my little pots. Pokey was sitting on the rail in the sunshine. She showed up dressed in normal clothes: a black shirt with fishnet sleeves, a black skirt with fishnets on under those, and black chucks held together with duct tape. She had on a studded bracelet and a choker.

No one in a million years would guess that this twenty-year-old punk worked in corporate security and knew Krav Maga.

Right away I noticed her face; she had a gnarly black eye.

"Whoa, holy shit," I said. "What happened?"

She looked confused. "What happened to what?"

"What happened to *what*?" I repeated. "What happened to your fucking eye, man."

"Oh, that!" She laughed and pointed at it. "Work shit."

"That cult?" I asked.

She laughed again. "No, actually. The cult thing was easy peasy. This happened afterward. I slipped on the loading ramp to the armored truck and smacked my face on a latch."

Of all the combat shit she goes through... "So you slipped."

The joy in her face faded and she crossed her arms. "There was blood on the ramp. I wasn't watching."

"Well." I pointed at her eye again. "It looks cool."

"It looks punk as fuck is what it looks like." She put up her fists and waved them at me. "You want me to give you a matching one?"

"Psh. Ilana, there is not enough Krav in all of Maga for that."

She laughed. "I know."

Ilana dicked around on her phone while I finished up my gardening and moved everything inside. Afterwards, Corolla drove us to Estaban's, this taco place up in SoHo. Ilana loved Esteban's because it wasn't like that pretentious hipster food truck bullshit where they throw darts at the food pyramid and invent something stupid like "mashed potato tacos," whatever the fuck that is. Esteban's was the real deal; a tiny, dirty, hole-in-the wall place that sold bean tacos for a dollar, chicken tacos for a dollar fifty.

"A dollar fifty," Ilana said. "In SoHo. I mean, how are you ever going to beat that?"

Corolla said, "You can't."

You can't eat inside Esteban's. They don't have the space for tables or chairs. There's just barely enough room to stand at the counter and there's a tiny kitchen behind that. We sat in Corolla and ate with the windows down. Corolla was nice enough to let me sit in the driver's seat so Ilana could sit in the passenger seat, otherwise she would have had to sit in the back.

"Did you get my chips and queso?" Corolla asked us.

"Yeah," Ilana said as she dug through the brown paper bag. Inside was a smaller, grease-soaked bag of chips and a styrofoam cup of cheese.

"Here." I reached for his food.

Ilana held onto it and opened her door. "Nah, I'll do it."

She got out, put the queso cup inside the chip bag, then held the bag against his open door frame. She slammed the door, destroyed the bag, and blasted chips and melted cheese all across the sidewalk.

"Oh, yeah," Corolla said. "Cheesy."

Some tourists walked by and gave Ilana the strangest look.

Ilana glared at them and said, "Keep walking."

And they kept walking.

After that, Corolla drove us to the "water bar" so we could spray paint their outside wall. What a stupid idea for a business. A water bar? There are homeless people all over New York and this bar wanted to pander to jackoffs who have eight dollars to waste on osmosis-filtered, flavored water?

I spray painted EAT THE RICH on the wall.

Ilana went for TIME FOR GUILLOTINES.

We were going to do more, but some snitch told the people inside what we were doing and this jamoke in a white waiter outfit came out to yell at us.

We flipped the dude off and bolted, jumped in Corolla, and he sped away.

Mission accomplished.

Despite the fact that I physically cannot get drunk, Corolla insisted on being our designated driver for the night. I think he just didn't want to be left out. We got to the bar around 10. We got inside at 10:06 because I had to argue with Corolla, explaining over and over that it was literally impossible for him to join us inside. Eventually Corolla agreed to wait parked out front, as long as I came out to talk to him sometimes.

The door guy didn't card us. No one charged us cover. The bartenders may or may not have recognized me, but they definitely recognized Ilana. She spent a lot of time at that bar.

The inside was dimly lit and packed wall to wall, front to back with spiky-mohawked punks and girls with clothes so torn up they looked like survivors of a panther attack. The place smelled like piss (as expected) and blasted local punk rock music so loud, it came out like pure static.

Once every three minutes, when the playlist changed songs, there were five brief seconds of silence where Ilana and I could exchange two sentences, then back to blaring deafness.

Ilana ordered us both PBR tallboys and each a shot of whiskey. I'd drink to keep up appearances, but I wasn't going to get drunk. We leaned against the bar and surveyed our surroundings.

"See that guy over there?" Ilana pointed across the bar. The place was crowded, elbows and assholes. It was tough to tell who she was actually pointing at. It could have been the tall thin guy with the beard. It could have been the bigger tattooed guy next to him.

"Which one?" I asked.

"The big guy with the tattoos."

"Yeah. What about him?"

She smiled at me. "I could kill him if I wanted to."

"You know him?" I asked.

"Oh. No. I'm just saying. He's the biggest guy in here and I could kill him with my bare hands."

I looked around and said, "I could kill everyone in this bar all at once."

She gave me a frustrated look. "Well, yeah, you have powers. I'm talking about just pure human skill."

"Okay," I said. "Well, if it comes to it, I'll kill everyone in here except him so you can have something to do."

She looked away and sipped her PBR. "Fuck you."

4

From time to time, I went out front to check on Corolla so he wouldn't get bored and drive away. He had been listening to one of his talk radio stations where they just go on and on about stupid New York politics. Honestly, he listened to so much talk radio when he sat around parked, he knew more about the in's and out's of New York than I did.

Around midnight, when Ilana was stumbling around the bar five beers and four shots deep, I dipped out to check on him again. That time, he had a black SUV parked next to him. It was Denali. They had their windows down so they could talk to one another.

I hadn't seen Denali in a minute.

"Oh!" I called out. "What's up, homie?"

"Penelope!" she said. "Corolla was just telling me all about your trip! It sounds like it was so much fun!"

"Fun, sure," I said. "Dangerous, too."

"Grr. Sorry I missed it!" she said. "Next time, take me!"

"Sure thing," I said. "So what's up? What are you doing here?"

"Ilana told me you two were going to come out tonight," she said. "I thought I'd drop by and see if Corolla was here and hang out with him and tell you happy birthday!"

"No, no, no," Corolla said. "Don't wish her happy birthday."

"Why not?" she asked. "It's-"

"It's fine," I told her. "Thank you, Denali."

"How are things going inside?" Corolla asked, quickly changing the subject.

"It's cool," I said. "Ilana's already drunk. If she's planning on staying here till three, she's going to be destroyed A-F."

Denali said, "I can give her a ride home if you need me to."

"I'd like to say that won't be necessary," I said, "but, yeah, you should probably stick around for that."

Yeah. Stick around to take drunk Ilana home and also keep Corolla company so he won't get bored and bail on us.

"Well, you two stay out of trouble." I headed back in.

"We won't," Denali said.

Corolla laughed at her. "You're hilarious."

I walked back into the bar with a smile on my face. Good for them. I wondered if Corolla and Denali were becoming a thing or if they were just friends. I wasn't going to bring it up to Corolla. If he wanted to talk about it, he would bring it up to me.

I went back in the bar and searched for Ilana. She was hard to find. The crowd was even more packed than before, plus people were way more drunk and moshing around. I pushed my way through the crowd, searching for her.

I spotted her posted up at this largely ignored corner table over by the broken pay phone. She was talking to some dude. He had his arm, not *around* her shoulder, but across the back of her seat. He was leaning in close because he could barely hear her.

When Ilana spotted me, her face lit up and she shot out of her seat. "This is her! This is Penelope! It's her birthday!"

I opened my eyes wide at her. "Dude."

"Oh, sorry. Sorry." She hugged me and looked back at the guy. "It's not her birthday. She hates her birthday."

I grumbled, "Oh my god."

This guy had to be in his mid-twenties. He had hipster glasses and a beard and hair down to his chin. He wore a black tank top and skinny jeans. I have a pretty good sense of people and everything about this guy screamed CHUMP. He got up and came over to stand a little too close to me.

"Hey." He attempted a flirty smile and failed. "Haven't I see you here before? I feel like I've seen you here before. I'm Boyd."

"You're the coolest guy I've ever met in my fucking life, *Boyd*," I said as I shifted away from him. I looked at drunk Ilana. "What are you *doing*?"

Ilana leaned in and whispered-shouted right in my ear. I could smell the booze on her breath. "He likes you. He asked me who you were. He wants to meet you."

"You're shitfaced," I told her. I turned to Boyd and waved him off. "Thank you. You're dismissed."

He scoffed. "You're going to be like that?"

"Yeah, dude, I don't know you. I don't owe you shit. Sucks to suck. Byee."

He walked past me. He muttered, "Cunt."

Cunt? Did this fucking tool just call me a cunt?

I grabbed him by the back of his shirt and yanked him down to the floor. He landed flat on his back. I kicked him in the side at one-percent power. I heard some ribs crack. He yelped in pain and rolled into the fetal position.

No one could hear him over the music.

I said, "Enjoy your hospital bill, you piece of shit."

Boyd didn't look at me as he dragged himself to his feet and limped off into the crowd. He's lucky I didn't kill him.

Ilana got us another round of beers and shots. She was all over the place, dancing, talking to strangers, disappearing off to the bathroom and randomly showing back up at my side. She walked through the bar with all the confidence in the world; no one could fuck with her. She wasn't a combat monster - far from it - but she *was* the second deadliest person in the bar.

If anyone messed with her, even when she was drunk, she could snap their neck.

5

Just a little before one in the morning and in a bizarre turn of events, Carl walked through the front door of the Gold Mine.

"Whoa." I elbowed Ilana to get her attention and pointed. "Carl is here."

She spotted him. "Oh, yeah! I told him to come."

"You invited Carl to the Gold Mine?"

"It's your birthday!"

"God dammit, Ilana. You promised."

She smiled and met my eyes, took a drink of her beer, then said, "Sue me."

Carl looked like a total narc in his Westland suit. There was absolutely no reason a middle-aged businessman should be at a rough-and-tumble punk rock bar. At first it didn't even look like the door guy was going to let him in, but Carl stuck some cash money in the guy's hand and his mood instantly changed. He waved Carl right in.

Despite all the chaos and noise, everyone noticed Carl right away. You couldn't help it. God, he was going to come over and talk to us and everyone was going to see us with him. How was that going to look?

But it was unavoidable. I sighed and said, "Well, let's get this over with."

We got to the bar and stood next to him. He was in the middle of ordering.

He leaned over the bar and shouted to the bartender, "Do you have Macallan Imperiale?"

The bartender turned around and grabbed a bottle of Macallans. It wasn't Imperiale, it was just some regular bottle. Carl ordered a double, neat. The bartender poured it. Carl put down his black Westland credit card.

"Cash only," the bartender said.

Carl put his credit card away and pulled out a hundo. He put it on the bar, pointed at me and Ilana, and said, "And whatever they're drinking."

430

Macallan, two PBRs and two shots of whiskey. The bartender tried to give Carl change. Carl laughed and slid it back over.

He turned to us and said, "I didn't really think they'd have Imperiale. It's 600,000 dollars a bottle. But, you know, it doesn't hurt to ask."

He raised his glass. Ilana and I cheersed him with our cans of beer. We all took a drink.

Carl made a face and looked at his whiskey. "Huh. Macallan 12 year." He swished it around. "Not the worst."

"I didn't think you were actually going to come," Ilana said to him. She lost her balance for a second, then steadied herself with he hand on his shoulder.

"I wouldn't miss it," he said. He looked at me and said, "I hear it's your birthday."

Defeated, I said, "Yeah."

"Well." He reached inside his jacket and said, "I got you something."

He took out a crystal cluster. It had six crystal points jutting off of a mass of tinier crystals. It was dark gray, almost black, and reflective like polygon mirrors. He handed it to me. It was dense and heavy and beautiful.

"What is it?" I asked.

"Osmium," he said. "One of the rarest metals in the world. It's used to make reflective mirrors for telescopes in space."

What was I supposed to do with a lump of Osmium? It was a weird gift, but Carl was a weird guy. I said, "Thanks."

I guess he could read the confusion on my face. "I know you like to eat gold, but this is the rarest metal in the world. I thought you might like it."

Oh, yeah, it's *food*. I looked at the metallic crystals with new perspective. It probably was going to be delicious. There was only so much of it, I'd have to be careful not to eat it all at once.

With more sincerity, I said, "Oh. Well, thanks, Carl."

He turned to Ilana. "I heard the Transylvania job went well."

Ilana hiccuped. "Yep." She mimed shooting a gun. "Psshew."

"I read some good things about you in the report," he added.

She pushed his chest. "I read some good things about *you* in the report."

He turned to me. "Keep an eye on this one," he said. "She's a rising star. She's on track to becoming the youngest team leader we've ever had."

"That's what she said." I drank my beer.

Carl sipped at his whiskey. "I hear you made it to Hell," he said.

"Where'd you hear that?" I asked.

"Penelope." He held out his hands. "It's my job to hear things."

Fair. "Okay, yeah."

He stared at his glass and tried to seem disinterested. "So did you find Theodore?"

"I did."

"Did you bring him back with you?"

"I did not," I said. "Isobella Westland is taking over Hell. Theodore stayed behind to lead a revolution against her."

Carl sipped his whiskey and nodded. "But he's doing okay?"

"He's fine," I said.

"Well, good."

"And I saw Voel."

He kept his eyes on his glass. "Did she ask about me?"

"No."

He nodded. "Well." He downed the rest of his whiskey and looked at us with a smile. "I just came for the one and to wish you a happy twenty-first. You ladies have a good night."

"Yeah, thanks for coming," I said. "Thanks for the Osmium."

"Carl," Ilana said. She could barely keep her eyes open. "Carl. Carl. Carl."

"Miss Rittenberg?" he said.

She put her hand on his shoulder. "Bye."

He laughed a little bit to himself and said to me, "I hate to be a Nervous Nick, but do see that she gets home okay. She's very important to the operation."

6

By the time the bar closed, I had to physically walk Ilana's stumbling, drunk ass out the door. I loaded her into Denali's back seat where she laid down and passed out.

Denali asked, "She's not going to heave, is she?"

"I don't know," I said. "If she does, make her clean it up."

"Oh, don't you worry about that," she said.

Denali wouldn't be any help getting Ilana into her apartment, but she promised to park there and wait for Ilana to sleep it off.

Stone cold sober, I rode home with Corolla.

"Well, that was fun," he said.

"Yeah, it was."

"It's nice to have you back," he said.

"It's nice to be back!" I said. "I missed you."

"I missed you, too! When I thought about how you might never be coming back, I got all depressed. It made me really appreciate having you as a friend."

"Aw, that's sweet. I appreciate having you as a friend, too."

"Thanks," he said. "It'll be nice to finally get everything back to normal."

"Yeah, it will."

Up in the New York sky was the moon. But something was wrong. It didn't glow it's normal white. It glowed green and blue. It looked like those pictures you see in some science article called *What Mars Would Look Like Terraformed.* The moon looked... *alive.* It floated there, bright and colorful, like Earth's little sister.

"Weird," I said. "Look at the moon."

Corolla saw it and said, "Huh. That's new."

THE END

EPILOGUE

"He just let her leave," Zophiel said. She sat on a flat bench of solid silver. She was clad in her armor except for her right leg, which was naked. A line of radiant gold circled her thigh, a scar from where Penelope Salvo had blown it off with some strange fire attack. A physical wound like that was superficial to an angel, especially one as powerful as Zophiel, the Spy of God.

"That he did," Metatron said. He stood over the seated Zophiel, arms crossed, fuming over their humiliating defeat.

She said, "In his wisdom, he allowed her to return to Earth."

Metatron grunted unhappily and repeated it. "In his wisdom."

Zophiel looked up at her brother. It wasn't in their nature to question *him*. They were his children. Their job was to obey and act on his behalf. But she couldn't honestly say that she would blame Metatron if he disagreed with the Almighty.

She asked him, "You think differently?"

Metatron took a moment before he answered. "It is not my place to question the infinite decisions of our Lord."

She nodded. "But if it were."

"It's not."

"But if it *were*."

Metatron was one of the most prominent angels in all of Heaven. He lived as an example to the other angels, a benchmark for how they all must live. No angel would dare oppose the will of God. That had happened only once, and the offenders were cast down into the fires of Hell.

434

But if Zophiel truly wanted to press the issue - if she truly wanted to know his opinion - he would tell her.

He said, "I would have... *suggested*... that he obliterate the mudblob right down to her very soul."

Zophiel said, "I would have suggested the same."

"But," Metatron said. "He requires not our suggestions."

"No," said Zophiel. "He does not."

They fell silent. Zophiel traced her thumb across the golden scar on her leg. The mudblob had bested them. The Daughter of Eve had deployed some type of explosive power they did not yet understand.

Metatron was no more pleased with the injury than Zophiel. He had not seen his sister sustain such a wound since the War For Heaven. Reattaching her leg was a simple process: she placed the end of the amputated appendage up to the stub of her leg. Golden blood flowed out of her body like honey and into the wound. Her body pulled itself into place. Just like that, she was whole once again.

Zophiel would have to craft new armor.

"Can you see her now?" Metatron asked. "Can you see what she is doing?"

Zophiel looked at him, then turned her attention down to the clouds. They parted for her and created a window to Earth, revealing images that only she could see. Her eyes glowed bright white.

"She cavorts in some tavern," Zophiel said, peering into a drinking establishment in New York City. "A modern day Sodom. She is surrounded by filth. The air reeks of excrement." She looked up at her brother. "Why would he allow this blasphemy to continue?"

"Mercy," Metatron said. "It is because he knows mercy."

The clouds closed and Zophiel's eyes returned to normal. "I lack mercy."

"I, also."

"Continue to watch her," said Metatron. "The opportunity will present itself where true justice will trump infinite mercy."

"If he wanted her obliterated, he would have done so."

Metatron thought for a moment, then said, "Perhaps he spared her only so that we might do it instead."

With seething disgust, Zophiel said, "Perhaps you are right."

www.ingramcontent.com/pod-product-compliance
Lightning Source LLC
Chambersburg PA
CBHW030546020726
47494CB00005B/1503